SUCCUBUS
in the
CITY

SUCCUBUS
in the
CITY

NINA HARPER

BALLANTINE BOOKS • NEW YORK

Succubus in the City is a work of fiction. Names, characters, places, and incidents are the products of the author's imagination or are used fictitiously. Any resemblance to actual events, locales, or persons, living or dead, is entirely coincidental.

A Del Rey Books Mass Market Original

Copyright © 2008 by Nina Harper

Published in the United States by Del Rey Books, an imprint of The Random House Publishing Group, a division of Random House, Inc., New York.

DEL REY is a registered trademark and the Del Rey colophon is a trademark of Random House, Inc.

ISBN 978-0-345-49506-8

Printed in the United States of America

www.delreybooks.com

OPM 9 8 7 6 5 4 3 2 1

This book is for those wonderful, irreplaceable people who feed me chocolate and floofy drinks when I'm miserable and depressed, and celebrate with chocolate and floofy drinks when things go well for me. Who take my calls at 3 a.m., who listen to my miseries and tell me that I'm still good company, who will tell me when the jeans are not flattering, who will notice all my weight loss but never notice a gain and who always give me a ride, mascara, or carfare home when I need it.

This book is for my girlfriends, the most excellent buddies any woman ever had. I love you all, and without you my life would be unbearable.

Acknowledgments

I would like to thank John Landers and Tom Major for putting me up, and John Irvine for putting up with me. Liz Manicatide and Karen Marcovici were invaluable in research. And always, Cecilia Tan, Sarah Smith, and Vandana Singh for critical advice on writerly matters. I also would like to thank Bill Fawcett for making everything happen.

chapter
ONE

There I was on a Saturday night, dressed up in Prada and ready to go out, to our new favorite club in the Meatpacking District when the phone rang. It was my friend Sybil, very contrite, to say that she was down with a nasty cold and really could not make it out. And that I was welcome to come over and share her chicken soup and her germs but she was planning on bed before the A crowd would even arrive at the velvet ropes. So my choices were to stay home and watch reruns or hunt. I'd already seen everything in the latest Netflix order and I was already dressed. And I just didn't want to look at the stack of dishes in the kitchen sink or admit to wasting forty minutes on my makeup.

So hunt it was.

A convention is always easy hunting. Like any New Yorker, I don't like the invasion from out of state, gawkers who stand in the middle of the sidewalk staring up at the high buildings and blocking traffic, to say nothing of display windows. The out-of-towners are so wary, watching their wallets and their keys and trying to look behind their backs—but they never worry about me when I show up.

I took a taxi to a hotel near the Port Authority with

a scuzz factor to match the address. The lobby and bar were crowded with bored-looking men in Arrow polyester shirts and bad toupees. Old Spice overlaid but did not mask the scent of disinfectant and I had to resist the impulse to gag.

They turned to look at me. They always do. I am a succubus, and they can't help it. But I knew that my clothes were way over the top for this crowd. Suddenly I was tired and depressed and thought the reruns looked appealing after all. Then I spotted my prey.

I don't make the judgment calls, I just deliver the goods. That's the way I think about the job. But like everyone else, I'm trying to make the world a little nicer, a little safer, so I choose men who make it . . . less nice. There he was, sitting at the bar, hooting and leering and whistling when I entered. He did it again when another woman made the mistake of passing the doors and that decided me. I walked over to him and leaned against the faux leather edging and tried to get the bartender's attention.

I ordered a Jack Daniel's. Somehow with these guys, that seems to indicate that I'm available and not quite respectable. I always order Jack Daniel's but I never drink it, and it did the trick again. Before I could get the change from the twenty into my wallet he was all over me.

"Hey baby, come here often?" he asked.

And that clinched his fate. I hate to be called baby, hate it more than almost anything else. Then, to seal it in stone, he reached around and fondled my ass. Yes, the women of the world could definitely do without him.

I smiled. "What's your name? Where are you from?" They always talk about themselves and never notice that they hear nothing about me. They think that they fascinate me and they've thought it for thousands of years. And for nearly that long they have been my prey, my mission.

His name was Brad and he was from . . . someplace that wouldn't miss him. Suddenly I was bored and wanted it over. No use playing the game, luring the prey, making it appear that I had to be caught and seduced and that I was overwhelmed with his charm. Or charisma. Or whatever. "Shall we go upstairs?" I asked when he paused to breathe.

And then he blushed and looked at the condensation on the bar. "I, ummm, well, my friend said we could save money on our per diem if we shared a room and he's a serious Christian and friendly with the boss . . . could we go somewhere else?"

"We could go to my place." I hate taking them to my place.

He followed me out and lit a cigarette as soon as he cleared the door. Then he balked when I hailed a cab. "I don't think that's covered in my per diem," he said, fingering his wallet. Cheap to boot. I sighed. "I'll take care of it," I said. I'd hit the trifecta: called me baby, cheap, and a smoker. The only good thing about this evening was where he was going and that he was going there as fast as I could manage.

My doorman noted that I'd returned, and with someone in tow. He looked away as I dragged Brad into the elevator and then into my bedroom.

At least he'd had a shower in the last forty-eight hours, I had to give him that. Though as he peeled off the layers of his Kmart suit I could see that his body was even flabbier than I had imagined.

They have to come before I can deliver them. That's the deal, and I was hoping he'd be a fast one. Fortunately, he was. I had him on his back and stripped carefully, teasing and not letting him touch as I hid my breasts with my mass of auburn curls or turned and slid my panties over my thighs. Oh, he was more than ready when I turned back and hovered over him. He lay looking up at me, plenty ready. It only took a few short strokes before he groaned.

He got his moment of pleasure, and then he ignited, bursting into screaming yellow flames that flared under my hands. In less than five minutes he was a few ounces of ash cooling on my sheets.

I dustbusted, changed the sheets, and then took a quick shower before settling in for season three of *Friends*.

On Sunday morning the alarm got me out of bed before noon. I turned on NY 1 for weather and news, and started some Costa Rican shade-grown dark roast in the French press. There was still some housekeeping to do. The dirty sheets that I'd tossed into the corner belonged in the laundry pickup bag. Brad's clothes, which also still littered my carpet, went into another bag to be dropped off at the Salvation Army on Fourth Avenue. Imitation Gucci shoes and bad knockoff of last season's jacket and tie, pants, a polyester-blend shirt, and underwear. Yuck. Bad clothes. But someone would buy them for three dollars and be glad and no one would trace them back to me.

After removing the cash from his wallet I set the driver's license and credit cards aside to be left on a subway bench later. All organized and cleaned up from the night before, I poured my first cup of coffee just as Wolf Blitzer started on the latest Washington scandal.

Vincent the doorman rang for the ashes.

Well, he's Vincent this week. Next week it'll be Jose or Michael or Vitale. Likely Vitale. Satan seems to like names that start with V, at least for doormen. Anyway, this was his first day so he came up to introduce himself and pick up the bag himself.

"And if you need anything, Miss, remember that my number one priority is to look after you."

Ack! Had this guy been in advertising or retail? Where does She find them?

And I know his number one priority is to look after me. Literally. Watch my movements, see who I bring home, take out the ashes in the morning, and send the sheets to the cleaners and drop off the clothing donations and wallets in anonymous locations. I mean, I can't complain about the service and it does improve my quality of life. After all these centuries I should be used to it by now, but there are just some aspects of the job that I've just never become really comfortable with, and having a doorman who knows way too much about me is one of them.

At least he's cute. They're always cute. This one had chestnut curls cropped short, and sherry-dark eyes. I do have to bow to Satan's class—She has never given me a dud doorman yet.

He stood there, smiling. "My name is Vincent."

"You said that already." I was late. Was he waiting for a tip?

"Will you be wanting a cab this morning? In fifteen minutes, perhaps?"

I was running late and Sybil would kill me, because there wouldn't be a table open at our usual restaurant and they won't even take us in line until the entire party is there. I'd made a real effort this morning, actually got up with the alarm and had even picked out my Seven jeans and the rose-colored lace camisole the night before.

"Thank you, Vincent. Fifteen minutes would be perfect." He smiled as broadly as any of the gentlemen, excuse me, creeps, I picked up for the delivery service.

I was in the lovely white marble lobby of my building in thirteen minutes flat and Vincent already had a cab waiting. Efficient and useful. I hoped he would stay around for a while, but if he discharged all of his duties so well he would be promoted by the end of the week. Well, I'd enjoy it while it lasted. So I sailed out the door and relished the sight of the young man running from the building to get the door to the cab as well.

"I knew you'd be late." Sybil sighed as I ran up to her on the sidewalk. She stood in front of the steps leading up to the restaurant and shivered slightly in her thin spring jacket. She should have worn a coat, but it was one of those perfect almost-spring days that New York has in the late winter, just to tease the natives who should know that there are at least six more weeks of slush to go. But when the sky is a clear, perfect blue and it's warm enough to wear a jacket instead of a coat it's easy to pretend that spring is just a few weeks away.

Of course, Sybil looked disappointed at my late arrival. Her large blue eyes were almost brimming with tears at my delay. Guilt, guilt, who could help but feel horrible at making this lovely, sweet-looking woman so miserably dejected by the ultimate sin of Being Late.

"Wait a minute," I said, looking at her. "What about your cold? You were too sick last night to go out and—Sybil, we're demons. We don't get sick."

She shrugged. "I really felt awful. If you'd come over you would have seen it. I'm not like the rest of you. I'm not a sex demon, I'm just a greed demon. So I do catch colds."

Sybil always seems to feel left out because she's the only one of us whose duty is not sex. Maybe she did have a cold. Or maybe she had just been feeling sorry for herself, which happened at times.

"What about Desi and Eros?" I asked, trying to distract her.

"Already inside, trying to pretend that we're all here so that we can keep our place in line. They lied and said that we were just outside having a cigarette." She shuddered delicately, and I agreed. Tobacco, ugh! I couldn't abide the smell. It was all I could do to swallow my revulsion if one of my deliveries was a smoker. I cannot understand why anyone smokes anymore. It's such a social liability.

We raced inside and joined our friends in the crush at the trendy poured-concrete hostess station that was separated from the entrance by a glass wall. Desi waved us over. She had snagged one of the dark wooden seats in the waiting area that was artfully reminiscent of a cross between a Victorian gentlemen's club and a Victorian train station. Though the press of bodies obscured the antique brass lockers and the deep mahogany desk, I could see the hostess shaking her head and studying the seating book that lay open in front of her. "Probably twenty minutes," Desi said, "Did you have a hard night?" That last was directed to me, and was genuinely sympathetic. I love Desi for that kindness more than anything. The others all think that I've got the easy gig, but Desi understands that the ashes-to-ashes business has gotten very old.

"At least this one had taken a bath," I said, and watched with some satisfaction as my friends winced a little. "I think he was with some convention. He wore a polyester-blend shirt and Drakkar Noir."

"You are so strong," Desi said, patting me gently on the shoulder. "I couldn't have managed that. I'm allergic to Drakkar Noir."

"We're all allergic to Drakkar Noir," Eros announced. "And I'm starving. Pancakes and French toast and Bellinis, everybody."

There are advantages to being an immortal succubus. To make up for the miseries of vigilant doormen (named Vincent or otherwise) and being required to take home men who wear drugstore perfumes and polyester, I can eat all the cake and chocolate and steak and French fries I want. The body is a requirement of the job so Satan has given me a permanent size four. At least until the style changes. One hundred years ago I weighed two hundred pounds and was considered exquisite. And I had a collection of Worth gowns that were the envy of more than one duchess. Well, some things don't change.

We were seated in ten minutes and had our order in less than five minutes after that. For a few minutes I simply savored the glory of fluffy blueberry pancakes swimming in sweet wine sauce and relished my poached quince, a crisp counterpoint to all that gooey goodness.

"So how many this week, Lily?" Desi asked me.

"Three," I answered. "What about you?"

Desi smiled. "Oh, for me it's not numbers, it's all the little provisions of the contract I get them to sign. I have to bring them along, you know, before they're ready to sign up for eternity in Hell. So I'm still working on Peter."

"The one from last week?" Eros asked. "The investment banker with the mole on his hand?"

Desi rolled her eyes. "Yes. That's the only Peter at the moment."

"Well, I certainly hope that's not the only peter," Eros replied tartly.

We all laughed. Maybe the Bellinis made it funnier or maybe just being in the company of friends made us laugh at the lame joke. Knowing them for hundreds of years and knowing that they wouldn't abandon me no matter what was about the only thing that had kept me sane.

I know, I know, no one has any sympathy for the immortal sex demon. Especially if she doesn't have to diet and gets to wear Jimmy Choos all the time. Which is why we all need each other, because my girlfriends know that my life is not all Prada. There are the polyester guys. And there is the fact that no man acceptable to Satan has loved me, not since I was mortal. And I don't think I want to tell you how long ago that was. Suffice it to say that She was known as Ashtoreth back in those days.

Satan is like our den mother and we are Her Chosen. No one can help but admire Her—everything about Her is so perfect. Her clothes, Her apartment, the hors d'oeuvres at Her parties, everything is just half a second before the fashionistas pick up on a new trend. When She's in feminine form She's really one of us, only better, more pulled together, more in charge. Kind of like what I imagine a big sister is when you're a sorority pledge. So when She's being the supergirlfriend and ultimate fashionista we call Her Martha. This decade, anyway. Once upon a time we called Her "Jackie," and before that "Peggy."

"I'm just flattered you like my taste," Martha said once, chuckling softly, when we were ooohing and aaaahing over her latest place, a penthouse on Lexington in the East Seventies. "I sometimes wonder if I'm a little, you know, too classic."

There's no such thing as too classic, and I told Her so. I wish I looked that sophisticated and elegant in Chanel. Martha can wear a Chanel suit like no one else. And She is the only woman I've ever seen who makes an Hermès scarf look like a scarf and not an advertisement for the size of her bank account.

We all have our own styles and best looks, and while we all envied Satan's perfect polish, I, at least, have learned that I do best sticking to what suits me. Which tends to be au courant, mostly Italian, and not tailored. I have vaguely messy hair and lots of it, very dark auburn with natural copper streaks from the sun. I look silly in a suit, but great in jeans or a little slip dress.

And while I adore cutting-edge fashion, I can't pull off Comme des Garçons or Issey Miyake the way Eros can. But then, she's got the very willowy, dare I say almost spiky, figure that is perfect for the avant-garde designers. Of course, that four-hundred-dollar haircut that looks so elegantly hacked and bleached that it could be on the cover of *Vogue* does help. Her pointed face and pointed hair are *très moderne*; no one would believe that she hasn't been a goddess for two thousand years. Well, demigoddess, but who's counting?

As demons, our job is to tempt humans into giving their souls to Hell. We cannot tempt those truly obedient to God, but most people have their iffy moments and we are there to exploit them. We can offer what our prey want, so long as they're willing to sign over their immortal souls (in blood). Except for me. I don't have to get willing consent with a contract and a signature. I tempt men with sex they can't resist, and deliver them when they come.

Once upon a time Christians thought that succubi preyed only on good, devout husbands, back when the definition of a good Christian husband was elastic on issues like wife beating. Now any man who responds to my pheromones is valid prey, so I don't have to select for religion and public approbation. My prey were always sleazebags, don't get me wrong, and one of my great faves is still to hit up a convention of gospel-quoting hypocrites and deliver a few. But there aren't a lot of them in NYC, so I tend to target drunks and the kind of men who treat women badly.

Eros used to be a demigoddess and looks it. She's

nearly six feet tall and is always just a little ahead of the curve on everything. Her temptation is eroticism of all kinds, including porn and fetishism. Desi, Desire, is—you guessed it—a demon of desire. She personifies and tempts by a more complex set of desires; sex is certainly part of it, but so are class and social status and sometimes even respectability. Desi is the most versatile of us, but it takes her a bit longer to bring her prey to where they are ready to sign. Sybil's specialty is greed. She was once an Oracle of Delphi with a true gift from Apollo himself, which makes her the wonder worker of Wall Street, where she is a very highly placed account manager. Which does not mean that she isn't beautiful—she is—but she doesn't have to have sex with anyone she doesn't actually want to date. And, unlike the rest of us, Sybil has been married. Something like fifteen times.

So these are my friends. Being Satan's Chosen is something like being a lady-in-waiting. We're Her friends, Her companions when She wants someone to gossip with or to sit with Her during a manicure. We shop with Her, drink with Her, and enjoy Her company. She has favorites all over the world and from every specialty in Hell, of course, but when She's in New York She enjoys relaxing with us. Why us? Maybe because we're congenial and adore Her taste and admire Her for who She is personally. We don't just love Her because She's Satan, we love Her because She likes Bellinis and clothes and art shows and the Hamptons as much as we do.

"Is Martha coming today?" Sybil asked.

"I don't know. You know how busy She is. If She drops by, it'll be later."

That's the advantage of being Satan. She never has to wait for a table.

"I want Her advice because I hate my wallpaper," Sybil moaned. "I sat all morning looking at it and I wanted to throw my coffee all over it just to make it different."

"Coffee is a very hot color now," Eros said in that knowing tone she uses when it comes to anything artistic. "But I'd rather talk about guys. Who cares about apartments?"

We all turned to glare at her. Everyone cares about apartments. Especially in New York, where they're just about impossible to find. A decent building where the pipes don't make thumping noises and you can't hear the people upstairs, one with a nice view of the park or the river maybe, or a fireplace, can take decades of careful searching.

The problem is that Eros has the perfect apartment. She found it during the Depression, when no one could afford an Upper East Side co-op with four bedrooms and a separate suite for the maid. The building was built at the turn of the century, and has fourteen-foot ceilings on the main floor with elaborate crown moldings and a fireplace with an Italian marble mantel carved in the Deco style. We all envy her apartment, even if she does invite us up to roast marshmallows and make s'mores on nights when we're just feeling a little down.

"So tell us about Peter," I said to Desi. Des is such a romantic, and besides, it would get the conversation off real-estate envy.

Desi sighed. "I don't know, I think that this one may like me. Maybe," she said. "He's an investment banker and has an apartment on East Seventy-seventh Street and a dog. A chocolate lab named Jazz. And he does tai chi."

"How does he dress?" I prompted, to get away from any description of an apartment in the perfect location.

"He's a banker. Probably Brooks Brothers," Eros said dismissively.

"No, Ralph Lauren," Desi defended her new beau. "Do you want to meet him? I can bring him on Friday."

Friday was the opening of the Michelos show at the Martindale Gallery. We were going because Eros adores Michelos and promised on the death of her immortal soul that there would be interesting and attractive men there (the fact that she no longer has an immortal soul notwithstanding). If Desi brought her latest it would be counterproductive, but it was her call, not mine.

"Oh, Lily, don't look so sad." Desi interrupted my thoughts. "You'll find someone lovely, I know it. You've got the hardest job of all of us and I couldn't manage it in ten zillion years."

chapter
TWO

"Ohmyghod, that's Franco Massilano," Desi gushed, turning in her seat.

"Who?" Sybil asked.

"Don't be so obvious," Eros hissed. "It's ridiculous. So what? It's New York."

"The famous architect," Desi answered Sybil, turning her back as if he were of no interest to her. After all, we are not only immortal and have lived thousands of years, but we're also New Yorkers and we're not impressed by anyone, no matter how famous.

Then Desi pulled out her compact and trained the mirror so that she could stare at the famous man all she wanted without losing cred. I have to hand it to her, Desi has brains and originality to go with her class. Eros really wouldn't have cared and if I'd known who it was I would have craned my neck like any out-of-towner. But Desi just went straight for the technology. A mature technology, to be sure. I bet she did things like that when she was in Catherine de Médicis' court in France. Of course, then watching your back was a whole lot more necessary. That crowd made modern NYC look as innocent as an after-school special on the Disney channel.

"Okay, he's a famous architect, what's the big deal?

Lots of famous people come here." I never have learned to be ashamed of my inability to recognize celebrities. Really, three thousand years and I still can't tell who's actually done something important and who just has a stunning sense of style.

Eros, much put upon, sighed at our ignorance. "Franco Massilano is probably here to accept his award for designing the new annex to the Brooklyn Museum. There was a fabulous party last night to celebrate. I went with Jason, that pretty twentysomething I picked up at Gehenna last month, and he was suitably impressed. All the glitterati were out in their best. Even Martha was there."

Yeah. Eros gets to go to a fabulous party, even if it's in Brooklyn, and I'm stuck at a convention bar picking up a guy in a polyester-blend shirt named Brad. Why couldn't I go to the fabulous party?

"What was Martha wearing?" Desi asked, momentarily distracted from the famous.

"Oscar de la Renta," Eros informed us. "A cream ballgown in duchesse satin cut down to *there* in the back. And pearls and diamonds."

I sighed. With her smooth, straight brunette hair and her large dark eyes, Satan had probably looked exquisite. A class act all the way. I'll bet that dress would look great on me, too. I wondered if She'd lend it, if I had a good enough occasion.

Desi was still looking into her compact mirror. "Oh, come on, Des, he can't be that interesting. Besides, he's in his fifties and he's with a woman," Sybil said.

"Oh, I'm not looking at him anymore," Desi replied with some surprise. "But some really cute guy just walked over to his table. Damn. He's probably gay."

He did have a great butt and nice shoulders, but then the Armani jacket emphasized the difference between the shoulder and the narrow waist. Desi was right, he was definitely worth a second look.

Sybil, who was seated in the optimal spot for observing, studied the situation. "Maybe. I don't have good gaydar. But he's not your type Desi, trust me. He's—"

She stopped cold and her face went blank. When she spoke again her voice was about an octave lower and harsher, with a bit of an accent making her usually middle-American English sound guttural and exotic, and not in the most appealing way. "He has a gun under his jacket. He will try to get the famous man to leave with him."

When Sybil used that voice she was never, ever wrong. She could not be wrong. Prophecy was her curse just as being a succubus was mine. She couldn't control what she saw any more than I could control the way men were attracted to me.

But that didn't mean that she always had the right explanation for why things were the way she saw them.

We watched the men intently. The younger man talked to the older one at some length, and then gestured widely enough that we could see his shoulders. Yeah, a gun was bulging under his jacket. And yeah, Mr. Famous Architect went with him. The guy was a plainclothes cop. Maybe even a detective.

"What do you think it's about?" Desi began spinning fantasies. "Do you think he was involved in a drug ring? Or maybe helping the police with a sting of corrupt officials. Or—he's Italian, isn't he? Maybe the Mafia?"

"Probably fixing a parking ticket," I said tartly as the two of them returned to the woman who had waited while elegantly sipping her mimosa. "It wouldn't do for a famous guest who just designed the newest la-la annex to the Brooklyn Museum to get his rental car towed."

Both men sat, the older famous one first saying something complimentary to the woman. She smiled and her cheeks got just the soft rosy glow expensive blush tries to re-create.

"I'm going over there," Desi announced. She got up, turned, and walked past the table headed for the Ladies'. The room was noisy and crowded, and even if the first wave were leaving it was easy for Desi to pass just a little too close and manage to drop her (open) handbag at an advantageous moment.

"Eeeep," she said, and leaned over to start picking up her fourteen lipsticks rolling under the cute cop's feet along with her handkerchief, keys, Treo, Luna bars, and just about anything a person would need in an emergency (including a collapsible cup, a bottle of Motrin and a tiny travel-size bottle of Scope). With amazing luck, neither her wallet nor her Tampax left the deepest confines of her Coach bag.

Desi bending over in her jeans is a sight to behold. Her legs go on forever and her butt is the product of not only supernatural tampering but hours in the gym. And her cleavage was displayed to excellent (but discreet) advantage as she tried to gather up her things.

The cop immediately understood his role, and began to chase stray lipstick cases that had gone astray on that helpful flagstone floor.

"Oh, thank you," Desi said breathlessly as he handed her the four that had gotten farthest under the table. "I really appreciate it. I would have felt like a total idiot scrambling under that table."

"No problem." He smiled at her and held out his hand. "I'm Steve Balducci. And you are?"

"Desi," Des answered, shaking his hand.

I had a sudden jealous flash. No one ever smiled at me like that. When they smiled at me it was all loaded with lust, not with warmth or kindness.

"By the way, let me introduce my uncle, Franco Massilano, who designed the new annex to the Brooklyn Museum, and his wife Paola. Aunt Paola is a textile designer."

"Very pleased to meet you both," Desi said in her most demure and proper voice. "I would invite you over to our table, but my friend was just complaining about her apartment and I know she'd start asking all kinds of questions while you just want a pleasant brunch."

Sybil gasped and might have said something if I hadn't kicked her under the table. "Don't," I hissed.

"Don't what?" she whispered back. "What would I have done? I would have liked to have met them, too . . ."

"To the courageous go the spoils," Eros said. "Besides, don't you like the young guy better?"

"He's hot," I agreed.

"Desi seems to think so," Sybil observed, acutely. Desi was standing with one hand on his shoulder as she sorted through her bag, making certain that they had collected all her belongings. Woe be it to all if one of her precious Laura Mercier lipsticks was missing.

Then we were quiet and could actually hear what she was saying again, though I'll admit that demonic hearing is far better than human. And though all of us share this particular trait, we oddly often forget that the others can overhear us when we're distracted by attractive masculine company. Naturally, we did the only loyal girlfriend thing: we shut up and listened in.

"I wish I'd met you before. We could have gone to the party last night and you could have seen the designs," Steve told her.

"But aren't they on display for the rest of the month?" Desi asked sweetly. "I could still see them sometime."

"Stop salivating," Sybil hissed. "It's not any nicer when you do it than when she did. And green is definitely not your color."

It's hard, is all. I want to be all happy for my buds. They've been with me through everything, and I do mean everything, and I really want the best for them. In every way I want the best. I want us all to have it.

But sometimes I can't help being jealous. After all, they are also immortal and perfectly (and effortlessly) beautiful and eternally young. They also have great jobs (both their paying jobs and their unofficial but more important positions in the Hierarchy) and apartments and bank accounts big enough to support both their shoe and handbag habits. They have all the same perks I've got, but they can have some romance and love, too.

Me, I just get lust.

I like lust, mind you. I like it a lot. But after three thousand years, a girl just wants a little more sometimes. For my friends, an offer of help or an invitation to coffee didn't automatically mean bed. For me, that experience would be a huge novelty. A really nice novelty.

So I'm jealous of my best girlfriends, and I hate that about myself. Rule number one, always, is that you're for your friends. They were all for me. Like Dumas said, "All for one, and one for all."

Oh, right, they were Musketeers. Our weapons are a little more subtle.

chapter
THREE

If I hadn't been drowning in jealousy I would have enjoyed watching Desi work. The sheer audacity of her approach, the precisely lowered eyelids—not closed all the way, and certainly never batted—Desi combined seduction and innocence in irresistible proportions.

Desi is the reason people buy Ralph Lauren. She personifies Old Money, the Upper Crust and the Upper East Side. She is, after all, a desire demon, and what do people desire more than beauty, youth, and wealth? She makes navy blue box-pleated skirts look sexy. Her hair is smooth and toffee-brown, just the color for the country club or the executive suite. It's thick with only the subtlest hint of wave, just enough to give it volume and bounce without ever looking messy like mine. Which has not always been an asset—back in the French court of Catherine de Médicis she frizzed her hair into a fashionable mass of burned curls, a fashion statement wisely discarded until an unfortunate revival in the 1980s.

Because she personifies desire in its many forms, she is also intelligent and powerful.

But now, with this hunky example of New York's Finest, she was all interest and confidence and carefully ambiguous glances. Mr. Detective never had a chance.

"The museum's open late on Thursday," Steve was saying. "If you're free that evening we could go over there and take a look, and maybe catch a drink on the way back if it's not too late."

"Thursday?" Desi asked, as if she hadn't a clue. "I'd have to check my calendar. Hmmm." She thought for a few moments, then pulled a ladylike filigree gold Mont Blanc out of her bag. Interesting that that pen hadn't appeared on the floor with the lipsticks.

She pulled out a scrap of paper from her wallet—it looked like a grocery receipt—and scribbled something on the back. Whereupon she handed it to Detective Steve with a flourish. "My e-mail address," she announced. "Send me a reminder tomorrow or something, and I'll check and see if I'm free."

Honestly, the poor guy looked like he'd died and gone to heaven. Hmmm, given the context he was going to be very surprised where he ended up when this was all over.

Uncle Architect had watched the entire byplay as Aunt Mimosa pointedly ignored the interaction, but as Desi handed over her e-mail the Great Man cleared his throat. Apparently he had been out of the limelight too long, and had to direct the attention of his ravening fans back to where it belonged. Namely, on him.

Detective Steve remembered that the good people of New York were paying him for his time as he flirted with Desi and excused himself. Desi smiled innocently, like a schoolgirl. Like a nun. Steve was about to be toast—well, metaphorically speaking. I'm the only one who toasts them for real, and I make good and certain to eliminate all traces of evidence.

"So, what do you think?" Desi asked breathlessly

when we were certain that Hunky Steve was really gone and Important Uncle was paying the bill.

"About what?" Eros asked. "He's just some guy, after all."

"He seems really nice," Sybil said. "And he's employed."

"He's got a great butt," I added, and the others glared at me. "Well, he does. It bears listing in the catalog."

"He has yummy eyes," Sybil sighed.

"Would you like anything else?" the waiter (who also had a cute butt and great eyes, and would probably say he's an actor if you asked what he did) mumbled by rote as he laid the bill on the table.

"How about a hunky guy with a cute butt?" Eros quipped.

Desi looked mortified, but the waiter laughed. "Honey, I've been waiting on your table all brunch. And you're saying you haven't checked out my butt even once. After all that time in the gym, too." He pouted. Cutely. Had to be an actor.

I laughed. "Baby, what's the good of looking at what I'm never gonna get?"

"Well, you didn't specify a straight hunk with a cute butt," the waiter positively flounced. "Talk about picky, difficult customers. I'll bet you wanted the butter on the side, too."

We all laughed and the tension broke. For all that life can be rough, I'm lucky and I know it. I've got three great girlfriends, a sympathetic uberboss with impeccable style and no worries about my figure. With all those advantages, any woman should be totally happy, right?

So why did I still have this sliver of sadness inside?

Mostly I knew life was wonderful, but I was lonely and had been for too long. So what if I was beautiful and thin and immortal and lived in New York and had fabulous shoes? No one loved me, not in the romantic way that had led Sybil down the aisle fifteen times.

We paid and left, and even left a decent tip. I wasn't in the mood to go home and I felt restless. I didn't know why nothing sounded like fun.

"Do you think Steve will ask me for a date today?" Desi asked.

"I just want to get my mind off feeling like I'll never have a real date. Ever." The dark mood had struck and I was wallowing, I admit it.

"You have plenty of dates," Eros said snippily.

"I mean the kind where they wake up in the morning," I moaned. "I am sick of deadbeat dates. Emphasis on the dead."

Suddenly Desi yelped and pulled out her Treo. "Can you believe it, he's already sent me an e-mail about Thursday night!" She could barely contain her glee. "Now I've got to think of something to wear . . ."

"What? Thursday?" Eros had not been paying enough attention in the restaurant, clearly.

"Steve. Famous uncle, cute butt," I reminded her.

"Have you told him you're going yet?" Eros asked pointedly.

"Oh, she couldn't possibly do that until Tuesday," Sybil replied blithely.

"Maybe Monday night," Desi said, almost pleading.

"Tuesday," Sybil announced firmly. "You can't appear too eager."

And suddenly, surrounded by wallpaper pattern

books that specialized in English floral pastels, I started to feel terribly sad.

Last night. Brad. He wasn't the worst I'd ever delivered, either. When they were awful I felt fine. I didn't care about the creeps, the ones I took home and turned to ash as soon as they'd gotten naked (or near enough to it that I hardly noticed). But Brad had just been some ordinary guy, the kind who didn't respect women or maybe just didn't know how. He probably hadn't had much of a bank account, either. He'd come in from—now I forgot, was it New Jersey or upstate?

Maybe I was getting old. Maybe I'd been at this too long. They were pathetic, the guys I found.

Most of them were lousy lays.

But Brad hadn't been one of the worst, which may be why I was so sad this time.

I was also sad about the fact that he was one of the better ones that I'd had in hundreds of years. At least Brad had tried. He had used his fingertips on my breasts instead of kneading them like bread dough.

I wouldn't have felt sad about one of the kneaders.

They incinerate at the moment of their climax, not mine, so most of the time I'm not only sleeping alone but I'm still frustrated and have to finish myself up, too. Alone.

Yeah, I was always going to look like I was twenty-eight. My hair might be messy and I have a few freckles from before immortality but still—I find men. When I'm on, they can't resist me. Succubus pheromones are completely compelling to the mortal male. They can't help it. Even the nice guys can't say no.

It's no compliment to me. Their interest isn't because

I have almost as much green in my eyes as brown, not because I can talk about movies or new media or where to find the best cocktails in New York. They don't notice the elegant bleached hardwood floors in my apartment, or the Philippe Starck Louis Ghost chairs around my dining and worktable. They don't recognize the Scalamandre silks on the windows or the thousand-thread Frette sheets. My taste, my mind, my personality are all irrelevant. It's just pheromones, magic, and lust.

To have sex with me without loving me—and without satisfying me—is to turn to ash and go directly to a minor level of Hell. With a signed contract, Desi's and Eros's and Sybil's prey are condemned to a major level. Some of my deliveries can even end up in Purgatory if the only wrong thing they ever did was go with me. I haven't done a Purgatory delivery in over a hundred years, and I hope never to do one again. I don't get any points for those.

The men I deliver usually become simple souls in torment in Hell. If they happen to be exceptionally good (except for sleeping with me), they may reside in Hell for a time before moving on to Purgatory. They never become demons. A person must make a contract with Hell, knowingly and deliberately, to earn demon status.

I do have one option that I have exercised at times. If I have sex with a man and he is generous and attentive, if he makes sure I have pleasure before he does, I can let him live. In all the thousands of years I've lived, there have been only a few men like that. And they never want to actually date me. We have mind-blowing sex and they never call me again.

I want someone to think I'm special, not just for my

perfect body or my Pantene-ad hair. Someone who'll think I'm special even in the morning before I put on my makeup, even on the days when I feel fat and frumpy, someone who won't ditch me because I get PMS and who thinks that I should go shopping when I'm feeling down.

In short, I want a boyfriend, a real boyfriend.

Satan has agreed. If someone falls in love with me and dates me without having sex with me for at least a month, and knows that I'm a succubus and loves me anyway, then I get back my soul and can be a mortal again. That's in my contract.

Big if. In a few thousand years I've never even come close.

"You seem to be in some kind of mood," Eros noted. "What's wrong?"

"Everything," I said, keeping my voice down although really I just wanted to wail. "Nothing. It just feels so meaningless. And lonely. You are the best friends on the planet, the best friends a girl ever had. But I'm tired of waking up alone every morning."

"Oh, honey, yeah," Desi said. "You've got a real hard time of it, we know. And it's worse when you've got a bad one. Are you going out tonight? What say we rent some silly Bollywood musical and get takeout?"

"We can go to my place and make s'mores," Eros suggested. "And paint our toenails."

"But don't you all have plans tonight?" I couldn't bear any more guilt right now.

"Nothing that can't be rescheduled," Desi told me and Eros nodded. Even Sybil looked up from her decorating magazine and agreed.

I've got the best buds in the world.

chapter
FOUR

"We'll call Martha and paint our toenails and relax," Desi announced. "Like a pajama party. No boys," she added with a faux junior high school sneer.

Satan, of course, was too busy to make it at the last minute. "I'm so sorry, dears, it sounds like a world of fun," She told us, and I could hear the real regret in Her voice. "But I have some appointments that I just can't reschedule, no matter how much more I would rather spend an evening eating s'mores and painting toenails. Next time, I promise."

I felt badly for Her. Being the Prince of Evil was a 24/7 gig and She never got any downtime. If She didn't have a weekly appointment for a massage and a facial at Bliss She would never get pampered just for Herself.

Once some sorcerer did a ritual in Australia right when She was in the middle of Her pedicure and tried to conjure Her to appear for some Satanic worship service. She sent Mephistopheles instead and was old Meph ever furious. He had just gotten seated for dinner at Morimoto and hadn't even gotten his appetizer yet. That was one unhappy day in Hell, let me tell you. With the popularity of *Iron Chef*, it's almost impossible to get a reservation at Morimoto, and

Meph had been looking forward to that dinner for months.

That was one of the very few times I've ever seen Satan actually use straight-out magic just to please a minion. She created a reservation at Morimoto for Meph for nine p.m. on a Saturday night and made damn sure that the table was ready and waiting, too. She does take care of us. And She knows the value of a topflight dinner reservation.

These so-called magicians and sorcerers and such just get things so wrong. They think that we of the Underworld can make things happen according to their desires, and some we can. Sex and wealth, no problem. Can do looks for slightly more, and eternal youth is in the portfolio but only with the right specialists at the top of the line.

Love is much harder.

Dinner reservations at nine on a Saturday night at the most popular places are almost downright impossible.

Which is a long way of saying that Martha is horribly busy and never gets any downtime for Herself, and we were more sorry for Her that She couldn't hang out with us than sorry for ourselves for not having Her around. Satan can be so much fun.

So in a much better frame of mind I went home to pick up my pj's and check my e-mail and MagicMirror before going over to Eros's at seven.

MagicMirror is like MySpace or LiveJournal for Underworlders. Actually, I have a LiveJournal, too, mostly to read what the humans I know are doing, but MagicMirror is my real home territory. It's secure—only Underworlders have accounts, or can even find it. The URL doesn't even exist without the right magical interface.

In fact, it's based on the old magical Magic Mirror that we used to use before it was easier to get online. The old method, which some of the less savvy demons still use, works with a real mirror and blood and takes up loads of energy. Ours. The old-style Magic Mirror still works, but it's limited and blood is impossible to get out of good linens. Frankly, with all the spells and magical hoopla to make it work, the system is such a bother that no one ever used it to announce movie outings or post food porn.

There were no new updates on my friends' list. Desi probably wouldn't mention Steve, at least not until she'd had a first date. And then it would be locked to her "Girls Only, TMI" filter.

A lot of demons don't even bother with Magic-Mirror because they can't handle the technology and don't see the benefit. Most of us are from an era before telecommunications, let alone the computer. Truth is, many of us date from before written language.

In my own mortal existence, only a very few could read and write. Literacy was a form of magic, and a very powerful one at that. Since I was a priestess of Ishtar before Satan chose me as one of Her (high ranking) minions, I did, in fact, learn to read and write. While most men in Babylon were considered unworthy to be initiated into this most secret of arcane arts, the High Priestess and her few chosen acolytes did learn.

Maybe we were the only women in Babylon who could read and write, though it wouldn't surprise me if the Queen and maybe one or two of the royal wives learned as well. Wives, daughters of foreign kings who had real status in the Women's Palace, not concubines.

Princesses were not taught to read. I'm not even sure all the princes were, except the sons of powerful wives who were most likely to inherit. I know a lot about being a princess in Babylon; I had been one. It was a fairly unspectacular position. I was the thirty-fifth daughter of the King by a minor concubine. My mother was not from one of the noble families of Babylon, nor was she a princess married off to secure an alliance. That would have given her the rank of a wife, anyway, and would have made me valuable enough to possibly marry off to some foreign satrap or one of my father's nobles.

My mother, though, was just an exceptionally pretty girl who was bought by the Palace at the age of fourteen and served the King maybe two or three times ever. I mostly remember her as plump and satisfied with her lot. No great love, of course, but the King had over a hundred concubines and some he never even saw. Since my mother had borne him a child, even a lowly girl child, she had high rank among the concubines. She had a private room in the women's quarters and several pieces of good jewelry that were gifts from the King.

She had come from a common farm family, so the beauty of the concubines' quarters in the Palace, though not so fine as the wives' residences, delighted her. She didn't have to till and hoe and harvest, grind grain, beat flax, weave, cook, brew, make pots, milk sheep, make cheese, or bear thirteen children. She didn't have to worry about going hungry due to famine or drought or just bad luck. She scoffed at some of the other concubines, those who complained about never having had love or a man of their own.

"They eat every day," she would say. "They have a home, with thick carpets and even a bed, and slaves to clean and a bathhouse with lilies in the water and they're whining? We eat meat three or four times a week and cheese every day and we have beer and wine, morning and evening. We are very fortunate, girl, never forget that."

And she was right. I've lived over three thousand years, and I've seen what life is like for most people on this planet. And it sucks. And women usually have it worse, married off too young, having baby after baby until they die in childbirth, eating only the leftovers after the husband and sons have eaten their fill, and still having to work the land or weave the cloth. Even today this is true in most of the world, so I try never to forget what I learned from my mother. I relish the good things I have, and I appreciate the fact that most women in the world do not live in a beautiful apartment (or palace) or have enough to eat every day, let alone food at the best restaurants in New York.

Anyway, minor princesses like me were prized applicants for the Temple service. I knew that's what I wanted even when I was very young, so I became an acolyte at the age of seven and a novice at twelve. By sixteen I was a full priestess and was being initiated into the deep secrets of written cuneiform. Then Satan came along and offered me immortality, eternal youth and beauty, and power over men. All I had to do was sign over my immortal soul. I did take a few days to consider the offer, but being a succubus sounded very much like being a Priestess of Ishtar, only with better options. Before the week was out I'd signed the contract with Hell. With a little extra bargaining, of course, demanding my escape clause for love and a few additional perks not included in the boilerplate.

Anyway, if I can learn to use MagicMirror, someone who was born in the fifteenth century certainly should be able to master it. I have little patience with Renaissance and Age of Reason types who are constantly confounded by technology while an oldster like me can figure out how to download the shareware to manage my schedule from my laptop.

Now, if I could just remember to sync my Treo and my computer more than once a month I'd be in great shape.

Nothing new on MagicMirror, like I said. Well, it was Sunday. Everyone had been busy Saturday night, and those who weren't weren't going to admit it and show up online like losers when they should have been out at a party or club or something. No one would start posting about the weekend until tonight. Except a few really boring Wrath posts about demons who started fights on Saturday night and couldn't wait to wash off the blood to post about it.

Starting a fight in a bar on a Saturday night is nothing to brag about in my opinion. Mortals manage that well enough themselves without demonic intervention. I just do not understand demons who have to show off when they haven't even done anything. Satan has to praise their efforts, too. She feels it's good management practice, even when the Wrath in question merely escalated a shouting match to a fistfight. "My minions always should feel that they are valued and their efforts are appreciated," She has said many times.

I only turned to e-mail after the blog, and almost missed the one actual e-mail in the pile of spam I had to clean out. To my shock, there was an e-mail from someone who wanted to talk to me about a missing person. Probably one of my guys, and I did not want to be traced. In fact, I take great care that no one has any idea of where the guys go, and that no one who sees them leave with me can remember me. And I'm very, very good, though today's technology does sometimes worry me.

There's more magic to being a succubus than sending a creep up in flames. I automatically fuzz myself on any security camera or device and my phone number and the other e-mail address appears only for my prey. Once the bait gets taken, any other indication of my passing immediately dissolves. When She's in work mode, Satan is unbelievably efficient. And She has got the entire Security Division to do the work, and they're very good—among the smartest, most efficient demons in Hell. Under the leadership of Beliel, Security has become one of the premier divisions, which has escalated the rivalry between him and Meph, who is Satan's first lieutenant, and Beelzebub and Marduk and Moloch.

So no one, especially no human, should have been able to trace me. The e-mail spooked me for a moment and I deleted it. But not before I took note of the address and the name of the sender: one Nathan Coleman.

Deleted.

I got my cute aqua pajamas with the fish on them and last year's embroidered slippers with sequins and threw them all into a Dean and DeLuca's bag. Vincent waved at me when I came downstairs again. "Do you want a cab?" he asked, all eagerness. I should see if he has an account on MagicMirror.

"No thanks," I said. I was planning to hit the bodega on the corner for a couple of pints of Ben and Jerry's as my contribution to the sweetfest. I'd get a cab when I got to the avenue, but I did appreciate the boy's enthusiasm.

I got to Eros's place a little past seven, which was being really early for me. The doorman here isn't a minion, but he knows us, so we don't have any problems going directly upstairs. Once I arrived I dropped my bag and took the ice cream into her outrageously luxurious kitchen. Unlike my little closet with appliances stuck together and only enough countertop to cover the dishwasher, Eros had a kitchen where four people could comfortably congregate. I stashed the Phish Food and Cherry Garcia in the freezer, where it kept company with a stack of frozen pizzas and a tiny tub of Godiva Raspberry Truffle ice cream.

I got to the living room where Sybil was already arrayed in a white cotton April Connell antique-style nightdress with enough pin tucking and lace insets to keep a Victorian seamstress at work for a week.

I thought it was a bit early for the pj's just yet, so I started leafing through the pile of take-out menus Eros had set out on the glass coffee table. Our hostess was in front of the fireplace carefully studying the position of her Duralog.

Desi was the last to arrive, flushed and smiling with her packages under her arm.

"You didn't," Eros said flatly.

"Didn't what?" Sybil asked.

"There were already three e-mails, and I knew I was going to go. It just made sense," Desi defended herself.

"You didn't actually send it already, did you?" Sybil demanded.

Desi looked at the polished oak floor.

"Desire, Minion of Hell, I am ashamed of you," Eros said in her coldest voice. "Six hundred years old and you can't put a guy off for even a day or two? Still? You know that's the fastest way to lose him!"

"But his e-mails were so nice," Desi defended herself. "And we're going to the museum on Thursday and I won't see him before that, so it's okay."

"It's not okay," Eros said. "I can't believe you."

"Come on," I tried to intervene. "We're here to hang out and enjoy ourselves tonight. No boys was the rule. How about no getting down on our sisters, also?"

All three of them stared at me. "No one was getting down on anyone," Sybil said. "We're just afraid that Desi could get hurt. You can't send them an e-mail the same day. Even the next day is not good. You know that, Lily."

No, I thought, *I don't know that.* A succubus does not play hard to get. Maybe that was part of my problem. Maybe if someone I liked had to work at it for a while he would think about me and what I was worth, and not just be so overcome with lust that he couldn't help himself. Maybe I had been using the wrong approach all along.

This thought lingered in the back of my head as I changed into my pajamas and painted my toenails "Mermaid Mint." It stuck with me as I debated the merits of General Tsao's Chicken versus Crispy Orange Beef in the take-out order and Eros lit the Duralog.

My mind wandered back again as we waited for the food to arrive, as Sybil talked about more home renovation plans and Desi tried to clear her reputation by not talking about Steve. When the log was blazing nicely, Eros laid out the supplies for s'mores on the table and pulled out the rotating, extendable marshmallow toasting sticks in brushed steel with a ball-bearing turning mechanism. Eros doesn't cook, but she's got every food-prep toy ever made that will fit into her oversized kitchen. She has the KitchenAid mixer and fancy blender, she has a whole set of All-Clad pots, and every gadget Cuisinart makes. And rotating, length-adjustable marshmallow sticks.

"So, Eros, did you hear anything from Beliel?" Desi asked as she judged the perfect golden color of the marshmallow.

"What's Eros doing with Beliel?" I asked. Beliel is one of the Big Five in Hell. He's the Head of Security, which is one of the most efficient, organized, and covert groups in the Underworld. Satan has been very pleased with their progress lately, but we don't hear much.

Eros just shrugged. "I'm not doing anything with him," she said. "Just like you and Mephistopheles. We chat sometimes."

"Beliel is a foodie?" I asked. Because most of my relationship with Mephistopheles centers on restaurant reviews in MagicMirror. Really. He and I don't actually get together, we just read each other's food porn. And that's about all.

Eros shook her head. Her long chandelier earrings swung around her otherwise bare neck. "No, but he's interested in real estate and this building is going condo. I'm buying five apartments and he was interested in investing. At the inside price."

"Of course," Sybil said sagely. "You're buying five? Do you think I could get in? That's going to turn an excellent profit in a few years."

"I'm not just buying them for the investment," Eros said. I could understand that. Only Sybil is really savvy about money. The rest of us hand over our portfolios to her and she manages everything. And makes us very tidy returns. But . . . then why was she buying so many?

"First of all, if any one of you wanted to live here, we could arrange it. The apartments are all beautiful, and I would so love to have all of you in the building. Think of it, all of us living under one roof. It would be wonderful."

Sybil sighed. "I just bought all this new wallpaper."

Eros was buying five apartments. In this superbeautiful luxury building. And she was willing to rent them to her friends, to us, at a reasonable rate.

"It's not like I really need the money," she said, and we knew that was the truth. The fact is, none of us need the money. Live long enough with the support of Hell and you can put away quite a nice nest egg. Acquiring property like Eros was about to do was one of the most reasonable ways to keep the cash flow large enough to support a full-blown Manolo Blahnik habit.

But, much as I like the building and much as I love my friends, I didn't quite see us all living together like college girls in a dorm. We're a little too old and too independent, for one thing. And for another, well, I love Eros's building but I really like my apartment. It suits me. And I hate moving, even when the packers do the worst of the job.

Even with chocolate and graham crackers set out elegantly on the table and high-tech roasting sticks in our hands, we were all stunned into immobility and shocked to silence. An eighteenth-century German clock ticked loudly on the mantelpiece for minutes as we all tried to find words and thoughts to put together.

"Oh, come on, it's not as if none of you have ever bought property," Eros finally said as if she were exasperated. "You all own at least an apartment in Paris or a ranch in Texas."

I wondered who had invested in Texas. I had bought commercial property in San Francisco right after the Big 'Quake in '06—nineteen oh-six, that was. That, and the villa in Tuscany and the coffee plantation in Hawaii were keeping my bank account very happy, along with my nice investment portfolio. But I had never bought a New York apartment.

For a moment I wondered why I hadn't, why I'd lived in this city for decades but hadn't committed to a single property. Maybe because there were so many temptations and I just wasn't a settling-down type of gal. Maybe if NYU didn't own everything worth having around Washington Square Park I would have taken the plunge, but really I had to remember that back in the '70s that had been a kind of sketchy area full of drug dealers.

No, it wasn't the building or that she was buying that was the shock. Or even that she had already planned for us all to live together here. It was that Eros was being her old demigoddess self, making the decisions and arrangements and assuming that we'd all go along with what she'd decided. You'd think that after a few hundred years she would have figured out that we're pretty self-reliant and independent and sometimes need our space. And that just because she'd been a goddess once didn't mean that she got to tell us all what to do.

"So, who's in?" she asked cheerfully. "I'd already had some ideas on who might like which unit best."

"I just bought wallpaper," Sybil reminded her again. "So I don't think I'll want to move, at least not for a long time. But it's a great investment, Eros; you're a financial genius to think of it!"

"C'mon, Eros, it's awesome that you're doing this and I'm really impressed. But I think we're all kind of settled in our places," Desi said diplomatically. "It would be fun, and maybe one of these days we'll all move in, but I don't think that would happen soon."

"What about Beliel?" Sybil asked. "Is he going in with you, or is he buying as well?"

Eros shrugged. "He's going with me, since he'd need me to get the insider price. It was really between the two of us to get the five apartments, but I thought it would be a great idea for us to all live together. It would be fun. But if it isn't going to work out . . ."

"Is Beliel moving in?" I asked, more out of curiosity than anything.

"He wants a place in New York," Eros admitted. "Not that I think he'd be here all that much, but there are a lot of security issues in this area and he's tired of the Pierre."

At that, all of us, me included, stuck our marshmallows on the fancy sticks and rotated them carefully over the Duralog until they were evenly dripping and brown (but not burned). I dutifully constructed the chocolate and graham sandwich and made appreciative noises, but I didn't taste a thing. Even with my best friends, the isolation threatened to overwhelm me. As soon as it was reasonable, I changed back into my street clothes and said my good-byes.

chapter
FIVE

Monday morning the alarm got me out of bed. Alone, as always, but at least there were no ashes to clean up. No, I'd come home and taken a long hot bath in my clawfoot tub (why would I give up my perfect bathtub and move to Eros's building?) with a Lush bathbomb fizzing and scattering fine scent and flower petals in the steamy water. I lay back with cucumber slices on my eyes and a box of Godiva truffles on the floor next to me and tried to simply enjoy the sensations. The scent and warmth of the water soothed my muscles and the cucumber made my eyes feel less itchy and swollen. And the truffles were strictly medicinal.

Do not think, do not think, I commanded myself. Just feel the water, smell the flowers, remember that Lush products are all organic and fresh and you could eat them if you wanted to. Except they'd taste like soap. Taste the truffles instead. Mmmmm. Chocolate.

I slept deeply that night and woke up and went to work on Monday dressed in a new Versace blouse with my favorite tweed pencil skirt.

I actually love my job. I'm the accessories editor at *Trend*, a famous and important women's fashion magazine, and today I had to sort through two stories and a photo shoot for our next issue, get the writer and stylist moving for the issue after, and decide on the page, writer, and photographer for the month after that. Not to mention the regular monthly updates on accessories and bags, which I usually work out myself with the help of one of my favorite photographers and the art department.

So I was leafing through the press releases from various companies when I saw the most adorable Kate Spade bags for spring in woven wicker with different-colored leather accents. Those wicker bags, they were the stuff of my lust. One set even had the leather trim in a pale metallic bronze. It would be perfect with everything in my wardrobe and it just flattered my complexion. I admit that I spent more time fantasizing myself with this new bag than going over photos for the next issue.

Yes, I work. We all work. Sometimes, on the really bad days, I wonder why I bother, why I don't stay in bed all day eating chocolates and watching DVDs. I don't really need the money, which is good because in publishing I don't earn enough to live the way I live anyway. That's on the bad weeks. Mostly, though, I work because sitting at home all day gets lonely and dull after the second week. And I've made mortal friends in the office and it keeps me in touch with the way the world is today. Whenever today happens to be.

Back in previous eras I'd done different things. Of course, being in the Court (Ottoman, Russian, Dutch, and English under Charles II) was always a proper job along with the perks. How else could I establish my credentials among the decadent nobility? Then in the Victorian period proper women didn't work, but we were expected to spend a lot of time supporting Causes. I helped organize charity balls to assist fallen women. Being one myself, I felt that I was uniquely in a position to assess their needs. Besides, I rather liked organizing charity balls.

Truth is, without a husband or children and without any friends who are free during the day to meet for lunch and museums and shopping, life is just too dull without a job. Work also gives me a sense of who I am when I'm not being a succubus. I mean, I can't be all succubus all the time. I don't have the stomach for that many men in Arrow polyester and even Satan doesn't ask for more than three deliveries a month. When I was a Priestess there were things to do besides sex (which was a sacred part of our duties in Babylon) and ritual worship, singing and chanting and decorating altars. The Temple was a business, and as a prospective High Priestess I had to learn to run it, to deal with tradesmen and schedule deliveries and decide on allocations. How much for sacred oil this moon, and were we going through the sacramental beer too quickly.

Honestly, a lot of my life in the Temple was straightforward management, no different from any manager in any company in modern New York. No different from running a brothel, either, which I'd done a few times when I'd had to train a few of Satan's newer recruits.

I thought about the many experiences I'd had as I sat through an afternoon marketing meeting. How many hundreds of thousands of meetings just like this one had I endured in my long existence? At least I'd perfected the pretense that I was paying attention while I let my mind wander, and chimed in just on cue about the new line of bags and how I thought we needed to target more accessory houses for advertising. Which was what they all expected me to say, and then the conversation went back to the age-old argument of whether we should try to develop a strategy to get rid of drugstore cosmetic support.

So I listened to the same arguments again and then went back to my office and spread photos of chunky bracelets over my desk, circling the best ones with a blue marker and making notes on the appropriate places to insert in the single page of text. It was diverting enough that I forgot I was, in fact, a personal courier to the Prince of Hell Herself, and mostly considered myself an ordinary accessories editor at *Trend* magazine.

Which was still the way I felt as I took the subway home and stopped in the bodega on the corner for some fresh flowers to brighten up the living room. After working on Spring and Summer collections all day (not to mention scheduling a page of beach totes and the best in dressy flip-flops) I needed something to counteract the dark and chilly reminder that it was still February.

Vincent saw me half a block away and had the door gaping for my entry. "Would you like me to help you carry those up?" he asked eagerly.

"It's okay," I told him. "It wouldn't look right if you're not here in the lobby, especially after dark. I mean, really, we're counting on you for our safety, not to carry flowers around."

That straightened his shoulders. "Oh, and I have to

tell you," he whispered as I got my mail. "There has been a man asking for you. Says his name is Nathan Coleman. He said he called but you were out, and said that he'd try to drop by again. I'll get rid of him if you'd like."

Nathan Coleman? The name rang a bell—yeah, the e-mail about the missing man. Guess he wasn't a spammer then. I was going to have to get rid of him.

There were ways to deal with this. The easiest was probably the most direct. I could just meet with him and act confused, and it would be all over. I couldn't help him. If he persisted, I could use my attraction on him and that would end the situation immediately. He'd be missing then, and I might have to think about moving, or change my name or something. I'd had to do it before and I really hate that, though with Eros buying five apartments at least there was a place I could go on short notice.

The one thing I did know from all my experience was that putting off the inevitable didn't make it any easier. Or better. Better to just get it done with. "If he comes back, call me on the intercom," I told Vince.

"But he could be dangerous," he protested.

I smiled. I could be dangerous, too. And it was better to appeal to the doorman's sense of honor and protective nature rather than make points for feminist self-determination.

"I think I know who he is," I mollified my would-be knight. "It's really okay, he just wants to ask about a friend. And if there is any trouble, I just have to hit the intercom and I know you'd be up in a second."

Vincent smiled. Oooh, Martha does pick the cuties. Anyway, much as having Satan's minions in the lobby can annoy me, they really do take care of a lot of my needs. And they're always eye candy, and I'll bet would happily be more than eye candy if I asked. And since they're already dead and in Hell I don't have to worry about the incendiary consequences.

Hmmm, so why had I never considered dating another demon? There were more than a few that were cute and smart and fun. It wouldn't make me mortal, though, wouldn't change me from being a succubus because a demon doesn't count as a man. Not worth the bother.

I managed my keys between the flowers and the bag with my Ben & Jerry's and a take-out box from Benny's Burritos on Fifth and Avenue A. Yeah, it was a bit out of my way, but I'd really been jonesing for one of their steak-extra-cheese burritos in salsa verde, and none of my posse were really Benny's freaks. Which I do not pretend to understand. Sybil doesn't like Mexican at all, and Eros only wants the very elegant stuff. Benny's is too low class for her, though she's all over the Cowgirl Hall of Fame (though I think it's the roasted garlic there that she can't resist). Desi likes burritos just fine but thinks that if she's going to the East Village she really would prefer Indian food on Curry Row, which is what everyone calls that one block of East Sixth Street between First and Avenue A. A number of guidebooks have called it the best-smelling street in New York, and if you're in the mood for Indian food that's probably true.

So Benny's is a solitary delight for me. Since tonight is a delivery night, I could have hit Benny's on the way out for service and sit-down, but I don't like to eat alone in public. Maybe because when I know I'll have my mojo on, I won't be left in peace. The prey will swarm around and I won't be able to just relax with my burrito and chips before hitting the clubs. Besides, I'd been busy at work and I wanted to catch up on MagicMirror before going out.

It was one of those nights. At particular times, which are predicted by a complicated formula that includes the aspects of the Moon, the Earth, Venus, and Mars, along with specific hours not only of astrological conjunction but "witching hours," I am irresistible. I am lust incarnate, and any man who sees me desires me. On those nights I am demon succubus, the deliverer into Hell of whomever enters my bed. That's in the contract.

The hours are specific and limited. Ten to three a.m. on the nights when the particular astrological alignments are in the correct degrees. Once upon a time it took a fair bit of work for me to calculate the time; these days I've just got it running on my computer, all neatly entered into my calendar in red. Hunting nights.

What makes me irresistible during these particular and limited times are my pheromones. During the correct astrological windows, whatever changes about me specifically affects the subtle underlying scent that is more instinct than actual attraction.

But not for a couple of hours yet. So I nuked my burrito and booted up the laptop in the living room. I ate while I read the blog and caught up on the doings of Hell.

Okay, so I got a little distracted. It happens online. I'm reading and there's some really exciting food porn that just makes me salivate. This time I ran across a flamewar in Marduk's topic about the Orders of Precedence, and whether Mephistopheles ranks Marduk. Well, easy enough to imagine what Marduk thinks about the situation, but there is good reason for Meph to get top billing even if Marduk is another Babylonian, so I spent some time composing a conciliatory post pointing out that really the incident did take place in Meph's territory and that Marduk shouldn't take it personally. Marduk is the head of the Treasury of Hell, after all, and if he's no longer a god he's got one of the top gigs in the Underworld. Along with Beelzebub, Beliel, Moloch, and Meph, he's in the next layer of organization directly under Satan Herself. Though Moloch's specialty isn't really directly in line politically, he's mostly included out of courtesy because Satan has been so pleased with his performance.

I like Meph, truth be told. He's smart and interesting and a lot of fun, to say nothing of being Satan's second in command. Marduk can be a stuffed-shirt prig, and I don't dare drop him from my friends list because he'd whine all over Hell about it. But he expects my support because he was a Babylonian deity and I did at one time pay him homage. That was back before I knew the Orders of Precedence of Hell and got to hang with him one on one. Face-to-face, Marduk is a has-been who can't change with the times. It's surprising that he's on MagicMirror at all—I always thought he'd be one of the Luddites who refused to master the tech. And hey, maybe he hasn't. Maybe he's impressed one of the newly delivered (and I certainly could supply enough of them myself) to do his setup. Maybe someone's made him a cuneiform keyboard.

Part of the problem is that since Pride is the greatest sin, most of us minions excel at it. Which means that there are a lot of prickly egos out there on Magic-Mirror, and it's very easy to rub someone the wrong way unwittingly. Emoticons just don't replace the smile and the sarcasm that can take the sting from what might appear to be a personal affront.

Really, it's not so different from a human business office, except that you can't quit and everyone has a memory that goes for millennia. And even among the immortals, there are always a few who don't twig to that and end up making everything much more uncomfortable for the rest of us.

Then I remembered that I hadn't bothered with the Ben and Jerry's and I craved at least a taste. After that I had to get dressed to go out and hunt.

I may have the pheromones from Hell, quite literally, but I still dress the part. I don't have to, really, though the more skin I show the more my succubus scent permeates the area. If I wanted to damp it down I could wear layers of clothing that covered me from head to toe, but Satan doesn't approve. This is my mission for Her, and while She's the greatest big sis in the world, I do have a contract with Her.

So I tried on four different outfits, all of them a little short, and finally settled on a silk Prada slipdress that was cream-colored but had a subtle pattern in a metallic purple that hinted of copper in the right light. I had a bag in the same metallic purple that I threw on the bed to make sure I didn't forget it, and was hesitating between copper sandals and dusky purple stilettos when the intercom rang.

chapter
SIX

I buzzed. "A Nathan Coleman to see you," Vincent informed me from the lobby.

Oh, damn, not *now,* I thought. The mojo was on. He would fling himself at me and protest and say he was in love, or at least overwhelmingly in lust.

I could, of course, just take him. That would be the easiest thing. I wouldn't have to go out and I wouldn't have to make a decision about the shoes. And no one would know but Vincent.

But unlike some guy in a bar who couldn't be traced to me at all, this Nathan Coleman had come looking for me. More than once. He must have made notes somewhere. Maybe he had told someone.

Maybe I was being paranoid.

No matter. It paid to be paranoid. Remaining untraceable was getting harder all the time, and I needed the cooperation of Hell and the support of Satan's power to do it. Someone who had been trying to track me down and had my address (almost definitely written down somewhere where a hunky detective like Desi's new Steve could find it with his eyes closed) was not prime succubus bait. Not when he had come directly here. Not when someone might know where he was.

"I'm going out," I said into the intercom.

"Too late," Vincent said. "You said send him up, so I did. Do you want me to get him and bring him back down?"

"I may need help to get him out of here," I admitted. "I've got my mojo on."

"Wow," Vince said with admiration. "Maybe I should come up just in case."

"I'll call if I need you," I said and cut off the intercom.

Actually, knowing that Vincent was ready to come and help me out was a great comfort. But I've been a succubus for three thousand years and I've learned some tricks of my own. I went back to the bedroom, stuffed my bare feet into oversized fuzzy slippers and threw a heavy, full-length terry cloth robe over my tiny dress that covered me up fairly thoroughly. I tossed a towel over my hair, as if I'd just come from the shower. Hair is especially rich in the succubus scent during my power windows, so covering it up would definitely damp down the attraction.

Okay, it wasn't perfect. He would still find me unbearably desirable. But I'd be able to get rid of him. And if I couldn't there was always faithful Vincent waiting down in the lobby to play the White Knight of Hell.

The doorbell rang. I looked out the eyehole. In the fish-eye lens it was hard to tell for sure, but he seemed awfully attractive. Pity to have to send him away. I opened the door a crack and kept it on the chain. Not because I was afraid of him—I did plan to invite him in or at least open the door more onto the hall—but because he would expect that. A woman who lives in the city alone does not just open her door to a stranger, not even in a building with a doorman on duty.

"Yes?" I said through the inch-wide gap in the door. I made sure my voice dripped suspicion.

"I'm really sorry to bother you, but I was hoping that you could help me," he began.

"I'm not buying anything and I'm already a member of the Sierra Club." I cut him off.

He held up a laminated picture of himself. And yes, he was indeed very handsome. I knew I would do so much worse if I went out. I had a sudden deep urge to throw open the door, throw off the bathrobe, and drag him inside.

Instead I made myself study the card he displayed. It appeared to be a PI's license, though I didn't trust anything of the kind. There are plenty of novelty shops that will make up all kinds of realistic-looking credentials for fifty dollars.

"Look, I'm really sorry to come by so late. I sent you an e-mail and I tried to come by earlier, but you weren't home and you didn't reply to my e-mail," he pleaded. "This will only take a minute."

"Okay," I said, keeping the door on the chain.

He sighed and handed a paper through the crack. Then he blew his nose loudly and I was flooded with relief. A cold! He had a cold! He might not be entirely immune to my pheromones, but with me covered up as I was and with his cold he wouldn't fling himself through the door and at my feet. I wasn't entirely safe, but I was much more in control. No wonder he hadn't battered the door down already. I had started to worry that I was losing my touch.

I plucked the paper from his fingers. It was a picture of a fairly nondescript man. Cheap haircut, medium sandy hair, mustache, watery blue eyes.

"Look, this won't take long but it might be easier if you open the door. I'm not going to attack you."

"I'll bet that's what all the serial killers say," I muttered back. Not because I was worried, but because worry was expected.

He laughed. "Fair enough," he agreed. "But could you look at this picture and tell me if you've seen this man in the past two weeks? He's disappeared and I'm looking for him."

I looked at the picture carefully and really, truly, to the depths of my highly mortgaged nonexistent soul, I could not say if I'd ever seen this guy or not. He wasn't Brad. He wasn't any of the ones in the last week, I was pretty sure of that. But more? I didn't remember. And he was so terribly ordinary.

"I don't think so," I said. "At least not recently. Why would I have?"

"Your name and address were in his Palm Pilot."

"What? Was he going to see me? Did it say why? Could you tell me his name? Because really, I don't recognize him," I answered perfectly truthfully. And, feeling utterly innocent and completely candid, I slipped the chain off the door and opened it more widely.

This Nathan Coleman was much better-looking in person than in his laminated license picture. Though his nose was red and there were dark circles under his eyes that attested to his current viral state, his wide mouth turned up with wry humor and his eyes were a startling blue that I told myself probably came from colored contact lenses. The dark hair contrasted with his very pale skin, which made his long lashes and straight eyebrows look strong and direct. Dark hair, pale skin, blue eyes—I wondered if he might be black Irish, though his features didn't look Irish at all.

He blew his nose again, into a monogrammed linen handkerchief. My heart melted. He was wearing an Armani overcoat, but it was the monogrammed hankie that made me go all weak in the knees. Real men do not use Kleenex. The very best use fine Irish linen with woven tone-on-tone stripes around the outer edge, just like Nathan Coleman's. And the crème de la crème have thick, elegant monograms with all three initials, custom embroidered and not bought twelve to a package with just a cheaply stitched single letter for the last name. No, these had a big C in the middle with a stylized N and R on the sides.

I wondered whether the R stood for Robert or Richard, or maybe something a touch less ubiquitous like Ryan or Roger. I almost asked, but that would be nosy and would keep him around too long.

I pretended to study the picture more carefully. "I can't say that I've ever met him," I said honestly. "I have no idea who he is or why he might have my address. He doesn't look like he's in the fashion industry."

"No," Nathan agreed immediately with a slight smile. "He's certainly not in the fashion industry. His name is Craig Branford and he's a pharmacist from Huntington, Long Island. He was last seen on February tenth boarding an LIRR train for the city. We're checking out everyone he might have known to try to find him."

"I've never been to Huntington," I said weakly. "I went out to the Hamptons for a couple of weekends last summer, and for a party in October."

The entire situation was ridiculous. Here I had been all concerned about someone tracking down a missing man because I'd possibly delivered him, and it turned out to be someone I truly couldn't recognize. Not that I would have recognized all of the men I'd delivered to Satan, but this would have been in the past two weeks at most. That would include Brad, who had been clean-shaven and nothing like this guy, and someone named Derek, who'd had a shaved head and tattoos and had said that he was a DJ. There had been one more, chubby and balding but with a scraggly ponytail all the same, the week before. But he'd been some kind of computer guy, not a pharmacist. He'd offered to set up automatic wireless syncing between my Treo and my computer, but only after he'd had sex with me. Which meant it never got done and I could really use an automatic sync program. That was my total for the past ten days.

"Don't worry about it," Nathan said. "He probably just took off. People do."

"But why would he have my name? My address?" I was feeling very put upon. "I didn't know this guy. And it was my home address, not even my office."

"Where do you work?" Nathan asked, very businesslike. "If I need to contact you again, you might be more comfortable at the office."

I told him, and he whistled.

"And what do you do there?" he asked, sounding impressed.

"I'm the accessories editor," I admitted.

"Being any kind of an editor so young is an achievement," he said. "I had some ambitions in writing once, but got sidetracked. A few people I went to school with did end up in publishing, though. Maybe you've heard of Stephanie Widenow?"

I practically yipped. "Of course I know Stephanie. Everyone knows her. She's the wunderkind of Condé Nast." I thought for a moment and narrowed my eyes. "Stephanie went to . . . let me see, not Columbia . . ."

"Yale," he supplied. "We were in Trumbull together."

"Trumbull?" I was confused again but I didn't expect to understand the intricacies of the modern American educational system.

"It's a residential college at Yale. A dorm. That's what we call our dorms."

"Oh." I guess I should have sounded more impressed. "I didn't think that Yalies became PIs. And what has this got to do with the missing Mr. Branford?"

"Not much," he confessed gamely, and blew his nose again. I could feel the shimmering in my veins that told me that my powers were on, that I was completely and utterly irresistible to anyone who liked women. Except for this guy with the serious head cold. Thank goodness. But time was wasting and Satan would be expecting Her delivery sometime soon. I knew that I should get rid of him, and I didn't want to.

Did I like Nathan R. Coleman? Find him attractive? Appealing?

Or was my desire to keep him another minute or two really an act of procrastination? I just didn't feel in the mood for another pickup, another loser, another set of lies (they all say they're single, or that their wives don't really care anymore) or another sniff of Old Spice.

"Being a PI isn't what people think," Nathan was saying hoarsely. "It's mostly research, and research is something I'm very good at. I leave the guns and the excitement to the guys on TV. Works better that way."

"Oh." I couldn't think of any good reason to try to make him stay.

"Well, thanks," Mr. Coleman said. "If you think of anything, give me a call, okay?" He handed me his card, which identified him as an associate of the Perkins McCauly Investigative Agency with a pretty foiled crest. Cards like that could be had for fifty dollars from the same folks who'd make up the PI license. I wondered how many different kinds he carried, and under how many different names. I wondered how good a deal he got on volume business and it crossed my mind to ask. After all, I could use some fake cards.

"And I may call back sometime, in case I've got some ideas of where he might have gotten your name," the fake PI continued. "We might be able to triangulate on the source, which could help us understand where he might have gone."

"Sure," I said. Whatever.

"Well, thanks," he said, and then turned from the door and walked down the hall. I watched as he called for the elevator, and then locked the door.

I hit the intercom to inform my overeager doorman. "I'm on my way up," he said as soon as he came on.

"No, Vincent, I'm calling to tell you that everything's

fine. He's leaving now. There was no problem. I didn't even know the person he was asking about."

"Oh." My doorman sounded so disappointed I felt that I had to think of something to cheer him up and prove that I still needed him.

"Could you get me a cab in fifteen minutes?" I asked. Usually I don't mind the half-block walk to the avenue to catch a cab, but poor Vincent really did need some reassurance that he was being helpful, and the request seemed to cheer him up considerably. Or maybe he'd just seen Nathan Coleman leave the building.

I finished getting dressed, made sure that my wallet, keys, lipstick, and cell phone were all in the purse, and made a snap decision to wear the metallic copper Vivienne Westwood shoes that Eros had talked me into last season that I almost never wore.

At *Trend,* shoes are a separate department and Danielle is the shoe editor. But Danielle is one of the nicest people at work and always makes sure that everyone knows what wonderful shoes and boots are just their style in the coming seasons. For a mortal, Danielle is a real friend. I've even considered inviting her to meet the gang one night for s'mores. Much as the demon gang are my closest buds, it's really good to have someone to call a friend at work, who's willing to gossip about who is being impossible this week and who is about to ditch her SO. And who's about to get ditched.

Okay, time to stop stalling. The cab was waiting outside as Vincent held the door for me almost ceremonially. And then I was in the yellow taxi and on my way to Gehenna, which is one of the more hip bars this week.

Bars for the cool twenty-something crowd were not my first hunting ground. Succubi are traditionally thought to target good husbands, to seduce the men of Heaven into Hell. Demons, understand, cannot tempt the truly righteous. I'd had enough of the self-righteous bad and the boring, and there's no reason why some arrogant creep who thinks that getting drunk is the only pleasure in life shouldn't take the short road to the Underworld. There are all kinds who deserve my services and I wasn't going to specialize too much. At least at Gehenna the music didn't suck and the drinks were tasty.

At eleven the bar was full. I ordered my mojito and noticed that half the bar was drinking the same. Hmmm, I was going to have to discover the next cool drink before I became too pedestrian. I avoided the two young women in imitation Juicy Couture jeans who were eyeing the room like vultures. I saw them size up my dress, my bag, my shoes, and tried not to listen as one said something deprecating to the other out of sheer envy. Okay, they were maybe twenty-four or something, and most of the way to being drunk. And they should be grateful to me, really, because whoever I picked up this night would be one fewer toad for either of them. Not that they knew that, or would appreciate it if they did. But then, they were typical hipster wannabes, a little too cheap and a little too New Jersey.

I scanned the men in the room, knowing that anyone I chose to pass near and select would have no choice but to come home with me. Maybe the gentleman with the tribal tattoo down his arm—but I liked the art. Then he put on a pair of glasses and started reading the *New Yorker.* Too appealing in some ways. The glasses made him look kinder and more vulnerable.

On one of the red sofas in the back I noticed two beefy boys with buzz cuts who seemed to be holding a competition over which of them would get drunker faster. Definitely unappealing. I wandered closer and picked up the unmistakable scent of Axe. Prey indeed.

I felt the burning through my skin that meant pheromones and enchantment were pouring out of me. Okay, one of them would have it; oh yes, one of them would get exactly what he thought he wanted. What he felt he deserved and certainly had coming. I made my decision. Whichever one of them called me "baby" or "honey" or "darling" first, that one would not get to insult a woman again.

Maybe my job is to deliver souls to Satan, but I also adhere to a feminist agenda and She most definitely approves. She's often said that I should consider myself a crusader, removing men who are potential hazards from the population. Which I could relish if only I didn't have to bring them home and get naked with them.

"Hey, baby, I got what you're looking for," the one on the left said, sealing his doom.

I walked over to him, smiled, and ran a finger over the back of his hand. "I'll just bet you do," I purred. "Want to show me?"

"What about me?" the other wailed.

I shook my head. "Only one of you gets lucky," I said, not defining what lucky would mean in their case. I turned back to the first one and raised one eye-brow. "Why don't we go someplace more private?"

He got up like an automaton, though I don't know if that's the enchantment or how much he'd had to drink. Oh, no, I thought, I hope he isn't so drunk that he can't function. Or throws up in the taxi.

He managed to stagger to his feet and get his coat on, though he didn't offer to hold mine. He lurched after me awkwardly as we made our way through the press to the door.

As we were leaving, I turned to make sure that he hadn't fallen on the long trek from the bench to the door. Every man's eyes were on me. I felt it. The mojo attracted them even if they weren't close enough to be overwhelmed.

chapter
SEVEN

"Come on, lover." I encouraged my prey to move toward the door. Since he was barely vertical this took some effort on my part. Fortunately, I am stronger than a human and could hold him up and steer him along.

Cabs were thick on the avenue near the bar, and I had no trouble hailing one that took us uptown. As I dragged my newly acquired candidate for damnation into my lobby, Vincent approached looking all natty in his uniform. "Do you need a hand?" he purred.

"No," I told him. "No problem. Do this all the time." Which was true, and depressing, and suddenly I felt sad. But not for this jerk, who was trying to yodel and wake up my neighbors. I was only doing the world a good and valuable service.

"Hush!" I told him as Vincent rang for the elevator. It was a long ride to the sixth floor. I crossed my fingers and only prayed to Ishtar (because I really can't bother Satan with these minor things) that he wouldn't throw up. I hate it when they throw up.

The doors opened and I herded him down the hall to my door. Once he was inside he sat down heavily on the floor holding his head.

"I don't feel too good," he admitted.

Whoops. "Bathroom's this way." I pushed him up and dragged him the last few feet to the bath. I did not want this creature vomiting on my carpet. For once my luck held and I got him over the tile before he lost it. Then he groaned and sank to the floor holding his head. "Just be a minute," he said. "You won't be sorry, nope, gonna do you good when I feel just a little better."

It was my own fault. I should know not to pick up drunks. Not only are they messy, but if they can't function, I can't deliver them. Well, maybe the next morning, but I didn't want this puling example of unattractive humanity in my apartment that long. I wanted him blasted, flamed, and gone. And if that meant cleaning him up a bit, then so be it.

"Hey," I said in my most chipper tone. I turned on the shower full blast and proceeded to strip in front of him. At least that got his attention. When I was down to my La Perla bra and matching thong, I leaned over him and started to tug his baby blue polo shirt over his head.

"Mmmm, up?" I lifted him under his arms, noticing that he had no definition and what might generously be thought of as athletic bulk was well on the way to fat.

"Can't," he protested.

"C'mon," I said, wiggling my hips a bit to encourage him. "It'll be fun. In the shower."

He groped my breasts, kneading me as if trying out koosh balls in a toy store. I backed into the tub, entirely regretting my new pale pink bra with Venice lace. I'd been so pleased when I'd tried it on and now

I only hoped it would survive the pummeling it was about to get.

He followed me into the tub and sat down again in his wet jeans. I hadn't been able to get them off in the three steps from the door, and he didn't have enough coordination to remove them himself. Which was only going to make it harder. Wet denim is impossible, and I wanted him out of those clothes before he dripped all over my hardwood floors and antique carpets.

Unless—no, it was too good to hope for.

I slipped my fingers under the waistband of his jeans and undid the buttons. They were 501s, no zipper, buttons all the way down.

He leered at me, and attempted a grin. "You can't wait for it, can you?" he said, his arrogance entirely comparable to the major minions of Hell. Damn, I'd hate to think of him in the Hierarchy. Yuck.

Under the jeans he was wearing Tony the Tiger boxers. I am not making this up. My imagination might be prodigious, but there are just places I can't go and Tony the Tiger boxers is one of them.

The shower was going full blast now and I had managed to leave the new lingerie on the floor and well away from the toilet (just in case). I took my prey by the hand and made a low humming sound in my throat. "Let's get all hot and wet and slippery," I purred in his ear as I held up a fresh bar of Provençal sage soap.

Wonder of wonders, he actually managed to hold himself upright in the spray. I soaped him all over, slipping my well-lathered hands over his chest and up his legs. I pulled off his boxers and used my fingers to stimulate him gently without expecting any results. He was too drunk, and I'd probably have to keep him until morning.

There are some decent guys out there. There are the smart ones and the kind ones, and a few who actually like and respect women. There are men who love kids and want commitment. I've condemned a fair number of reasonable men to the afterlife in damnation, and I've felt some degree of regret about them. In the past few hundred years I've been avoiding the nice ones. There are enough self-righteous louts, arrogant jerks, and self-involved narcissists that I don't have to deplete the supply of genuinely worthwhile men in the world.

Nothing about this particular specimen prompted my sympathy.

"What's your name?" I purred. Not because I cared but because I had to have something to call him.

"Kevin," he said hesitantly, as if that much pronunciation had been a burden.

"Well, then, Kevin, I hope you're feeling good. I hope this shower is making you feel better."

He grabbed my breasts again in his ham hands and proceeded to squeeze. "Hey, remember Mr. Whipple," I reminded him, but he was too blitzed to get the reference. "Don't squeeze the Charmin," I added.

"Your name is Charmin?" he asked, unsurprised.

"Yeah," I lied, but for some reason his mistake bothered me. Maybe because he never did ask my name.

Suddenly I wanted him gone as quickly as possible. I didn't want to have to make him come in order to go, but that was my inescapable burden. My prey have only one way to Hell, and that's through Heaven. Or at least one really spectacular orgasm.

Sighing, and knowing it was only a preliminary promise, I started to caress his cock with my soapy hand. Big shock, he started to get hard. I would have bet money that he had been too drunk to get an erection, but clearly I was wrong. Maybe it was his capacity for alcohol, maybe it was that he had a quick metabolism, or maybe he was just lucky. Maybe it was me who was lucky.

He had slumped to the bottom of the oversized tub and was stretched out as if on a bed. He sighed and leaned his head back against the high-contoured tub wall as I wrapped my fingers more firmly around his hardening member and began to squeeze in earnest. If I were lucky, if I were very lucky . . .

I helped him to stand and started to give him the hand job of his life in the shower. When he sagged against the tile I supported him with my hip and shoulder because if I were very, very lucky I wouldn't have to do any more.

Just a few more good, firm strokes.

"Oh yeah, oh yeah, baby, don't stop," he moaned.

I didn't. I didn't dare hope but I pumped my hand like a prayer of deliverance and licked into his ear for good measure.

He just leaned against the tile and let me do him. Since he'd stopped squeezing my breasts, he hadn't bothered to touch me, except to hang on to my shoulder when his knees went weak. Not even an attempt to turn me on, to do anything for me at all.

I held his balls lightly and then massaged softly

behind them with my left hand as my right kept going. I tightened my grip and added a bit of speed, of insistence. I wanted him to come. I wanted him gone.

And then he came in the shower, all over my thighs and his. Not a huge orgasm but I didn't care. He had been so drunk I was shocked he could manage at all. Desperation, it had to have been.

He came and he cried out, and suddenly he disappeared in a flash of flame and a swirl of greasy gray ashes down the drain.

Now I only had clothes to hand over to Vincent in the morning.

Even though it was near three in the morning, and I had to be at work in five hours, I turned off the spray and got out the Scrubbing Bubbles and scoured the tub immediately.

Then I took a long and very hot shower with my favorite lavender soap and shampooed my hair twice.

When I felt fresh and decent I toweled my hair dry and then wrapped a clean towel around it. If I could get it mostly dry, I would only have to blow dry for a few minutes before I went to sleep. Then I took care of business.

First, I wrested Kevin's wallet from his wet jeans. He had almost two hundred dollars in cash, which went into my wallet. I looked at his driver's license. I was right, he was from New Jersey. Twenty-six years old. A gold MasterCard with a NASCAR sticker filled out the rest of the contents of his billfold. No pictures, no business cards, not any he had collected or any of his own. Not even a phone number written in pencil on a cocktail napkin.

His jeans and boxers were soaking, so I laid them

over the shower rail to dry. I'd give everything to Vincent to take to Lighthouse International, the store for the sight-challenged on East Fifty-ninth Street. No rush on this, and I am careful to rotate charity shops. I wasn't expecting company for a day or two at the least. I'd leave the wallet without the cash on the seat of the cab that I took in the morning.

By the time I'd finished these little chores my hair was ready for a touch-up with the blow dryer. Then I settled into my soft luxury sheets, blissfully alone.

chapter
EIGHT

Desi was sobbing so hard that I was having trouble making out her words. I caught "Steve" and "Satan" and "museum" but I could have been wrong about any of them. Maybe I really should change carriers again, I thought, as I asked her to repeat herself for the twentieth time. Or buy a phone separate from the Treo. The Raz-r is really cute in an edgy kind of way. I wondered if it worked any better.

"Argggh, eeee, Steveeeee, rrrrrr, glbglb," came through the handset.

"Cafeteria," I shouted, twice. "Cafeteria. At one."

I hoped no one in the office could hear me. The door was closed, but the walls are thin. I wish she'd called on the landline, but Desi is nothing if not addicted to her speed dial. Since it was Friday and 11:30, a fair number of the staff were already starting on lunch, and most of the rest of the office were on their phones finalizing their weekend plans. I hoped.

There were a few more incoherent noises before there was nothing. I hoped she'd heard me. Just to be sure, I sent an e-mail to her work address. Not that she would be sitting in front of her computer at the moment, given the condition she was in.

Since Cafeteria at one was one of our usuals, I

hoped at worst she'd opt for the default. Oh, what the hell. I picked up my office landline and looked up her office phone. When she didn't pick up I left a voice mail. "Look, Desi, I think you need a shoulder. Cafeteria at one for lunch, I'll see you there." Then I hung up and hoped she could make it through the next hour and a half.

Desi is a desire demon. I had once understood that to mean that she created unquenchable desire in her prey. They adored her, they could not exist without her, and she got them to sign a contract with Hell for their souls in return for having their desires, or at least some of them, fulfilled. They want her so badly that they don't even hold out for a demon contract; no, they sign their souls over to eternal torment just to have whatever she will provide.

Eros and Sybil work the same way, delivery by contract. Which rates more highly because it is ostensibly willing. Ostensibly only because my friends inspire such desire, lust, or greed in their prey that their prey are only too happy to sign. The very best of their recruits (though only about one percent) are eligible to become demons, though that has to be bargained and in the contract in advance. Almost none of their victims even realizes this alternative is possible, and we don't advertise. If they don't ask for it, in writing, in full legal format in all six of the appropriate paragraphs, they don't get it. And since we've got all the best lawyers, we can usually get contracts interpreted the way we want them.

In reality, it appears to me that Desi feels as much desire for her current object as he feels for her. She angsts, she despairs, she gets all giddy and loses her sense. And she is constantly in this state because this is her position. Embodying desire for others means that she experiences it herself in far greater measure, and a whole lot more often.

Poor Desi.

I wondered what Steve had done to her.

Friday was a quiet day at the office and I'd finished most of the work I really had to do. So I had Magic-Mirror up on my computer. Asura, Lady of Vengeance, had taken a vacation to Aruba where she drowned two divers and complained about the cuisine. Which seemed like it was mostly American chains and steak houses. Well, what do you expect, going to a Dutch island? I was really tempted to write that in her reply column, but you don't say things like that to the Lady of Vengeance.

I watched the freezing rain splatter the window. Aruba sounded nice. Two days now without sun and constant precipitation—no wonder Desi was a mess. What's the good of being a demon with a pile of cash when I couldn't take off and go to Aruba for the weekend? Everyone else on MagicMirror was someplace warm and nice. Asura in Aruba, Beelzebub in Rio, even the Furies were off in Baghdad, which sounded a lot nicer than New York in the rain. Of course, they were just loving all the war and chaos and were hoping to take credit for some of it. As usual. They really liked to go where everyone else had been in on the action and then talk like they were responsible.

Hi everyone! Ohhhh, this is one of those travel posts just like sending picture postcards but so much faster! We just couldn't resist war and mayhem!

Bombs, mines, all the fun and none of the bad weather. Restaurants are a little scarce and most of them aren't very good at the moment. Journalists have such pedestrian taste—it's all lamb and roast beef and rice. And no drinks! When we finish up stirring up the crazies here, we're off to someplace where cute young waiters serve drinks with umbrellas in them.

Anyway, having loads of fun! Wish you were here! Well, you probably wish you were here, but look at all the souls we've delivered in so little time. So easy. *sigh* It's almost like a vacation.

I mean, really! At least they write with capital letters and punctuation and have not succumbed to IM abbreviations.

I was so fed up with their posturing that I closed down the site and went to zappos.com instead. And after a thorough perusal of how various companies are trying to copy the best designs it was time to go to lunch.

The restaurant is in Chelsea, very trendy with the twenty-something set and very loud. It also serves amazing lychee Bellinis, blood orange martinis, and the kind of comfort food that a demon in distress really needs. There are elegant selections on the menu as well, but I thought that Desi could use a burger or mac and cheese, and how many cool and trendy places can offer lychee Bellinis *and* mac and cheese?

Desi was already seated at a table when I arrived. She was in a back corner, as private as anything could be in this room. A large bright cocktail sat in front of her.

Good. At least she was taking some kind of care of herself, then.

"Hey, I thought this should be a three-martini lunch," I quipped at her as I took a seat.

A waiter appeared immediately and I ordered a blood orange martini and another of whatever Desi had. She would probably need it, and it was better to be prepared.

For a desire demon, Desi looked a mess. Usually her shiny hair, a perfectly exquisite but understated shade of warm honey brown, bounced in gentle waves to just below her shoulders. Now it looked stringy and dull. Her eyes, usually as large and round and blue as an anime character's, were red, surrounded by dark puffy circles. Her white blouse, the one with the extravagant cuffs, looked wilted, and washed out her complexion. She looked like she'd been up all night.

"Hey, Des," I said, and I squeezed the hand that lay limp on the table.

And she began to cry. "I don't know, Lily," she said. "I don't think I'm heartbroken; I think mostly I'm just angry. Or am I losing my touch? Am I all washed up? Am I a *failure*?" Her voice went up at the end in a long wail.

"You're certainly not a failure," I stated firmly. "What happened?"

"You remember Steve, that cute cop I met last Sunday at brunch? We had a date last night to go to the Brooklyn Museum, to see the display of his uncle's designs."

"Did you go?" I asked.

She nodded. "He picked me up at six and we went for sushi and then we went to Brooklyn. It seemed like everything was great. We were having a good time and he took me through the museum and for a cop he really understands art. He gets it in a big way. We even talked about that, and I found out that he studied architecture at Cooper Union."

I whistled, impressed. "Why's he a cop, then?"

"His uncle. He's a cop because his uncle is this world-famous architect and he wanted to take Steve on and make Steve move to Rome."

"That's not the end of the world," I pointed out. "What's so bad about Rome?"

"His uncle is a tyrant and Steve felt like he was never going to leave the family. He wanted to get out on his own and do something himself."

I nodded. So far there was nothing to explain Desi's misery, the mascara blotched from tears and the misapplication of tissues. "So what happened?" I asked. "What's the problem?"

"He's Catholic," she wailed, and then sobbed into her sodden hankie. "I don't know how he knew what I was, but he knew. But we were in the museum and I went to the ladies' and before that we were talking about stopping for a late snack afterward. And then I got out of the ladies' and he was talking to this guy and then he saw me and he looked like he'd seen something awful. Like I had turned into some kind of monster. And then he hissed at me, I mean he really actually *hissed* and said 'I abjure thee, creature of Satan, servant of darkness.' And the rest of the formula, too, only I can't bear to repeat it."

Then she broke down again, sobbing anew. At least this bout of tears cleaned off some of the runny bits of makeup still clinging to her lashes.

"How could that be?" I asked. "Whoever that man was you saw in the museum must have told him."

"I'd figured that out already," Desi said. "But how did he know? How did he know where I'd be? How'd he know Steve was my date? And mostly, how did he know that Steve would know the full formula to reject me?"

Reject. What a mild, puny word for what he'd done to Desi! Had she been some minor minion, his formula (along with the appropriate paraphernalia and faith) would have cast her directly into Hell. But she is old and strong and one of Satan's girlfriends, so she was only desperately hurt and mauled and in tears.

"But when you didn't explode in a puff of smoke or something, didn't he figure out that he was wrong and apologize?" I inquired. Not that he was wrong, of course, but usually when they try that and we don't disappear according to schedule they decide that we're not monsters at all and that they got it wrong. Clearly Steve had not followed the mainstream line of thinking on this.

"He didn't. He didn't even take me home. He stranded me in Brooklyn."

Just then the waiter appeared and I ordered our lunch. "Two macaroni and cheese, another lychee Bellini, and two Banana Nilla Vanilla puddings for dessert." Desi was definitely in need of comfort food. For a moment I wondered if I should have just ordered dessert and have done with it, but Desi needed vitamins and protein as well.

I waited until the waiter was well away before I asked my next question. "Have you told Satan?"

She shook her head.

"We've got to tell Her," I insisted. "If someone is hunting us, then this isn't just about you and Steve."

"I don't know. I'm just so humiliated. A guy abjured me and dumped me in Brooklyn. Martha will think I'm a failure. I'm no good anymore. I'm fat and ugly and old and I can't incite desire and I'm no good to Satan or to anyone. I'm so miserable—"

"Calm down, Des, it's not you. It's not even a little teeny tiny bit about you. Drink your drink, come on."

As she sipped obediently I buttered a slice of crusty French bread from the basket and handed it to her. "Now eat some bread until the food comes. I'll bet you haven't eaten anything since last night."

"Did so. A whole pint of Cherry Garcia. All by myself."

"Good for you," I praised her. "You need to keep up your strength at a time like this. And ice cream has protein and dairy and all that good stuff. And even cherries, so you had fruit, too, and we're supposed to eat more fruit. Now eat your bread and then our mac and cheese will come."

She dutifully ate some bread and I tried to wrap my mind around what she had told me. Because no matter what Desi thought of the situation, I was dead certain that we were being systematically hunted. What about that strange PI who'd turned up at my place on Monday? Okay, I hadn't heard anything from him since, but that didn't mean he was entirely gone. He had my home address and my work address and my e-mail. And I shivered and thought that I probably wasn't even close to done with Mr. Nathan Coleman.

We had more bread, and as we ate I told Des about

my strange visitor. "The thing of it is, he's not like any kind of real PI," I told her. "He's deadly good-looking and way too educated. I mean, do you really think that guys who look like movie stars and graduate from Yale take jobs tracking down exes for child support and poking into people's private lives for potential employers? I think not."

"Really?" Desi asked. She had eaten two pieces of bread, which was respectable under the circumstances. "You're not just saying that to make me feel better?"

"Des," I told her as I laid down my knife. "You have known me for six hundred years and I have never ever lied to you. Not about anything important."

"Except that gold dress that you borrowed and ruined."

"Except the gold dress," I agreed. What else could I do? "But that was a hundred and fifty years ago and I paid you back and I took my punishment from Martha for that. And once in six hundred years is pretty reliable. That should count for something."

"Except for white lies, too," she added.

"Not lies," I insisted. "Those were the fashions of the day, and when I told you I thought some of those dresses were fabulous on you, I was telling the truth. Just because we think some of those things look ridiculous now is beside the point. Everything looks ridiculous after thirty years or so. So I did *not ever* lie about any of that.

"Anyway, the PI is perfectly for real. Well, the guy himself is, though whether he is a PI or not is questionable. Deeply questionable. I don't believe it for a minute, I don't think. And I don't think that any of this is coincidence, either. There's something going on here."

"You really think so?" Desi asked tearfully, but with the first hints of recovery in her tone. "Really?"

"Really," I told her firmly. Then I thought for a moment. "And we met both of these guys within a day of each other. Hmmmm."

"But I liked Steve a lot." Desi sniffled.

Then the waiter reappeared with our lunches and we both dug into our mac and cheese with relish. I've heard comfort food is the next major trend, and for demons who don't have to worry about calories it's a great idea. Of course, when I was a child my comfort food was a barley cake with walnuts dipped in honey. No one makes them taste right anymore.

Desi was slowly coming to grips with her disappointment, and good food, along with sympathetic friends, lots of dessert, and distractions go a long way to recovering rational thought.

I waited until we'd both made a good dent in our main courses before I began to speak. Desi had actually paid attention to her food and wasn't crying anymore. Rationality was slowly returning and she would be able to grapple with her emotions soon.

"Des, Steve is one of five million guys in this city. Yeah, he's cute and smart, but he's a complete loss. If he thinks you're a minion of Hell, there's no way you can recover. You've only had half a date with him, and sure, you're used to men falling at your feet with protestations of eternal devotion after ten minutes. This one's a total loss. Chalk it up and move on. There are so many much more attractive, attentive, interesting men out there. What about Peter? You don't need to waste one minute of your life on this jerk, because that's what he is. Only a jerk strands a girl in Brooklyn."

"But, I *am* a minion of Hell," she said softly.

"No way. You are not even close to a minion. You are one of Satan's Chosen. You are of the First Rank of the Underworld and you deserve someone who will adore you. Someone who understands that you weren't just handed this position, you achieved it through centuries of dedication and hard work. You are Desire Incarnate.

"Face it, you were just too much for the guy. You're way out of his league."

"You really think that?" Her voice was small and high, like a child's.

"Yes, I do," I answered firmly.

And then our Banana Nilla Vanilla puddings arrived and I deferred to a major mood reconstruction effort.

chapter
NINE

I dialed Satan's private number as soon as I got back to the office, but only got voice mail. "Martha, it's Lily and I'm really sorry to bother You. I know You're insanely busy now, and I wouldn't call if I didn't think it was important. But I've just had lunch with Desi and someone told her date last night that she was, well, one of us. And I've had this fake PI nosing around me, too, and I think there's something up. So I thought we should tell You—"

I was going to go on, but the tape cut off. Time up.

Since I was back in the office, I tried to pay attention to charm bracelets, but they weren't doing it for me. I thought I was too upset about the possibilities of what was going on, but there was also the distinct possibility that I just didn't like the charm bracelets.

I like things that are unified and create a complete look. In accessories, I look for items that will update last season's great outfit. Or will pull together a look. Or will make clothes from H&M and Target look like they might have come from Barneys, because our readers need that. Most of them can't afford the kind of designer clothing they want, and a lot of what I try to do is show them how to get that look on a budget with a few well-chosen accessories.

I got distracted as I was musing on my career and
the possible places I could go, and did I want to stay
in accessories and should I start looking. But looking
is hard and I was at such a great magazine—was I
really willing to go to someplace with a little less pres-
tige in order to get into a better position? And really, I
like accessories. A lot, truth be told.

Scarves. And shawls were going to be big in the fall.
So maybe not sunglasses in June, but I could certainly
push a feature on shawls and scarves for September.

I was deep in planning, both the feature and how I
would approach the editor, when the phone rang. I
picked it up half expecting to hear Susan (our editor's
assistant) on the line. So when I heard Martha's voice
so full of concern I was disconcerted.

"Are you certain that he was told?" Martha was
saying before I could quite catch my breath.

"That's what Desi said, and I don't have any reason
to think she'd be mistaken," I answered. "Though of
course it could be that the fact that she saw someone
talk to her date right before he blew her off could
have been coincidence. But that would be a stretch."

"Indeed," Satan agreed. "I think I need to talk to
you girls, all of you, and immediately. Tonight. Dinner would be good. Dinner at Aquavit at nine. Tell
the others, and I'll see you then."

I was suddenly cold. Satan was very serious to
make the appointment immediately this evening, at
prime dinner hour at such a popular restaurant. And I
knew She was going to have to use some serious mojo
to get us on the list. Though of course, whenever
Satan really wants something She gets it. I guess it
was a good thing I didn't have a date that night.

Relieved that Satan was onboard and taking care of things, I was able to concentrate on my work and put together a rather exceptional proposal for my scarf and shawl feature to present at the next editorial meeting. I could coordinate with Samantha in Outerwear, and maybe we could even bring in Danielle with a forecast on boots and do a huge centerpiece. Perfect for the season and just what our readers wanted to know just as the clothes hit the stores.

It felt good to do this work. In the moments when I'm flying, when I'm really good at it, I feel like something bigger than myself. As if all the thousands of years I've spent observing and participating in humanity, all my love of fashion through all these years and the many places I have lived, all of it has come together seamlessly. Then I don't think about how lonely I am at home. Being a succubus fades into the background and I'm Lily the editor, Lily the fashion setter. So I actually paid attention to my job and was glorious for at least four hours. Then it was time to go home and get ready to go to Aquavit.

Aquavit is justifiably one of the great restaurants of New York. I arrived at ten to nine. One does not keep Satan waiting. Desi was already there, and through the glass doors I saw Sybil get out of her cab. Martha arrived last and swept us all behind Her, and we followed along to the hostess desk. We were seated immediately at a prime table, next to the windows, far from the waitstand.

Martha ordered vodka martinis all the way around. This conversation was going to require serious drinking. Of course, She also ordered the caviar and gravlax appetizers, which arrived with dense rye bread.

"Now, girls, tell me what has been happening. I'm terribly worried for you," She said, and Her voice was full of comfort and concern. She looked at each of us closely, warmly, and encouraged us to taste our drinks.

Eros and Sybil looked confused, and Desi immediately launched into the story of what had happened at the museum.

"Oh, but he was so nice," Sybil cried.

"What a damn prick," Eros said flatly. "You're better off without him."

Desi started to sniffle again and Martha patted her arm before putting the blueberry martini in her hand. Desi sipped as Martha addressed us all.

"I'm just collecting information to start," She reassured us, "but trust me, we are not letting anyone get away with insulting or upsetting my Chosen Companions. We are not interested in this idiot at all, we only need to know how he was contacted and convinced. We, and I mean all of Hell, need to know who these people are. Who met this Steven Balducci in the museum, are they members of some organization or confraternity?" Martha studied each of us and nodded, apparently satisfied.

"And you, Lily, what's this about some private investigator who showed up Monday evening? And he didn't fall for you immediately? You could have simply invited him in," She mused. "But yes, I suppose that he could be traced to you. I'm very proud you managed to dissuade him."

"Thank you," I said, my eyes on the remains of my caviar. One didn't get praise from Satan so often that one didn't cherish the moment. Besides, it didn't seem like it would be polite to pick up the last of the caviar with my fingers, and I needed to concentrate. That took more discipline than I'd shown in weeks.

So I told Her about Nathan Coleman, about his e-mail and how he came to my place and had a cold so he was less susceptible to my magic. And how he said he'd gone to Yale and that didn't match up in my worldview to a PI. Something just seemed off to me, and after Desi's incident the timing looked awfully suspicious.

Our entrées arrived then. I had ordered haddock because it was so good with the leek sauce and truffle oil that I seriously doubted this was traditional Swedish food.

"This is insupportable," Eros said, and I didn't think she was talking about the dinner. "This kind of thing hasn't happened in over a hundred years."

"Here," Satan corrected her softly. "There are plenty of areas in the world where our range of operations is fairly limited by these secret societies and cults. Even in this country there are states where we have to be careful and stay on the move. I have only two succubi for all of Georgia, not counting Atlanta. Of course, I save the plum jobs like New York for the elite. You've proved yourselves and you certainly don't need to be inconvenienced by these narrow-minded bigots. I think only the greatest cities are deserving venues for my stars. Which is why it is more disturbing to see the forces of opposition gathering any following here, in my cities."

The way She said "my cities" made it quite clear. They were Hers in every way that mattered: the people, the pavements, the pulse and tenor, the signs and colors and astronomical rents. All of it belonged to Satan, here in New York and London and Paris and Tokyo and Buenos Aires and Rio and Los Angeles. All the fun and fashionable places, all the places one wanted to be, with the best food and the most wonderful shops and the trendiest people.

Sybil had turned white and put down her fork. Since there was still food on her plate, I assumed that something else was wrong. "Nononono" she muttered softly, her eyes blank and her concentration inward. I thought she was having a vision of the future and waited to hear what she would pronounce. Whatever it was sounded like it wouldn't be too good.

"Is it them again?" she whispered. "Is it them?"

"Who, dear?" Martha coaxed her.

"The Burning Men," Sybil replied, and then I realized that what terrified her so was the past, not the future. Sybil had lived through the English Civil War when the Protestant fundamentalists under Cromwell had ousted the King and had vigorously purged and burned anyone who didn't follow their dictates to the letter. So in the course of routing out Catholics and less rigid Protestants, and those few intellectuals who cared more for evidence and scholarship than toeing the party line, Cromwell's men had also managed to eliminate a not-insignificant portion of us. I think Sybil had been imprisoned by them for some months, and it was only the end of Cromwell and the restoration of Charles II to the throne that had saved her.

The experience had traumatized her horribly. PTSD would be today's diagnosis, and she would probably do well to see a therapist. Only how could she tell a therapist that she really had lived for almost two thousand years and had been perfectly happy until her arrest by Cromwell's men? Sybil had been one of the last Oracles in Delphi, one of the few truly gifted. She had been recruited, as I had been, from the ranks of the pagan priesshood to a calling not too different from the one she had held. Only this one delivered immortality, and more magical power than we ever could have wielded as mortals.

Desi might be a closer friend and more emotionally in sync with me, but Sybil and I shared a parallel history.

But Satan did not reassure her immediately. Instead, the Prince of Darkness hesitated and patted Sybil's hand. "They are certainly not the same Burning Men," Satan said finally. "And whatever comes, I will protect you. Be assured that I shall always do my best for you. As I would have done then."

And I knew then that I had not been the only one to try to help Sybil back in the bad old days, and surely Satan was stronger than I. But done was done and nothing could be changed now. Not even with all the power at Her command could Satan change the past.

"If it comes down to it, we can always call in Admin," Satan reminded us.

"Move?" Eros asked, aghast.

"There are worse things than relocating to London or Paris or Rio," Satan said. "And everything would be taken care of, as always."

I didn't want to move.

Not that Admin didn't take care of us here, too. Wherever we are assigned, Admin fixes all the details, like birth certificates and passports and leases and memories. They make sure that all of us speak the current language like a native (only we don't forget languages we use regularly, so I still have decent French, Italian, and Spanish. My Chinese has improved since coming to New York, too, since I try to pick up a newspaper in Mandarin every few weeks or so. My Russian has suffered badly, though it's still serviceable if I listen hard enough. Everything else is gone except my native tongue. I still dream in Akkadian, and keep my diary in cuneiform. Partly it's because no one else could read it, but mostly to keep in touch with my past. I don't want to forget who I am, that I was once a royal, if very minor, princess and priestess. I don't want to forget that I was mortal).

Admin takes care of all the necessities, like making sure we can keep our leases and that no one around us realizes that I've been living in this apartment for twenty years and I don't look any older.

Satan has to apply to Admin for services on our behalf, since we share services with Heaven and they sometimes outrank us. Which is one reason She hates applying to Admin for special services. Besides which, Admin charges outrageous fees for emergency rush. Expensive, and Satan finds it just a touch humiliating, which is very hard for Her. Satan's central sin is pride, after all.

Sometimes being the Prince of Hell is really hard on Her and we can only admire the way She manages. Poor Satan. Poor Martha.

"Well," Satan mused. She certainly didn't want to go beg Admin for four full reorientations.

"If we could have one research librarian with Akashic credentials, we might be able to track them down without going through Admin," I mused aloud, wondering what the Akashic record would turn up about one far too frighteningly attractive fake PI.

Satan raised an eyebrow. "Excellent idea, my dear. That we can do immediately through our own organization—no need to notify the Angelic Council about a little research. You, my Lilith, have earned my approval today. I give you the gift of one boon."

Eros blinked. Even Desi whistled through her teeth. Satan almost never gives boons. I was so stunned that I couldn't move, not even to pick up my drink. Me? A boon? It was a blank check, a get-out-of-jail-free card. I could ask at any time in the future for anything, anything at all. Well, almost anything. I was still bound by my original contract for my soul. But aside from that, Satan was honor bound to grant my request.

Satan pulled out Her Treo and tapped out an e-mail. "There," She said. "Since this was your idea, Lily, I have put a demon under you, reporting to you directly. You will be responsible for the Akashic research. Eros, you will be in charge of the central investigation as to who these people are, who their leader is, and how they are funded. Desire, you are too close to matters now, but when you are feeling stronger I expect you to lend a hand."

"Of course, Martha," Desi agreed. "I would be ready to help out today, if only to get back at that Steve guy for leaving me in Brooklyn." Her voice went up on that last word.

"And me?" Sybil asked.

Martha patted her hand. "You've had a bad time with these types. I don't want you involved for now.

If you get any prophecy that could be useful, call Eros. Otherwise I would prefer if you stay away from the threat."

Sybil looked at her napkin and I thought she seemed a bit ashamed.

"Come girls, we've beaten them before and we'll do it again. And we'll start our investigation tonight. So now, dessert," Satan ordered.

One does not disobey the Prince of Hell, so I paid careful attention to my lingonberry crème brûlée, along with bites of Desi's Arctic Circle dessert (made with blueberry sorbet and passion fruit curd), which Martha had declared a medicinal necessity. Seratonin levels and all that. And Satan ordered ice wine all around for all of us, sweet and cool and just the right bit of alcoholic tinge to the very scary evening.

chapter
TEN

It wasn't until I got home and signed on to Magic-Mirror that I realized that I'd gotten a new job. Along with being a succubus and an accessories editor, I was now the head of a research team. Great. It's a good thing that I had a decent education when I was mortal—or what passed as an elite education back in Babylon, though at the time even the Dewey decimal system and microfiche were beyond imagination, let alone Internet search engines. I started to hope that our assigned demon would be as good with them as with the Akashic record.

My laptop was sitting on the coffee table where I'd left it that morning. I threw my coat on the floor next to the sofa, reached over and booted up. As I waited for the programs to check that they had all their parts I ran my palms over the gold and rose silk upholstery and studied the walls. But I still liked my deep bronze paint and architectural white moldings.

Being good, I checked the e-mail left for me at my MagicMirror dump, which was different from my work or personal e-mail addresses. Nice touch of Satan's, to have my new minion get in touch with me here and leaving it up to me whether or not I should give out other personal methods of communication.

And, indeed, there was already a message in my in-box bearing the Akashic ISP address.

Lilith Ad-Hzar, Princess of Babylon, Priestess of Ishtar, servant of Hell, was the first line of the e-mail. I had to admit that I liked the style. Obviously this demon, in the hour it had taken me to consume my dessert, hug my friends, and get into a taxi uptown, had already done a good solid search on me.

> *I am the Librarian Azoked, assigned to assist your investigation. Let me say first that it has been my privilege to serve Satan with my specialized abilities and training for two thousand years. While I have been in charge of a research project for the past five hundred years, Satan Herself has requested my personal attention to this matter. As I have not been fully briefed on the situation, I will need the particulars, both of the conditions and the context in order to resolve your predicament.*
>
> *Azoked, Librarian*

Okay, Azoked, how about let's get started now. I hit Reply and typed out the words, hit Send, and then went on to my friends' page.

I'd barely read the very first post (Melanie, one of Eros's clan, was taking a vacation in Corfu and wanted shopping and packing advice—I didn't even have time to tell her that Barneys had just gotten in some great beachwear—when I smelled a sharp strike of sulfur. I turned and there was an elegant Bastform demon librarian plugging the power supply for her Thinkpad into my socket.

I was suddenly grateful that I'd been sitting on the

sofa in the living room, fully dressed. Thank all Hell and the engineers for wireless connections, though usually I felt that way when I was online in bed, wearing an oversized Ozzy tee. (Okay, they'd been handouts all over Hell about twenty years ago, though really he never was one of us. Talk about a poseur! But he tickled Satan all the same and She made sure we all had that No Rest for the Wicked promo shirt—which by now had been washed to soft and cozy and which I sometimes like to wear in utter defiance of the entire world.)

After all, I have all the wonderful, beautiful things a girl could want. But sometimes I don't want to feel like I have to be beautiful all the time. Sometimes I just want to curl up in a soft XXL tee shirt that's been through the wash for twenty years and eat ravioli and Oreos. Sometimes it is comfort over style, and I was insanely relieved that this librarian hadn't caught me out. Because if there were a time that I really wanted comfort and normalcy and to forget the people who would hunt me and my friends down and destroy us, it was right then.

She was a Bastform, which means she looked rather like a four-foot-tall Siamese cat. This one was a blue point, which gave her the air of a stern librarian who was on the lookout to hush anyone who dared to talk. The (cat's eye, naturally) reading glasses that hung around her neck on a beaded cord added to her air. Her silk robin's-egg-blue robe looked like it came from the wardrobe of one of the Harry Potter movies, and it flowed around her elegantly elongated form as if she were Professor of Akashic at Hogwarts. Tree of life designs wandered around the collar and down the front rendered in raised silver embroidery and adorned with a scattering of pearls. Either she was high in the Library hierarchy or had been outfitted with some thought to my rank and reputation for elegance.

When I turned my attention to her, she waited for a long moment before acknowledging my presence with a slight nod.

That's the problem with Bastform demons. They have the personality of cats along with the looks, which means that they think they are superior. And this one was a librarian, which meant she really did have some very specialized abilities. Damn.

"Welcome, Librarian," I said formally and in Akkadian. "Your aid is most valuable and we are grateful." I hate hate hate having to flatter and play humble, but if you want anything out of a Bastform you have no choice. And if you act like you're equals they'll make you wait forever.

She deigned to blink in acknowledgment and immediately took up the Thinkpad, which had booted and displayed a welcome screen that I'd never seen before. Pale blue just the shade of her robe, trees and vines in ghostly echos of pastels twined themselves through the usual log-in boxes. It was quite an elegant piece of programming, no doubt about it.

"I didn't know you used the Internet in the Akashic," I commented.

"Only for the first pass or so, to eliminate the most obvious dead ends. We've been working on going fully computerized for decades now." Her tone was bored and just as superior as I had anticipated.

The Akashic record is the *Great Book of All*

Things. All events, all Fate, everything a person has ever done or thought or tried and failed, all of it is recorded in his or her Akashic file. And not just people, either. No, everything that lives is in the Book. Every ant, every tree, every milkweed and luna moth and feral tabby cat, every tomato plant and pigeon is in the Book.

Which in itself is just a metaphor, since it's not a book in any sense of the word at all. It's more like a database, only it encompasses a magical space larger than New York and London and Tokyo combined. It is possibly the hugest thing in existence.

Magicians, human, Underworld or Upperworld, had to undergo years and years of training and privations to be accorded access. And once admitted, they had to study for years and years longer to learn how to locate the information they sought.

Those with particular talent learned to call upon the Demon Librarians, like Azoked, or the Angelic Librarians, who were simply out of reach for any of the Underworld.

I knew little about the Akashic other than the few courses offered in Advanced Demonic Skills. The Librarians, of either the Demonic or Angelic Hosts, were highly specialized professionals who were always in short supply. My last interaction had been before the use of electricity, let alone computers. So I ended up asking the only question that came immediately to my mind.

"Windows?"

Azoked sighed. "I prefer Oracle myself. The Angelics use it, of course. But—" She shrugged. "We support our own, you know."

I rolled my eyes. But then I'm a Mac user, ever since the very first Apples came on the market. Maybe no one in Hell knew quite how devoted I was to my lightweight titanium Powerbook.

"Now, just a few preliminaries and I'll start immediately. I'll need names, of course, and all the contact information, and anything else you have. Also, some personal item of the search target does help us narrow things down far more quickly."

I'd have to ask Desi if she had anything of Steve's. A personal item, or even better, something that had been part of him—like a hair—would be best. I obediently gave the kitty demon all the information I possessed about Steve Balducci and Nathan Coleman. Which was very little indeed.

"But I don't think I have anything of his," I said, trying to remember if he'd left me anything. Oh, right, he'd given me his card. I dragged out my Treo, input the information, and then handed the card over. "For all the good it will do. It's not very personal."

"Hmmmm." The Librarian studied it and, miracle of miracles, actually appeared interested. "Well, we'll see. It was on his body and in his hand for a while, though your emanations might have overridden the original information. I'll have to see what I can do. And the other, this Steve Balducci?"

"Just a sec." I hit Desi's speed dial number in the Treo and prayed she'd pick up. Sometimes when she's in a real funk she hides the phone or just lets it ring and then doesn't retrieve the voice mail for days.

"Pick up, Des, pick up," I muttered. I didn't realize I'd said anything aloud until Azoked gave me a startled glance.

Finally Desi decided to answer her phone. Or maybe it was buried in her purse again and she hadn't found it too easily.

"What?" she asked abruptly, as if I hadn't spent most of my day trying to take care of her.

"I've got a librarian right here this minute, Des. Think. Do you have anything of Steve's? Anything at all that would link to him."

"No," she answered too quickly. "And if I did have anything I'd have thrown it out."

"Think, Des." She'd been better at dinner, but had obviously come home and indulged in a good cry. "A librarian could use it to trace him. It would make our pursuit much easier."

"Oh." There was a long pause, and then she asked if she could call back. I shot a glance at Azoked, who stared down her nose stonily, and said if she found anything she should let me know.

"I have about two thousand possible Nathan Colemans and Nathan R. Colemans, but this one looks promising." The Siamese cat Librarian had that lilt to her voice that meant she had something you really wanted to hear and that she was waiting and holding out and maybe would tell you if you treated her particularly nicely.

"Would you like some coffee?" I offered. "Shadegrown Kenyan, and I grind the beans fresh."

"That will do," the Librarian took the bribe. "You do have real cream, don't you? And some biscuits? I would love a biscuit."

"Biscuits?" Where was I going to get biscuits at this time of night? As if I ever had such things in the house anyway.

"Yes, of course. To go with the coffee. You don't even have any chocolate chips in the house?" She sighed as if she were much put upon.

"Oh, cookies!" I said. Why was an Akashic Librarian using Britspeak? "I have Oreos and Pepperidge Farm Mint Milanos, if those will do."

"The Milanos are acceptable," she agreed. "Though I prefer bakery biscuits. Especially Florentines. Next time please see to the Florentines."

What a bitch! She was in my apartment and I was brewing her coffee and then she ordered me to have her favorite snacks on hand whenever she calls. And who knew when that would be. She worked for Satan, same as me.

I was steaming mad, but there wasn't a lot I could really do about Miss Thing's attitude. The waiting list for an Akashic librarian ran to decades. Maybe Pussyface was available because no one could stand her. I fumed as I ground the beans and set up the French filter. I arranged the cookies on a plate, not one of my better pieces, and added some Oreos because I liked them. In an act of absolute contempt, I left the cream in the cute little pint carton instead of putting it into a creamer the way I would have if, say, I were serving the homeless in St. Joseph's. The finishing touch to my revenge was a handful of pink Sweet'n Low packets that I tossed on the table. No sugar. Let Ms. Snot cope.

Truth was, I would hardly have treated an enemy that way and this was a librarian whose skills I desperately needed. Truth was, she wasn't any worse than any Bastform demon I'd ever met and a lot more useful than most. Truth was, I was scared and pissed and needed to take it out on someone, and she was just the last straw in a generally unpleasant day.

She took her coffee, glared at the Sweet'n Low as if it were radioactive, touched the cream carton like it was coated in something noxious and smelly, and gobbled down all the cookies, Milanos and Oreos both. No, I'd been right. She wasn't just Bastform, she was a major pain in the nether regions.

After she had finished her snack and licked her paws and face so many times I started to hope the fur would rub off, she turned back to the computer.

"Now this one looks promising," she purred. "Graduated from Yale, 1996, hmmm, Magna Cum Laude in Near Eastern Languages. Odd. Interesting. Hmmm. *R* stands for Rhys. Born in New York City, February 19, 1974, hmmm, an Aquarian. Aquarians can be difficult, you know. Very cerebral, often not emotionally mature. Prone to valuing ideas above people. And, hmmmm, looks like he's overly attached to Mama. Or at least hasn't cut the apron strings nearly so much as someone his age should have."

At that point the Librarian gave me a look that could only be thought of as sisterly. Though she was a bitch in silver fur, she could still feel some bond over the emotionally immature males.

Rhys, I thought, almost chortling. Gotcha! That explained the pale skin and black hair. Welsh, I should have recognized it straight off. But that was bad, too. There is a strain of magical sensitivity among the Welsh that can be dangerous to the likes of me.

Well, there are sensitives in every population group. Only they are more common and more pronounced in some than others, though there is a definite nature–

nurture controversy in this area. Some cultures promote other-physical awareness, while the more rationalist Western cultures deny their existence.

In the past, especially in eras of great faith, in places where faith was the default, my job was so much harder. Men would try harder to resist me. They were aware that creatures like me existed and that I was not only the end of their mortal life but that their souls were forfeited to Hell through my ministrations.

Now so few New Yorkers believe that they have souls, saved, forfeited or otherwise. So they don't worry about it and they aren't suspicious.

My librarian was hmmming again. "Odd, odd," she muttered, staring at the screen.

"What?" I asked, trying not to sound as impatient as I felt.

"Interesting," was all she answered, which made me want to rip her head off for the twentieth time in the past hour. Except then I would never get any cooperation from the Akashic Division and Satan had pulled a lot of strings to get this one.

"Please?" I was begging, not my usual style. "Pretty please?"

She turned slowly and shook her head. "Young lady, you must understand that I have only the most cursory information at the moment. I need to cross-check things, to look up references. This is only the most preliminary skim of only the most public bits of knowledge. Indeed, you could have looked it up yourself. Did you Google him? Because that's most of what I've done so far."

The Akashic librarian uses Google? I wanted to put

my fist through the wall. I could have done that days ago if I'd thought that Mr. Coleman had any relevance to my life at all.

Azoked regarded me more kindly than before. Though after calling me "young lady" there wasn't anything she could do to make me like her. I didn't need to like her. I only needed to be able to work with her, and hoped that most of our work would be done at a distance. "They do not stop being programmers after they die, you know," she said as if I were a child of limited intelligence. "The Akashic Library has acquired a few top people recently, and we expect more. We do have first call on any programmer admitted to the Afterlife. And if it's any consolation, I was using the internal Akashic version of Google, which isn't available without our authorizations."

"Oh." That makes it all better. Not. But I wasn't going to risk alienating the demon. It did seem that she wanted to do her job; it wasn't her fusty schoolmarmish attitude that I found so irritating; it was her Bast-like personality. But it stood to reason that an Akashic librarian would be all about the process of digging out detail. She probably couldn't understand that some people—namely, me—are just not detail-oriented.

"I expect that you shall be seeing Mr. Coleman again rather soon," Azoked said, shaking her head again. "Yes, I expect quite soon. Well, I expect that you can get hold of me if you need to. And if your little friend Desire does find some item that I could use as a sympathetic link, please do let me know as quickly as possible. I can send a servant to collect it, or she can even drop it with your doorman. He is a most efficient minion. I expect that he will make full demon in record time. Excellent young man, young Vincent.

"Well, then, I'll be off. A laptop and a slow connection through our firewall means that I am not at my most efficient. And I have access to resources that do not leave the precincts of the Library, as you understand. I can't do more than the most surface kind of search here, not to mention the fact that I am starving again. You wouldn't happen to have any Starbucks Espresso ice cream, would you? I thought not. In our own research facilities librarians have amenities. And full librarians like myself have twenty-four-hour service, and of course the management keeps all of our preferences fully stocked. No, I will return to our main facility, and shall communicate when I have some reasonable data. I expect that e-mail is the best way to get hold of you."

I think I sat there with my mouth open for a full minute. Not because I wasn't anxious for her to leave. Truth to tell, I was dying to remove my Manolos (which were four inches high and hurt like holy water after the first hour or so), my hose, and my very confining jacket. I hadn't had a minute to just sit all day without someone throwing problems at me, and I was craving a bubble bath like my prey craved me.

So I told her sure, I understood that she had better access to her tools at her desk. I knew she was a miracle worker, et cetera, et cetera. And how should I contact her if I suddenly needed her?

She grinned, an expression I had thought was not in the Bastform repertoire. Ever.

"Magic," she quipped, holding up a BlackBerry.

I must have blinked, since I didn't consider a Black-Berry magic at all.

"Oh, please." She gave me that look that communicated *Look at what I have to put up with and all these nonBast demons are so stupid* much more effectively than any words ever could. "All the varieties of instant communication? And information retrieval and note taking? If this is not magic, what is?"

I had to get her out before she started another lecture. So I just agreed and mentioned that it was getting late and that she might want to pursue this investigation where she had Florentine cookies and Starbucks ice cream and all the necessary comforts. Finally she was gone and I was free to shed my clothes on the living room floor and head to the bath.

chapter
ELEVEN

My apartment has a lot of great features. The building has a beautiful lobby with a conscientious doorman. In my opinion it probably has the best location in the city, on the Upper East Side just half a block off an avenue with plenty of cabs and three bodegas within a three-block radius, and that's not counting the bagel bakery, the reasonably good pizzeria, and the two newsstands that carry flowers and chocolate for those late-night emergencies. I have hardwood floors, twelve-foot ceilings with the original 1904 moldings, a kitchen with counters and a door, a living room with windows on two sides, a bedroom large enough for my king-sized bed, and a walk-in closet that could be billed as a second bedroom.

All these advantages are secondary. I love the place because of the bathtub.

My bathroom has the original black-and-white tile with an oversized pedestal sink and the huge claw-foot tub that had been installed in 1904. It was long enough that when my head rested against the rolled edge my toes didn't touch the opposite end. And it was so deep that I was immersed to my neck, where the hot water could work its spell on my knotted shoulders.

A Chicago shower had been installed over it and I

had found an elegant Battenberg lace curtain that tied open when I wasn't keeping water in. The wall above the shoulder-high tiling had been painted a very pale green back in the 1920s and I'd kept the color.

I turned on the hot water and took down my jar of Lush bath bombs. I had the pink ones and the sexy ones and the ones with flower petals, but tonight I wanted mostly comfort. So I decided on a yellow Butterball, set it on the ledge and put the rest of the jar back in its decorative spot on the windowsill.

I turned the water off and sank down into the deep hot water. It hadn't even been twenty-four hours since I'd delivered Kevin from this very tub. But if I were to be sentimental about every delivery job I did, there wouldn't be a place I could live or a city I could endure for long. I dropped the bath bomb into the water and watched it fizz as the delicious aroma scented the air.

By the time I left the bath, dried, and was ready to slip into bed, I had put the events of the day behind me. I embraced the bliss of sleep for at least six hours until the alarm rang.

Wednesday started much better. I arrived at the office late but no one seemed to notice. The place was in an uproar with the Big News about a designer who had just announced a move from his own line to take over design duties at one of the Great Old Fashion Houses. Danielle had left a huge pile of shoe boxes next to my desk and I spent the first hour of the (admittedly, very late) morning trying on next season's metallic sandals and wedgies. Danielle was so good to me.

I called over to her office and thanked her effusively

for the shoes. "Oh, no problem, Lily," she said. "They sent them over for us to look at for a shoot, but nobody else wears size five. Really, what else would we do with them?"

Back when I was mortal, I was considered a tall woman. The kings of Babylon were large men, physically as well as diplomatically and militarily, and I carried their genes. I was accounted a towering beauty with rather large feet—three thousand years ago. Now I'm considered petite. At five foot three, I am the shortest person who works at the magazine. I may be the shortest person in the building. And I definitely wear the smallest shoes.

"Well, I really appreciate it, though," I told her. "And when those new Chanel bags come in, the oyster's got your name on it."

She almost squealed, but that would be undignified in front of the interns. I was happy for her. Myself, I just can't get that worked up over oyster.

Then I went to lunch with my boss and two of the fashion editors and I got their support on the shawl feature. My boss even said it was "an excellent idea" and thought we should maybe run it in November and include the evening-wear shawls to go with holiday finery. It looked like my special feature was getting bigger and better. I called around to a couple of fashion houses and started ordering garments for the issue, which they were all excited to supply. As usual and as expected, but I was delighted to see that at least four of my favorite designers were featuring shawls and scarves in the winter collections. Then, to top it all off, my first-choice writer for the assignment was available and agreed immediately.

I called Sybil to check up that she was doing okay after her upset yesterday, and she was fine and had a date for tonight. Sybil dates less than we do, but then her service to Hell is not based on her love life. So the date was a real one, not an assignment. Lucky Sybil.

"I'm a little nervous," she admitted over the phone. "I met him on one of those dating sites and I've never done that before. I mean, it seems so strange to know these things about a person I've never even met before. And what if he's ugly? What if his picture is ten years out of date? What if he's bald? What if he lied?"

"Well, where are you meeting?" I asked. First things first.

"Oh, just at the Cathedral for coffee. And he doesn't have my last name, even. He should recognize me from my picture on the site, and I'm supposed to recognize him the same way. So if we want to disappear, we can."

"Who suggested Cathedral?" I asked. It wasn't Sybil's usual haunt, being down in the East Village. The Cathedral was next door to what had once been a church. When it had gone on the market, the coffee house had bought up a load of stained-glass windows that were installed as their walls. So you sipped your coffee surrounded by stained-glass suffering saints. Très goth. But very pretty if you're into that kind of thing.

"He suggested it, actually," she said. "I was surprised but it seemed like at least no one I know would be there. And it's convenient."

"Well, call me tomorrow and let me know how it

goes," I told her, only a little bit jealous. "Have a great time."

I refused to let my mood be dampened by the fact that I didn't have any plans for the evening. I was going to sit at home and read MagicMirror and maybe rent the whole first season of *Buffy the Vampire Slayer*. We're all big Buffy fans. In lots of ways she's so much like us.

On the way home from work I decided that a treat was in order and I took the long detour to Benny's for one of their steak burritos. Mmmm.

"Hey, Lily, isn't it?" a voice asked from behind me.

I spun around to find Nathan *R*-for-Rhys Coleman standing behind me in line. "What are you doing here?" I demanded. "Are you stalking me? Are you following me because you can't find your runaway pharmacist? I suggest you go off to Nevada or Iowa or wherever it is runaway husbands go."

"Sorry," he said, raising his hands. "I'm getting dinner. Okay, I happened to see you on the street. But I was in the area because I wanted to pick up their chicken enchiladas in tomatilla salsa. I can't even admit it to my friends, but they've got the best tomatilla salsa in the city."

"Why can't you admit it to your friends?" All my friends knew I loved Benny's, even if they thought I was nuts. And I thought all guys liked Mexican food and beer.

"They'd think I was crazy for going twenty minutes out of my way for these when there are plenty of very good Mexican places in my neighborhood. But none of them make salsa verde like Benny's."

"Do you want a table?" a waiter asked, gesturing

to one of the spaces available. Okay, it was way early for dinner. And I had been planning to go home with my food, but—all of a sudden I thought, *Why not?*

I never do things like this and I should have known better. A strange guy was such a risk. But, when I thought about it, I was the immortal one with Satan and the backup of Hell and it was only a burrito dinner at Benny's, which is as unthreatening a place as I could imagine. And this guy did have my address and my work phone and my e-mail. So if he wanted to stalk me or do something dangerous, he wouldn't have to meet me at Benny's.

Of course, he could be doing this just to put me off guard.

But I was hungry and immortal and the place was just so normal and safe and—the truth was, I was jealous of Sybil's date and even of Desi's aborted date last week. I wanted to pretend, just for a few minutes, that I had an actual date of my own.

And Nathan was so cute in his Diesel jeans and leather jacket. He looked so perfect, as if he had been put together by one of our stylists, and he definitely was as hot as any of the models we used, though definitely a few years older. Which meant that he might have learned to order wine, do his laundry, and hire a cleaning service.

We gave each other a few quick quizzical looks.

"Do you think?" I asked.

"Whatever suits you," he replied.

"Well, we're both really busy," I stated because I suddenly realized that I could not admit to being without plans for an evening, even a Wednesday, to a man I hardly knew. Eros and Desi and even Sybil would disapprove. I'd heard them lecturing each other on the subject often enough.

"Easier than washing dishes," he countered.

"Sold," I agreed. Even Eros and Desi and Sybil couldn't fault the logic of that.

And so we were seated at a lime green table with pink and orange napkins on our laps waiting for margaritas that had not been in the game plan half an hour before.

"So tell me about this detective gig," I said after my first few sips of a drink that could have filled half my bathtub.

He shrugged. "It's not really a regular thing. I graduated from Yale and went to grad school there for a few years, but dropped out after I passed my comps when I realized that there really weren't jobs in Akkadian."

I nearly choked on my drink. Akkadian? My mother tongue. Fortunately, my mouth was full of tequila and lime so I didn't say anything that would have been a mistake.

He misinterpreted my reaction. Which was no surprise, given that he was hardly going to figure that he'd been the first person in over a century to mention my native language to me. "I know, I know," he said, waving his hand in a self-deprecating manner. He had the good grace to look abashed. "It was totally nuts. My mother called once a week to tell me that it wasn't too late for me to go to law school. So I've got a masters in Near Eastern Languages, which is useless except to make me overeducated for almost any job that interests me. I keep thinking of going back to school, getting an MBA or going into law like my mother wants me to. I like languages and I've been playing with taking the test for the State Department, but right now I'm just weighing the options and trying to figure out what I want to do, when I can't seem to do the thing I wanted to do most."

"Which was?" I prompted. Guys love to talk about themselves and it's usually a good tactic to let them do it. They feel happy and they don't ever ask much about you, at least not in my experience. Which sometimes I resented, but mostly it was just safer. The less they asked, the fewer lies I'd have to tell.

He sniffled and blew his nose again.

"You still have that cold?" I asked.

He nodded. "It's not getting better. If it keeps up for another week I'm going to a doctor."

I shrugged. "It could be allergies."

He laughed. "Oh, no, it's too early yet for allergies. I have horrible allergies. Grass, ragweed, flowering trees, the whole shebang. What I really wanted to do was finish my Ph.D. and teach. Get to go to Iraq, Syria, Iran, and Turkey to dig in the summers, translate texts, do the things my professors did. But there are very few students who are interested in studying ancient languages and now all the sites where I wanted to dig are war zones. For a while I thought that by the time I finished a Ph.D. the wars would be over and I'd be able to go. I know people who are working in Syria but I don't think they'll have permits for long.

"It's really too bad because there's a lot we don't know about the ancient world, and we should know. We need to understand not only what happened then and how we've changed, but also how we haven't changed. As people, I mean. It's important for us to remember that Babylon was the New York of its day. The Ceremonial Way was as wide as Fifth Avenue and the walls were decorated with gold- and cobalt-glazed bricks, with lions and griffins and a magnificent gate called the Ishtar Gate."

He went on talking, but I remembered it. He was right, it had been as grand as anything built today, and more beautiful. I remembered victorious generals at the heads of their armies, all washed and polished, carrying heaps of riches from their conquests and leading the newly enslaved and soon to be executed. We threw flowers from the roofs, so that a great snow of petals pelted our heroes.

We weren't ashamed of conquest in those days. Land, riches, slaves, wealth, all came through the great gates and down the Ceremonial Way and Babylon cheered.

Today, Babylon is seen as degenerate and cruel, though not so developed in either degeneracy or cruelty as the Empire of Rome. But in our day some of the choices were simpler. We vanquished our enemies because otherwise they surely would have destroyed us. They would have marched our wealth through their streets, would have put our women and children in chains and brought our men to their temples to sacrifice to their gods.

"I'm boring you," Nathan said flatly, cutting into my reveries. "I do that to people. I'm used to it. No one is interested in the ancient world."

"No," I said. "I'm more interested in Babylon than you can possibly imagine. Just that what you were saying brought back some . . . thoughts to me."

"Really?" he asked, suspicious.

I shrugged. "About how war and conquest were viewed very differently then than now."

He went still and regarded me for a moment that stretched into the next. Then he spoke very softly. "Tell me what you were thinking about conquest in the ancient world."

I drank some of my margarita and our food arrived, leaving me a little time to formulate an answer. "I was thinking about how there was little guilt about the notion of empire then, about how people were simply glad to loot what they could from their neighbors and enslave them because they knew that anyone who could would do the same to them. That's all. That's just the way it was. The Babylonians and the Egyptians weren't the worst of the lot, or the Greeks or Romans either. At least they had laws, some concept of social order that they spread with their hegemony. The people they conquered were usually not much worse off than they'd been before, and much better off than if a less ordered enemy had gotten there first."

He nodded slowly, his eyes gleaming. "People today don't understand the conditions or the mind-set. The world has changed so much. And that's one of the reasons I love reading the ancient texts, being able to read from the original writings without interpretation, without anyone between me and them. There's something almost magical about that."

He sneezed again and I waved the waiter over for more chips and salsa.

"But why the PI thing? That's because my mother's friend's son is doing Mom a favor by hiring me as a consultant to do some research. I almost never do the thing that I did with you, going to question people about a case. Mostly I do research, computer searches, translations. I'm good at it and it gives me something to do. Sometimes it's even interesting."

"So why did you come to my apartment, if mostly you're just doing computer research?"

"The boss is trying to train me and give me more opportunities to do more of the actual job a PI does. I think he thinks that sending me to interview beautiful women will make me more interested in the job."

I smiled at the compliment, and nibbled on my enchilada. Nathan was right, the tomatilla salsa was amazing, and I was glad that I had decided to try something new. Besides, I could get a steak burrito to go and put it in the fridge for tomorrow.

"So what's the deal with the pharmacist, and how did I get into it?" I asked after I'd finished a hearty bite.

"That whole case is entirely weird," he said after he had thought for a moment. "I don't know what else to call it. Okay, so the guy disappeared. We did the usual missing persons/runaway search, studying his habits and hobbies. My boss once found someone because she had a thing for organic vegan food and wouldn't shop in normal stores. I admire that; that's good research. So I was interested and started to trace the same way. But I found nothing. It's like he really disappeared into the ether, and I'm starting to wonder if maybe this is all just a smokescreen for something else. I just have this sense that I'm just seeing a little piece of a bigger pattern."

"Hmmm," I said as I pretended to concentrate on my food.

I understood what he meant, but more, I had a feeling that his piece of a pattern somehow intersected some other pattern of mine. He'd arrived just at the same time as Desi's bad date and the Burning Men and I don't believe in that much coincidence. I was certain there was some connection, and if I couldn't see it there might be information in the Akashic.

I wondered if our librarian had turned up anything yet.

I thought about how Nathan would love the Akashic. If Nathan became a demon he'd want to be a librarian.

That thought made me very sad, for no reason I could identify.

"Hey, something got you down?" he asked softly.

"Yeah. Just . . . stuff." There was nothing I could explain. "I just have a morbid imagination." Suddenly, I had a very weird thought. Insane, actually, but hey—he was being nice and was interested in Babylon and that's a sure way to my heart. "Do you have a copy of that picture you showed me? Because if he had my address maybe he knew someone I know. I could ask around a bit, just to see. If you'd like."

His hand froze in midair, cheese dripping off his fork as he held it poised a foot above his plate. "You'd do that? You don't have to. I mean, that would be great, but you don't have to."

"I know," I said. "But if you have an extra one that you can spare, if it works out and comes up, I might be able to ask. It's probably terribly unprofessional and I shouldn't say anything like that and you probably want to interview people yourself—" And I shouldn't be chattering on in that idiot fashion.

"I would very much appreciate it," he said. His voice was quiet and serious. "And you are a wonderful person, Lily. I would like to spend some time with you and talk about ancient civilizations. You don't know—it's been ages since I met anyone who thought my interest was anything but a waste of time when I should be trying to work on Wall Street or get into law school. Which I haven't totally discounted, you understand, but you're the first person I've met just about since I moved back here who doesn't think I'm crazy."

I shook my head. "No, I don't think you're crazy at all. And if I could get a job translating ancient texts— well, let's just say I do understand and leave it at that."

"Where did you go to school?" he asked, utterly innocently. "What did you study?"

All the expected questions. Fortunately, Admin had set me up. "I went to Mount Holyoke." And I had, too. For a summer. But Admin had me in their alumni system with a transcript and a picture of me in the yearbook, and I get regular letters asking for money. Which I give. "Comparative religion and romance languages," I said. "I was really interested in the Italian Renaissance. If I'd gone to grad school, that's what I would have studied."

He looked at me quizzically. "So why didn't you go to grad school?"

I shook my head. "No jobs. Come on, Italian Renaissance history and literature?"

"More call for that than ancient Near Eastern." His tone was bitter.

I shrugged. "I'd think that there would be more call

for ancient Near Eastern. It's a whole lot harder to learn those languages than Italian."

Both of our plates were empty, which is saying a lot. Benny's does not believe in small servings.

"So tell me, are you free Saturday or Sunday? We could go to the Temple of Dendur at the Met and have lunch."

A date. He was asking me on a real date. A museum date, no less, during the day. A very appropriate first date, not a bar or a movie, but the Met no less.

"Let me check my schedule," I said after a moment. "Saturday might work, but I have to check. Sundays I usually meet my girlfriends for brunch, and we have a solemn pact. No guy gets in the way."

He grinned. "I can respect that. But check on Saturday and let me know. If I don't hear from you by tomorrow I'll ping you."

The waiter brought the check and Nathan threw down his credit card without even looking at it. I pulled out a few bills, enough to cover what I thought was my share.

"No, not to worry," he said, refusing my money.

Sometimes it's hard for me to know how to deal with which world I'm in. Only a few decades ago I would have been insulted if he hadn't picked up the tab. Now it was my turn. "I insist. We just ran into each other. I can't let you take me out."

He opened his daytimer and pulled out a picture and handed it to me. It was a slightly better version of the one he had shown me over a week ago of the fair-haired fortyish man who was still a complete stranger to me. "You're helping me out by offering to show this around," he said. "Dinner is on the company."

Well, it would be churlish to refuse that kind of an offer. "Thank you."

"Don't forget to show it around," he said. "And send me an e-mail about Saturday."

"I will," I said as I waited for him to sign the credit slip. He walked me to the door and turned north. Once on the street I bolted around the corner before I started to grin.

I had a date, but I had better check my schedule for sure. Because the last thing I needed was a date with Nathan during a mojo moment. I couldn't spoil this, and I couldn't risk Nathan. No, I had better make sure that the stars were going to cooperate.

But I was still dizzy with desire, with the delicious joy that comes of being paid court by a handsome, intelligent, personable man. He liked me, he wanted to see me again, he liked *me*. The real deep me, the me who had been a Princess of Babylon and a Priestess of Ishtar, who had chatted with Aspasia in Athens and had cheered the gladiators of Rome. And it was for this, and not just for my perfectly proportioned body and my pheromones that he wanted to see me again.

For a creature of Hell, I was in Heaven.

chapter
TWELVE

"You can't go," Eros said flatly. "Look at what happened to Desi."

"That has nothing to do with it," I answered defiantly. We met for lunch at the ABC café, where the food was almost as wonderful as the décor. Twenty Murano chandeliers in various color combinations littered the ceiling. It was a crazy quilt of whatever they had at ABC at the time and there was no telling just what it would look like from one meeting to the next.

I had called and asked her to meet me. I needed support. I needed advice. I needed a girlfriend who would listen to me obsess about a guy I'd just barely met.

"But the schedule works, and it's a daytime date," I protested. "That doesn't count like Saturday night. I'm being busy on Saturday night."

"It's still Saturday and you can't," Eros repeated.

"Screw the rules, I want to go." I probably sounded as petulant as the Librarian had made me feel.

Eros sighed and blew on her tea. The way she ate you'd think she had to diet to keep her figure; she eats very little and drinks plain unsweetened tea. Sometimes I wonder if she even likes food.

"You'll do whatever you want, in the end. But you

know that if you appear eager you'll lose him. Men want to chase, that's their nature. It may feel stupid, but the more you make him work for you the more he'll value you in the end." And then she cocked her head. "But for you the end really is the end. Remember that? Why do you ignore that?"

Because I hadn't been thinking of that. Because I had just enjoyed being with Nathan. Because I thought he was the most attractive man I'd seen in ages, decades probably. More because he'd heard of the Ishtar Gate and the Ceremonial Way. He cared about Babylon and he cared about the past. For him it might all be ancient history, but it was my history, and it mattered.

I wondered how badly he spoke Akkadian. I wondered if he liked pomegranates.

My home is gone. The land is still there but the language has been dead for thousands of years. The music, the buildings, the warm familiar things are all dust in a desert today. Sometimes I miss it so much it's like a big gaping ache inside. My home, my past, my childhood. Sometimes I want the comfort foods that my mother fed me, but today I'm not even sure I would know what they were. I certainly don't know how to make them (and neither did my mother—even a minor concubine was served by cooks) or what went into them. But I miss them all the same.

I shrugged. "It doesn't always have to be the end. I can let them live if they satisfy me. I've even done it more than once. And I like Nathan because he knows all about my people. He knows who Ishtar is and about the Ceremonial Way and he even says he can read Akkadian."

"You like this guy because he reminds you of home?" Eros asked, clearly perplexed.

"That's a piece of it," I admitted. "That's not all, though. He's frighteningly attractive and smart and he likes Benny's, too."

"I should have known." Eros shook her head. "You're infatuated, which feels great. But if you're going to make this work then you can't go on Saturday. Not when he asked on a Wednesday. You know better than that, and if it were me you'd be telling me exactly the same thing."

Only it would never ever be Eros because she would never in a million years say yes to a Saturday date on a Wednesday from a new guy who wasn't a steady boyfriend. What Eros forgets is that I have never really dated. I went straight from being a priestess to being a succubus.

Priestesses of Ishtar were not celibate. Far from it, in fact. Ishtar was a fertility goddess and her priestesses were expected to take lovers and have children. But they were to take many lovers, although their allegiance was to the Temple and the Goddess and not to any man.

So here I am, three thousand years old, and I have never had a steady boyfriend in my life. Well, not a regular boyfriend, at least not one Satan would recognize. Niccolo had certainly been a lover and partner in every way, but he doesn't count in the grand total of my life.

Self-pity joined homesickness. I wanted Niccolo. I wanted Nathan. I wanted my mother. I wanted—something.

I got the bread pudding.

"You'll do whatever you want, but you'll be sorry. Honestly, Lily, remember that you don't have a lot of experience where romance is concerned. Especially big-R Romance. Guys don't get it unless they have to work for it, and work hard. Otherwise they don't value you. These are things that most girls learn at fourteen."

Yeah, well, at fourteen I was learning how to keep the Temple books in a neat hand (having mastered the intricacies of written cuneiform and basic arithmetic, which at the time were Mysteries). There was no concept even close to romance.

"Besides, I have a very good reason you can't go on Saturday. Sybil, remember our totally paranoid terrorized Sybil? She needs us to help hide in the etheric."

"I wish she'd stop being such a baby. That was four hundred years ago, and she shouldn't keep freaking about it," I said.

"Sure, she's always going off about her Burning Men, but that doesn't mean they're not a real threat."

"What are you saying? Do you think this is bigger than we thought? They're just another bunch of conspiracy nutcases and they'll disappear when the next big thing comes along."

Eros shook her head. "Beliel is concerned for our safety. He sent me an e-mail about that after Satan contacted him, because Satan thinks that there really is a conspiracy against Hell, and you know how She gets when She thinks there's a turf war. Why do you think She dealt with Admin to get that librarian on the case pronto? You know how much She loves dealing with Admin, and I'll bet they charged plenty."

I wouldn't take that bet because, Admin being what they are, they probably took twice as much as I'd imagine. And it's not something as crass as money, either, since they have no use for it. No, Admin gets paid in favors, which is how they keep up their inventory. As I understand it, they work something like eBay. They provide a forum to match up the magics needed and what they have on call to do whatever it is that needs to be done—for a percentage, of course. With all the potential that Satan commands they could be sitting on quite a pile of future magic and potential favors.

Fortunately, my specialty is not in demand outside of the original use. So I'm no good to anyone but Satan and my magic doesn't get loaned. Desi and Eros and Sybil, though—they have had to go on Admin assignments when needed. I wondered whether they had been part of the bargain for the Librarian. Looking at Eros chewing her lipstick, I thought perhaps they might have been in the deal.

Suddenly I felt a little sorry for my best friends, and had some sudden insight besides. No wonder they wanted this cleared up as soon as possible and with as few uses of other resources as they could manage. Doing it ourselves would mean that they might not be called on to perform for Admin.

"Okay," I agreed. I would have to tell Nathan I couldn't make the Temple of Dendur. I'd stand by Sybil instead, to keep her from becoming the pawn of her fears. Because, bottom line, a girlfriend is forever.

I got back to the office but couldn't concentrate on work. Instead I flipped through photos of sunglasses without seeing them, thinking about poor Desi and

Nathan. Eros was wrong, I told myself. There was no reason not to go to the museum with Nathan on Saturday.

But somehow I managed not to actually hit Send on the e-mail, as I recomposed and tinkered with the wording, first to accept and next to decline. But decline in a way that made it very clear that I wanted to go and suggest a different time. It was hard. Finally it was late enough that I could reasonably leave the office and go home. Maybe there would be voice mail from Nathan, I thought. Or maybe that snot of a librarian would come through with something useful.

One can always hope.

Vincent was on duty when I arrived home. He held my bags while I got my mail. I had the usual pile of junk and bills and one thick creamy envelope that looked almost like a wedding invitation, but the calligraphy was too regular and had to be computer generated. Besides, I didn't recognize the return address.

I dumped the rest of the mail on the table and my big bag on one of the dining chairs and opened the ersatz wedding invitation.

> *Succubus, we know who you are.*
> *We know what you are.*
> *We know where you are.*
> *You and your kind will not escape us.*

I started to scream. The pain raced up my fingers and infected my hands. I couldn't hear myself shrieking, couldn't think.

I hit the intercom desperately, waving my hands in the air to cool the burning that came off the paper, which was slowly being reduced to embers on my eighteenth-century Aubusson carpet.

Vincent was at the door three minutes later. When I thought about it later I realized that he must have raced up the stairs all the way to the sixth floor because the elevators in my building are so slow. He had to pound on the door, and I was afraid to touch the knob. My hands were burning as if there had been acid on that rich, creamy, twenty percent rag.

And there as good as had been.

Vincent screamed at me to open the door, and by the time I managed the knob I saw several of my neighbors ranged in the hallway. I didn't recognize any of them, but of course I wasn't seeing straight.

"Help, help, my hands," I sobbed as Vincent entered the apartment.

"Nothing to worry about, folks. Looks like a little accident with the iron. I'll take care of it. No problem," he assured the other residents as he closed the door behind him.

"What happened?" he asked urgently and all I could do was point to the floor.

The evil note was still there, the words now outlined in glowing red clearly legible in the gray ash. Vincent read them and even scribbled down a copy before he stamped them out with his heavy boots.

I was whimpering by this time, my mascara running down my face. The palms of my hands were bright scarlet and blisters were forming on my fingers where I'd touched the letter.

Vincent pulled me up and took me into the kitchen, where he held my hands under the cold water at the sink for what felt like forever but was probably more like ten minutes. Then he washed my palms very gently and sat me down on the sofa, wedged me in with embroidered cushions, and took off my shoes.

He went to the bathroom and emerged with some Betadyne ointment and gauze bandages. Funny, I remember him going into the bathroom but until he came out with the first-aid supplies I couldn't imagine why he'd gone in there. Shock, endorphins, fear, whatever it was, I wasn't tracking very well.

"Tell the others," I said.

"Let me get you taken care of first," he protested, spreading the ointment so gently over my burns that I felt only cooling relief. Then he applied the bandages expertly. I raised an eyebrow; his skill was professional and unexpected.

He shrugged. "You get a lot of experience with the gangs" was all he told me.

"Tell the others." I couldn't dial the phone, couldn't even think of talking. "My Treo is in the bag. It's got their phone numbers. Call on their cells."

"Don't worry, I've got it," he said soothingly.

But he wasn't on the phone. Instead he returned to the kitchen, took one of my knives and nicked the inside of his wrist. In the thick ichor that dripped into my white enamel sink he added some dragon's blood root and sulfur and muttered a few words. I was too weary to actually move so that I could see, but I knew the procedure. And weak as I was, I could feel Satan's magic flow into my apartment.

Then She was there, not in Her aspect of our den mother/big sister Martha, but as Anger and Vengeance, as Kali and Coatlique and as all the goddesses of destruction who ever lived.

Sometimes I am almost too used to Satan as She is with us, in Her Chanel suits. I can forget that She is one of the most powerful angels in the Hierarchy, that in some ways She is destruction incarnate. Hurting and weak as I was, I was overwhelmed with the urge to do Her worship.

"Lily," She said, coming to me directly as She manifested.

I tried to kneel down, though moving from the sofa was a great effort. "Satan," I greeted Her.

"Tell me what happened." Her voice was hard and commanding, but She did soften Her aspect so that we could gaze on Her. This was indeed Lucifer, the Light-Bearer. Sometimes with our girlfriend it's easy to forget that.

So I told Her and Vincent filled in where I hesitated. He showed Her the copy he had made of the message.

"My poor Lily," She said, and She touched my hands.

The pain abated and suddenly the blisters were gone. I felt calm and light and in perfect health.

"The others?" I asked. "They may have gotten letters, too."

"They have been informed," Satan said in that voice that brooked no argument. She was utterly, perfectly, completely in command. If She said the others knew, they knew. I just hoped we'd been in time.

Then Satan took one long last look at me, there was a sound like a soft popgun, and She was gone. The scent of sulfur remained in the air.

chapter
THIRTEEN

"Aren't you supposed to be at work?" I asked Vincent about half an hour later, after we'd finished the pint of Chunky Monkey between us. Then I realized that he'd been in my apartment for a long time and asked, "Don't you have to be downstairs? Is this going to be a problem?"

He smiled broadly. "No prob, Lil. Her Evilness has a simulacrum of me down in the lobby even now, guarding the residents and delivering the packages. No one knows I'm gone."

I licked my spoon again. I'd scraped out the carton twice already, and wondered idly whether the bodega on the corner would deliver more, if only I could find the phone number.

"Who do you think attacked me? And how? And with what?"

"Well, the what is easy," Vincent said dismissively. "Holy water. Clearly. Burn pattern. Who and how is a lot harder. The letter came in the mail with the regular mailman. No one besides our regular mailman opened the mailboxes. And the UPS and FedEx deliveries were also by the regular route drivers. I know them all; they greeted me by name. So it wasn't like someone snuck in and dropped that thing off. It went through channels."

Which made sense. Holy water wouldn't hurt a live human, so the letters could be processed through the mail like anything else.

But how did they find me? And who were they?

I wanted to cry.

I wanted more ice cream.

"Look, my shadow is downstairs," Vincent offered. "If you're okay with being alone for a few minutes, I'll go and buy a couple more pints. Just Chunky Monkey, or what other flavors?"

I thought about it for a moment. I just wanted comfort and safety. "Cherry Garcia and Fudge Brownie. They should have those in stock."

My ridiculously handsome and resourceful doorman disappeared. He didn't even ask me for the cash.

I was about to dial Sybil when the phone rang. I picked up; it was Desi. "Are you okay?" she demanded abruptly.

"Satan took care of me," I said, aware that she knew the full story. Okay, sometimes magic is more effective than technology. It takes a lot more energy, but sometimes the additional expenditure is worth the impact. "Did you get a letter?"

"Yes, but I heard from Satan first and turned it over to an Enforcer. And before you ask, yes, so did Sybil and Eros and neither of them opened theirs and everything has been turned over so they're on it."

"They" were the Enforcers, which is what passes for the demon police. Mostly they just break up fights and demon exhibitions and clean up after they catch minions who aren't doing their jobs. Easy grunt work, so most of the Enforcers are not exactly geniuses.

"The Enforcers won't figure anything out," I said, speaking before I thought.

There was silence on the other end. What else could Desi say? There are plenty of brilliant denizens of Hell, but none of them would stoop to Enforcement. The smart demons work for Beliel in Security, but it didn't look like Satan had called him in on this one. His area was more internal in Hell rather than the mortal world.

No, this was not going to get solved by anyone but us.

"How's Syb?" I asked. Desi was upset and unhappy, but it was Sybil who had me really worried. She wouldn't be able to cope if she knew who was pursuing us.

If she knew who was pursuing us we could catch them and get rid of the problem. The problem was that in this teeming island, to say nothing of the four other boroughs, it could be anyone. And they would think that they were doing Heaven's will, too, without any real directives from On High. Because, trust me, On High has no percentage in making war on us. That's a human perception. We're part of the Hierarchy and of general use to the Upper Orders, even if they detest our methods.

Anyway, that's all for the higher-ups. I've never quite been able to wrap my mind around the good/evil dichotomy, and even less able to understand why something perfectly lovely like sex gets put under the general subheading of evil.

When I was human we worshipped the power of creation.

"Sybil is not thinking about this, but I think she's terrified," Desi said. "Truth is, I'm terrified, too."

"Why don't you both come over? We can have ice cream and Frangelico," I invited.

"I'm—I think I'll be okay," Desi said softly. "But why don't you call Sybil?"

So I did call Sybil, but she was too scared to leave her apartment. I told her that Vincent would come and fetch her in a taxi and she could stay over and we could both call in sick to work tomorrow. Clearly relieved, she agreed to the plan, so I was alone again with no ice cream in the freezer.

Nathan kept coming back to my thoughts, Nathan and Desi. Was Nathan one of them? Had he sent them to me?

But I couldn't bear that and I had to know. I liked him so much. And we just clicked on things that weren't about my looks and sex. He cared about the ancient world and knew my background, my home, and that touched me in a gentle soft place that I had mostly forgotten.

I was all alone and I'd been hurt and I wanted to talk to Nathan. I wanted assurance that he had nothing to do with the mess, and that he'd find the people who'd hurt me.

He was a detective, after all.

The thought wouldn't leave. But how would I explain without letting him know what I was? How could I hire him to find people who attacked us unless he knew the basic battle lines?

Still, I was alone. Vincent couldn't babysit me while he was out fetching Sybil. I pulled out my Treo and looked up Nathan's number and, well, so it was ringing. I hadn't meant to dial and I could still hang up. I could always hang up.

"Hello?" He was on the line. His voice was warm and deep and slightly raspy with congestion.

"Hi, Nathan, it's Lily." I felt like an idiot. Eros would be horribly disappointed in me if she knew.

"Hey, Lily, great. Thanks for calling. What's up?" He sounded ridiculously happy for a mere phone call.

"Oh, I just wanted to say hi and that I checked my schedule and I can make it on Saturday as long as it's early. I've got plans at six, but if we go early we can have lunch."

"Great!" He sounded quite enthusiastic. "Temple of Dendur. Not quite Babylon, but maybe one day we'll go to Berlin."

"Berlin?" I was slightly confused.

"The Pergamon Museum," he said. "They took the entire temple from the top of the hill of Pergamon and rebuilt it, stone by stone, in this museum in Berlin. And they have a re-creation of the Ceremonial Way with the real bricks that lined the walk. Not at full scale, but it's still wonderful. I went there back when I was an undergrad. A bunch of us went to Berlin. Everyone else wanted to go to the Love Parade and the clubs, and all I cared about was this one museum. They all laughed at me. But hey, it was great." Then he paused for a breath. "I'm sorry, I'm rambling. I'm just thrilled that you can make it on Saturday. How about if we meet at ten on the museum steps on the Fifth Avenue side?"

"Can we make it eleven?" I asked. That was still too early for me to wake up on a weekend, but it would be worth it.

"Sure. Eleven it is. I can't tell you how much I'm looking forward to this," he said cheerily, signing off.

Okay, I was being stupid. He could be like Steve, be in on the plot. I could have given him way too much information by calling. He would know that I was fine. Maybe the date at the Met was a setup and something awful would happen to me on the way there, or on the way home. They would have some knowledge of my movements.

Paranoia chased hope around in my brain, and if Vincent hadn't shown up with Sybil and three more pints pilfered from her collection I might have been inconsolable and afraid. As it was, Sybil was afraid and I had to pay attention to her.

Fortunately, I could obsess to her about Nathan to distract her from her own fears.

"Eros is right, you know," Sybil said solemnly. "You really should have made him wait longer and call a few times. And you should have sent an e-mail instead of calling."

We had changed into pajamas and banished Vincent downstairs. I had given her the short version of meeting Nathan and the possible date, my very first ever real honest date.

"But I wanted to call," I said. "I wanted to talk to him."

"Exactly. Of course you wanted to talk to him. Which is why you shouldn't have," she chided me gently.

"But I had this other thought about it," I went on. "I wimped out, I was too scared really to ask, and it would probably mean telling him way too much about me, about all of us, but you know, he is a detective. Or at least pretends to be. So I thought that maybe he could help us. With these people who are following us. Or whatever." I suddenly remembered that I had to be careful. Sybil is the most timid of us. I almost wished it were Eros here—she would be planning a nuclear holocaust. And she's the one who talks to Beliel. Desi would be analyzing them, figuring some way to turn them from their plans. Sybil just couldn't cope. Which made it harder, but in some ways better for me because I had to keep her on subjects that wouldn't frighten her. So maybe it was just as well that she was focusing on my bad dating behavior. That certainly managed to distract her.

"The reason there are rules about these things, Lily, is that we don't need to reinvent the wheel. Men haven't changed in three thousand or six thousand or ten million years. They want to hunt. The less interested you appear, the more interested they become. The more available you are, the less they have to work, and they don't value you unless they have to work for you. So you're just undercutting yourself. I've had dozens of boyfriends and more than a dozen husbands and I'm telling you, you have to play it cool."

"But I am," I protested, wailing. "It's not Saturday night, it's daytime."

"Lily, you're hopeless. Totally hopeless." Sybil moaned in despair. "Forget accepting a Saturday date the first time he asks, and in the same week, too. You called him. You never ever call guys until the relationship is established or if you have something urgent to say. Like, your cat died and you can't make the date you had that evening. Emergencies. I can't believe you've been living with your head in the sand for three thousand years. I think we need to send Vincent to rent a whole season's worth of *Sex and the City*."

"I watched that show, it was one of my favorites," I told her.

"Who did you relate to?"

I shrugged. "I didn't. Well, maybe Samantha some."

Sybil shook her head and looked sad. "Lily, Lily, Lily, that is the problem. You need a different role model. You want love, not a one-night stand. I'll send Vincent out for my DVDs."

I called Vincent again on the intercom, but the doppleganger answered. Damn. I never thought that Vince would take advantage of having a simulacrum for the evening but hey, he is one of ours.

So at least I was off the hook for the dating dos and don'ts, which was no end of relief. No doubt Sybil was right and I'd made a complete mess of things, and I started to feel nervous that she was thinking of how inexpert I was in one of her areas of accomplishment.

No, she was flipping through the listings on my TiVO.

"They're doing reruns of *Rome*," Sybil suggested. "You lived there, didn't you? You might find it funny."

As usual, she was right, so we stayed up and reminisced about dear lamented days of yore. I love watching modern interpretations of what the world was like more than two thousand years in the past. Sometimes they try to get it right and sometimes they don't, but it doesn't matter because something always turns out wrong. So Sybil and I had a good giggle over the year that kind of mustard yellow stola with glass beaded fringe was just the hottest fashion item. Glass beads were more expensive than pearls in those days, actually—I remembered wearing that stola every single time I went out that season.

Governments rise and fall, ideologies are born and die. Religions conquer, impose their morality and turn to dust only to sometimes rise again. Fashion is always just this season and is as reliable as the moon. It will change; it will look wonderful; and three years later we will all wonder how we ever wore those stupid things. The year after the mustard yellow stola the hot color was dark blue and the only people wearing dull yellow were slaves and the poor, who got the castoffs.

I left Sybil sleeping on the sofa bed in the living room when I left for the office the next morning. Yes, I had told her we'd take the day off, but by the end of the evening she had been giggling and six empty cartons of ice cream sat on my dining table. Vincent would let her out and lock up. If he'd come back. It certainly looked like him when I grabbed a cab and headed to my office, where I immediately called the writer of the shawls piece and told her to include some history, maybe discuss the Roman stola. She agreed groggily and I felt vindicated.

Unreal as the whole thing felt, I was still unsettled. Bad things had happened to me in the past. Okay, bad things have happened to everyone in the past, but I was getting tired of being pursued and alone and afraid of the Burning Men. Away from Sybil I could admit that, like governments and thieves, bad restaurants and must-have shoes, the Burning Men were forever. No matter what we did, there were always a few who refused to believe their eyes and insisted on thinking that there was more to the old stories than uneducated fears and rumors. They organized, generation to generation, and identified us. Somehow.

If only we could get into their database, I thought, idly fingering the keyboard on my desk. If only we could erase all our traces. Satan paid dearly to Admin every time, but somehow, generation to generation, the Burning Men tracked us down.

I was sick of hiding. Why was it always the demons and immortals who had to keep our heads down while those prejudiced, self-righteous little men remained on the offensive? Why shouldn't we hunt them back?

I was shocked that I had never thought that before. In three thousand years, it had never occurred to me that we could fight the forces of Organized Faith. We are, after all, subcontractors for Upstairs. In the greater picture we serve their purposes. Why did we have to take the blame while the Angelic Host got all the praise?

I almost giggled, thinking of how I would love to tell one of the righteous that they were, in fact, perpetuating the Albigensian Heresy. Which would have our own dear Satan on a par with God and fully able to fight Him. Clearly utter nonsense, though She really doesn't like to be reminded that She functions in this world as She likes only because it serves His purposes.

But much as She is the Prince of Evil and Darkness and we serve the Underworld, the truth is that we're actually a division of the Heavenly Host. If people weren't tempted, if they weren't led astray, then they couldn't profess their faith or use or even discover their virtues. Hell is the ultimate service organization and our job is approved and vetted by the On High.

I do good in the world, too. I deliver creeps and liars, unfaithful husbands, men who don't respect women, and brawling louts. If they weren't worthy of me then I couldn't find them. Yeah, yeah, the old saw goes that a succubus seduces good husbands and pillars of the community, but how many pillars of the community are wife beaters and child molesters? How many of the so-called righteous sin on the side and expect that their good reputations will save them? Well, all the hot air in the world won't save them from me. The truly good, the truly righteous and caring cannot be tempted by any of us. Those are the rules.

And these Burning Men, they were no different from any of the men I'd ever known. They might think they are the Army of God, but really all they listen to are their own desires. I'd delivered at least five or six so far as I knew, so I could say that from experience.

I wanted to call Eros. No, I wanted to call Nathan but Eros would talk me out of that, which was a good plan. Bad enough to call last night. Even I realized that to call again today would be pushing it.

I am a succubus, beautiful and terrible, sex incarnate. I do not have to run after anyone, let alone some mortal man who probably would end up responding to succubus pheromones just like all the rest.

I have in all my life had only one proper boyfriend, and Martha and the girls didn't count him as proper at all. I became a Temple acolyte at the age of eight, a novice at twelve, and was initiated a priestess at fifteen. One year later I was one of the inner circle, chosen as the possible successor of the High Priestess herself. And would very likely have gotten the appointment, too, had I not taken a better offer. From Satan.

I had never had a normal boyfriend in the thousands of years I'd been immortal. I was due some indulgence in mooning. So I can be forgiven for sitting in my office, staring out the window, and thinking of Nathan. How he had an adorable dimple in his left cheek when he smiled and how his aura sparkled when we talked about the ancient world. How he had table manners better than most of the kings I've known.

And how could I ask him to help us with the Burning Men without telling him what I am, what my girlfriends are? That was another dilemma entirely.

But we were under attack and he's a detective (and very good at research, and this looked like the kind of thing that needed research) and ridiculously smart, and it wasn't like the Enforcers were going to do any good. They probably didn't even realize that it was just some new iteration of the Burning Men who were after us. Again.

I was feeling all mixed up and like I couldn't even think straight. So I did what any reasonable, rational woman does when she's afraid and overwhelmed and at the edge of her rope.

I went shopping.

chapter
FOURTEEN

I went to Barneys, unsupervised and with one goal in mind. I bought a pair of Citizen jeans and a fine-gauge green sweater with lace trim, the color that makes my eyes look greener and brings out the auburn in my hair. For some reason, modern Americans think that everyone in the ancient world had black or dark brown hair and dark brown eyes. The women of Babylon were known for their red hair and green eyes; from modern Iraq to Istanbul the red-haired siren is both admired and not entirely uncommon. I so often envy Sybil her very blond Anglo-Saxon looks—she has perfect peaches-and-cream skin and huge blue eyes and I have to be very careful in the sun or I freckle.

I returned to the office feeling centered and refreshed and ready to think. Somewhat reassured by my new purchases, I wasn't even upset when I saw an e-mail from Azoked in my in-box. I opened it idly, and it was as terse as I would have anticipated.

I am making progress and may have some information that could be of use soon. Will be available next week, Monday and Wednesday between five and eight in the evening.

Wow. Two whole windows to make an appointment, almost a full week from now. She must have known what had happened. Or maybe she was just showing off her OCD. Having met just one librarian, I had decided that they must be required to be obsessive-compulsive. Otherwise they would get bored and cross-eyed.

Reluctantly I rescheduled my facial and asked the Librarian to come on Monday. Then, since I was already booted up, I checked out MagicMirror. No one had posted about the attack. Even Eros had said nothing.

Sybil's post from last night was most interesting of all, though.

> Had a lovely evening with Lily last night. And met a yummy young demon who actually is cute and has brains and understands about serving a girl ice cream. Hmmm . . . *smile*

No. Nonono. Couldn't be. Sybil liked Vincent? I held my head and groaned. That was too crazy. He was just a newbie demon. He might be smarter than an Enforcer, but it was my idea to send him to fetch her last night. And now he was getting all the credit.

It was just embarrassing, especially all the replies congratulating her and asking for details. At least it was a locked friends-only post. I should be grateful for small things. Didn't she realize that Vincent could perfectly well have his own account on MagicMirror? And that you never should post anything on the Internet, not even on our own private little corner of it, that was not mortal-friendly.

"Never post anything that you wouldn't want to see on the front page of the *Times*," Mephistopheles had told me when he first friended me online.

After her little lecture last night, I thought she was being just a little hypocritical. It was locked and maybe he didn't know that she liked him, but he would know soon enough. Okay, maybe she wasn't being as foolish as I'd thought.

I didn't want to think about that, so instead I went looking to see if Azoked had a topic. That took a little searching, since there was nothing under her name, which I didn't expect. She was too sly to post openly, from what I could see from our one short interaction. I had to link through interests in Akashic Library, Librarians, research and Bast before I located a user who seemed to have all the right elements.

There it was on her user page, Bastform demon, female, highly intelligent and engaged in vital research. Interests mostly of an intellectual nature, though she did list needlepoint. Needlepoint? Okay, well, Eros took up china painting for a while about a hundred and fifty years ago. It was quite the rage then, though, and she dropped it after a couple of decades.

And once upon a time I'd tried to learn the violin. But that was in Venice and there were extenuating circumstances.

I went in and started reading. Fortunately, there is no way to trace someone just reading a journal entry, not unless you post a reply. So I could read what Azoked thought.

Quite annoying, though of course I am quite honored by the direct command of Satan Herself. Still, a silly little desire demon thinking that some man not following her into Hell means that there is a conspiracy is probably going to turn into a waste of time. I'm in the middle of the biggest project of the past six hundred years, converting our public records into digitally accessible formats, and I'm interrupted because one of the minor minions has a hissy fit.

Minor minion? *Hissy* fit? It took all my three thousand years of self-discipline and then some to refrain from writing a withering response. And there was still more!

If only that silly succubus had figured out how to use a search engine, I wouldn't have been needed. But you know how it is with these Luddite demons. They can't even use a remote, let alone do a keyword search on Google. So I'm doing all the legwork on this one.

I wanted to put my fist through the screen. Not able to do a search on Google indeed! I hadn't done one on Nathan because I hadn't thought he was important yet, that's all. Why would I bother?

So I fed his name into the computer and saw what I came up with on my own, without that supercilious librarian making snide comments about my computer literacy.

There were about thirty hits straight off, most of them published papers on Akkadian. I followed the links and read the papers and realized that he was wrong about a couple of grammatical nuances. How do you tell a guy he's wrong about something where he has a formal education and you can't explain the origins of your expertise. How could I say, "Nathan, really, trust me, it's pronounced like this and I know that because this is my first language. And, by the way, you've got the case wrong in the second paragraph." How do you say that to a guy who almost had a Ph.D. in the field and didn't know that he was talking about your mother tongue?

Sybil was right, it was hopeless.

Suddenly I felt like my heart was going to break. My friends thought I was stupid and the Librarian hated me and the man of my dreams was going to disappear because I accepted a date for a Saturday too quickly and his Akkadian grammar wasn't quite up to mine. The world seemed like everything was going to close in on me and I felt like a mess.

I wasn't going to get any work done. I'd already done my shopping and even the best blast of retail therapy had only delayed the misery, not beaten it. Work was useless. Everything was useless. I blew my nose, left the office and hit the video store on the way home. At least I still had a great selection of ice cream in the freezer.

Why had I ever agreed to a daytime date? Especially one that started at eleven in the morning? I am not functional that early on a Saturday. Usually I'm still sleeping off the vodka and the club and wouldn't even think of getting up until noon at the very earliest.

It was one of those perfect crisp winter days where the sky sparkled cerulean. It was cold enough that I wished I could wear a knitted cap for my ears and big fuzzy mittens. Unfortunately, fashion does not bow to the mere flourishes of a New York winter, and so I made do with my shearling coat and Gucci gloves. If it hadn't been for the boots I could have walked over to the Met—three long blocks in sneakers when it wasn't biting cold would be lovely. But it was miserably cold and I was wearing stiletto boots, so I took a cab and tipped extra since the driver wasn't thrilled about going from Eighty-eighth and Lexington to Fifth and Eighty-first.

I arrived at the stairs leading up to the Met at precisely ten past eleven on Saturday. He was standing on the top craning his neck trying to cover all the approaches. Good sign, I decided, and I ran up the stairs, all twelve million of them.

He wasn't wearing a hat either, but did have an elegant burgundy cashmere scarf and an old East German military greatcoat that I lusted after, the kind that belted in close and almost swept the ground but still managed to look almost menacing.

"Your ears must be freezing," he said. "Let's get out of the cold."

Which we did. We went into the museum, to the Egyptian exhibit. The Met has one of the best collections of Egyptian artifacts in the Americas, including an entire temple. It's a small temple, to be sure, but it had been donated by the Egyptian government for aid in salvaging buildings and monuments from areas that had been covered by Lake Nasser when the Aswan High Dam had been built. So the Met has an honest-to-Satan Egyptian temple. The Temple of Dendur.

It sits in a perfect Eastern orientation, just as it had along the Nile in a hall built especially to show it off with a pool situated at just the distance where the river would have been. I reached out and touched the stones carved when I was a girl and used as a place of worship when I was being trained as a priestess myself. The path winds through the claustrophobic rooms and with the crush of visitors on a Saturday there is little time to linger. Still, Nathan did not rush, and managed to ignore the shrieking child running up and down through the room. He caressed the stones reverently, his fingers barely brushing the rough-hewn surface as if it were skin.

"So so old," he sighed. "And I can't read the hieroglyphs. Which is frustrating."

"Neither can I," I said before I realized quite how strange that statement would be today.

He only looked at me and smiled wryly. "You know, knowing you, I'd almost believe that you might." I felt the compliment in his voice.

"Hey, you in there, you're holding up the line," someone said from behind us. So we had to observe in haste, appreciate on the fly, one minute per millennium, until we exited the third and final room.

"Do you want to see the ancient Near Eastern exhibits?" he asked after we'd finished the Egyptian wing. "That's the Babylonian and Sumerian and Hittite exhibit, which was my area of study in grad school."

"But you didn't finish," I said gently, wondering what I should do. Go? Say that I wanted to see the Roman statues? No, that would be ridiculous, if I wanted statues at least I should choose the Greek—or something modern.

"I'm technically on leave and in dissertation. I

could still finish," he said, and I could detect just a hint of resistance in the hopelessness in his voice.

"Sure," I agreed cheerily. "I've never seen that wing." Which was perfectly true. I'd avoided it like it was infected with the Spanish flu in 1918.

We went to the Babylonian wing. Great stele and slabs of black basalt with bas relief figures lined the dimly lit walls. It was cool and quiet.

"Look, here," Nathan said, squinting at one of the giant slabs. I recognized my great-grand nephew's chief adviser's face.

Nathan pronounced something that sounded vaguely familiar but garbled. "Of course, we don't know how it was really pronounced." His voice was full of excitement. "No one alive today has any idea of how the language actually sounded, but my professors were among the best in the world. Though I won't vouch for my accent."

I looked at the writing carved deep into the rock and I realized that he had been trying to read aloud for me in the original. No, clearly they had no idea of how the language had sounded. I wanted to correct him, to speak out the words the way they should be said, the consonants softened and the vowels more complex than Nathan's gibberish.

My mother tongue, I thought. I wanted to reach out and stroke the stone, connect with my very personal past.

He would want to know how it was really said. I knew that, but I kept silent. I could almost hear Eros dripping sarcasm in my head. *If you're going to be stupid and go on a Saturday date with him the first week, you might as well go correct his Akkadian as well. After all this time you should know that men like to show off for women. They like to be experts. If you insist on showing them up, they leave.*

I hadn't taken Eros's advice before, either, and it hadn't mattered.

For some reason, though, I hesitated. Not Eros, but my mother's voice came back to me—and her Akkadian was as elegant and refined as her brothers' tutor could manage. "Even a great king, even your father, needs to be reassured that he's right. That's what they want from us, child. Not our ideas, but our confidence. Because they often don't have quite enough of their own."

Mother was right, and I bit my tongue.

"This writing says that this was erected by the grand vizier to King Ea-mukin-sumi, in the year of his illustrious reign, to advise the people of this . . . place . . . that the following is due to the gods and to the Great King, and to his divinely appointed representatives and their overlord," Nathan continued, with only a few hesitations.

Some of the words were not quite the English equivalents I would have chosen, but I had to admit that he was more accurate than I would have anticipated.

"And then it goes on to list the taxes due and various regulations of public life, and who was allowed to wear certain . . ." Here he hesitated while he puzzled out several words that specified the two lower grades of jewelry, neither of which I, as a member of the royal household, would be permitted to wear. In fact, the first highest grade (which I was permitted as the daughter of the King, but my mother was not), and the second highest (which were permitted to all the King's women, and all dedicated priestesses serving any main temple site) were not mentioned in this document, which certainly implied that it had been from some outlying neighborhood or even a fairly prosperous village outside the capital.

"Costume jewelry," was the term he finally decided on for the translation, and my respect for his abilities went up a fair bit. So he understood the concepts and was trying to translate correctly, accurately, and allow for idiom and embedded meaning rather than lecturing me on the various regulations of who could wear which gemstones. Which I certainly knew better than he did, though I was impressed that he understood that the concept had been important in my world.

"But here, later on," he continued, pointing to another portion of the slab, "it also says that the overlord, under the direction of the vizier and the King and the Priests and Priestesses, are to provide just settlement of disputes and to keep the village safe. That the overlord is responsible for the maintenance of the two wells and the road, and that these must be kept in good repair and that all people of the Kingdom shall have free access." His eyes glittered and his entire face glowed. "Isn't that wonderful?"

He had certainly translated accurately, but I couldn't see why it was wonderful and said so.

"Because it shows that even then, so many thousands of years ago, the government and the nobility had responsibilities to the people in return for the taxes and work the peasants paid. That it was not all top-down management, but that the common people were acknowledged to deserve certain benefits for supporting the structure."

"Well, of course," I said, still confused. "Isn't that what civilization is? Orderly society has to exist at every level or there is chaos." Not only had I been trained as a king's daughter (though an extremely minor, disposable one), but I had lived through the kind of chaos that occurred when the social order broke down. The cruel and violent extorting what they could, the majority suffering in frustration, the collapse of any kind of trust or humanity had been horrifying. Even the most destructive wars had rules; the world where the social contract failed was more frightening than the mustard gas in the trenches nearly a hundred years ago. I certainly know, having lived through all of them and then some.

Nathan Coleman looked at me and smiled. His eyes were deep sapphire and full of mystery. He reached out a hand to my hair but drew back from actual touch. "You are so good, Lily. You don't even accept a world where some people are beyond redemption."

I'm a succubus, I thought. *I know more of Hell and evil and the possibilities of redemption and damnation than you could imagine.*

And then I had to pull back, back to the immediate now, back to the thought of the first date and how much I enjoyed Nathan's company and how I didn't feel like he talked down to me although he had no idea I knew anything at all about this ancient world and he nearly had a Ph.D.

I was good at shoving the memories aside, locking them away until I could take time in private to sort them out. Sometimes the only way to survive so long was simply an act of will, to concentrate only on the now and force all other considerations aside.

I'd never been to a museum with a man before, at least not a man I liked and found attractive. In my first centuries as a succubus I loved the fact that I could have any man I chose. Once. And I took advantage of all the bennies, all those beautiful, strong, well-dressed men. I loved my power over them. I reveled in the fact that at the right times they could not resist me, none of them could.

Over the years I had begun selecting men who would not be missed, who deserved their fate, whose elimination would benefit the women around me. I felt like the protector of my sex, weeding out the undesirables.

And the truth was, even though none of the girls counted it, I'd had one boyfriend once. Niccolo had been a castrato in Venice. Satan and the girls agreed that the fact that he wasn't intact meant that it wasn't a real relationship. Satan always insisted that She discounted the relationship because of the hormones, not the actual cutting. Since his hormonal levels were never in the range for a normal man, he couldn't respond to my succubus pheromones; my being a succubus didn't make him lust insanely for me, and so the fact that he loved me didn't count. To Satan. And even to my friends.

Well, maybe Niccolo and I didn't exactly have a porn DVD sex life, but that doesn't mean that there wasn't love, and caring, and morning coffee. And sex too, and he took care to please me in what ways he could, and there were plenty. The truth is, I had had better sex with a castrato than I had with ninety percent of the men I picked up and delivered. More like 99.999 percent, actually.

He had almost known what I was, my Niccolo, and still he had loved me and sang for me and cosseted me. And I never did take his money, though as the leading man in the Venetian opera of the day he was very well paid. No, he thought I was a courtesan, one of the famed red-dressed women of Venice, and I was.

But it didn't matter in the end because he was found floating in a back canal near the opera house one morning. No purse was found on his body, so people assumed that he had been killed during a robbery. Maybe. It happened often enough. But maybe it was jealousy in the opera, or something about a rich patron of his.

Which was another reason why Satan and the girls always insisted that it wasn't enough to void my contract. Not because the count paid him and slept with him, but because Niccolo had been truly fond of the nobleman. I had never cared, and in the Venice of that time no one would have noticed. And his relationship with the count did nothing to lessen his love for me.

But the count had been political and very rich and had enemies. Any one of them could have had Niccolo killed as a threat. Or maybe the bravos had been hired by his two rivals in the opera companies—that is how such artistic differences were settled in those days.

"You look so lost in thought." Nathan called my attention back to the here and now. "What were you thinking about?"

I forced my brightest smile. "Venice," I said. "How it's not really Roman, not like the rest of Italy."

"I've never been to Venice," Nathan said. "But you're

putting me in the mood for Italian food for lunch. Would you like that?"

"Mmmm," I agreed. "Nothing like pasta on a cold day."

So we left the museum and took the subway from Eighty-sixth Street to Bleecker and then walked the cold blocks into the West Village, which is packed with Italian bistros that all look like the set of the *Godfather* movies. We chose one at random on the corner of Macdougal, where there were at least three similar eateries, and ended up seated across a red checked tablecloth with a hunk of crusty bread and a dish of olive oil while we perused the menu.

It's easy to make small talk ordering food. It's easy to say how the cold makes you want soup and pasta and how you adore cannelloni and how you can't resist mushroom ravioli. And he talked about how linguini with clams is his favorite comfort food in the world, and I got to tease him because he ordered the veal instead.

"But I don't need comfort food," Nathan said, laughing. "I'm with the most beautiful woman in New York and she calls the Babylonian world civilized and supports the notion of reciprocity in the ancient world. The world is so perfect right now that maybe I should have just ordered the tiramisu and called it done."

I grinned. "Not cannoli, then? Tiramisu has gotten so clichéd. And they have those mini cannoli with chocolate chips in the cheese. I saw them in the case up front."

"Not prefilled, I hope. Only a Hittite would prefill a cannoli," he said, rolling his eyes with mock horror.

"Or a Greek," I added.

We both laughed. And we did end up ordering the cannoli as soon as our meals came. The food was good, too, and we ate before we resumed the conversation.

"So how did you end up at a fashion magazine?" he asked. "After studying Italian at Mount Holyoke."

I rolled my eyes and wiped my plate with the last bit of bread. I shrugged. "I always liked fashion and I knew someone who knew someone. She set me up with an interview and I started as a lowly editorial assistant." Which was perfectly true, though saying that I knew Satan, who really did know just about everyone and could guarantee any job, was not precisely first-date material.

Then the cannoli came with our coffees and Nathan took the moment to savor the perfect pastries, their crisp fried shells flaking onto the plates, the cheese so smooth and sweet it was like ice cream that doesn't melt. Nathan closed his eyes and sucked at the spoon with the abandon of any of my girlfriends. One thing I have learned is that men don't usually swoon over desserts. They might like them and tuck right in, but they don't play with the food and don't lick minute portions almost a molecule at a time, trying to make a truly glorious sugar experience last as long as possible.

Nathan talked like a man and ate cannoli like a girl. He was not one of the Burning Men.

Burning Men do not believe in self-indulgence in any sense. They don't treat a cannoli like a momentary idyll in the garden of delights. Which, of course, is exactly what a perfect cannoli is. Burning Men punish themselves for pleasure, for experiencing any kind of pleasure or any joy in the world.

I don't have a lot to do with the On High, but I do know the Angelic Orders find the dismal righteous bigots rather a trial. All that lovely Creation, all those good things of the world, that these self-righteous little men reject and call sin, all gone to waste. Cannoli are meant to be enjoyed. Great food and wine and perfect weather and love and free time and fun are all gifts from the On High—gifts that the kind of people who spend their time hunting us reject. From a few things I've overheard (standing in line waiting for some paperwork at Admin) those On High find it even more frustrating than we demons do. After all, the people who adore us at least know how to enjoy themselves. Well, most of the time.

Anyway, the important fact was that Nathan's pleasure in his food, in the museum, and in being with me proved he was not one of the attackers. I could trust him.

Maybe.

I certainly wasn't going to tell him that I'm a succubus, though.

"So I really don't know what to do, Lily," he was saying. "I'm technically still able to finish my dissertation and get the degree, and I've got this detective gig. Which was not supposed to mean running around all over the city. I was hired mostly to do computer searches and look up histories and things like that. And mostly I just think of it as something to do while I figure things out, but for some reason this case bothers me. Chris, my boss, thinks that my missing guy, Craig Branford, was probably selling prescription drugs on the side. Oxy has amazing street value these days, and if he was compounding, well—anyway, all the facts would fit that theory. But he's disappeared entirely and why would he do that if he had a nice little drug operation going? Why jeopardize it?"

I shrugged. "He thought he was going to get caught?"

Nathan shook his head and the lights reflected brilliantly off his too-black hair. "I don't think the police were on to him at all, even if he was dealing. So why would he think he was going to get caught?"

"Paranoid?" I offered. "If you're doing something wrong, you might be afraid of getting caught even if there's no actual reason to think that. The guilt just builds and gets overwhelming. Or," and here I paused, partly to think it out and partly for effect, "it wasn't the police he was afraid of. Maybe some Colombian drug lord killed him and dumped him in the river and that's why he's disappeared." Hey, no one had told me that *Miami Vice* was going to rate as educational one day. I just thought Don Johnson was entirely too cute and wore Armani besides, and how many cops had spiffy power boats and really knew how to dress?

That show educated a whole generation, come to think of it. One TV show was the turning point for American men understanding that dressing well was masculine. That changed the entire culture. Which sounded like a feature article for the magazine, which would fit in perfectly in our menswear issue. I pulled out my Treo and made a note to mention it at our next editorial meeting.

Nathan raised an eyebrow. "Oh, I just got an idea for a magazine article," I said.

"It's Saturday. You're not supposed to be working."

I laughed. "And we're talking about your case, so you're working. And I suggested that he was hit by the Colombian drug lords and is dead. Which I think sounds pretty good, honestly. Since you can't find any trace of him."

Nathan suddenly looked somber. "I hadn't thought Colombians, but yes, it did occur to me that if he were dealing drugs he had stepped on the wrong toes. But something about this all just feels so wrong, and there haven't been any unidentified bodies that fit his description since he disappeared."

"And it's Saturday and you're out with me and you're not supposed to be working." I smiled broadly.

He smiled in return, and then turned serious. "But really, Lily, I appreciate your thoughts on the subject. You're smart and original and I think I've been kind of limited with this whole thing. Like I got so caught up with the details that I should be able to put together a picture that makes sense, but I can't."

"You need to not think about it so much," I said quite seriously. "I read an article in the *Times* just a few weeks ago. Researchers in Germany discovered that if there are a lot of factors to consider, the subconscious mind makes better decisions than the conscious mind."

Which was the perfect way to distract him, and we went off talking about psychology and neurobiology, with a good deal of bashing the outdated and disproved theory that there was a change in the ability to think abstractly in the Golden Age of Pericles, and before that everyone was very literal. Which just makes me furious, and made Nathan as furious as I was, and we experienced a deep and violent agreement before I noticed the time.

"Oh my goodness, Nathan, it's five thirty and we're in the Village and I have to meet my friends at six on the East Side and I won't even have time to change—"

When I had planned the day, going to the Village had not been part of the picture. There was the museum, near to my house and not all that far from where I was meeting the girls. Now I wondered how I was going to change for our charity event after our little ritual at Sybil's. Being on the other end of the island had not been part of my original calculation.

We ran out of the restaurant and over to Sixth for me to hail a cab. "I've had the best time, Lily," he said, looking deeply into my eyes with his arms wrapped around me as three cabs cruised by. "I want to see you again. Soon."

"Me too, Nathan," I said. "I want to see you again really soon . . . This week? Dinner?"

I could hear Eros now. She would be apoplectic. I knew I shouldn't, not ever, ask for a date this early. I should have played it a bit cooler and I really should have let him send an e-mail and ask me and deny him a few times before we could settle on a time. I was doing everything wrong. I couldn't possibly tell my friends but they would know, I knew they would know.

"Monday?" he suggested.

Monday? Yes! No. I was seeing Azoked on Monday. "Can't do Monday," I said, feeling some reprieve.

Eros couldn't think I was being too terrible. No, she would and so I couldn't possibly let her know how badly I'd slipped. "Send me an e-mail and I'll check my calendar."

And with that I raised my right arm and a yellow cab cut across three lanes of traffic to pull up in front of me.

I opened the door and then Nathan pulled me in to him in an embrace that smelled of soap and warmth and home. I lingered in his arms for a moment, wondering if he would kiss me. I wanted him to kiss me, and I guessed that would be against Eros's rules as well.

"Lady, I'm blocking traffic. Get in the cab," the driver yelled at me through his open window and the moment was obliterated by the blare of at least three horns.

chapter
FIFTEEN

We met at a bar near Sybil's with a huge selection of umbrella drinks and an even better selection of hard-bodied men in Helmut Lang. The plan was to meet up at the bar, have a little fun, go to Sybil's and do a protection spell of warding, and then hit a charity event where Desi hoped to drown her sorrows over Steve by meeting some attractive fashionable man who would succumb to her magic.

I looked around the room quickly when I entered to find that Eros had already claimed a table and a chocolate martini. "You saw him," she said almost accusingly. "Didn't I tell you that was a bad idea?"

"You told me," I agreed. "Now I need one of their chocolate raspberry truffle martinis."

"You might want to order two," she said. "I don't know if you've heard about Sybil—"

Suddenly I was terrified. "What about Sybil? What's happened to her? Is she all right?"

Eros laughed. "Oh, the only thing she's in danger of losing is her heart. And her head. No, I meant what is this thing going on with her and your doorman?"

But before I could answer, Sybil and Desi appeared flanking a very chic Satan. If She weren't the Prince of Darkness it would be thoroughly disheartening to see all our fashion finery eclipsed by Her utterly stunning Yves Saint Laurent pantsuit. I didn't think She'd planned to go to the charity event—some fund-raiser for a children's hospital. They made their way over and, of course, since Satan was now among us, waiters and drinks materialized immediately, large and strong and perfect and made up of lots of things that weren't on the menu.

"I can't linger," Satan said when She sat down. "I just wanted to make sure that you all know that the Enforcers have studied the documents you turned over and this case has their highest priority. Our librarian has been working overtime and will be reporting in soon, and hopefully she will be able to trace through connections to unravel this new infestation. And, the important thing that you all need to know—the Enforcers are going to be keeping an eye on you until this is all resolved. I do not want any of you harmed or in danger again, and some big mean burly demon Enforcers are not going to let anything happen." She smiled, laid four hundred-dollar bills on the table, and stood up. "Have a lovely evening." And then, without even touching Her drink, She disappeared. Literally.

"Enforcers?" Desi wailed. "Watching us? That's the worst, the absolute worst."

Sybil blinked. "I feel much safer knowing that there are Enforcers watching out for us. I don't have a heroic demon doorman to come to my rescue if anything should happen."

Heroic? Vincent was now heroic? For what? Fetching Sybil from a couple of blocks away, or for getting us more ice cream?

Eros rolled her eyes at me, and I winced in sympathetic reply. "I wish it were Security watching out for us," Eros said. "Beliel knows what he's doing."

"Unfortunately," I added, "Beliel isn't interested in catching Burning Men. He's more interested in background checks for the Treasury." I'd heard plenty on that score from Marduk.

"Which is part of the reason I wanted help to ward my apartment," Sybil continued. "Oh, you are all just the best best friends!"

"And we're eating rubber chicken, too," Eros reminded her. The charity dinner and dance were sponsored by Sybil's office and she had generously picked up the tickets for all of us.

"Oh, no, it won't be rubber chicken," she said, aghast. "Rive Gauche is catering."

We finished our drinks and then ordered a second round, and by the time we arrived to do the warding ritual we were in, hmmm, shall I say, not precisely a ritual state. Not that two drinks is enough to put any of us off our magic, but even Sybil was giggling and not appearing to be as worried as she had sounded when she made us all promise to show up.

We entered her apartment and I noticed immediately that the new wallpaper really did make a huge difference. The place had been charming before, but the shimmer of the silk organza overlay created a subtle play of light that made all of Sybil's admittedly overstuffed and vaguely Victorian furniture look sophisticated and even verging on postmodern. I was impressed.

"So let's start. I'll need some time to get ready for this party afterward," Eros announced.

"Oh, but Vincent isn't here yet," Sybil protested.

"You asked the doorman?" I was aghast. "He's barely been a demon for a month and hasn't even started his first magical tutorial. He's still on probation."

"He's been a demon for four months and has been doubling up on tutorials," Sybil corrected me. "He's already through Level Three, Intermediate Locator Spells and is working on Etheric Manipulation, and has already had nibbles from Security and Oversight. Satan's top lieutenants know he's talented, smart, and dedicated. He's going to have a brilliant career in the Hierarchy."

The great majority of demons don't have careers. Most have functions, and most of those functions are low-level and boring. Top demons are mostly fallen angels and old gods who Satan has recruited. A few of us impressed Her enough that our original contracts specified high position, wealth, and attention. A handful like Desi worked their way up from the bottom, but that took a superhuman level of ability and commitment. Vincent may be cute and smart, but he'd have to do a whole lot more if he wanted to reach the ranks of a major demon.

Eros gave me a quick raised eyebrow before the intercom buzzed. Sybil let Vincent in and in a few minutes I was impressed to see him standing in the living room wearing couture. I'd never seen him out of uniform before, and the tight cashmere turtleneck showed off a body that had been carefully sculpted in a gym when he had been alive. Though now that he was a demon he got to keep it without the endless hours of crunches and bench presses that had gone into the creation of that perfect physique.

Okay, chalk one up to Sybil. She could spot them. And I'll lay money that she was the one who took him shopping for the clothes.

He was carrying a familiar garment bag and a bigger train box, which he brought over to me. "Your dress for this evening," he informed me. "And your makeup. I didn't know what shoes you wanted, so I brought several pairs. I hope that's okay, but I thought it would be easier for you than having to return home. Shall I put them in the bedroom for you?"

Oh my. Oh my my my. I have never, ever, in three thousand years, had a doorman bring me my dress without my expressly asking for it. I wondered what dress he had brought, and if I was pleased or annoyed by this development. But, oh, he was being so useful. And it made me feel like a princess again, and a high priestess besides. Being a succubus doesn't always mean that you actually get service.

"The bedroom would be lovely. And, Vincent, thank you." I reached up on my tiptoes and gave him a sisterly peck on the cheek.

"You've been drinking!" Vincent was clearly offended. "You're not supposed to do magic when you've been drinking. It affects the concentration, and means that either you're too grounded on the earth plane or that you can't access Yesod. Or you get confused by the etheric and can't control it."

Wow, he'd certainly caught on to the jargon. Give him another couple of months and he and Meph will be geeking together on the Technical Magick topic on MagicMirror. Myself, I stay away from that most of the time. I've got my cred in some of the higher levels, but I don't like to sit around and talk about the details as if I were some overweight guy in a faded Linux tee shirt talking about computer gaming.

"That's just for mortals or the lower order of demons," Eros said, sweeping her hand grandly. "We're cool."

Vince was clearly confused. "Well, if you say so . . ." Clearly he didn't quite believe us.

"Really, Vincent, it's okay. We've done this before," Sybil reassured him, holding his arm and curling up against his chest. "And when you've gone beyond the intermediate level tutorials you'll start to see exactly how we do control the etheric forms, and sometimes a bit of alcohol is useful. And we're doing a specific Hell working here, since I want to make sure that nothing of the Holy gets anywhere near this place."

With that, she pulled out a few thick, smoky gray candles. She showed Vincent where the big brazier was hidden, and he lugged it to the center of the room after Desi and I moved the coffee table, which weighed far less than the brazier. In fact, either one of us could have taken it alone, but it wasn't well balanced and we were being lazy and didn't want to take all Sybil's knick-knacks and big art books off the top. Eros marked the cardinal points, arranging the candles and checking the incense. Two passion fruit mojitos didn't make her appear even the slightest bit inebriated.

Then we each took a quarter, with Vincent standing in the doorway in the shadows. "No, no, you take the North," Sybil directed him. "I have to be the priestess." Which was not strictly true, but it didn't hurt to have a full complement.

Since I was West, Vincent was next to me. "You know how this works?" I whispered. He nodded, and

Sybil began. She lit the incense, a kind of nonentity aroma whose main ingredient I think was lavender or soap. She carried the smaller basin around the circle and lit each of our candles, starting in the West and circling South, East, and then North. She returned the small censer to the central brazier and took a chalice of salt water, which she sprinkled in the same circle.

The interior of the circle changed. The light had a different quality and there were darting bits of color and lights that blazed like incandescent miniature fireworks. Tiny creatures flitted at the edge of our vision, and something like wind chimes sounded just at the edge of hearing. This was the etheric level of existence, the Realm of Yesod, if I were trying to use geekspeak. This was the world of energy and magic, where thought and desire were real and created a template for what was expressed in the physical world.

Sybil threw something into the brazier and I could see her apartment as it appeared in the etheric world, brilliantly lit in greens and golds, a shimmering beacon of magic. There were other beacons around, some far brighter and others very pale, all pulsating different hues and humming different notes. It was very pretty and easy to get distracted here, easy to wonder what that soft shimmering pearl blue represented and what was the blazing orange sun. At times I've been known to get a little too close, and sometimes one can penetrate and sometimes a demon can't. Some of those points of light are cults and secret organizations, and some are Esoteric Orders who study high magic and work on this plane. If we had time to drift and watch and look around, we might find the pinpoint that was the Burning Men's focus. We might find it and we might not; it was dangerous in any case.

We weren't here to hunt. Sybil, true to her nature, wanted only to hide.

And so we constructed a veil around the soft green-gold light that was Sybil's place. The gray candles were the antithesis of light—we held them and circled around, each time shrouding the beacon that was Sybil's address. Around and around and around, layer after layer of protection we wove so that Sybil no longer appeared in Yesod.

It was clearly effective, though I thought a bit wrongheaded. The Burning Men could find us in the physical. They could use Google as well as the rest of us. And they could find us through the threads that seemed to disappear into the soft haze where Sybil's place had shone before.

Personally, I thought that it was easier for enemies to identify the absence or hiding wards as easily as the normal etheric presence. There are so many entities in Yesod—and none of them look like they do in physical manifestation—that I think this exercise is entirely counterproductive.

Well, counterproductive in any real sense. It was really about reassuring Sybil. So long as she felt she was safer and wasn't hiding under her bed all the time, the exercise would be a success.

Finally the tiny glow that had been Sybil's place faded entirely, a rubbed-out negative space in the shimmering that is Yesod. We circled our candles into the center and snuffed all of them in the giant brazier in the middle of the room. Sybil poured the rest of the salt water over the glowing coals, extinguishing them as she completed the ritual.

There was only one more thing she had to do to set the final form. She picked up a small paring knife and nicked her wrist open, letting three drops of ichor drip into the mess in the brazier. We are demons, and our blood seals our pacts with Satan and marks us for what we are. Our blood itself is a magical ingredient, used in some of the more daring works of high ceremony. Very few magicians can call a demon and get enough blood to perform certain workings, which is why most humans think they can't be done. Not at all true, but if you don't have the right ingredients you don't get the cake.

"Well, now that's done," Sybil announced with a wide smile. "Thank you, everybody! Now we can get dressed to go to the party."

Sybil giggled and hugged Vincent. "Except you. You look perfect."

Gack. It was true, I thought. They were dating, or on the verge of dating. Or at least Sybil had a wild crush on my doorman. And it was all my fault because I sent him to fetch her when she was so scared and vulnerable.

Though maybe Sybil wasn't so silly, falling for Vincent. The garment bag he had brought from my house had three dresses, one long and pale silver, one sedate black, and a very short one that shimmered in dark green and burgundy with an overlay of bronze lace. And he'd included the bronze shoes that I had bought with just this dress in mind. Okay, the guy was a genius when it came to women's clothes.

How did he get to be a demon, anyway? Why wasn't he a fashion designer?

And for Sybil's sake, I hoped he wasn't entirely gay. For someone who could see the future, it was amazing that she couldn't see what was right in front of her face. She would be heartbroken for at least a week before she tried to find someone to fix him up with. Sybil can be so sweet about things when she's in the right mood.

Dress, shoes, hair, makeup, I looked . . . okay. Well, much better than okay, but it all felt like wasted effort. There was no one at this charity event that I cared to see me looking so fine. I could hunt—even when my mojo isn't entirely on, I can hunt and deliver if I have the intention to do so. But I didn't feel like that, either.

I wanted to see Nathan. I wanted to go back and have our date again and get to stay for dinner and maybe rent a stupid movie together. It had been only a few hours and I missed him already. I wanted to call him.

At the very least, I wanted to check my e-mail and see if he'd suggested a time to get together next week. I knew I could check it on my Treo, only the girls would all know what I was doing. And I could *not* be sending him an e-mail on a Saturday night. Even without Eros's prompting, I knew that was carrying things too far. It was Saturday night and I was going to a fancy party with my best buds, and I should be happy.

The five of us piled into a cab that Vincent hailed and made it over to Park in ten minutes. As promised, the food was delicious. I hardly tasted it. I looked at the crowd, all beautifully dressed and smiling, sipping champagne and nibbling canapés. It was all a horrible waste of time. Sybil was clinging to Vincent and introducing him around, Desi was chatting to a tall blond investment banker (one of Sybil's copartners in the firm, probably), and Eros was fending off no fewer than three gentlemen who vied for her attention along with multimillion-dollar accounts.

I hid behind a particularly attractive arrangement of pink lilies and tulips, fuming. And then I wondered why I was so upset, and got an answer I didn't want to acknowledge. Nathan. It was fine being with my friends taking care of Sybil's apartment, but here in the social milieu they were each on their own and doing fine. Except me.

And I'd felt so pretty earlier, in the museum, with Nathan's approving eyes all over me. Here all my friends were getting attention and I was a wallflower. Literally, hiding behind the flowers.

"Hey, babe, what's a fox like you doing hiding behind the tulips?"

There is very little that turns my stomach more quickly than some total stranger addressing me as "babe" or "baby" or some other insulting diminutive. Lousy come-on, cheap clothes and all, he was precisely what I was in this corner to avoid.

Besides the bad come-on line, he had a toupee and was wearing a shiny synthetic shirt with an ancient double-knit jacket that had pilled. Garments that have pilled belong in one place only and that's the trash. This combination of unappealing traits just curled around my mojo and I could feel the succubus start to rise.

Yeah, this night was a loss as far as fun went. But delivery—I might be able to make Satan happy, along with every woman who wouldn't have to listen to this creep again.

Some badly dressed men have nice manners, or at least are pleasant people. They can have a conversation with a woman and not treat her as if she is a piece of meat with the IQ of a doorknob. I've met some brilliant, interesting, and socially adept men who had yet to figure out that the leisure suit had died back before they were born—or at least should have. And even more charming, personable, pleasant gentlemen who thought that the height of fashion meant that their jeans and tee shirts were clean out of the wash that day.

While I appreciate people who take the time to dress, who understand the niceties of fashion, I know that not everyone worthwhile is going to spend hours every month perusing our magazine to make sure they are at the very cutting edge.

I do expect people to treat each other with some basic respect. I do not expect to be called "babe" by a random stranger.

I smiled grimly. Not that he noticed the subtle flash of canines or the murder in my eyes. He didn't appear to believe that a woman like me could do anything but worship his powerful manliness.

They all think that, and that's what condemns them.

"So, what do you say we go off and have a little real fun?" he suggested.

"Oh?" I asked, keeping my tone innocent. I wanted to see how far he would go on his own to condemn himself.

He leered. "We could go to my place and get horizontal." He'd just done it. Now I wasn't the evil soul-sucking succubus, I was a member of the Justice League making parties safer for all women.

I smiled wider. "Sure. Lead the way."

He immediately ran his hand over my backside and squeezed. It was all I could do not to wince.

We got into a cab and he gave directions—to the PATH station.

Oh no. He was taking me to New Jersey. I wanted out. "You didn't tell me you lived in another state," I protested mildly. I could still deliver him just as effectively, but I had no idea how I'd ever get home.

"It's nice," he assured me. "Hoboken is very trendy, really upper-class, and right on the PATH. Which runs all night."

I had never been on a PATH train. I didn't think I'd ever even been to New Jersey. I was starting to get worried about this whole out-of-state thing. Could I get a cab in New Jersey and would they be able to take me home?

The PATH train was nicer than the subway, truth to tell. It was cleaner and newer, and quieter too. Which made me even more suspicious. New Jersey was not a good idea, not for me, not on the spur of the moment in the middle of the night. Probably not ever.

"You know, I'm not sure this is such a good idea," I said as the train approached the Christopher Street station. Moment of decision here since, according to the handy map over the doors, this was the last stop before the train headed under the river. Leave now or follow Mr. So-Unappealing into another state. I had a split second to make the call as the train stopped and the doors opened, and decide I did. The night had been bad enough without this delivery. I wanted to go home, I wanted to put on my Ozzy tee shirt and watch *Buffy*. I wanted to be anywhere and do anything other than stay on that train and endure one more minute of this loser's company.

The doors slid open and the moment was at hand and I called it. I bolted out and ran up the stairs and had my arm in the air for a cab as soon as I hit the street.

"Hey, wait, you can't run off like that." I heard him yelling after me. It didn't occur to me that he would get off the train and come after me. But no matter how much I knew he deserved to be delivered into Hell, I could not bring myself to cross running water. Not into Hoboken, anyway.

I heard him running behind me as a yellow taxi pulled up in front of me. I hopped in, locked the door, and told him to take me to East Eighty-eighth.

The man I had abandoned punched the car just as the cab squealed away into traffic. "That guy give you a bad time?" the driver asked in heavily accented English.

"Uh-huh." I couldn't keep the whimper out of my voice. I felt tired and angry and I wondered if I had enough money in my wallet for the fare. And Vincent was still at the soiree with Sybil, so he couldn't go up and get my mad money. But yes, okay, I did have the extra twenty squirreled away for an emergency just like this. I'd be fine.

"Mens should be nice to ladies." The cabbie kept up his one-sided conversation. "Too much I see this, ladies run away. I pick up the ladies. I save them. I do not like these bad mens who no respect their mamas. Every woman be treated like my mama, that's what I learned."

"Thank you," I muttered. So here I was, a damsel

in distress saved by the yellow cab knight. It was all so funny, so absurd, that for a moment I wanted to laugh. But I knew that my gallant knight would take it wrong and I wanted to build him up.

My choice. Two thousand years ago I delivered men like this cabbie who were only trying to help me out—more than once. But now, now I think it's better to let the decent ones live. Who knows when I'm going to need a cab again in a desperate situation?

So he took me home and I had just enough cash to pay the fare and include a very generous tip. I staggered out of the cab and through my lobby, where a strange young man in a doorman's uniform looked at me suspiciously. I showed him my key and he called the elevator for me. I would have felt better if Vincent had been there.

When I got in I wanted to call Nathan so badly it hurt. I wanted to talk to him, wanted to hear his sane, soothing voice. It was one in the morning. I didn't need Eros's rules to know that this was not the time for me to call.

So I did what any reasonable, sane New York woman would do on a late Saturday night when she has just barely avoided being abducted to New Jersey. I ran a very hot bath with a bath bomb and settled into the fizzing steam with the two men I could always trust, who would never let me down. Yes, Messieurs Ben and Jerry know how to soothe the wounded and care for the downtrodden.

There is nothing, nothing at all in this world, like eating a pint of Napoleon Dynamite in a very hot bath up to your shoulders. It almost makes all the disgusting creeps of the world disappear.

chapter
SIXTEEN

Sunday morning I went through my usual routine. No delivery this time, no bag to dump down the disposal, no check-in from the doorman, no leftover clothing to clean up from the night before. By eleven thirty I was on my second cup of shade-grown fair market Kenyan. The radio said it was cold out today, in the twenties, so I pulled a heavy sweater over my jeans, restocked my wallet, and made it out the door with six minutes to spare.

Vincent was in the lobby, looking perfectly well rested though I knew he'd been out late the night before. "Good morning, Lily," he said when he saw me. "Cab?"

For once, I was not the last one there. Eros and Desi were waiting at the entrance, and they immediately dragged me in. "Come on, let's get a table. Sybil will be here in a minute, I guess," Desi said.

"What happened to you last night?" Eros asked after we'd been seated. "I went to look for you and you had completely disappeared."

So I started to tell the story of my near abduction and they were properly horrified at the thought I could have ended up in Hoboken with no way home.

"So what happened with you guys? What about

Sybil?" I asked after I'd finished. Sybil was never this late. "Vincent was on duty when I left this morning."

Desi giggled. "He didn't get any sleep then, I'll bet. He and Sybil were still on the dance floor when we left."

"They were the only ones on the dance floor when we left," Eros specified. "Romance." Eros practically spit the word.

"What's so wrong with a little romance?" Desi asked. "I love romance."

Eros shook her head. "That's not what I mean. Sybil falls in love too easily. Too often. But before now it's always been with mortals, so it wasn't going to last. But with a demon? Disgusting. Demons do not have torrid passions for each other. The point is that humans have torrid unrequited passion for us."

"But Sybil's not a sex demon," I pointed out in her defense. "Her specialty is greed, when she isn't telling the future. And isn't knowing the future a form of greed no matter what people ask?"

"Greed is every bit as good a sin as lust," Desi chimed in on my side.

I was about to go further in my defense of our colleague when she came in the door. And every thought I had about protecting her fell apart when I saw what she had with her.

There, on her shoulder, was the cutest wicker Kate Spade bag with bronze leather fittings.

That was my bag. I had seen the picture a week ago on my desk and I didn't even think that they had them in stock. How had she managed? The spring collection wasn't out yet. I knew that; it was part of my job.

First my doorman, then my bag. I felt betrayed. I

couldn't even look at her. My eyes were riveted to her bag.

"Don't you love it?" she was ingenuous enough to ask.

"How did you get that? That's this spring's collection." I'm not sure I managed to keep all the venom out of my voice.

"I just wandered into the shop yesterday and there they were. Not even on display yet, but the salesgirl showed me when I asked. They had just arrived, they were still in the cardboard packing box. There were so many colors and it was so hard to choose, but I thought this would go—"

She looked at me, and suddenly her mood fell. "Oh, no, Lily," she said, throwing her hands up to her cheeks. "Oh, Lily, was this a bag you'd been planning on?"

Slowly I nodded. "I didn't think they'd be out yet. And I didn't think that was quite your color."

"I'll take it back," she offered immediately. "I'll exchange it for the pink, or maybe the orange. Those will go with more of my clothes, really. Or the lighter gold, that's better with my coloring anyway."

I felt really awful. Sybil was being a real friend, and I was behaving like an idiot. "No way," I insisted. "That's a great color with your stuff. It doesn't match but it coordinates perfectly. I can get the smaller one. I've been trying to carry smaller purses anyway, since my shoulder started to hurt."

"That's because you put too much into the big bags," Eros said. "If you didn't stuff them full of papers and magazines and old shopping receipts your shoulders would be fine."

But really, it wasn't about bags at all. It was about me and Sybil. She looked at me very gently. "You know, Lily, I think you really need this bag. And it really isn't my color anyway. Not to mention a wicker purse is pretty silly when it's twenty-six degrees out."

Suddenly I began to laugh. It was like the dam broke and all the tension and misery from the night before, and all the worry about the rules and Nathan and my friends, all of it just dissolved.

On the table, as the waitress brought our mimosas and took our orders for banana stuffed French toast and sides of sausage and bacon, Sybil unloaded her bag. Lipsticks, wallet, keys, sunglasses, sunscreen, and tissues (in a cute little quilted packet embroidered with penguins and baby ducks) all lay on the wooden table. The purse was empty.

"Here," she said, presenting the bag to me with both hands. "For you."

"No, no Sybil," I protested. "You can't. You don't need to. I mean, why can't we both have the same purse?"

She smiled broadly, honestly, as if she were really, truly happy. "Lily, I don't need this purse. I can get a pink one. If I think about it, I really wanted the pink one more and couldn't admit that I made a mistake when I made that poor salesgirl sell me something that wasn't even checked in yet. And it's too early for wicker anyway. I want you to have it, really I do."

She would not take no for an answer. She stuffed the lipsticks, the keys, the tissues and all the credit cards into her coat pockets. I started to cry.

There is nothing and no one like a true girlfriend.

* * *

Monday was terribly busy at work and still cold. And when I arrived there were six Kate Spade purses on my desk from the spring collection. I nabbed a wicker with hot pink leather trim and a metallic gold and pink tote for Sybil and the turquoise for myself. They hadn't sent one of the bronze.

There were also piles of photos to go through, the month's column to prepare, and sets of accessories for the upcoming shoots. Fashion editors might arrange the shoots, select the photographers and models and the outfits, but I arrange the purses, jewelry, and other accessories for each feature spread. Really, that takes much more of my time than working on my own column and the accessory page in every issue. Mostly I feel like I'm at the beck and call of the six editors and stylists who put together the photo spreads that make our magazine so popular.

On Monday Samantha was putting together the beach issue so I had totes and sunglasses along with the usual jewelry. Danielle came in with piles of sandals and espadrilles (tied with gossamer ribbons this season, some of them decorated with beading). Samantha laid out the swimsuit and cover-up that she had chosen, and then I suggested sunglasses, tote, jewelry, and maybe a hat, and Danielle would add the shoes. Then we would critique the completed set, swap pieces in and out, and think about who hated whom at the moment and then go over the whole thing and think about the overall composition. Had we gone too much for the blues? Were the sunglasses all too heavy? Were there too many bikinis and not enough maillots? Had we included enough flat sandals? Danielle was often hard pressed to show a shoe with under a three-inch heel.

"They make your legs look like potatoes," she had pronounced once upon a time, but really it's hard to walk in the sand in stilettos. So Samantha and I insisted that at least a few of the heels were wedges that could possibly navigate a beach.

I didn't even really get lunch. The three of us, closeted all day over the shoot, ordered from the deli across the street. I don't remember eating, only that we did just so that no one could say that we had eating disorders. That was important in a world where everyone associated with the fashion industry is accused of driving teenagers to kill themselves in the name of a slender figure. An edict had come from on high (Amanda, our editor in chief) that everyone will eat a lunch or at least take a lunch hour every working day.

When we finished at seven, it was all I could do to get a taxi to take me home. Home. The thought of kicking off my shoes (chosen by Danielle, so they had the requisite heel) and calling out for Chinese sounded like Hell, in the very best way.

Vincent smiled cheerily at me as I entered the building and handed me my mail. Not that he was supposed to have my mail key, and that was tampering with the U.S. Mail, which was a felony. But Vincent was used to felonies; from what I knew he had committed a fair number of them, and very successfully, before he met his demise from a seizure while playing a completely innocent game of pickup basketball.

I opened my door, ready to slip out of my shoes, when I saw her. I had forgotten. And then I wondered how she had gotten in and whether Vincent had let her in, and then I got angry at Vincent for not saying that he had done so. Though, to be honest, an Akashic librarian can probably manifest on the Earth plane wherever she chooses. Maybe, if I were very charitable, it wasn't Vincent's fault.

"You're late," she hissed. "And there are no Florentines. This is not acceptable behavior and I will complain to my superiors. I am not used to being treated in this manner."

Thank Satan for MagicMirror. "How about some Cherry Garcia?" I asked with a cheer I definitely did not feel.

"Do you have any fudge sauce to go on that?" she demanded, but there was a hint that she could be mollified.

"I've got U-Bet syrup," I offered. It doesn't get better than that, and even our evil librarian agreed. She accepted the offer and I fixed her a large helping.

Really, I didn't want to see Azoked at all, but I was also hoping that she would have some information for me. And she may have even sent me a reminder but I hadn't had a chance to look at my e-mail since ten in the morning, and then I'd only scanned the work-related information.

I waited while she daintily licked her way through almost half a pint of ice cream, wondering the entire time whether I wanted to order lo mein or orange beef. I was pretty set on the orange beef by the time she deigned to address me.

"As I told you, I have made some progress, though I cannot say that I have completed the investigation by any means," she began. "In a search of this nature, we of course have to follow the multiple threads of possible threat, past and future, and see where they intersect with those of our demon element. The problem here comes in part because demons are not represented in the Akashic. Those of you who, like yourself, began as mortals, have records of your existence in life. But the activities of the Hierarchy are not recorded, so discovering the intersections is an exercise in looking for negative space."

"Oh," I said, trying to look interested. "What did you find?"

She blinked at me, picked up the bowl in which I'd served the ice cream and licked it clean. Then she handed it to me and asked for more.

"How about Phish Food?" I asked. "That was the end of the Cherry Garcia."

"I do not eat fish food!" Her offended dignity could be heard across the Hudson.

I hit the Intercom. "Vincent," I hissed when he came on the line. "Did you let the Librarian into my apartment?"

"Yes, of course," he admitted readily. "She had an appointment, and you were quite late. She arrived at five on the dot."

So she'd been wandering around my place for two and a half hours. Who knew what she had discovered about me? Not that there was anything Satan didn't know, but the thought of Her Cattiness pawing through my stuff angered me. There was nothing to be done, though.

"Can you run out, or call out, for another pint of Cherry Garcia? And some Florentines, while you're at it. There's that good bakery over on Eighty-ninth—"

"I'm on it," he answered and hung up.

Miss Priss sat there and refused to say a word until the rest of her dinner arrived. Vincent had gotten not only what I'd asked for, but several other flavors of ice cream and a large bakery box of cookies tied with string that contained mostly Florentines but also included the green and pink leaves stuck together with chocolate and the butter cookies with the maraschino cherries, both red and green, in the middles. He had also included two large lattes.

"How much do I owe you?" I asked.

He waved his hand. "I put it on account," he answered grandly, and then spread out the paper napkins like a tablecloth on my coffee table and presented the food with all the flourish of room service at the Sherry Netherland.

Azoked nibbled one of the Florentines delicately, as if expecting them to disappoint. Then she looked surprised. "These are adequate," she admitted. Well, it is a very good bakery.

"There have always been societies dedicated to the extermination of the more, hmmm, tempting levels of the Hierarchy," she began to expound when there were no more Florentines left in the box. "That is nothing new; indeed, it is expected. The real question in this case is how one of those groups was able to identify you. It is the passing of information so highly classified that has Satan so displeased, and, indeed, the upper Hierarchy as well. Which is why I was taken off vital work on a major project and assigned to your case. This is not about you and your friends, you understand, but about a breach of security. We cannot have humans knowing that we are among them. That would be a disaster for all of us, not just a few self-important sex demons."

I really wanted to slug her. The only thing that held me back was that I was sure she was trying to provoke me deliberately so she could get taken off the job. Oh, Satan would get someone else (who might not be any more palatable, and might not be quite as competent), but She would be displeased with me and we'd lose whatever progress we'd made.

"And have you discovered who it was who gave out the information? Or to whom it was given?"

Her expression changed drastically, as if she could hardly credit me. I forced myself not to smile. Of course she was a grammarian, had to be. I had her. She was recalculating her position.

"The hunting organization your names and addresses were given to is called the Knight Defenders."

"Templar descendants?" I asked.

She cocked her head. "Possibly. I did not trace their history past this current iteration. Previously their main focus was a Bible study class that changed only when they began receiving information that is privy to the Hierarchy."

I didn't for a moment believe the "I did not trace their history," not coming from her. Probably, if pressed, Azoked could not only tell us precisely what this organization had done and funded, but the amounts in their bank accounts, their membership data, and their full schedule of activities for the past two hundred years. But I didn't really need to know that. I just had to know why they were dangerous to us and why we had been targeted. And how to stop it.

Preferably without another visit to Admin.

Yes, we could get our lives made over, kind of like the Witness Protection Program. We'd have to split up, the four of us, and leave New York. And I would never see Nathan again. In a really thorough job, his memory of me would be wiped. I would never have existed.

I did not want that to happen. Suddenly something shifted inside me and I realized that I was going to stand and fight. In the past, the times I've been threatened I'd always let Satan and Admin take care of it. And that always meant a change of identity and location, and I'd always been fine with that. Admin always managed to transfer at least most of my securities and accounts, liquidate my real estate or turn it over to a holding company. I'd never lost much, and after a year or two the four of us would find each other again. Sometimes it took a decade or more to arrange transfers so that we were all in the same city, but with enough persistence we had always managed.

But I deeply did not want to leave New York, at least not until I had worked things out with Nathan. I didn't know what I wanted and I didn't know what I could have, and I hardly knew him. That didn't matter. I wanted—maybe not Nathan at that moment so much as the opportunity to get to know Nathan. To see if there was a relationship worth pursuing.

I was perfectly clear that I didn't know if anything would come of this first date. I'd had a lovely time with him and it was possible that things would work out for us. It was far more likely that they wouldn't, that I would find out that on longer acquaintance he was addicted to Monday night football and hated Chinese food and left the toilet seat up. He might like my clothes but turn out to be horrified at what I considered a reasonable price for a pair of shoes or a jacket. There were just so many ways a relationship could fail, and I knew that.

So probably it would fail.

That didn't matter. I wanted the chance to find out on my own. I didn't want to just run away because someone was trying to hunt us down. We had to fight back.

"Of course, the best thing would probably be for you to disappear." Azoked spoke as if she were reading my mind. "Satan could arrange that fairly easily and it would be less expensive than much more of my time."

Which was true. "But this isn't about us at all. If someone is giving out privileged information, then we have to trace the source. This is an attack on Satan, and we cannot let that stand."

I was surprised by how ardent I sounded. Even more, I believed it. Yes, I wanted to stay and see if I could make things work with Nathan. But it also was clear that someone had hurt me, had tried to destroy all four of us, to get at our boss. I was almost touched. But I was also right. We could not let an attack on Satan go unchallenged. Leaving New York would change nothing, especially if the demon betraying us were sufficiently important.

Azoked showed even more approval of me, and it looked like her face would break with the effort. "You show admirable loyalty," she finally admitted.

I deserve an extra helping of something particularly luscious, I don't know, maybe a new pair of Christian Louboutin stilettos, as a reward. Because I did not make a face or roll my eyes or react in any way to the insults that Bastform demon chose to heap on my reputation. Succubus and sex demon I may be, but that is no reason to be surprised at my loyalty or the fact that I am not an idiot. I get really tired of these people and demons who think that anyone who looks good and knows how to put an outfit together is an imbecile and flighty and doesn't have any values.

"Satan is our overlord," I said calmly. "She deserves all of our loyalty. And all of our support and aid in tracking down those who would do Her harm."

"Indeed," the Librarian agreed. Not that she had any choice. "I simply do not know why I am instructed to report to you in this matter. I should be speaking to your superior."

I squared my shoulders and narrowed my eyes. "I was personally asked by Satan to coordinate research on this investigation. She is my only superior in this matter."

"Very well," Azoked said, mollified. Or at least I hope she was mollified. "This particular group, these Knight Defenders, are a small organization run out of an apartment in Grand Army Plaza."

Brooklyn. Right near the Brooklyn Museum. Unless we cleaned this up in the next couple of months, there would be no lying out under the cherry trees of the Brooklyn Botanical Garden and no visits to the Zen meditation garden either. Much as I hate to admit it, there is nothing quite like them in Manhattan. And some of the clubs and galleries in Williamsburg are getting very trendy, too. Truth is, there are some pretty exciting spots springing up on the other side of the river and I did not want some group of pathologi-

cal self-righteous twits to stop me from shopping in
Park Slope.

"It is a sex-segregated organization, currently
recorded as headed by one Lewis Taggart. At least, his
name is on the papers, though in the Records he is a
ghost, which is quite curious."

"Oh?" I asked. Clearly Azoked expected me to
inquire.

"Yes. Very curious," she answered, clearly ready.
"We call them ghosts, people who come up in
searches but whom we cannot find in the Records.
There are one hundred seventy-nine Lewis Taggarts
currently living in the Records and I have searched
each of them, and none of them are connected with
either this organization or this particular part of the
world or time period."

"So he's a cutout," I said.

"I have not heard that term," the Librarian countered, clearly disappointed that I followed the concept so easily. "But in the Record of All Living, there
is no Lewis Taggart who is living now in Grand Army
Plaza, or any other place in Brooklyn. There is no
Lewis Taggart who is affiliated with any secret society
or organization, and none in the current time frame
who are involved in any charity besides the RSPCA
and Habitat for Humanity."

Something was stirring at the base of my skull, tick-
ling my memory. There was no Lewis Taggart. That
was no surprise. And in some ways, the Knight
Defenders were not the issue. There had always been
small groups among the Righteous who were fanatics
and dangerous.

No, the real problem was on the demonic side of

the equation. Who was trying to undermine Satan? Who would have the nerve, the arrogance, the means, and the desire?

Satan treats us well. She says it's good business and I believe Her. Working for Satan is a very lush gig—loads of perks, plenty of money, great addresses, food, sex, and indulgence in the extreme. If the work was at times unpleasant, the compensation was more than generous.

There is nothing here on Earth that Satan can't get, make, give, or provide. Nothing. And She is not stingy with Her Chosen favorites. My friends and I are all proof of that. She believes in rewarding service and in taking care of Her own.

Who would not be content with this arrangement? Who would want to rebel? No wonder She has Enforcers watching us. And while I don't relish being bait, we do need to get to the bottom of this.

Well, there is the matter of eternity, service, and one's immortal soul. But eternity is pleasant and most of the service is enjoyable and light. The stuff about selling your soul, though, that can get a bit sticky. Although Satan has a special clause for each of us, should we wish to leave Her employ. It's hard to fulfill Her conditions, but that is always agreed upon at the onset of the contract. And Satan keeps Her word. Absolutely. Sometimes in ways that surprise the recipient, but that's their fault. Satan may be very good at twisting the meaning of a clause in the contract, but She always delivers exactly as stated. Bargaining and negotiating are the most highly regarded skills in Hell.

Someone who wanted out? Someone who couldn't

figure out the release clause? Someone who couldn't meet the conditions of the release clause?

But then, why hurt fellow demons? None of us is better off that way. Some might be happier than others in serving the Prince of Darkness, but in the end a job is a job. Hurting us might annoy Satan, but doesn't cut into Her power in any real way. And it won't help someone's release clause.

So what if it's not a release clause the demon wants to activate? What else? What could someone want?

All my Agatha Christie was coming back to me. We had to find a motive, because we were never going to track a demon through the Akashic. As Azoked had explained earlier, only the living had Records. We could look into the future there, or into the past, or into every level of existence, but only for those creatures who had mortal existences. And souls. So I had to discover what the demon wanted.

I wondered what Nathan would say about all of this. He was a detective, or at least was trying to be a detective of sorts. He had heard of real cases, I guessed, unless this missing person was his first. But there was no way on Earth I could possibly explain the situation to him and get some feedback.

"I am currently tracing all members of this organization through the Records. We have found that Desire's gentleman, Steve Balducci, is a member. In fact, he had been instructed to go to Public for brunch to meet one of you. So not only your addresses, but your movements are known."

Whoever had betrayed us knew about our brunches, intimate details of our personal lives. I was incensed. Was nothing sacred?

chapter
SEVENTEEN

"There's nothing sacred about Public," Eros announced. "We can find another place for brunch."

We had thought long and hard about where to meet for lunch to discuss Azoked's information. I thought we should go somewhere different, someplace that we hadn't been for a long time. Balthazar was perfect. It was right around the corner from the Prada store on Broadway and since its sister restaurant Pastis had opened, we (along with seven-eighths of fashionable New York) had transferred allegiance to the new eatery. Truth was, though, Balthazar was still the place we had swarmed three years ago, with the same perfectly Parisian atmosphere, reliable food, and an attendant in the ladies' room.

While the antique mirrors that lined the walls and the hard tile mosaics on the floor made the place almost insufferably loud, that meant that likely no one was listening. Or rather, that no one would make out what we were saying. It was hard enough to hear companions at your own table. Most important, though, is that none of us had been in Balthazar for years, except for a midafternoon blood-sugar crash while shopping in SoHo.

Besides, I was really in the mood for fennel ravioli

and duck confit. So I ordered the large-size appetizer along with the duck confit with wild mushrooms, and if it was a lot of food, dealing with betrayal and politics was hungry work.

Eros poked at her salade Niçoise.

"You really need to keep up your strength," Sybil encouraged her. "When we're under attack we have to be extra careful to eat well and get enough sleep and facials, or else we're going to collapse. And that would mean they win and we can't let that happen. We are Satan's Chosen. We owe it to Her to crush Her enemies beneath the heels of our Manolo Blahniks."

"Well, if you put it like that . . ." Eros was not about to be outdone by Sybil. Certainly not when it came to daring. Eros was always the leader, the fearless one, and Sybil was always the fraidy-cat in the back.

"We could have Sunday brunch here," Desi suggested, licking her fork one more time for the last possible morsel of her hand-cut frites.

I had not known until that moment that it was possible for Eros to get any more pale than she was. But she did. She blanched. "No. Absolutely not. We were here regularly a few years ago and that was fine. We can move on."

"It's not about our brunch specifically." I wanted to get the conversation back to the problem at hand. "It's about Martha, and about who could know enough about us to set us up at brunch the way Desi was targeted. Clearly there is some inside information being leaked to our enemies. It doesn't matter how thoroughly we eliminate this group, some other will crop up. The problem is the demon who is feeding them our secrets."

"Why do you think there's some demon involved?" Eros demanded again. "I just can't imagine anyone actually going to this length to betray Satan."

"Maybe she's jealous of us," Desi suggested. "Maybe she wanted to be one of our sisterhood and Satan didn't choose her. That makes more sense to me than someone trying to attack our Master."

Hmmm. I hadn't thought of that. I leaned into the plush red leather banquette and twisted the linen towel pretending to be a napkin in my lap. Most of Hell would be jealous of us, except for the old guys like Meph.

"What would you say to asking Mephistopheles?" I suggested. "He's been political and at Satan's left hand forever."

"He doesn't travel much in our circles," Eros mused. "None of us knows him too well, and it might be out of place."

"He's friended me on MagicMirror," I said. "I'll bet that if we invite him to someplace with really spectacular food he'd meet us. He'd go to Nobu. He loves Nobu. And he likes being consulted as an expert."

"Unless he's the one doing it," Eros protested.

Sybil shook her head and perfectly cut blond tendrils brushed the shoulders of her lace-collared blouse. "Not Mephistopheles," she pronounced with absolute conviction. "Meph is loyal and has no reason to betray Her or us. He's hardly aware of us, I'd guess, except for Lily's Mirror posts."

"Well, if Lily knows him best, then maybe Lily should meet with him." Eros waved her hand with imperial disdain.

Okay, Eros was a semi-divinity. But that's no reason for her to act snobby and withdrawn with her friends.

Still, I would be happy to have dinner with Mephistopheles. He is witty and urbane and he knows all the very best places to eat.

Mephistopheles, Satan's prime deputy, was rumored to be a fan of gluttony. Not nearly so respectable a sin as lust or greed or wrath. Not that any of them could compete with pride, but that was Satan's very own baby. Gluttony was down there with vanity, almost verging on the venal. Or maybe more merely the ubiquitous. It's just not that exciting a sin when everyone is doing it.

Not that it's his specialty or anything. He, like many of the old-time elite, would insist that his specialty was pride. And the truth was, I was certain that that was where his work was. Gluttony was just more a hobby for him.

Our waiter showed up again wrapped in his Parisian-style long apron and a saucy smile. "Dessert?" he asked, passing out menus.

Well, of course dessert. I ordered crème brûlée. What else would anyone choose in a bistro? Especially one that really does look like it belongs on the Champs Elysées, with a restroom attendant who personally passes out paper towels and has a tip basket at the door. Though when our desserts arrived, Sybil's Tarte Tatin looked awfully appealing.

So order number one was to set up a meeting with Mephistopheles. But that wasn't going to be enough.

"MagicMirror," Desi said. "We should go through all of our friends' lists, and take a more careful look. Also at some of the junior sex demons who might feel passed over, especially those who have been junior for a long time. It could be that one or two of them deserve promotion, and we could let Satan know. Sometimes She gets really overworked, you know. She can't be expected to know when every junior demon should move up in rank, and if they have a sloppy superior. . . ." She shrugged.

Desi was the one who had actually worked her way up through the ranks. She had started as an apprentice and had patiently gone through each of the grades of service, making promotions because of her excellent record and results and her staunch loyalty and hard work. As a Priestess of Ishtar, and a royal princess, I had been recruited to the higher levels immediately. Sybil had been an Oracle of Apollo before she had been tapped by Satan, so she had always had high status. And Eros, well, Eros had never even been human. She had been created semi-divine from an illicit relationship between one of the great old gods (who were now among the elite of the Hierarchy) and a human. But even half-divinity packs more power than most demons ever amass in eons of service.

Anyway, Desi was more likely than any of the rest of us to understand what an ambitious young demon might feel and had to do to get noticed.

"So I'm going to set up a meeting with Mephistopheles and we're going to all do some research on Magic-Mirror," I summed up. That didn't seem like a lot of progress for an entire lunch cabal.

"And we're going someplace new next Sunday," Sybil added. "I'll take care of finding a place."

"But I keep feeling like we should do something else," I said. "I want to ask Nathan. He's a detective so he might have some ideas on how to handle this. He's got experience solving crimes and stuff like that, and that's not what we do. So having his expertise might give us a better idea of what we need to do next. Because I keep feeling like we're missing something."

"Lily, you're in too deep too fast," Eros chided me. "And I mean with Nathan. You have had exactly one date with the man, and you shouldn't have had that. He approached you about some missing guy. How can you be sure he wasn't one of your deliveries? I think that you're just using our situation to make excuses to call him and see him. If I wrote bad TV, I would twist this so that it was you who had been sending those letters, just to have a creditable mystery for your lust object. Or that he was doing it in the hope that you would turn to him and then he could 'catch the perpetrator' and make you all grateful for his having saved us all. Or something like that. I don't think you should see him again."

"What?" I was blindsided. These were my very best friends. Why couldn't they support me and be happy for me in finding someone I could possibly care for?

"Lily, listen to us," Desi said, laying her hand on my forearm. "You don't have a lot of experience with romance. You're head over heels over this guy and you really don't know anything about him."

"I Googled him," I protested, having learned my lesson from the Librarian. "I know that he did study ancient languages and he even did a creditable translation in the museum."

"I'm sure he did," Desi agreed softly. "But you don't know anything about *him*. Whether he's honest and trustworthy or if he could be setting you up. I was set up and I'm more experienced than you in these things. And we just don't want you to get hurt."

"Not hurt that way," Sybil spoke up. "Lily, you're innocent. You don't know what men can be like, even if they really like you. The only one you ever were involved with was that castrato back when? The seventeenth century?"

"It counts to me," I protested. "Niccolo loved me."

"I don't doubt it," Sybil said, smiling. "But he wasn't, you know, full of testosterone. You don't know what they'll do. Hormones. And they say that women are all at the mercy of chemistry. But guys get really weird and I'm sure it has to do with their hormone levels. That's what makes them all violent and macho."

"Nathan isn't violent and macho," I insisted.

"They are all violent and macho under the right circumstances," Eros said flatly as she threw her credit card on top of the long curling bill attached to a postcard. "Just like all mortals are susceptible to one of us. You know that. Find the right temptation at the right time and even the most perfect will fall. As long as they have been disobedient in any way. And you know almost every living being has been."

Sybil had already bitten off all her lipstick. "Eros is right," she said. "We're not saying don't date him, Lily. We're not saying that at all. We're just saying to take your time and be careful. Don't be taken in by good manners and a case of the sniffles. That might mean that he won't fall for your mojo immediately, but it doesn't make him that far off your prey. Just . . . be careful."

"What if you met him?" I asked. "Then you could see for yourselves."

"No," Eros insisted. "What part of no don't you understand? You are *not* asking him on a date this early in the game. You are going to wait it out and let him suggest the next three at least and you are going to be *busy* for the next time he picks. Do you understand that? You are going to be very very busy and you are not going to be able to see him until next week. Which means after next Sunday."

"That's a week from now," I wailed. "Too harsh. Eros, you're overdoing it."

"No, she's not," Desi said. Her face was soft and concerned and she reached across the table to touch my arm. "You're really too trusting. And I know what we can say about me and I know I was wrong, so this is partly my fault. But Eros is right. You need to take it slower and find out more about this guy."

"We should get out of the city," Sybil said in her scary predictive voice. "They are searching. We should not be here."

"Well, that's convenient," I muttered.

Three pairs of eyes turned on me. "Sybil never, *never*, fakes her predictions," Desi said. "You know that. If she says we should be out of the city for the weekend, then we should be out of the city. The end."

"And I, for one, do not want to deal with another attack," Sybil added. "I want to go away, someplace safe where no one knows who or what we are and there are no Burning Men looking for us. Especially if they are planning something for the weekend. I'll bet they know about Sidonie's gallery party! That would be ripe. All of us in one place and the gallery opening is very public and no one's going to confront them and Steve's uncle is a famous architect, he's probably on the guest list. They'll be fawning all over him."

I wanted to stay in the city. I wanted to see Nathan. I had totally forgotten about Sidonie's gallery opening, which I would much rather skip anyway.

"We could just skip the party," I suggested.

"And wait for something else?" Sybil asked softly. "We couldn't have predicted the holy water in the letters. I don't know that they're planning something for the gallery; all I know is that the city is not safe for us next weekend. We can leave. We can go on a weekend getaway."

"It's the middle of winter," I groused. "Where can we go that would be any fun?"

"What about skiing?" Eros said, raising an eyebrow. I may be a thoroughly twenty-first-century New Yorker, but I'm also a princess of Babylon. I have never quite figured out how snow and ice can be fun. I'd tried skiing twice and hated it and reminded everyone of that fact. Which, since they had been present at my humiliation (coming down a mountain on my derriere flailing poles in front of every attractive man in a ten-mile radius, to say nothing of being so bruised up that I didn't dare show up at the hot tub to soak out some of the pain), they were not going to try to talk me around.

"A cruise might be nice," Desi said. "Maybe in the Caribbean. They have these singles cruises that sound like they'd be fun."

"Not a singles cruise." Eros nixed the suggestion. "We're not looking for guys who aren't New Yorkers. I mean, what if you met someone on the cruise who came from someplace else. Like Philadelphia?"

"Ask Meph for some restaurant recommendations?" I piped up. "I've been dying to try Morimoto ever since he wrote it up on MagicMirror."

"So if we don't go on a cruise, where should we go that would be fun?" Desi mused, more to herself than to the rest of us.

"Philadelphia?" I suggested. They looked at me as if I had really lost my mind.

"You've been reading too much of Meph's food porn," Desi said. "I, for one, am not willing to spend a weekend out of town for a single restaurant. No restaurant is that good."

"Aruba," Sybil said brightly. "I'd love to go to Aruba for a long weekend. Lie out on the beach and have cute waiters with big muscles bringing me Bahama Mamas. You could talk me into it."

Sybil had been to Aruba last winter for some investment seminar and came back utterly enchanted.

"I'd rather go to Martinique," Eros started. "The Empress Josephine, Napoleon's wife, was born there. I think the French have better food than the Dutch."

"But Aruba has real New York bagels." Sybil defended her choice. "And there's lovely Italian food and Argentine steak. You love steak."

"Would Vincent come with us?" I asked, suspicious. Sybil, right now, was my very specific example and she seemed to be doing everything with Vincent that my friends wanted to dissuade me from doing with Nathan.

"No." Sybil looked offended. "And yes, I am interested in Vince. He's very attractive and he's very nice, considerate, thoughtful. He brings me ice cream and he takes care of all of us. But it's only been a few weeks and I am definitely not inviting him to Aruba with us. Besides, I don't think he's got the money for it and I am not paying his way."

"Or at least, not yet," Eros said.

Sybil shook her head and her brilliantly blond hair shimmered in the light. "We'd have to be very serious for me to even consider that. Even if we marry, I'd make him sign a prenup. Back in the days when all of a woman's property became her husband's upon marriage, I always made sure that the bulk of my estate was well entailed and tied up with false identities that could not be traced. I had to pay Admin extra for that and you know that Admin will take everything they can get."

I had to admire her. I hadn't known that Sybil followed her own financial advice so carefully.

The waiter was hovering nearby and his smile wasn't quite as all-encompassing as before.

"It's two in the afternoon and there isn't a line," Sybil said directly to him, and then smiled to sweeten it.

"The point is," Eros continued, "you kill men. You have sex with them and you kill them. You don't have to analyze them. You don't ever have to make them stick around."

"Okay, okay, you're right!" I caved. "I get the point. I even agree that if Nathan weren't in the picture I would jump at Aruba."

"Then jump," Desi said. "All of us will go together. I'll call my travel agent as soon as I get back to the office. Can everyone get Friday off?"

We all nodded. And then, much to the waiter's relief, we left.

chapter
EIGHTEEN

Being immortal and one of Satan's Chosen has many, many advantages. Being rich is one of them. I could afford to just say yes and have Desi's travel agent book a first-class vacation at the last minute. There are always seats available for people who are willing to pay full first-class fare, always a few of the most expensive suites in the best resorts open at the last minute if one doesn't care about paying a little above the going rate.

I had a confirmation from Desi's travel agent in my e-mail before I got the next note from Nathan. Which was probably exactly what the girls had planned because I certainly would have seen him if I hadn't just plunked down my credit card for round-trip airfare (business class) and a deposit on a five-star beachfront resort. To say nothing of the fact that my girlfriends would totally kill me if I bailed on them—if the Burning Men didn't get there first. And truth was, the memory of the holy water on my hands was enough to make running away for a weekend that could be dangerous sound better even than Nathan's invitation.

Nathan's e-mail was for dinner Saturday night at some restaurant I'd never heard of and live music at some club in Williamsburg.

Okay, so they call Williamsburg the new SoHo. It can't be. Nothing can be SoHo, but I did give him a few points for being a little ahead of the curve.

Still, it worried me. Williamsburg is in Brooklyn, where our ersatz Templars had their headquarters. It could be coincidence. Or not. Whatever, it worried me just a little bit, which made it easier to tell the truth. Which is, I had prior plans with my girlfriends for a girls-only weekend.

Maybe Eros (and Desi and Sybil) would be disappointed in me, but I did say that I was sorry and that I would love to see him, and maybe he'd be interested in doing something when I returned. So even if I asked, I was playing by the rules. I hoped.

I'd hardly had any time to work out some accessory ideas for a shoot one of the fashion editors was putting together when I got a reply from Nathan. He was invited to a gallery opening in Chelsea a week from Wednesday and would love me to go with him.

Okay, so Williamsburg was proving that he was cutting edge and in the artistic know, not dragging me out into questionably demon-killer territory. My faith was restored and now I had two events to anticipate. Aruba *and* a date with Nathan.

By the time I was ready to leave the office, having chosen at least ten handbags and seventeen necklaces for two different photo shoots, I had a dinner appointment with Mephistopheles, too.

My friends and I might be among Satan's Chosen, but Meph is one of the Great Old Ones. He was created in the Hierarchy before there was a humanity to tempt. There are only a very few like him—Beliel and Moloch and Baal-Beryth are the others—and then some of the Old Gods, who were also members of the Hierarchy but were actually worshipped as deities in other places, like Marduk. If what had happened to us was a result of politics in Hell, there were two possibilities. One was that a junior demon had attacked us, either out of piqued jealousy or to get Satan's attention. The other was that there were some machinations among the Old Ones, whose power and power politics went back before the Jurassic.

Some of the old gods didn't like reporting to Satan, had never liked answering to anyone, and resented their overlord. Others were content with Satan but had issues with other departments over what I'd call turf wars. Who got which allotments, budget, prime office space, pencils. All the things that people and demons snipe over inside an organization.

Sometimes I think that is one of the primary reasons that my friends and I are Satan's Chosen. We don't care about those things. We're not gunning for the next promotion, the corner office, the bigger staff, the high-visibility cases. We are the demons we are. Period. I don't want to oversee all three hundred twenty-seven succubi in North America, let alone the entirety of the Western Hemisphere. We don't use our relationship with Satan to bludgeon other demons with our access and power, and we don't ask Her for anything except Her company—and advice on caterers and decorators.

It was easier to get time with Meph than I'd anticipated. He had a reservation at Butter the next evening and his intended companion had canceled. So there we were, with a reservation and an opening and, well—I jumped. I was glad that I could talk to Meph

so quickly. I'd been worried that it would take a long
time to get an appointment. He's an important guy.

The bar at Butter is long and narrow. The seats are
low and appear to be hewn out of rough logs with
deep leather upholstered cushions on the inside to
contrast with that glazed bark exterior. Everything is
shades of golden wood and yellows, autumn in the
woods, and, well, butter. It was a quarter to nine so I
was a little early, but Meph outranked me and I
should not keep him waiting. The protocols were just
as strict among demonkind as they were in the palace
of Babylon, and I wasn't going to stint on the propri-
eties. Especially not when I had requested the meeting
and I was asking for aid.

Butter is an interesting place. It's a high-end restaurant upstairs but a club with a DJ in the basement.
Mostly I'd been here to eat lunch or down in the club,
which is very popular in its own right. While I know
the food is wonderful (all those lunches, yum!) I usually don't think about this as a place to go for dinner,
and I remembered to dress differently for the occasion. I kept that in mind when I chose a suit in a cop-
pery and olive tweed, with a slender skirt to the knee
and the new boots. I sat at the bar nursing a glass of
champagne. He arrived precisely at five past and I
walked to the hostess station to greet him. Of course
they had his table ready and it was in a quiet corner
near the mural of autumn leaves that dominated one
wall.

Mephistopheles, like a very few of the most elite of
Hell, can change his looks to some degree as he might
wish. Being ancient and powerful, he tends to appear

in more different shapes than those of us for whom this takes more energy. He always walks in the body of a man, usually in early middle age, naturally very fit and excruciatingly handsome. Vanity is a sin, after all, so it is almost a requirement to indulge. Mostly his look is fairly consistent and he's had the same face the last four times I've seen him.

In the most recent iteration, Meph is about six feet two of pure muscle. He moves like a dancer and has the same firm abs and arms, broad shoulders and developed butt as any of the men in the corps de ballet at ABT who appear fifteen years younger. His hair is thick, abundant, in a rich brown with just the barest hint of silver at the temples. His navy wool suit came from Brioni and cost about what Eros just paid for the apartments she's buying.

Mephistopheles exudes power and wealth the way I embody sex when my mojo is on. Only his mojo is always on. Heads turn whenever he walks into a room, in Hell as well as in New York. Even here in New York where people make a virtue of ignoring the outrageously famous.

"At least in New York no one asks for my autograph," he said, responding to my unvoiced thoughts. Most of the time it's too easy to forget that Meph can read thoughts—sometimes. Not always, which makes it difficult. But he is the most powerful denizen of Hell after Satan.

I nodded. "I really appreciate you seeing me, and especially that you made time for me so quickly," I said immediately. With a demon of Meph's stature, it's always best to acknowledge the favor quickly and often.

Meph smiled benevolently. "Oh, for one of our dear Prince's favorites I can always find a little time. Especially for such a delicious creature as yourself, Lily. I was quite distressed when our Master told me about the attack, and I was glad to read in Magic-Mirror that you had suffered no lasting harm."

"Satan was most generous," I demurred. "I expect you know that She's appointed me to help investigate the attack, which is why I wanted to consult with you."

He nodded once, graciously, a royal in an expansive mood. "I am only too happy to help if I can," he said. "I don't know that I have anything useful to add. Certainly I don't know the creatures who would attack such lovely, hardworking demons as yourselves."

Our waiter materialized even more magically than Meph, and laid open menus in front of us. I glanced down, looked up at him and smiled. "Could we see the dessert menu as well, please? I just can't plan an entire dinner without knowing what's for dessert."

The waiter immediately complied. Mephistopheles laughed deeply, his eyes crinkling with delight. He raised his water glass to me. "You are perfect, Lily. I have never even thought to look at the dessert menu before ordering, and that's so clearly utterly brilliant."

My eyes widened in surprise. "But how else would you know? I don't know who started the idea of not putting the dessert on the main menu. It's horrible. I need to make sure I have room for all the dessert I want. I don't want to fill up on salad when there's something like—oooh, look at this. Now I'm really glad I asked for this first. Maybe I'll just have it for my entrée and again for dessert."

Meph raised an eyebrow. There it was, the very first dessert listed. "Look at this, honey tangerine crème caramel with lemon sorbet and ginger crisps. Is it really as good as it sounds?" I was drooling. Suddenly the wild salmon in a ginger crust or the Colorado rack of lamb with rye berries didn't sound nearly as tempting.

"I don't know," Meph confessed. "I've only ever had the cheese plate. It's wonderful. I love cheese."

We are demons of Hell. It is our duty to live out all the things that mortals desire in their deepest, most secret fantasies. Meph was being too traditional, too hidebound, and I was feeling very defiant.

"How about this?" I suggested, my voice full of evil anticipation. "We order the oysters and the foie gras and the raw tuna salad and the calamari. And then we have the cheese plate and two honey tangerine crème caramels and the Turkish coffee napoleon."

"No entrée?" He looked shocked.

I shrugged. "If you want one. I'd rather have three desserts." I waited for a moment for him to absorb the shock. "Come on, Mephistopheles, we are Satan's elite demons. You are Her second in command, and I'm Her shopping buddy. If we can't eat whatever we want and break all the rules, what are we good for?"

While Meph is clearly a traditionalist, he could see the point of my argument. We ordered the dinner I had outlined, and then he chose a bottle of Sauvignon Blanc to complement the seafood.

Once the waiter took our order and disappeared, Meph leaned over the three butters in the middle of the table. "What precisely can I help with?" he asked seriously, as if we were having a conversation about investment banking. "I don't know who these attackers are and I don't understand what use I may be, but of course I am at your service."

"We know the name of the group who actually sent the letters," I told him. "They call themselves the Knight Defenders."

"Boring and pretentious," Meph commented.

I nodded and continued, "We know where they are headquartered, even, under the aegis of a Lewis Taggart who doesn't exist in Grand Army Plaza in Brooklyn. The question I want to answer is how they found us. We aren't easy to track down, you know. Desi's date had some kind of prearranged rendezvous while they were at the museum, and he ran into her at our brunch. I would have thought it was really coincidence, but after we all got letters at home I'm thinking that this isn't possible. Someone had to tell this group where we were and who we are. Someone told them the name of the restaurant. Someone who knows."

"You think a demon betrayed you?"

I'll give this to Meph, while he was shocked he was also ready to accept the evidence as presented. Even when it was ugly.

I nodded. "Exactly. Which means that to find that demon we need to know why. Desi thinks that it may be some junior sex demon who's jealous of us, and we're looking into that. But I think that it could also possibly be someone in the upper echelons making a political move."

"Against Satan?" He was alert, considering.

"Maybe. Or maybe against someone else, jockeying for position closer to Satan."

"Hmmm," he said, tapping his fingertips on the table. "You realize that would be a plot against me."

I shrugged. "Possibly. Or possibly a layer or two down."

The assortment of appetizers, which really had been excellent, were gone. The waiter arrived with my honey tangerine crème caramel and I was not about to permit worry over the possible politics of the attack—after all, this was one out of many possible motives; personally I was leaning more toward a junior sex demon being jealous of our positions close to Satan—to interfere with my enjoyment of this dessert. No. I have my standards.

Fortunately, the crème caramel lived up to my imagination. After three thousand years, very few things do.

Meph smiled and gave the cheese selection the same attention I was giving the crème caramel. And he seemed about as appreciative, too, so I decided to sample a bit of the St. André and a très leches which, I had to admit, were stunningly good. Then Meph took his first taste of the crème caramel and it was all over.

"This is truly . . . art." He sighed. Then he signaled for the waiter and ordered two more of the crème caramel and two more glasses of ice wine to accompany it.

"Now, back to your conjecture," he said when the waiter disappeared with our order and the empty dishes that had held the desserts we had just devoured. "If some demon wanted to advance through the ranks, I normally wouldn't get involved. It's Darwinian, let them fight it out, try to destroy each other and protect themselves, and whoever wins rises by merit. But, and this is the central problem, we can't have demons in one area of the Hierarchy attacking those outside of their direct line. Destroy their competitors, that's fine. We encourage that. They can weed through the chaff and expel them and we don't have to worry about screening. But if someone from my division, say, was victimizing you, that would be intolerable. We don't permit that kind of thing. You, especially, are not pawns."

"Darwin in action," I muttered.

Meph raised an eyebrow. "They hurt us, they're eliminated. They didn't understand how to play the game, not all the subtle levels, so they're out. But they'd better be out before they hurt me or my friends, because I don't know if we could endure anything else. Sybil, you know Syb is already at the end of her rope. And Desi isn't far behind."

"Sybil has that very promising young demon to protect her," Mephistopheles observed, his voice rich with approval. "Vincent? Very talented. I'm watching him. Don't let him know. I don't want to make him nervous, thinking that he's being observed for higher things when he's only been dead for five months. We have all eternity, no use letting it go to his head."

Our second round of crème caramel and ice wine arrived and we took another short break to savor them yet again. And they were just as good the second time around as the first.

"So, is there anyone you can think of who might be in that kind of junior position and trying to rise through the ranks?" I recalled Meph to our topic from wherever out in the astral the experience of honey and tangerine had sent him.

He blinked rapidly, recovering. "There are two demons, maybe three, who come to mind," he confessed. "But I wouldn't want to accuse anyone until I had a better idea of which one it might be."

Great. But that left me and my friends sitting in a trap.

The thought must have showed on my face. "I'll be watching them very closely," Mephistopheles reassured me, and there was steel in his voice. "Trust me, if any of them even thinks of endangering you or your friends again, I will intercede before anything happens. And that I vow to the Prince of Darkness."

Which is as solemn and serious as it gets.

And then Mephistopheles picked up the check.

"Oh, no," I protested. "I asked you, I begged you for your advice. The least I can do is pay for our dinner." I was junior to him; I had asked him for a favor and he had given me his time and his thoughts generously. He had also promised to look out for us in the future, at least if the threat was coming from his department. That was far more than I could have hoped for, and he offered it all freely. By all the protocols of Hell, I had to pay for the dinner.

And the truth is, we both have enough money that it hardly matters.

"Not at all," he said gallantly, handing his American Express Black Card to the waiter. "You are Satan's Chosen and under Her protection, which means you are under my protection as well. What is valuable to our Master is mine to guard. So I am very grateful that you brought this matter to my attention, and I am glad to serve our Prince in this and in all things."

Mephistopheles has class. He's a gentleman of the old school, and I felt safer than I had in days.

Meph got both of our coats from the coat check,

helped me into mine, and escorted me to the door. "I'll help you catch a cab," he said, "and then I'll return to the office and do a little investigating on my own."

I felt so good, so safe. I leaned against him as we exited into the chill of Astor Place.

As usual, outside there was a line to get into the downstairs club. I had stood on that line enough times in the past, though usually we could get through to the bouncer and get in before most people, and I had always been glad of the privilege. Now I walked down the line with Meph holding my elbow, feeling sorry for the ordinary hip New Yorkers wanting only to spend an evening dancing in a popular club. The cream of single young New York was waiting to get in here—or at five or six other clubs in town, if they weren't taking an evening for a facial and a foot massage.

I thought briefly about hunting. It wasn't a mojo night so I wasn't required, but I was angry enough at whoever had attacked us that the thought of luring and killing some obnoxious male was appealing.

"Lily!" a familiar voice called out from the line. I had been so wrapped up in my own concerns that I hadn't even noticed people in the crowd as individuals.

And there was Nathan Coleman, decked out in his Communist overcoat and thin leather gloves rubbing his hands together to keep circulation in his fingers.

"Nathan," I said. Then I realized that Mephistopheles had me by the arm.

I wanted to melt into the pavement. Nathan looked Meph over as if he were in the Armani trunk show, trying not to let the jealousy and hurt show. "Nathan, this is my old friend Meph. Meph, Nathan Coleman. I think I've told you about Nathan. He reads Akkadian."

"Indeed, Lily has just been singing your praises," Meph said as he extended a hand.

Nathan reached over the butter-colored leather rope and shook it, his face sternly disciplined. Both of them had such class, such good manners, that my insides twisted up.

"I look forward to seeing you at the gallery opening next week," I said lamely. Only it was true, it was entirely true.

"Lily, I need to get back to the office," Meph murmured. "Shall I see you to a taxi?"

I nodded mutely. Why didn't Nathan ask me to join him? I could have gone out clubbing with him, even if I was dressed more for business than for dancing. There was nothing in the world I wanted more at that moment than for him to ask me to join him in that line. If I had a choice of immediately catching the demon who'd betrayed us and Nathan asking me to step over the rope and join the line, I would have taken Nathan's invitation in a heartbeat.

I wondered if he were meeting someone at the club. Maybe someone female and beautiful and not a demon, and that made me even more upset.

I hesitated, and I'm afraid that I wore my hope too naked on my face. Eros would kill me and she'd be right.

Nathan smiled, though not as deeply as he had on Saturday. "Yeah, see you when you get back from Aruba."

And then Meph whisked me into a taxi and I was on my way uptown—away from Nathan.

chapter
NINETEEN

"Aaaawww, baby," Sybil said, putting her arms around me.

"You are not, I repeat, *not* going to ruin our trip to Aruba because you're moaning over this guy," Eros insisted. "It's good that he saw you with someone else. They think you're more desirable if they think they have competition. Trust me, this is the best thing that could have happened."

I sat in my living room furious and upset. I was afraid I'd start to bawl like a baby, like Sybil, and I was a lot bigger and scarier than that. So I decided I wanted to smash crockery instead. Only—I really like my dishes.

Vincent had been on duty when I arrived in the cab and he saw my condition immediately. Without asking, on his own initiative, he called Sybil and told her that I needed her. She, in turn, had called Eros and Desi, but Desi had been out. Still, both Syb and Eros had rushed over to find me on the sofa contemplating mass destruction of Kate Spade dragonfly china. On the one hand, it would be a fabulous relief. On the other, I wouldn't have anything to eat off of and it would take six weeks if I ordered a replacement set yesterday.

Eros and Sybil arrived, ice cream in hand, just as I was weighing a bowl and thinking of hurling it at the door.

"Don't do that," Sybil said immediately, taking the bowl from my hand.

"Why not?" I snarled.

"Because we are going to need this to eat ice cream now," Eros said reasonably. "If you need to throw something, throw the dinner plates. They're more satisfying when they smash and you hardly use them anyway."

Having just eaten an extravagant dinner and just having my heart broken, I couldn't possibly think about food. Not even ice cream, not even Chocolate Dinosaurs.

"Eros is right, you know," Sybil said softly. "You haven't done anything wrong and there's nothing to worry about. He doesn't know what's going on with you and Meph and he'll wait for you to tell him, but he couldn't ask you to come out with him. You were with someone else and that would have been horribly rude."

"Meph could have challenged him to a duel for that," Eros observed.

"Nathan isn't a demon and humans don't fight duels anymore," I said. The image was amusing enough to make me accept a bowl of ice cream. It was Chocolate Dinosaurs, after all.

"You have been on all of one date. No matter how much you like each other, it's too early to even think of being exclusive," Sybil continued.

Eros snorted. "Lily can't be exclusive. She's a succubus."

"Not if Nathan loves me," I protested. "That's my retirement clause. If a mortal loves me and does not have sex with me for a month, and I can prove to Satan that he loves me for myself and not just for sex, then I don't have to be a succubus anymore."

"Why would you want not to be a succubus?" Eros asked, incredulous. "You get all the sex you could want and none of the complications. Every man and not a few women can't do enough for you in bed. What more could you want?"

Her complete lack of comprehension was entirely honest and heartfelt. But then, Eros was never human. And I'm not sure that Eros believes in love. She called it a pathology once and has boycotted every one of Sybil's weddings.

"I want love," I protested, standing like a politician delivering a speech. "I want this one guy to love me and want to see me without my makeup and to want to cuddle me when I've had a bad day. And to want me to make him happier on days that are hard for him. I want to be together with him and I would like to have sex with him more than once."

Eros's eyes opened wide and I knew I had her. "You see, if you only have sex with a guy once, he doesn't know how to really make you happy," I said, and I saw her nod. "Yeah, there's all the excitement of the first time, but I never get a second chance. And with some of them, well, I don't always pick the most appealing guys, you know. Mostly they're selfish in bed."

Eros nodded. "A lot of men are."

"A lot of men think that all women want to do is please them. A lot of men don't have a clue about a woman's body," I said flatly. "I've had enough of them and let me tell you, they think that you're supposed to come because they're doing their best to please themselves. Honestly."

Sybil sighed and patted my hand. "That's because you haven't had sex within a relationship. When a man cares about you, personally, then he cares more about pleasing you. That's what you've been missing."

"And now everything will be over with Nathan and I really liked him and I'll never have a chance."

"Lily, this is the best thing that could have happened for you and Nathan," Eros reiterated. "You were being too available for him. You weren't making him pursue you. You were making it too easy for him and you know it. You've heard me say it a million times." She cast a meaningful glance at Sybil. "You know that's the kiss of death. Don't call him, and I know you want to. You want to call and tell him that you were meeting with Meph on a business matter, or that Meph is your uncle or anything that you think will reassure him that you're available. Well, you're not going to call him, not tonight, not tomorrow, and then we're going to Aruba and you're going to soak up the sun and pick up pretty Dutch surfer boys and drink blue drinks. And you are going to want to call or send an e-mail to Nathan and we, as your friends, are not going to let you do it. And come your date next week he will be crazy insane for you."

"Are you sure?" I asked, weakening. I no longer wanted to hurl the china. The ice cream in my dish looked appealing. I could follow her logic. I had even said similar things when one of my friends had been in a similar situation, and I'd even seen that they were true. The advice worked.

So why couldn't I take it? Why was I dying to get on the phone or the computer? No, the phone would be better—closer and faster and more immediate.

Not that it would matter, I realized. Nathan would still be downstairs at Butter, maybe buying drinks for the blonde I'd made up.

"Now I am going to run a hot bath and set out the Black Pearl bath bomb and lots of yummy soaps and scrubs. And Syb will cut some cucumbers for your eyes, and don't you have one of those nice home facials? And you are going to take a bath and lie there with a facial and then we're going to call out for Chinese food. And then on Thursday you're going to meet us all for lunch and some shopping because we all need some beachwear and sandals because last year's are, well, last year's." Eros was ticking off all the necessary tasks on her fingers.

"And then," Eros continued, "I'll book us all for pedicures on Thursday after shopping because we can't go to Aruba with naked toenails. Because we are going to go to Paradise and lie out on the beach and have lots of sex with pretty boys who will serve us drinks and worship our bodies. And we will get golden enough to last us until summer."

Eros marched out to the bathroom to start my bath. Sybil massaged my shoulders. "I'm afraid that the three of you are going to get all the attention," she said. "Really, you know, it's always like that. You're the sex demons and I'm not. I'm not gorgeous like you three are. I always feel so outclassed. The three of you are going to have hot and cold running boys and I'm going to sit alone on my beach chair in front of my laptop and predict stock prices."

I sat upright and spun to face her. "Sybil, where do you get ideas like that? That's crazy. You're stunningly beautiful and you don't know how many guys can't take their eyes off you. You're so feminine and graceful and just . . . pretty. I don't know what you're talking about."

Sybil shook her head sadly. "I'm not, not compared to the three of you. Whenever I'm with you, I feel like I'm the official ugly one."

"You're insane," I said. I couldn't imagine where Sybil had gotten such a stupid idea in her head. She's got gloriously natural buttercup hair that waves just perfectly, the English peaches-and-cream complexion, and an hourglass figure that any lingerie model would kill for.

Sybil shook her head slowly. "I'm thinking of going to Admin and having a redo," she said softly. "Maybe get a thinner, leggier look. And slightly more interesting coloring, do you think?"

I looked at Sybil for a few minutes, just studying her. "You know, Syb, you're drop-dead gorgeous. What I do think, though, is that you've got this sweet thing in your head. You need a makeover. Your clothes aren't doing your face and body justice. I know the Jil Sander is great for Wall Street, but I think you need to just try something a little more elegant. You're a classic Princess Grace type, really. I always thought that the Laura Ashley look was to disarm your opponents, make them underestimate you so that you could spring a trap. If you don't want to look like a sweet English rose, you don't have to. But it's not you, it's just the clothes."

"Really? You're not saying that just to be nice?" Her tone was suspicious.

I shook my head, firm in my beliefs. "We're going shopping for beachwear on Thursday, right? So we'll be at Barneys anyway. Where better for you to try some outfits from some designers you don't ordinarily wear? Then you can see."

Eros announced that my bath was ready. I dropped my clothes on the bedroom floor and sank deep into the hot water. Sybil came in with the chilled cucumber slices for my eyes as Eros applied the vitamin C mask. I leaned back and let all the goodness soak in, my mind firmly fixed on Sybil.

There is nothing more fun than helping a girlfriend realize her full potential.

By the time I was bathed, masked, toes painted, and had finished my third cocktail (something Eros had made up with my selection of rum and fruit juice and liqueurs that tasted lovely and had a serious kick), I was ready to fall asleep. It wasn't until the next morning that I realized that I hadn't thought about calling Nathan at all.

We spent Thursday shopping. Fun, but exhausting. Seventeen hours from now we'd be heading to JFK, so a quiet evening and early to bed were in the stars for this gal. At least bikinis, beach cover-ups and sandals don't take long to throw into a bag. I included a nice dress too, on the theory that we were going out at night.

It was around nine in the evening, prime dinner

hour, when the intercom rang. Vincent's voice came through, clear and professional. "A Mr. Nathan Coleman is downstairs to see you," he said, with no inflection to give away his opinions. "Shall I send him up?"

"Uh, yes, sure," I said, flustered. What was I wearing? My jeans were okay, but I pulled off the ancient oversized (but oh so comfortable) *Bat Out of Hell* sweatshirt (Meatloaf really was one of ours) and threw open my drawers. No, no, and no. Clothes flew over the bed and the floor before I located my favorite forest green ribbon-knit tunic. And better bare feet than the fluffy bedroom slippers, so I left them in the middle of the pile on the floor.

Just in time, too, as I heard the bell and ran to the door. Had I washed off all my makeup already? Too late now. I hoped I didn't look too wretched.

He stood there with a boyish grin, his black hair combed back from his face and his nose red from the cold. His hands were behind his back and I smelled— something mouthwatering. "I know you're leaving early tomorrow, but I thought you might have already cleaned out the fridge and could use some dinner. You haven't eaten yet, have you?"

I shook my head, completely taken aback.

"You like Chinese?" he asked, grinning.

We're New Yorkers. Chinese is our native cuisine. Of course I like Chinese food.

He whipped the bag from behind his back. That had been what I was smelling, hot and sour soup, egg rolls, kung pao chicken and orange beef. And shrimp chow fun and white and brown rice. I invited him in and he unpacked the stack of cartons on my dining table, which was almost never used for eating and so was piled with books and papers that I had to throw on the floor.

I was really glad I hadn't smashed all my nice dishes. I brought out two of the dinner plates Eros was so ready to sacrifice along with bowls and chopsticks.

"It's so much food!" I gasped as the boxes appeared to multiply on the newly cleared surface.

"So you'll have some leftovers," he said.

"But I'm going to Aruba early tomorrow," I protested.

"Okay, I'll have leftovers," he said and smiled. I wondered if he'd planned it that way. "Good, I'm a lousy cook and I'll have something to eat for the next couple of days."

Nathan reheated the soup in the microwave and I found I was uneasy with him in my kitchen. I call myself an indifferent housekeeper, which is a nice way to say that I don't do anything and rely on my cleaning service to make sure that there isn't mold growing in my sink and that the sheets get changed. Between the service and the laundry that's picked up and delivered (and Vincent, who gives them my piles of clothes and linens when they call on their weekly rounds, accepts the pickups and hangs everything in my walk-in closet), my home has not yet been condemned by the board of health.

For the first time ever I was actually embarrassed.

I couldn't let Nathan into the bedroom.

There were many reasons I couldn't do that, but the pile of clothes and fuzzy slippers in the middle of the floor, the unmade bed and the clothes threatening to explode from the closet were certainly high on the list.

We ate our soup and eggrolls and he asked me about packing and flights and where I was staying. All the nice, normal things people talk about when you're going on a trip. Finally, after I'd had seconds of the kung po chicken, I couldn't wait any longer.

"About the other night at Butter—" I began, but Nathan shook his head and held his finger to his lips as I took a bite of orange beef.

"That isn't why I came and it doesn't matter," he continued, taking advantage of the fact I couldn't answer until I swallowed. "I came for two things. First, I wanted to see you before you went off. But I also wanted to celebrate, though it's not really a big celebration. I found my missing guy today, and I wanted to share that with someone."

I managed to get the beef down before I started to speak. "Oh, that's wonderful, Nathan. Where was he? How did you find him?"

"I found him on a ship's manifest, on a cruise to Mexico. It was just research, like I said. No one had thought of cruise ships because most of them leave from Miami and we would have thought he'd be on a passenger list from the airlines. My boss didn't think of checking for ships out of New York, but there are a number of them, and his name was on one of the lists. The funny thing, though, is that they docked this morning and he didn't get off."

"You've got the itinerary," I said needlessly. "So he jumped ship? Are you going to follow him?"

He shrugged. "That depends on what his wife wants and if she's willing to pay us to track him down. I think she's got enough information now to start procedures for desertion, and since he's left she probably can simply take control of the assets that are left. Though he did cash out a few bank accounts, so we assume that he's got a load of cash on him. And it was a significant amount, but I don't know if it's enough to pay us to go after it."

"Well, congratulations, that's fantastic!" I enthused sincerely. "Let me check and see if I have some champagne in the fridge. Though I don't think so. Will Ben and Jerry's do?"

Nathan laughed so hard he had to grab the side of the table. "Yes, Ben and Jerry's would be fine. Do you have Cherry Garcia?"

chapter
TWENTY

"And can you believe it, his favorite flavors are Phish Food and Cherry Garcia?" I was far too animated for seven in the morning at the airport. It also appeared to be Official Stupid Day at JFK as well. Check-in at American was a complete zoo, and even the first-class line snaked through the terminal. There was a backup in security and at least three people were upset about taking off their shoes and two others hadn't taken their laptops out of their carry-ons.

Airports belong to Satan. Once upon a time flying was elegant and daring and people dressed up for flights. Now all airport operations are under the aegis of Hell, under the direction of Moloch—a perfect assignment for the Prince of the Land of Tears. He was one of the Old Ones, like Meph and Beliel, but he is great with technology and new ideas. While his record with lost luggage is breathtaking and eliminating food on U.S. carriers was inspired, his greatest achievement was the hub system.

Satan had praised him and elevated him to Prince of Hell for that innovation, guaranteeing millions more stranded travelers unable to make their connecting flights. For which, naturally, the airlines don't pay and won't put them up in hotels. Sometimes passengers booked in first or business class have to accept coach to get to where they want to go. The miseries of the hub system are so great that there was even talk of making airports a Circle of Hell for the damned, which would be the first new Circle of Hell in over a hundred years.

Moloch's minions were clearly on the job that morning. There was a crowd at the gate already, and rumors of overbooking looked accurate. "Maybe they'll start asking for volunteers," someone near me said. "This always happens. I've taken so many bumps that I've gone to the Caribbean free every year since ninety-seven."

Sure enough, the flight was overbooked and they began asking for volunteers to bump at three hundred dollars. "I'll wait for six hundred, bottom," the voice said, cutting through the crying children and the irritated Long Islanders whose ideas of carry-on was about the size of a steamer trunk.

I refuse to travel steerage with no place for carry-on and only cheap alcohol available. Though it was so early that honestly, even with the actually good wine available in first class I couldn't face a drink. Well, maybe a mimosa once they served the breakfast.

We got settled and somehow our seats got changed around and I was sitting next to Desi, not Eros. I suspected that Eros had engineered this because, without adequate caffeine, she couldn't stand to hear anything about my evening before. Or maybe she didn't want to talk about the investigation.

Desi smiled brightly as if she enjoyed being up this early. Or maybe she hadn't slept last night either. "I think it's great you like the same flavors," she said.

"And it's very nice that he came over with dinner unannounced. Very romantic. Especially since you didn't have anyone else there at the time. It could have been embarrassing."

I shrugged and winced. The flight attendant looked at me carefully, concerned that I was expressing displeasure with the plane or some aspect of first-class service. I waved my hand wearily and she smiled brightly and moved on.

"Maybe, but it wasn't," I agreed. "He was so sweet. And he didn't even want to talk about seeing me and Meph."

"So you see, Eros is right," Desi said. "And you wasted all that perfectly good terror and misery and heartbreak on nothing. I'll bet that seeing you with another man inspired him to bring over the Chinese food."

"You really think he likes me?" I asked for what must have been the ten millionth time that morning.

"Yes, he likes you. He likes you very much," Desi said kindly, repeating what she'd said at least a dozen times since we'd arrived at the airport. "So did you ever find out about his missing man, and why the guy had your address?"

"Oh, he found the missing man on a cruise ship," I said. And then I hesitated, because Desi had remembered and I'd forgotten. How had Nathan gotten my address? Did Mr. Mexico really have it, or had Nathan tracked me down for some other reason?

Why would some pharmacist from Long Island have my contact info? Last night with the Chinese food and ice cream, I had only enjoyed Nathan's warmth and enthusiasm and company. I thought his presumption in just showing up with dinner was endearing and it made me feel loved.

I was startled out of my reverie when the pilot announced that we were flying over Tennessee. Then we were in Miami, incongruously hot and humid after the cold I'd left in New York that morning.

The Miami airport was worse than a zoo. I always thought that Kennedy was the worst. Miami has it beat by a mile and we had to go through security again before our flight to Aruba. Which was also overbooked and where they also had to call for volunteers. We didn't arrive on One Happy Island until well into the middle of the afternoon. Moloch must have been very proud.

But it was a gloriously sunny and perfectly warm afternoon when we finally disembarked at Queen Wilhelmina airport in Oranjestad. I was a mess. No one can stand up to two miserable airports and delays without a frayed temper and splotchy makeup.

Had Craig Branford of Huntington, Long Island, actually had my name and address? If he had, then why? If not, then what was up with Nathan? I barely took in the brilliant sunlight when we emerged toward the taxi line, and I paid little attention as the cab drove us out of town and toward the beach.

Desi's travel agent was a genius, no question. The hotel was gorgeous, with palm trees in the open atrium lobby and a pretty fountain in the center. My room was quite elegant in shades of pale blue with a Jacuzzi in the oversized bath. Huge patio doors led out to a balcony that overlooked the beach, which came right up to the hotel and stopped only for the complex set of pools, one with a swim-up bar, and a miniature golf course.

On the beach itself, lounge chairs and umbrellas were set with military precision. Two thatched structures defined the limits of the hotel's private sand, one a sit-down bar where waiters in Hawaiian shirts carried trays of colored drinks out to the lounge chairs by the ocean. The other was much smaller, with a signpost that gave times for scuba and sailing lessons. Women in starched, pale blue uniforms with aprons and frilly caps handed out freshly folded towels to hotel guests. No need to bother taking a towel from the room.

Who needs Heaven when you can go to Aruba?

My solitude was interrupted by some very uncivilized pounding on the door. "Come on, Lily, we're all ready to go to the beach."

"Go on, I'll join you in a minute," I replied, embarrassed. I hadn't even opened my suitcase.

It took no more than ten minutes to throw on the new turquoise bikini and cover-up, grab a pair of oversized sunglasses and tie the laces on my new sandals. The girls had saved me a lounge chair and it already had a towel folded precisely in the center.

"I ordered a drink for you," Eros said. "I don't even know what it is, but it's blue and has pineapple."

"Sounds great!" I enthused, just as the very cute waiter showed up with his tray and made a ceremony of serving us all.

And there, on the beach, enveloped in the warmth of the February day, I leaned back and sipped my blue and pineapple drink, and began to relax.

Burning Men do not go to Aruba. They don't believe in pleasure or fun, they believe in punishment and cold and economy. They don't drink, and even if they did they wouldn't touch girly drinks with stupid names with umbrellas in them. They believe that February in New York is an expiation of sins and they keep the thermostat at 63.

I was away from all that.

So I was quite surprised when a waiter appeared with a tray that contained a note and served it to me with as much flourish as he brought to my second drink.

All the relaxation, all the safety seemed to dissolve with that slip of paper. I picked it up and started to fume before I read it.

Which, as Desi or Sybil would have pointed out, would have been a complete waste of good anger. Because it turned out that the note was an invitation to dinner from a sister succubus.

There is one permanent succubus resident in Aruba. Her name is Margit. She'd only been here for a few years, since she'd relocated from Amsterdam where I'd met her briefly a decade or so earlier at one of the big fetish parties in her then hometown, and there had been dozens of succubi and incubi from all over the world in attendance.

It could have been a nasty competition, but Margit had turned it into something fun. "Plenty for everyone," she'd said when I'd arrived at the hotel in Amsterdam.

Then she and I and about thirty other succubi went out drinking in Amsterdam's famous Red Light district. Several of the girls almost started to bicker over who would bag the most deliveries for Satan, but Margit had squashed that kind of talk. "You are in Amsterdam," she had announced, as if there were more to the city than we understood. "And there is a fetish ball. All of us will be terribly overworked. There will be so many, many deliveries to be made. We cannot do it all. We may be Satan's best, but there are not a hundred of us and there will be three thousand attendees to the ball. So I suggest that you all remember to enjoy yourselves! Have a good time! Deliver, yes, but take some time to relax. I will take everyone shopping and we will go to the vendor fair at the ball, and tomorrow night we will have a large *rijstaffel* and you will return home well sated and with many wonderful new things in your luggage."

That weekend there had been no competition among us for souls. Margit had been right, there had been plenty of spare. Even the incubi, who usually avoid succubi like we were poison, went on Margit's tours of the old buildings and canals, and they joined us so that our group alone nearly sold out the English-language comedy supper club where she took us after most of the fetish ball guests had departed.

We'd stayed in casual e-mail contact, and she had sent me her change of information when she decided to leave cold, gray Amsterdam for Aruba. *It is still the Netherlands, after all,* she had written in her mass e-mail.

But it is warm and beautiful and I'm sure that all of you will be visiting often. So be sure to let me know when you'll be in town. I would love to see you.

I'd dutifully e-mailed her every time I'd planned to go to Aruba, but the past three times she'd been away. Where does one vacation when one lives in Paradise? Of course, Margit had to return to Europe to shop.

I didn't expect to find her in this time, either, but I'd sent her an e-mail as usual anyway. This time it turned out she was in town. She had called at the hotel and invited us to join her for dinner and then drinks on Saturday night in Oranjestad. "Because I know you'll be so tired and jet-lagged today, and you'll just need to rest in the sun and near the sea, and have a nice simple meal at your hotel. Your hotel has an excellent restaurant, so you can feel comfortable about eating there. Although it is more American and Argentine food, steaks and lobster, not Dutch food."

I laughed. That was just so Margit, really, to think that we'd be jet-lagged because when she flew it was always to Europe. In fact, we were in the same time zone as New York. That wasn't the kind of thing Margit could be expected to know. She never came to New York.

Everyone agreed that the dinner invitation sounded lovely, although Sybil showed some apprehension about Indonesian food. "It isn't very spicy, is it? I'm such a wimp, and I'd hate to seem all ungrateful."

"Nope. Lots of peanut and coconut and onions," I told her. "I don't remember any hot peppers."

Sybil sighed with relief and took another sip of her drink. "That's so lovely of her to invite us," she said.

"I'll be delighted to go. Greed demons just aren't as social as you sex demons."

A waiter appeared to gather up the empty glasses and make sure we had fresh drinks. I asked about a phone and he produced a cell phone for me on the spot. So I called the number in Margit's note, and she actually answered.

"Oh, Lily, I am so happy you and your friends are here. It will be so much fun tomorrow night to see you. And we will hunt if you like. There are two cruise ships in, and there are all those hotels. Really, can you believe that I could not get one single other succubus down here to help me? And the hunting is so easy. Do you plan to hunt tonight?"

"I don't know, Margit," I said honestly. "Really, I'm here for a rest and a vacation."

"Oh, of course," she purred. "You are certainly not to work if you are on holiday. But if you would like a little, you know, entertainment, there is a gaming room at your hotel that should be just perfect. And you don't have to go out and get tired. I'm sure the flight was miserable. Moloch is such a genius."

I assured her that the flight had been every bit as bad as she assumed, got the address of her house where we would meet on Saturday, and agreed on a time. I closed the phone, traded it to the waiter for another blue drink (my third? Or fourth?), and then I settled in to watch the sun set over the water.

I was in Paradise. All my problems could wait until tomorrow.

chapter
TWENTY-ONE

The hotel had something that pretended to be a club. Mostly it was full of overweight Americans from cold and boring places. No one from New York, but then we know what a club is supposed to be like, and that the concept has evolved since the eighties. So has the music, but you wouldn't know it in this resort.

Really, it was kind of fun.

A quick check in the full-length mirror reassured me that I looked fabulous. Which was a good thing, since my friends all looked wonderful, too. But Sybil was the real standout. Or maybe it's because we were all used to Sybil as the "nice girl" with the wholesome and sweet style. Normally Sybil wore pretty dresses with full skirts below the knee in floral patterns, or softly draped linen cut in classic lines. In the summer she wore linen ballerina flats in floral prints that matched. It was all we could do to keep her out of Talbot's, or not let her buy one more Jil Sander or April Connell outfit.

Tonight, no trace of sweet New York Sybil remained. Tonight she was in bold, primary red, in a tight skirt that barely covered (but oh so enticingly depicted) her rear end. She was all curves, dangerous and sexy, with her lips lacquered in brilliant red MAC vinyl that matched the outfit. She must have worked for the better part of an hour on her chignon, her honey-colored hair just barely tousled and messy.

"Sybil, you're going to put us out of business," Desi said admiringly. "Satan catches you looking like that, and you'll get switched over from greed to sex in a heartbeat."

Sybil smiled so sweetly that she ruined her vamp effect. "Really, you think so?" she almost squealed. "I did it right?"

"You did it more than right," I said. "I'm a little jealous, or I would be if you hadn't given me the purse."

We went to the silly so-called nightclub. The place made me think of a Long Island wedding reception without the smorgasbord. I'd been to a Long Island wedding factory affair once, only that had actually been in the eighties. This club had the same mirror ball. The music included Van Halen's "Jump" and Michael Jackson. And Bon Jovi.

I was wondering whether they were going to play the hokey-pokey and the bunny hop, and if someone's Aunt Bernice was going to get drunk and try to drag the DJ behind the potted ficus to attempt sexual assault. But what could one expect of a resort hotel, even a fancy one? Still, if the macarena came on, I was out of there. Some standards are nonnegotiable.

A little before midnight we were ready to leave. Maybe we could still go into Oranjestad, or maybe we could call it an evening. We were on vacation, and somehow a good book or a movie I'd missed at home on Pay-Per-View in the room seemed more amusing than this club. But we'd spent so much effort on looking good and I'd hate to have wasted it. Especially for Sybil. She might go back to flowered frocks forever if she didn't get ogled by someone more appealing than a fat guy with a gravy stain down the front of his polyester shirt.

Then, at ten to midnight, the wannabe lotharios (who spent their real lives working in cubicle farms, coaching Little League and mowing their lawns) disappeared and a second wave of gentlemen arrived.

Dressed in the Armani beach collection, sporting four-hundred-dollar sunglasses and carefully regulated tans, casual shoes, and carefully sculpted muscles, they screamed Eurotrash from across the room. I smiled and almost purred. Rich hunting indeed. Desi perked up, Eros looked bored. And Sybil's eyes got very big, as if she hadn't seen Euro surfer boys before.

"Do you think they're all gay?" Sybil whispered to the rest of us. "They look too good to be straight."

Eros turned her concentrated gaze to the newcomers, and there were more all the time. A few came in with women who matched, in tight Italian clothing and towering Italian heels.

"A few may be gay, or bi, but mostly they're just European," Eros pronounced. And she always knows. It's her gift, after all, to know what any human finds most erotic and to either embody that or inspire it. She doesn't care about minor questions of orientation, other than to make sure she provides the correct stimulation. And since she can entice anyone of any sex or preference, and can subtly shift into a glamour that makes her male to those who will be attracted to her as a man, she has no stake in any human having any preference. But she has a large stake in knowing what that preference is.

The four of us broke apart and each of us started to penetrate the crowd. Rich hunting here, no need to crowd or compete. I could feel the mojo shimmering on my skin, though I didn't feel any need for pheromones tonight. I could have my pick. And maybe, just maybe, I would even have a good time.

I wanted a cute one. I wanted one who wasn't drunk or stupid or mean. I wanted to pick up a guy who was actually attracted to me and made me feel nice and like I was valued and not just some random pickup.

And if the one I picked up tonight did anything for me, I decided that I would let him live. He would never know that he'd been succubus prey. I could do that. I was on vacation.

I was so caught up in my own decision that I hadn't noticed the blond hunk who'd sidled up to me at the bar. He said something that I didn't understand, and immediately caught my blank look. "Do you speak English?" he asked. His voice held only the slightest hint of an accent, the kind that made it impossible to place but impossibly sexy as well.

"Yes, thank you. I'm sorry, I do speak a few other languages, but not the one you used. Which was?"

"Dutch," he said. "You are in the Netherlands. You're American?"

"From New York," I said.

"And you speak other languages? Which languages?" he asked, and his eyes sparkled.

"French and Spanish and Italian," I said. Which was true, and Admin left more than that after my last reassignment. But he really didn't need to know that I also speak Russian, Polish, Farsi, and Arabic. Among others. I don't speak Dutch, though. Not even German. I'd never lived in the Netherlands and a language for a place I'd never lived wasn't generally worth owing Admin a favor. Though for this particular specimen I might be tempted to make an exception.

But since he was Dutch, he spoke English better than most New Yorkers.

"Three languages besides English!" he exclaimed and looked immensely pleased. "You are most unusual for an American. Is this your first time in Aruba?"

So we actually made small talk. I told him about the magazine and my friends. He told me that he was an accountant and he'd moved to Aruba two years ago because he wanted to live in Paradise. And then he smiled and asked me if I liked to dance.

We danced.

He was not at all like Nathan. His name was Marten and he was blond and tall and had clear eyes the color of the Aruba sky. His skin was light gold from the sun and he touched me gently as we danced.

"You are so very beautiful, Lily. Just like the flower of your name," he whispered into my ear between Abba songs. "How long will you stay?"

"I go back Monday morning," I said. "It's just a long weekend, and really I shouldn't have taken that much time off from work."

"No, you should take forever, the way I did. There is work here."

"I don't have useful skills," I said gently. "But we can spend some time, at least tonight."

"Tomorrow," Marten insisted. "Tomorrow night

and Sunday, promise me now. We will have a perfect island romance and you will see, you will come back to Paradise."

"I do have a dinner engagement tomorrow," I said, hoping that he wasn't so selfish that he wouldn't live until morning.

"No," he protested. "With whom? Is he your boyfriend? I will not let you go to dinner with another man."

I giggled. Really. Embarrassing, but true. I don't normally giggle, so maybe it was all the blue drinks with umbrellas. In part, it was necessary to cover up how much his proper use of the objective case made my insides feel all warm and squishy. Most native speakers of English, at least on this side of the Atlantic, had forgotten that the word whom exists, let alone use it correctly at all, let alone when drunk. "It's not with a man. It's with a woman friend who is Dutch and lives here now."

"Oh." He looked only a little mollified. "Then we will have to meet for lunch and drinks tomorrow before your dinner, so that we will have time for a proper date and conversation before meeting later in the evening. Does that suit you?"

I put my hand on his shoulder. "That suits me fine."

He got us both fresh drinks and led me over to a table as the music shifted to Europop. There is a great deal to be said for Europe and Europeans. They dress beautifully, have exquisite cuisine, elevated tastes, and comprehensive educations. They are usually far more cosmopolitan than Americans and the men are almost invariably better groomed. (Well, except for Nathan and a growing minority of New York men who have a larger range of comparison. And who don't define masculinity to mean a beer gut and a baggy tee shirt.) But Europe definitely lags when it comes to popular music. The Brits are great, Americans and Canadians rule, but I just don't get Abba. Or any of the other bands, but honestly, to me they just all sound like Abba.

We talked. We danced. He held me very close and we swayed back and forth to some indistinguishable mellow tune. I could feel the developed muscles of his arms through his silk Armani jacket. He molded me tightly against his body in the way that dancing is almost sex.

Almost, but not quite.

I wanted him. I wanted him the way I hadn't wanted anyone except Nathan for a very long time. I wanted to take him upstairs and rip off that nubby silk and see what he wore underneath. And I wanted what was under that, too.

He walked me back to my room with his arm around my waist, keeping me close. I could smell his cologne (Gaultier, expensive), subtle against his skin. We arrived at my door and I turned in his arms.

He stared down into my face as if he were memorizing my features. "I do not want to leave you," he said, brushing my curls with his left hand as his right held my waist.

Back in the real world I would have told him that I didn't want him to leave either. It was the truth. Let him think I was fast, what did that matter? This is the twenty-first century and modern women have a right to control their sexuality. If we want, and he's willing, why should we wait?

But wait I did. I muttered something about it being a long flight. I don't know what had gotten into me, but the thought of having someone who really wanted to spend time with me, who wanted to date me, not just have sex with me without preamble, was infinitely appealing. And I was drunk.

He leaned down and his lips touched mine for one innocent moment. Then the innocence dissolved and he teased at my lips with his tongue and I was open to him, drinking his desire and passion with his kiss.

"Tomorrow," I whispered into his mouth.

He came up slowly, his arms still wrapped around me. "Tomorrow. At noon. If you do not wait for me in the lobby then I will come up here and I will not let you go, Lily."

"And if you are ten minutes late I will call the hospital and I'll call hotel security because I don't think I can wait. And if you don't show up I'll have all the demons of Hell at your gate," I whispered. Not that he realized that I was uttering a literal curse, and that I had the power to do so.

By the time I staggered into my room, I was giddy with anticipation. This insanely handsome man had treated me like a lady, like someone he had to court and date, not like cheap sex. I kicked off my shoes and whirled around, laughing drunkenly, though I didn't think that alcohol had anything to do with my delight. Marten had kissed me. And, more important, he had gone no further than a kiss and wanted to see me in just a few hours.

I collapsed into bed and had delicious dreams.

* * *

"Okay, so who were you with and what have you been doing since last night?" Desi asked. We were all sitting in the living room area of her suite. Marten had left not ten minutes earlier, and we had a date for midnight at the club. The day spent with Marten had not disappointed, but I needed to check in with my friends and let them know all of my good news (and hear theirs) before we got ready for dinner with Margit.

"What about you? What have you been doing? Or whom?" I laughed as I said that.

"You wouldn't believe it, Lily," Sybil said, her eyes huge. She was still in red, in a maillot that pretended to modesty while it made the most of her assets with a matching pareu wrapped around her waist to make a long, elegant skirt. Her finger- and toenails were a matching hue, and she wore brilliant metallic red sandals with ribbon ties to her knees. She looked like a golden Greek goddess, which was pretty close to accurate, since she had been an Oracle at Delphi and had been granted her prophetic gifts by Apollo himself before she took a better offer.

Hmmm . . . Could Apollo be behind the Burning Men? He certainly had a nasty sense of humor and all the requisite pride.

I raised an eyebrow. "I can believe a lot, Sybil. Try me."

"I met two guys last night and I had a date with one today and I'm meeting the other one tonight after dinner. And they're both really cute."

"Cuter than Vincent?" Desi asked.

Sybil blushed.

"Oh, it's good for you," I said breezily with unworthy thoughts of getting my doorman back into my service.

"But there are two of them and we're leaving on Monday," she said. "What do I *do*?"

"Sybil, you have been married at least fifteen times. You ought to know what to do by now," I said, just a tiny bit exasperated.

"But I'm only going to know them for the weekend and then I'm going to go away," she wailed. "I can't sleep with them. I'll never see them again. It's not like I'm really going to date either one of them."

"What do you want to do?" Desi asked.

Sybil flapped her hands in the air, destroying all resemblance to the forties sex goddesses of the silver screen. "I don't know. I want to sleep with them. I want to date them. But I want to date Vincent. I don't know what I should do."

"You should definitely have sex with both of them," Eros said, moving directly to the point. "They're here, they're willing, and you like them. And this is Paradise, and can we have Paradise without sex?"

"But what about Vincent?" Sybil asked, utterly confused. "And if I have sex with these guys and I never see them again, does that make me a slut?"

The three of us blinked at her, confounded.

"Sybil, we're sex demons," Desi reminded her carefully. "Would you call us sluts?"

"Nnn, no," Sybil answered softly. "But two of them? In one weekend?"

"Do you think they could be bi?" Eros asked. "Then you could have a threesome. Well, you could have a threesome anyway, actually. But it's more fun if the guys are bi. It's definitely hot."

Sybil looked scandalized. "I can't think that way," she protested. "I have never had a threesome, ever, and I do not intend to start now. I just . . . can't. It's too awful. And . . . ick. It's not hot, not to me."

"Really, Eros, you're pushing it too far," I said. "Sybil gets married. She's not a sex demon."

Eros shrugged. "I take her investing advice, even if I don't understand it. She's almost always right. So I think she should listen to me in my area of expertise."

I couldn't fault Eros's logic, but Sybil still looked shell-shocked. "It's okay," I told her. "It's okay if you have sex with one of them, or both of them, or both of them together, or a third person, or no one at all. It's your vacation and we're here to have fun."

Desi came around and touched Sybil's shoulder. "Honey, if you want to have sex with them, then do it. Enjoy it. Listen to Lily, she's right, it's vacation and the guys know that. That's why they hit on us. They know we're going to disappear, that's the point. But on the upside, it will always be perfect. They will never be bad boyfriends who don't return your calls or forget your birthday. These guys won't break your heart."

Eros nodded sagely and Sybil blinked.

"Falling in love is a bitch," I said firmly, thinking more of Niccolo than Nathan, but truthfully a few little thoughts floated by.

"Falling in love is wonderful," Sybil responded, horrified.

"Falling in love means that you're probably in for a broken heart and possibly years of therapy," Eros stated flatly. "I hate the vulnerability, the judgment. All the time wondering if he feels the same way you do and if he's going to drift. He may seem wonderful right now, but what happens down the road when he decides that he's in love with someone newer and shinier and makes you miserable? What then?"

Sybil looked confused. She had married a large number of men, and claimed to have been in love with each of them. And then, being mortal, they died. And Sybil mourned and cried and carried on, and her loyalty to Satan sustained her until she fell in love again.

"Better to think about clothes than debate love," Desi said. "A good hot shower and a decent meal will solve half the problems in the world, and right now that sounds really appealing."

Desi was right. A long hot shower was a luxury. I stood under the water thinking of my afternoon date with Marten. In daylight he looked much better than he had the night before, his sandy hair precisely cut to fall into his eyes and his skin a smooth golden tan that made his eyes look just the color of the Caribbean Sea as it touched the beach. And he wore loose linen Versace pants with sandals, the perfect picture of island casual at its most elegant.

He had picked me up in a Jeep with a picnic lunch packed, and drove inland away from the beach. This was the real part of Aruba where the residents lived.

"We're going to the bat cave," he announced.

I'd been to Aruba a number of times and had never heard of a bat cave, but I let him take the lead and he drove us over rugged desert to an outcropping of rocks with several tour buses in the distance. He pulled off the road and unpacked the cooler chest that yielded bagels with sliced turkey, lettuce and tomato that had been professionally wrapped, several bottles of good Belgian beer, and a box of Dutch chocolates. Perfect!

"Since you're a New Yorker, I thought I would make you feel at home," he said as he offered me one of the bagel sandwiches. And, true to advertising, it was the real thing, crusty and chewy and dense.

"Sometimes I miss a real city," he told me as he unwrapped the chocolates. "After the first year I thought I knew just about everyone who actually lives here, and the island seems a little small. I get lonely." He sighed and shrugged.

There was little I could say to that. So I gathered up the empty wrappers and threw them into a plastic grocery bag. And then he stood up and pointed to the tour buses and said, "No more sad talk. Bats."

"Bats?" I asked.

"You aren't afraid of bats?" he asked, wary. "I was going to take you to a famous bat cave. It's a big attraction."

"Oh, no, I like bats," I assured him.

We got back into the Jeep and drove to the parking area. There were tour groups going in and out of the cave, and we tagged behind one as the guides explained how the bat population was declining and this was a problem since bats eat most of the insects that would otherwise plague us. And then they turned on bright lights and the bats woke up and flew around and I was fuming. Bats have a right to a decent day's sleep. How cruel, to wake them up every half hour so that tourists could scream while bats flew around. No wonder the bat population was declining.

I like bats even if they do belong to Upstairs. They're adorable, with their little rounded ears and their pretty soft fur. Most of them have cute faces, which I'd mostly seen up close on *Animal Planet* when I was channel surfing and feeling sorry for myself. The cute bats had cheered me up a little bit, and the knowledge that they ate tons of mosquitoes cheered me up a whole lot more. Though, actually, insects don't often bother demons. Something about ichor doesn't attract them the way human blood does. One of the minor unadvertised perks of selling one's soul to the Devil.

And then we returned to the hotel and Marten dropped me off and reminded me that he would meet me at midnight in the club.

Out of the shower. Clothes. Makeup. Hair. Do not think about Marten. Think only of the next ten minutes. Get downstairs. Get a taxi into town.

Demons are good at living in the present, keeping the mind firmly disciplined from either past or future. Or they don't make it past the second hundred years. They have breakdowns and end up in precincts of Hell in low-stress filing jobs where they don't have to cope with human mortality and their own lack of it.

The taxi driver delivered us to a discreet gate in a white stucco wall that was covered in flowering vines. Margit's garden was large and elegant. We followed a winding paved path around several large trees and by a pond where koi swam around the water lilies that scented the air.

The house itself was shrouded in vines, honeysuckle

and wisteria that appeared to bloom out of season. A maid in a peach-colored uniform ushered us inside, to where the shadow provided delicious coolness after the blazing sun. Through an archway we found Margit seated in a shaded courtyard. Inside and outside flowed together in this house. Here under the open sky there were large tree-sized ferns growing, shading the velvet upholstered sofas arranged like a living room. The effect was stunning.

Margit rose and burst into a smile. "I am so very glad to see you here, to welcome you to my island," she said as she crossed the courtyard. "Come, come in please. Rosario will bring us some drinks before we go out."

Whereupon, as if on cue, the maid in the peach uniform entered with a silver tray laden with tall thin glasses with ice and lemon floating on what appeared to be iced tea. Fortified iced tea, I discovered when I took the first sip. At least my island vacation was going to be awash in alcohol, which was perfectly suited to my mood. Curiously, there appeared to be one extra glass. Either someone else was expected or Rosario couldn't count. I rather suspected the former.

"Our reservation for dinner is in an hour, but I thought we might enjoy some quiet to catch up," Margit said after we were all served and Rosario had withdrawn. "And I have another visitor who has a message for you."

At that point a Bastform demon in a cloud-blue crochet bikini and matching blue pareu tied around her waist came in through the entrance where Rosario had retreated. She had cat's-eye glasses on a matching blue macramé cord around her neck and a remarkably self-satisfied look on her face.

Her! There was nothing, absolutely nothing, that was worth our vacation being destroyed by that librarian. No wonder we'd heard so quickly from Margit. This was not usual. And Azoked looked ridiculous in the bikini, although I'd heard that humans who didn't know about us saw her as just another human. Though short, I hoped, really short. I didn't want to contemplate how they would see her in her current getup. I surely didn't want to see her at all.

But I still had to be polite. She served Satan, same as me, and I couldn't immediately tear her to shreds for having shown up on Aruba. For all I knew, she had found the entire Brotherhood and consigned all of them to flames single-handedly and wanted only an umbrella drink and a few days on the beach as a reward.

Not likely.

She came in, took her drink from the tray that Rosario had left on the side table, and sat down on one of the deep cushioned sofas. "I am not pleased to be made a messenger, not even for Satan," she began. "I begged Her to send Vincent, who is appropriate for the task and of much lower rank. Sending a full Akashic Librarian on an errand of this nature is unprecedented and I protested most heartily. But our Master insisted, and did permit me to take a few days of personal leave time as long as I was here."

"Boondoggle," Sybil hissed under her breath. It takes a greed demon to see through the mask so easily. "Bet she begged for the job for an all-expenses-paid vacation in the islands." She raised her voice to a more conversational level and asked Azoked where she was staying, as if it were a pleasantry.

"Not on the beach," the Bastform demon replied primly, as if she were on a tight budget. "The Royal Sonesta in Oranjestad. They have several annoying macaws in the atrium who scream every time I enter. It is most disturbing."

The Royal Sonesta is not a budget hotel. In fact, it was nicer than the place we were staying, and has its own private beach with a shuttle and I think a private tiny island as well. Trust Azoked to make the most elegant hotel in Aruba sound like a dump.

"And you are here to tell us something?" Desi tried to return her to the point.

"Oh, yes, the message is that Lily's apartment has been searched by the current enemy. Vincent was off duty, so they used a glamour to get by the mortal doorman. We have no idea what they were looking for. Nothing was taken."

"Shouldn't you tell that to Lily first? Or privately?" Sybil stood up for me.

"Eros is the head of the investigation. I thought it important that you all know and that you are aware that your apartments could be searched."

"And you came all the way here to tell us that?" Eros asked. I couldn't tell whether Eros was shocked by what had happened or that Azoked had used that bit of information as a way to get down to Aruba in February, and get Satan to spring for the Royal Sonesta for the ride.

"There is one more thing," the Librarian said, looking extremely pleased with herself. "I have found the information on Craig Branford, Nathan Coleman's missing pharmacist. It appears that he has some ties to the Knight Defenders, or at least to Lewis Taggart, and might possibly be the organizer. He disappeared from his cruise in Mexico, but on Friday he showed up here in Aruba."

"Okay," I said slowly. This was interesting, and possibly important, but I didn't see why it was necessary to have the information now. He couldn't have followed us; he'd been on a cruise to Mexico and we only made these plans on Monday. We didn't even know we'd be going away, let alone where. "Is this just a coincidence?" I asked, wondering aloud. I couldn't see how it could be anything but coincidence, but it looked very odd to me.

"Now that is the odd thing about it," Azoked said, practically licking her whiskers with glee. "We, that is to say Satan and myself, think that he was probably tipped off."

"Which sounds like an inside job."

Azoked looked almost disappointed. "I have checked on who could have known, and it is a very short list indeed. Unless your e-mail or phone was compromised? How did they contact you to set up your dinner?" the Librarian asked Margit.

"I'm certain it was e-mail," Margit said.

Azoked gave both of us her professional librarian glare of disapproval. "I am not a specialist on computer security, but even children know that e-mail is not secure. And it can easily go astray and people can hack into your account."

"And cell phones aren't secure either," I agreed. "Or landline phones. And hey, if it comes down to it, people have been reading other people's mail for centuries. No, I did not want to use the magical pathways to set up a dinner among friends. Not that even the old-style MagicMirror is secure. There are plenty of magicians who can trace the etheric remains of a conversation. But I'm not going to stop talking to people.

"Besides," I added, thinking rapidly, "it might not have been me. Any one of us could have had our e-mail hacked. We all got confirmations from the travel agent. Maybe someone got into the agency records." I looked around at all of them and returned to Azoked's immobile face. "Don't pin it on me because I sent a private e-mail to an old friend asking if we could get together for dinner."

"I think we can be pretty sure it wasn't just a random human." Eros stood up for me. "Or a hacker."

"Why not?" Sybil asked. "Why couldn't it have been one of the Burning Men?"

Eros shook her head. "Maybe it could have been, but they would still have to know who we are online. They knew our addresses, about our brunch—they know too much about us. I'd bet that they didn't have to go after the information. I think they're being told."

That made sense. Only a demon privy to our plans could have given the information, and there were a finite number of them. The humans in this case were pawns; the real problem was that a demon wanted to use us for—well, certainly advancement. But precisely how?

As I contemplated the problem, I asked Margit if I could use her computer. I signed on to my e-mail just to check and clean out the spam. After a few days away it was often hard to find the actual e-mail I wanted to read among the pseudo-bank phishing, advertisements for Rolex watches and penis enlargers.

There were two e-mails from Nathan, one saying that he knew I was away and hoped that I was having a fun time, and he looked forward to seeing me when I got back. The second one was also decidedly cheerful, with a link to a notice about a very trendy book promotion at a club back in Williamsburg. Why did he keep suggesting places in Williamsburg? Still, it did look like a fun event and it was the week after next. I could certainly consider it.

Which brought me to the question of telling him about Branford. Who was here, at least for a few days. I didn't know if Nathan was still on the case, if the wife was willing to pay to actually apprehend the guy. (And do PIs do that, anyway? Didn't she just need to know where he was, or that he'd skipped the country or whatever?) Would he come down here? That would be nice. But I had a date with Marten for tomorrow evening. Would I break the date with Marten for Nathan?

And then I had to consider the ugly possibility that Nathan was the link between his missing person and my plans. Nathan knew that I was going to Aruba. He had a picture of this guy—and it was only his word that the pharmacist was actually missing. Maybe it was all a story and Nathan Coleman was really the head of the Knight Defenders and had sent Branford down here.

I was being paranoid. But with people like that hunting me, I thought it was reasonable. They'd been in my apartment. They'd been through my things. I'd have to send everything out to be cleaned. The thought of those self-righteous prigs putting their paws on my La Perlas was enough to make me explode.

They'd used a glamour to get through. Suddenly that fact became very important. Who could use a glamour? Burning Men found magic anathema. They wouldn't touch it. Suddenly my head hurt.

"Lily, are you getting anything useful?" Desi yelled in at me.

Then I saw she was in the doorway watching me. I shook my head and started to tremble. "What's the matter?" she asked as she put her arms around me and rocked gently.

I told her about my fears about Nathan and my own worries that the Burning Men might have left booby traps in the apartments. If that's who they were. I told her my fears about the glamour. But mostly I couldn't tell her that it was the feeling of being violated, knowing that strangers had been in my apartment, that it wasn't safely, entirely mine.

"Let's look at the rest of the e-mail," Desi suggested. "Let's see if there's anything from anyone else in the Hierarchy. I'm sure the Enforcers at least will go through the place before we get back. And while they're pretty stupid, I'm sure they'd manage to set off whatever trap there is. And look, here's something from Vincent."

She clicked on the doorman's e-mail, which reassured me that he had searched my apartment and Sybil's both very thoroughly and had found nothing that could hurt us.

Of course, you will need to go through and make certain that nothing was taken. The place was in perfect condition when I entered and I could find no obvious signs of intrusion, but then I don't know where and precisely how you keep everything. And I have taken the liberty of sending out all your clothes to your dry cleaners. I hope that was the appropriate action.

Satan bless Vincent! I almost wept from relief.

"I just wish it were Beliel and his boys handling things, and not those idiot Enforcers," Eros groused.

Truth is, Eros is vaguely friendly with Beliel from what I can gather, and that makes me uncomfortable. Back when the big split came between the incubi and succubi, Beliel supported the incubi and has had a good number of them in Security ever since. Not one single succubus has ever been allowed to join. Maybe Beliel has nothing to do with the anti-succubus feelings among our male counterparts, but it still makes me uneasy when she mentions him—and her friendship with him.

"There's nothing else we can do," Desi said. "So we might as well go out and enjoy our dinner with Margit and drink a lot, and you can continue to seduce that very pretty Dutch boy and I need to snag a conquest or two of my own before we go home. I don't know why that nasty Bast demon showed up here anyway. It isn't like any of this is useful to us. We can't do anything in New York now. Vincent is dealing with things there. The only thing she did was spoil our vacation, and I'm not letting her do that."

Desi had a point. There wasn't anything we could do

about the break-in back home. So what had been Azoked's purpose? Had she done it just to get the boondoggle trip? Surely she can visit where she chooses, and she must have access to enough money for a comfortable trip anywhere she chose.

On the other hand, she was enough of a priss that she probably wouldn't spend a dime herself if she thought she could get Satan to spring.

Desi was right. There was nothing I could do about New York. But I could decide to enjoy my last days on Aruba, have fun with Marten and not think about Nathan and the whole mess back home. Or I could sit around and cry and be miserable and obsess about Nathan and I still wouldn't get anything done except ruin the holiday.

I am an immortal and I've learned to live in the moment most of the time. I can concentrate on the here and now far more effectively than most mortals. Now was certainly the time to use this skill, to lose myself in what pleasures Aruba had and exist entirely within the moment. No thought of the future or past should interfere with these few days when I could rest without being pursued by Burning Men. If Marten was part of that package, so much the better.

"Indonesian food?" I asked, hoping I sounded as strong as I would like to feel.

We went out for *rijstaffel* at a pleasant restaurant just a block off the main street of Oranjestad, which made it only about two or three blocks from the Royal Sonesta. Of course, in Oranjestad nothing is more than a few blocks from the central square and the beach. And the town itself is a little too clean, a little too cheerful, a little too carefully groomed.

All the sidewalks are swept all the time and there is no trace of trash. Very Dutch, one could say, along with the brilliant orange, green, and blue decoration on the columns along the street and the crisp awnings over the shops. All I could think of was Main Street in the Magic Kingdom.

The real people, the poor people who work as maids and dishwashers in the resorts on the beach mostly live in a city at the south end of the island where tourists don't go. It's not as safe or pleasant or clean as Oranjestad, and there are only a few fancy shops to cater to the cruise passengers who spend a few hours on shore while the ships take on fresh water and produce.

We were at the restaurant in less than five minutes. An Indonesian lady in an elegant pink silk dress greeted us at the door, the walls were papered in a woven grass, our table had orchids, and the food was delicious, full of coconut milk and peanuts and subtle spices that teased but never overwhelmed the food. We ate. I ate almost too much, savoring all the nuances of a cuisine that I didn't often experience.

"And how do you find our One Happy Island?" Margit asked as we licked dessert custard off our spoons. "You are all having successful hunts, I hope."

"Oh yes," Desi assured her. "Really, if you are the only lust demon here you must be completely overwhelmed."

Margit shrugged her perfectly tanned shoulders. "I have tried many times to convince our sisters that they would find all these islands very rich indeed."

It was nice to just relax with the ladies, not to think about any of the more threatening matters. Even

Azoked behaved decently, bringing up the new Sonia Rykiel fashion book. Too soon it was time for us to head back up the beach. Margit had plans for later in the evening, and truth be told, so did we. Well, at least I knew that I did. Marten would be waiting for me at the hotel, and while I had dressed nicely for dinner I wanted time to change into something just a little more smashing for my date.

A date. A real second date with someone. He had taken me to the bat cave and had a picnic, and we had danced the night away when I arrived, and I still hadn't slept with him.

After I got dressed I met up with Desi and went downstairs. And there was Marten, looking even more elegant than he had last night, waiting near the fountain. Waiting for me.

And he looked beautiful, all Delft blue eyes and warmly golden skin and a pair of Helmut Lang trousers that clung and curved over a firmly developed rear. But he wasn't just displaying his assets to find someone for a quick fun and tumble tonight. No, he was scanning the area, eyes discarding every woman there even though some of them were breathtakingly beautiful.

He was looking for me.

chapter
TWENTY-TWO

His eyes lit up when he saw me and when he smiled I saw the deep dimple in his cheek. Oh my yes, he was lovely. And far more lovely because he was thrilled to see me.

He held out his arms and I moved into them and he hugged me warmly. "You smell as enticing as you look," he said. "Would you like a drink?"

We drank, though I was carefully moderate in my intake. I didn't want to get so drunk that I lost control and delivered him entirely by mistake when I didn't mean to.

We danced a bit, or rather swayed around to whatever the DJ was inflicting on the company. Mostly I was thinking of how firm Marten's arms were around me and how he guided me on the dance floor. How he nibbled so lightly on my ear and then whispered, asking if I would like to go someplace quieter, and led me off the floor.

I took the lead and led him to my room.

For a moment I hesitated, wondering whether I should just drag him to the bed. But he sat down on the white sofa and pulled me with him, close, almost in an embrace. He turned to me and put his arm around my shoulder. "I hope you are having a very nice time on our island," he said softly. The he leaned over and kissed my ear.

I made a deep noise in my throat, closed my eyes and leaned into his chest. His expensive cologne and scented soap did not disguise the warm masculine smell of sea and sun and sand that emanated from his sun-kissed skin. I leaned my cheek tentatively against his neck and felt the smooth, soft, freshly shaved skin.

Skin was the only soft thing about Marten. His arms tightened around me and I felt the hard muscle enfold me effortlessly. I leaned my head on his chest and found that, too was firm. I wanted to run my hands up under his shirt, to feel the interplay of flesh, the power in his shoulders against the sensitivity of his skin.

He nuzzled me gently, teasingly, breathing into my ear and flicking his tongue around the upper curves. Then he moved down, kissing my neck and stroking his fingers down the deep *V* of my halter top. His fingers barely brushed the top of my breasts, hesitant, hovering.

I was ready, but then I'm a succubus, and he was going slowly. He kissed the hollow in my throat and then, moving like honey on a hot day, slid his mouth down over my exposed décolletage. I could feel the heat of him. His muscles were tensed, powerful, but he was taking his time.

"Beautiful, so beautiful," he murmured into my flesh. "I could just look at you all night."

I smiled.

He traced the tracks of the ribbons, where the black and pink met and ran over my nipples and then the chevron pattern down to my stomach. Again, this time harder, I felt his fingers over my nipples and they stood erect. Then he smoothed his palms down over my stomach and I felt all warm and fluttery.

"Shall I?" I started to ask, but he shook his head.

"Shhh, we have plenty of time. Let me," he told me.

I leaned back and succumbed to his gentle insistence. He was still seated next to me on the sofa. Instead of working back down, he dropped his hands to my knee and massaged down my bare calf to my shiny strappy sandals.

He bent down and kissed the top of my foot, and then untied the laces around my ankle. They came away leaving marks, and after he removed my shoe he began to massage, very gently, from the bottom of my toes, relieving the discomfort that I had almost forgotten from dancing for even a short time on those high narrow heels.

His hands, his hands moving over my bare skin, were electrifying. He massaged my poor battered feet and then moved up to my calf. He explored higher, up to my knee, paying careful attention to the curves of my right leg as if there were nothing else in the world at that moment.

I sighed and sank deeper into the cushions, my head against the arm of the sofa and my leg across his lap.

He smiled, and there was a kind of innocent delight that lit him up. He stopped at my knee and reached for the other foot, and I was torn.

Oh, yes, I wanted him to massage the other foot and leg, and oh very yes, I wanted his hands on my thighs, under my skirt. I craved his more intimate touch and I quivered with desire and frustration.

Most men are done and delivered long before I felt

half the arousal Marten was inspiring. I made a little noise in the back of my throat and he froze, then looked up quizzically.

"You are happy?" he asked gently. "You are not worried that you are doing something wrong, that you have a boyfriend at home and you are having qualms of conscience? If you are worried I can stop." He said the last gently, bending down to kiss my knee.

"No, don't stop," I said. "Please, please, don't stop."

He leaned over me then and put his face close to mine. "I would not like to make you unhappy. I want to remember that Lily was only ever happy with me. That all her memories of Aruba will be pleasure in paradise and there will be no guilt or sorrow. Ever."

I reached up and pulled him against me. Feeling the length of his body along mine, I knew that he was as aroused as I was. I kissed him, deep and open and with a passion I had not kissed anyone in centuries. I explored his mouth and he replied eagerly.

When we finally broke for air I whispered to him, "I want you now, tonight, and I will only feel unhappy if you leave."

"No guilt?" he asked gently, one last time to be sure.

"No. No guilt," I assured him. "Just lust." Then, to prove it, I smiled and ran my hands down over that perfect rear, aware of the powerful muscles bunching in my grasp as he gasped.

I'm not certain quite how we got untangled, but he managed to get to his feet and picked me up and carried me into the bedroom. And, exactly as I expected, he could carry me with as little strain as if he routinely ported around a hundred-and-six-pound weight.

After lowering me to the bed, he carefully unbuttoned the twelve tiny buttons down the front of the ribbon top, and then unwrapped me as if I were the best present under the tree on Christmas morning.

Then he just leaned back and stared down at me, eating me with his eyes.

I was hot, dripping, panting, I wanted him so badly. *Don't make me wait, touch me,* I screamed in my mind. I would have said it, too, but his slow generosity had already brought me closer to the edge than any man had done in—way too long.

I thought I knew what would come next, and wiggled a bit in anticipation, but I was wrong. He didn't even attempt to remove my skirt. Instead he reached under it, bunching the fabric around my waist, and slid my panties down my thighs. He didn't remove them entirely, just took them down far enough to look at me.

And look he did. He examined me, ooohed and aaaahed as if he couldn't stare long enough. "You truly are a redhead," he breathed softly, lightly fingering my carefully trimmed pubic hair.

"Please please please," I moaned, demanding and begging together.

He chortled deep in his throat. And then he bent down and buried his tongue in my nether curls and flicked his tongue between my legs. And I was over the moon, waves of orgasm washing outward so that I felt shaken to my fingers.

He didn't stop. Instead he licked with more urgency, as if he had been dying of thirst on a desert

island and I was the oasis of his dreams. I came a second time before I could pull him up and try to get his
clothes off.

"Now, I want you inside me now," I said desperately as I struggled with buttons and zippers. When
he assisted it was easier and he was naked and he was
as beautiful and as endowed as I had imagined. And I
was hot and desperate, and even having had several
orgasms could not deter me from my need.

He efficiently slipped on a condom, which struck
me as terribly considerate since I had not asked.

And then I pulled him toward me and while he tried
to delay I could not. I wanted all of him inside me,
now. I'd been wanting him since I first saw him, and
now my need was overwhelming and insatiable. And
oh he felt so good, so hard and full, touching all the
overstimulated and needy flesh.

And he moved so slowly when I wanted him to
devour me. He moved inside me carefully, as if I were
delicate and he could harm me. And this, too, sent me
back over the edge yet again, to have what I wanted
and yet still have him holding back, holding off, and
using his body to please mine.

"I want, I want," I panted as I tried to make sense
through the overwhelming pleasure coursing through
me. "Harder, please, harder," I encouraged him.

But he stayed slow and deep until I had come a
fourth time before he began the hard thrusting that
presaged his own building orgasm and lack of control.

Yes. I wanted him wild, wanted all the hard power
in him. His excitement fueled my own, driving me
further into mindless joy.

Then, just as I was about to crest again, he pulled

out of me. With one strong arm he flipped me over onto my stomach and took me from behind. Holding with one arm like a vise around my waist, his other hand strayed between my legs and began to caress my clit while he continued to thrust into me.

Thought was gone. Only pleasure remained. My body convulsed again and again as he rode me. I was a demon from Hell in Paradise. Only one more thing I wanted, and I wanted that now more than I wanted anything, ever. I wanted his pleasure, wanted to feel him lose control and explode within me.

And so I begged for more, harder, until he couldn't resist, slamming into me with such force that had I not been immortal it might have been too much. But it was wonderful, glorious, and better still when he shuddered and rammed me hard and cried out hoarsely behind me.

Yes. Oh yes.

If my prey can make me come before he does, then I have the option to let him live. Marten had made me come more times before he did in one night than all my partners in the past decade had.

We lay panting in the bed. His arms were still around me and I enjoyed the nestled postcoital comfort that I had rarely experienced. I wanted him to touch me, to continue touching me although I had used all my passion, at least for the moment.

I turned in his arms and he gathered me close and kissed me. And then he got up as if he were going to leave.

"No, stay," I told him, but he pulled on his pants and buttoned up his shirt.

"I must work tomorrow," he said. "But I will see

you tomorrow evening, yes? We will meet again near the fountain?"

"Okay. What time?" I was disappointed and let it seep into my voice.

"Oh, my lovely Lily, do not sound so sad. I would stay if I could, but I must be at the office at seven in the morning, and I cannot arrive there in these clothes and with the delicious smell of you on my skin. I must go home and wash and put on working clothes and be able to take care of clients. You would not wish me to do less."

I conceded as much, though grudgingly.

"It is the price of living in Paradise," he told me, although he seemed a bit wistful. "But we will meet tomorrow evening, let us say seven? And we shall have dinner together and then spend a proper amount of time on our pleasures. But for now I must go."

And he leaned over and kissed me good-bye before he left into the night.

As I lay alone, reflecting on the pleasures I'd enjoyed and hoped to enjoy again, I found myself thinking of Nathan. What did Nathan look like without his layers of jacket and heavy shirts? Were his lips as soft and firm as Marten's? Were his arms as strong? Was he, hmmm, as well endowed?

And was he as skilled? Did he know a woman's body in the same way? Would he pass the succubus test?

I found myself wanting to know—and I was afraid. I wanted him so badly and I wanted him to be the kind of lover I didn't want to deliver. Who was generous and wanted to satisfy me for his own pleasure. There are so very few men in the world like that that our succubus leniency is almost never possible. Maybe a few dozen in all my demon life had qualified, and I had let every one of them live.

To my knowledge, all of my sisters did the same.

If only they knew, I thought. If only they knew it was so easy, if only they bothered.

They don't bother, and that is why we can so easily hunt them into Hell.

But Nathan was different. I hadn't even really touched him, but I wanted, so very much wanted, to know that he would survive. Even if he was like most men I wanted his company; I wanted to translate more Akkadian with him and listen to his funny accent.

I rolled over and drifted into dreamland, replete with Marten's lovemaking but dreaming of Nathan Rhys Coleman.

"You let him live," Desi said, and sighed.

"I most certainly did," I agreed. "How would I have a date tonight if I hadn't?"

All four of us were lying out in lounge chairs on the beach. We each had an iced-tea glass full of something blue and alcoholic with an umbrella in it. The cute waiter had joked with all of us as he brought the drinks and made sure we had fresh towels.

"What about your evenings?" I asked politely. Given the satisfied expressions around me, I wasn't the only one who had had a great night.

"Oh, it's mostly Sybil," Eros said. "Desi and I both found attractive men, enjoyed them. This was a very good idea, actually. Aruba, I mean. Lots of good-looking prey. But Sybil tried something new last night."

I turned politely to Sybil and lowered my sunglasses. "Something new? Oh, do tell."

Sybil blushed. "I can't. Just—it was really good. Really, really good. Fun. I didn't think it would be that much fun."

"She had sex with both of them," Eros said. "At the same time, two very pretty naked boys in the bed. One dark, one fair, excellent balance. I would have loved to have watched."

"Oh," I said. "Do tell. Did they both go down on you? Did they do each other? That sounds so hot."

Sybil shook her head. "I can't," she stammered. "I can't tell you that."

"Why not?" Eros asked. "We all talk about it all the time. I don't see why you should be so shy, it's not like you've never had sex before or have never heard us talking about sex. You heard all about Lily's night, and she didn't exactly edit."

"I can't," Sybil replied. "I just . . . can't. I'm not a sex demon like you. You don't talk about your bank accounts in public!"

"Well, if Sybil isn't going to tell us all about her adventure, I vote that we walk down the beach and get *tostis*," Desi suggested.

I did have to agree. No *tostis* in New York. Well, really they were just Dutch grilled-cheese sandwiches, only sealed at the edges and often with ham in with the cheese. And, like all truly Dutch things, they were cute and small. (Except Marten, who was cute and hunky.)

"Thinking about your hot date tonight?" Eros asked me.

I shook my head. "No. Not even a little bit. Thinking about home."

I wondered if it was just anticipation that fueled the images of Nathan.

Maybe. Maybe really all my interest was focused on Nathan because we'd spent a lot of time together, at least a lot by my standards, and we still hadn't gotten into bed. That was kind of hot, really, and new for me.

Anticipation. Not Nathan Coleman. Not anything special at all, except that I'd seen him three times and he hadn't even unbuttoned his shirt.

chapter
TWENTY-THREE

By the time the sun had started to turn the ocean bright red and gold I was thoroughly bored. The sun had warmed me to the bone in a way the New York winter, full of slush and chill, had made me forget. I had despaired of warmth and here I was, lying out in February in a bikini and feeling, finally, relaxed. Truly relaxed.

I had dressed for dinner and arrived in the lobby at the agreed-upon hour. There was Marten, waiting. I was surprised (and tickled) to see that he was reading the European edition of *Trend,* and made my way over. He seemed engrossed in his article and didn't look up until I stood over him for perhaps five minutes. Honestly, I didn't know whether to be insulted or be pleased that he was clearly engaged. Either way, I had his attention.

He looked up and smiled just as brilliantly as he had every other time I'd seen him, but there was something just a little less enthusiastic about his greeting. The anticipation was gone for both of us. Now there was only the assurance that we would go to bed and it would be a lot of fun, and he would leave and I would get on an airplane in the morning and we would never see each other again or send e-mails. Ever.

Still, he was an excellent host and we went to the casino after dinner. A little gambling, we agreed, would be just the thing.

I spotted him when Marten was placing a bet on the roulette wheel. There, well across the room, was Craig Branford. I recognized him from Nathan's pictures. I'd looked at that face so many times I couldn't be mistaken. And Azoked had warned us he was here—hunting us.

I am the hunter. I dislike being prey.

He looked exactly like some tourist from Great Neck in his Hawaiian shirt, baggy shorts and white sneakers. Hadn't anyone told him that white sneakers told the whole world that you were an American tourist? His hair was thinning and he'd done the classic comb-over. I wanted to deliver him for that alone.

I murmured to Marten that I was going to the ladies' room, but I kept to the wall where the slot machines were and watched. And, exactly as I had anticipated, he made his way over to my date.

Just the way Desi had described her experience in the Brooklyn Museum, Branford approached Marten and drew him aside. I watched them talk, Branford's intent expression, and Marten's slightly shaking back. I watched for minutes, until Marten finally turned around and went back to the roulette wheel.

I could not figure out Craig Branford. He didn't look at all satisfied or pleased. In fact, he appeared furious and maybe confused. In any case, Marten was precisely where I had left him. I thought that the time was right to return and see what happened. Certainly, unlike Desi's date, Marten hadn't disappeared—in fact, he had made certain that I could find him.

I touched his shoulder and he smiled at me and held up a finger.

He said nothing about the encounter until we got upstairs. And then, only after we were settled on the sofa with white wine from the minibar, like some old married couple.

"You will not believe the crazy thing that happened when you were in the ladies' room," he started. I raised my eyebrows to show interest without undue concern.

"This man, this very badly dressed American, came over to me. And he told me this story, that you were not a human woman but some demon from Hell, and he warned me that if I slept with you I would be killed."

"Oh?" I tried to keep my tone casual.

"And then I told him that I had already slept with you and that I was very much alive, so he was obviously quite wrong. And possibly insane, and should definitely keep his opinions to himself."

"I would say so," I agreed emphatically.

"But that is not even the strangest part of it," Marten continued. "The very strangest part is that when I told him that I had already had sex with you, that I was dating you in fact, he was so confused. 'But I know she has to be one of them, I had it on good authority,' he told me. He was so very clearly unable to process the information—he even asked if I was certain that I had actually had sex with you. Whereupon I told him that was a crude thing to say to a stranger about a lady whom he had never met and he was left entirely speechless. It was very odd, but amusing. I do wish the casino would be more selective about their clientele. At least institute a dress code. But they will not because really, they want anyone with the money to gamble. It lowers the tone of the place, I think. And then it lets in crazy people like that man, who should have been on the streets with his little religious tracts."

"I thought that religious crazies were our specialty in the States. I didn't think you had them here in Paradise," I said lightly.

He shrugged. "I thought that as well. Well, he was an American on holiday, but clearly just crazy. I only told you because I thought it was funny."

I agreed and then he put his hand on my waist and dropped it around to trace my rear. No slow seduction tonight, no delicious ambiguity, no fear that maybe it wouldn't happen or that one of us was going to be disappointed or disappointing. No, we'd gotten that out of the way.

Tonight was just sex. And it was good sex and he showed as much skill (if not quite the level of enthusiasm) as the night before. And he did make sure that I was well satisfied before he entered me, and so ensured his continued survival.

And yes, I enjoyed it. A lot. But I was also thinking about Branford and the Knight Defenders and wondering what he thought now about me being a succubus since he'd just gotten information to the contrary.

But most of all I was wondering who had told Branford who we were and that we were in Aruba this weekend. At this resort in particular. There were so very few who knew that—my friends and Meph and Martha . . . and Nathan.

So my attention was not entirely on the delicious sensations that Marten was eliciting with his fingers and his tongue. And I vaguely thought to wonder if I should deliver Marten tonight if he didn't satisfy me completely again, and then decided that wasn't fair.

Or rather, his tongue became rather more insistent between my legs and suddenly I was overwhelmed by the first wave of orgasm. I was so hot I broke a sweat and writhed under him, but he didn't let up, just took over with his hand. And oh, he was good. He knew what to do, did Marten. He was not so gentle now that I had already crested once, and I could barely speak, let alone gasp out demands that were probably incomprehensible.

I bent down, so much as I could manage, grabbed his shoulder and tugged. "Want," I managed to say between hisses and screams. But when he started to enter me too slowly, I gyrated and yelled and he got the message and gave me the hard, fast, unrelenting sex that I wanted. Oh yes, I wanted that. It had been so long—well, only last night, but it felt like so long since I'd had a man who was any good. Who could get me hot and get me off and last long enough for—

I screamed and arched against him. Couldn't keep count of how many times I'd come, or maybe it was only one long orgasm that went on and on and didn't end. I didn't know. I couldn't think anymore.

Finally I was so far over the top that I couldn't stand the intensity and the pleasure any longer. I couldn't stand knowing that he was holding back, that he was still in control when I was so clearly out of it. And I wanted him harder, wanted that moment of overwhelming release that happens only when a man completely lets go.

"I want you to come," I told him, and really I did. That happened so rarely; usually I only wanted them to come so that it would be over and I could deliver them. With Marten it was different. I wanted his pleasure and his lack of control.

His face changed as he stopped holding back. His body, already hard and pummeling mine with most delicious demands nearly convulsed with his own need and desire. I had driven him senseless. I could take now, deliver him, and he would agree to anything just for the release.

Instead I welcomed his demands and made more of my own, and let the desire and pleasure of both of us wash through me. And just as he yelled out at his own climax I peaked yet again, and tightened my legs around his waist and brought him even more deeply into me.

I did not deliver him.

He held me for a few minutes before he got up and started to dress.

"It has been lovely to know you, Lily," he said softly, taking my hand as I lay in the bed he had just abandoned. "I am sorry you will be leaving."

"No," I said. "You're not sorry. You like picking up tourists and having short little vacation affairs. No commitment, no strings, just a little holiday fling."

He looked horrified and abashed.

"Don't worry," I told him. "I knew what you were about. Did you have a good time?"

"I had better than a very good time, Lily. If you were to stay longer I would see you again. But I will always remember our days together." Then he bent down and kissed me and left.

I sighed. The little speech was canned and he probably made it twice a week. And he had no idea, none at all, that he could have been nothing more than a little pile of ash in the sheets had he been less a lay.

Well, I had a plane to catch in the morning.

I thought about calling Nathan as soon as I got into a cab at JFK. Only then Sybil would hear me and I'd never hear the end of it. I knew what she'd say, don't call, send an e-mail. I'd accused Sybil of getting into the cab with me because she wanted to come back by my building and see Vincent.

"Weren't your Aruba boys fun?" I asked, teasing. She blushed. "They were fun," she admitted. "But honestly, really, Lily. You know me. I didn't, you know, have sex with both of them. At the same time, I mean."

I grinned as we hit the bridge into Manhattan. Another gray February day enveloped the city, slush piling in the streets and New Yorkers bundled up in heavy coats. "Then you mean you did have sex with both of them," I chortled. "Just one at a time."

Sybil said nothing but her cheeks became even more scarlet and it wasn't the cold. The cabbie must have hailed from a warm clime because he had the heat jacked up high.

And, exactly as expected, we did get to my building first. And Vincent came out to open the cab door, something he does not do for every resident, I'm certain. But since I'm the reason he is placed at the building, I enjoy all the little extras.

Only this time it looked like he might have gotten

the cab door so that he could talk to Sybil. "Did you have a good time?" he asked.

I couldn't hear her reply but I was sure it didn't include the two men she'd met in Aruba. And I had to cough to get him to get my bag and wrestle it up the two steps and through the door.

As the cab pulled away, Vincent actually made an attempt to do his job. Or almost. When he finally turned his attention to me, he asked about how Sybil had enjoyed our little jaunt. "Do you think she relaxed?" he asked anxiously. "She said she wasn't taking the laptop or the BlackBerry, but she can get so wrapped up in work. She did sit out on the beach and drink funny drinks and did beach-with-the-girlfriends things, right?"

"I didn't see her with the laptop or the BlackBerry once," I assured him, smiling. "She drank and lay out in the sun and shopped and went to the casino. I think Sybil managed to forget about work."

"I'm so glad to hear that. Thank you for taking care of her, Lily. I really appreciate it." By the time we'd finished the conversation he had gotten both of us into the elevator and out on my floor, and dragged my luggage to my door.

"Do you need me to bring this inside?" he asked gallantly, the Vincent I had once known.

"No, I can manage," I told him. "It has wheels."

I smiled at Vincent and fumbled with the key, but he didn't leave until I closed the door and bolted it behind me.

Then I left the bag in front of the coat closet and ran for the phone, which had just started to ring.

It was Nathan.

"Lily, I'm so glad you're home," he started. "I tried half an hour ago, but I thought that you might have had trouble finding a cab or that the rush-hour traffic over the bridge was rotten."

"All of the above, and it took forever for them to get our bags on the belt," I told him, and tried very hard not to laugh with delight. "You have to add in baggage time."

He laughed. "I wasn't thinking. I don't usually bother with checked luggage for a short trip. I mean, you could fit a couple of bikinis in your purse. What else do you need in Aruba?"

"Even in Aruba you need to dress decently for dinner at a restaurant," I reminded him. The conversation was entirely inane, but it was easy and felt good.

"So I'll bet you haven't got any food at your place and you'll be starving in about two hours. What would you say to pizza?"

This time I did giggle. "With mushrooms and pepperoni?" I asked.

"Ahhh, you like mushrooms and pepperoni. Then that is what it shall have," he said.

"What do you like?"

"Clearly, you have never been to the secret center of pizza in the U.S. I, however, have lived there. And someday I shall capture you and drag you on a trek to deepest, darkest Connecticut and introduce you to the garlic sausage pizza at Sally's and you will never find pizza the same. Ever."

"You're on," I told him.

After I'd showered and put on a warm winter sweater, I booted up my computer and checked my e-mail. And there, about halfway through the spam, I saw something from Azoked. Much as I didn't want to deal with whatever she had to say, I knew I would feel better if I'd seen it already than if I tried to spend time with Nathan and worried about it.

So, feeling resigned and knowing that my reward was coming in the form of a black-haired, blue-eyed Akkadian scholar with pizza, I opened the message and read it through.

There are a number of strange rumors and inquiries among these Knight Defenders Burning Men, also echoed through the Information Technologies of the Hierarchy. This group is currently in a state of confusion and disorganization. They were shocked to discover that all four of you survived the holy water attacks with no apparent consequences. Further, the report that you had had sex, probably twice, with a certain gentleman on Aruba and he is obviously alive and healthy has confounded your enemies.

We had detected confusion and chaos among the brethren in the newest strands of the Akashic records. Clearly your presence, and more specifically, the presence of a living survivor, has created a situation among the ranks, and the followers are beginning to question their leaders and their leaders' sources of information. In return, those leaders, one of whom you encountered in Aruba, are questioning their sources as well.

Further, the fact that not only your "fling" survived, but all those assigned to seduce your full cohort survived, made the Knight Defenders review their strategy. And as you all emerged unscathed from the holy water attack, there are new questions about the quality of information.

We in the Akashic Division are monitoring the situation carefully, as the current situation appears unstable. Unfortunately, there is too little data at present for us to predict what might occur. Therefore we still advise extreme caution when dealing with this particular branch of the brethren.

There is one more issue that may be of some interest. Marten Loowens is a ceremonial magician who is aware of your position in the Hierarchy, and had obtained this knowledge before you arrived on Aruba. As his knowledge is more sophisticated than that of the Knight Defenders, it is possible that he targeted you in particular. I do not know if you have prior experience with ceremonial magicians, but they tend to work on a quid pro quo basis, so he may believe that you owe him a favor and he may have the magical means to compel you. I cannot firmly establish his particular skills and abilities, nor can I speculate on his motives or possible actions. But these possibilities exist and you should be aware that such situations are not unknown to us in the Library.

As Satan has asked me to support your investigation and assist you in any way appropriate for a Librarian of my abilities, I shall attempt to keep you informed.

Sincerely,
Azoked

I was so shocked that I couldn't think. Marten's a magician? Then he'd known all along! Or did he? And what did he want? Magicians try to command demons, to get things from us, but Marten hadn't tried to get anything from me. Yet.

Yet. No doubt he would.

I wanted to throw a glass at the screen. Marten. I had such nice memories of Marten, had enjoyed my fantasies of finding him again. And now I felt betrayed. And angry. And curious as to what he wanted from me.

I was still staring at the screen, trying to puzzle out what this all meant, when Vincent buzzed to announce a pizza delivery at the door. At first I was confused; I wasn't expecting a delivery. Only then did Vincent admit that it was Nathan, and sent him up.

I shut down the computer but couldn't close down my mind. I wanted to be fun and bubbly and sunny for Nathan, and tell him that I'd seen his mark, but I couldn't quite get Azoked's e-mail off my mind.

The Akashic couldn't predict? I thought they had the full *Book of Livingness* which was unbounded by time. They had access to the past and the future equally and could tell what was to be, or so I had always thought.

I wanted to talk to Sybil, no matter that I'd left her in the cab only a few hours ago. For one, I wanted to consult her in her oracular role. Not so much to get a prediction, but to understand how it worked. How could she see the future while it wasn't written yet in the Akashic record? I wanted her to explain how she understood that.

And there was something else, too, bothering me around the edges. Marten had known what I was? All of our boy toys on Aruba had not been honestly flirting with us, but were really planted by this Brotherhood?

That made no sense. Did Marten think that he was going to die? He didn't strike me as the self-sacrificing type.

Azoked said he was a ceremonial magician, but that really didn't scan. He was hot, young, good in bed. What I knew about ceremonial magicians is that they do long elaborate rituals that take years of preparation and include the most unlikely requirements. Often they are celibate. Some of their rituals are effective, and some can even compel a demon in the Hierarchy to manifest and perform favors.

But then, why was he known to Craig Branford? Religious fanatics and ceremonial magicians usually at best have no use for each other. More often they detest each other and consider themselves enemies. Burning Men generally think that anyone who practices any form of magic belongs to Hell—and often to some extent they are right. A fair number of the ceremonialists are perfectly willing to barter their souls for things they want. Though usually it doesn't come to that, and a good number are religious to some extent, just not in any way a burning fanatic could understand.

So when Marten courted me, he'd only been trying to discover whether I was a demon?

Then he didn't know a whole lot about demons, that was for sure.

For having just returned from a lovely vacation, I was in a rotten mood.

"You do not look like someone who just had a great time in Aruba," Nathan announced when I opened the door. I hadn't realized that it showed that badly.

"I made a mistake and checked my e-mail," I said.

He shook his head. "Always a bad move," he agreed, and opened the pizza box on the coffee table even though I have a perfectly good dining table only a few feet away. "Now come here and eat some of Ray's mushroom pepperoni and tell me all about Aruba. You sat on the beach. You drank girly cocktails."

"Brought by cute waiters right to the lounge chair. I never lifted a finger," I admitted. "But there's something else I need to tell you, Nathan. Something important."

He put down the slice of pizza he'd been annihilating and looked at me with an expression that was somewhere between hopeful and afraid.

"I saw Craig Branford in Aruba," I told him. "He was in the casino of my hotel."

"And you didn't call me right away?" he demanded.

"It was very late last night, and I knew I'd be home today to tell you. I was going to call you as soon as I got in, but you called first," I protested.

"Just last night, then?" he asked briskly.

I nodded, feeling as if I'd betrayed him. Eros was wrong. I should have called him immediately.

"You're sure?" he asked again. "You're certain it wasn't someone who might just have a passing resemblance?"

"I'm pretty sure," I said, thinking more carefully about what I'd seen. Maybe since Azoked had come to warn us I'd been seeing what I'd expected to see. "It's been a while since I've seen the picture, and of course he was wearing all different clothes, and was tanner."

Nathan nodded and then excused himself to the bathroom. I could hear him on his cell phone and figured he was talking to his boss. I wondered if they'd gotten more money from the wife, or if it were someone else who wanted this guy tracked down.

I thought it would be useful for him to know about the Knight Defenders in Brooklyn and why Branford had had my contact info in the first place. Because maybe with the right information Nathan could break this group apart and negate the threat to me.

My hero.

He would never believe me about the whole demon thing. They never do.

He would just figure that I was nuts and he'd dump me.

Suddenly I realized that I cared more for Nathan Coleman's good opinion of me than I cared about my income-producing properties in Paris and Tokyo. I even cared more for what he thought than about getting the Christian Louboutin spring line.

Only one being in the world mattered more to me, and that was Satan.

And that was something I could never tell Nathan.

Misery and confusion must have shown on my face when he exited the bathroom, slipping his cell phone into his pocket.

"Oh, Lily, I'm sorry," he said suddenly, and then swept me up in a long embrace. "I didn't know you'd be upset. I'm not angry with you, really truly I'm not. I was just—we've got a commission on finding this guy and if I can do it then I've got a nice bonus and probably I'll get to keep my job."

I didn't know that he might not keep his job. I didn't know that he needed a bonus. He wore Armani and Hugo Boss and Brioni. Surely he couldn't be entirely dependent on his salary as a private investigator. I'd read enough mysteries to know that they're usually not all that well paid.

And because I was feeling so open and vulnerable and confused, the words came out without my willing it. "I don't know, I don't know anything about you. You went to Yale, you're a PI, you wear expensive clothing. You talk about paying bills but—I don't understand, Nathan. I'm all confused."

He took my hand and led me to my sofa and sat both of us down. The pizza was still on the coffee table. I could smell it and somewhere I knew I was hungry, but that just didn't matter so much at the moment.

"I guess there are some things I should tell you, Lily. If we're going to see each other. And I want to. I want to spend a lot more time with you and I want to get to know you and everything about you."

He sighed deeply and took my hand. "I, ummm, my parents live fairly close by here. I grew up in this neighborhood. My mother organizes charity balls. My father, well, my father owns banks. I guess that's the best way to put it. I hated the bank. I didn't want to go into the business, so I went to grad school and studied something I loved and I try to forget the family and all that."

"Wait a minute," I said, wanting to slow down, wanting to make sure I understood. "You're telling me that you're basically independently wealthy. And you live with your parents? What are you doing playing PI?"

He shook his head. "It's not like that. I do not live with my parents. I have a nice place of my own in

Brooklyn, and I wanted to live in an area with artists and creative people and away from my mother's friends. I was bored to death trying to be the proper banker's son. I hated dating socialites. And I wanted the PI gig and I actually care about doing a good job. I'm good at research. But I had to take a year off writing my dissertation because it all seemed so pointless. No one cared about the ancient world anymore, only a very few people had any idea of what I was doing and, I don't know, I wanted to participate in the world. In life. I needed to find a place where I belong."

"And did you find it?" I asked softly.

He shook his head. "I'm trying. And my mother is trying for both of us." He laughed harshly at that. "But in spite of her directions, all I think about is how I need to get back to school and finish the dissertation because that's the only thing I've ever done that engaged me enough. That was interesting all the time and that was even sometimes hard. I liked that, liked the fact that I could do this and that it wouldn't happen by paying someone or using family connections or anything. That I could be effective in the world, and more than that, that I'm good at this. I'm really really good.

"And the worst of it is, no one cares. Well, except my adviser. But my family all think that intellectual investigation, especially of a culture that's been gone for thousands of years, is an idiotic waste of time. That everything I've ever done or wanted to do was stupid because it wasn't about making money or extending the family's influence.

"We have plenty of money. We have plenty of influence. I don't know if I can make you understand why it's so important to me, to be someone myself and not just my parents' son."

I sat quietly for a moment, absorbing not only his words but also the sense behind them. "I think I do," I said. "My father was wealthy and important, and I wanted to be my own person, too. I knew I had a lot of advantages, and I knew I pushed to see if I could make a mark entirely on my own, with my own talents and abilities and not because someone was just giving me something because of him."

Nathan nodded vigorously. "That's exactly it. I knew you would understand. I expect that you're an editor for the same reason I'm a PI."

But here I shook my head. "I'm an editor the way you're a graduate student," I corrected him softly. "You might have gotten your Ivy education as a legacy, but you didn't get into grad school on your parents' shoulders. You had to have the skills yourself or they wouldn't have taken you. And I've seen you translate Akkadian. You yourself told me that there are maybe only thirty people in the world who can read that language today. And you're one of them, and that was entirely by your own efforts."

"Lily," he murmured quietly. "Lily, Lily, Lily. You are the most amazing woman." He practically crooned to me, and gathered me against his chest and oh, it felt good to be in his arms.

And it felt terrible, too, because I wanted to tell him and I knew I couldn't. And I felt entirely dishonest, with him and myself.

I had a chance here, a chance with Nathan.

I knew what my friends would say. *Shut up, Lily.*

Don't tell him. He probably doesn't believe in demons anyway. He doesn't need to know.

Prudence won, but I wanted to indulge in the revelation as well. I wanted Nathan to know what I was and I wanted him to love and accept me all the same.

"Then why do you care so much about finding this guy?" I asked, honestly a little confused. I understood wanting to do well, but I thought that he was staking just a little too much on this one thing. "You just told your boss where he was less than twenty-four hours ago, and they should be thrilled with you. You've done more than your job, so why are you acting as if you have to go down there yourself and bring him back in irons? Isn't that a little old-fashioned? Why does anyone want him anyway, and what are they paying?"

He looked at me for a long moment. "That's the question, isn't it?" he asked and studied my face. "I don't really know. My boss seems stuck on it so I could only figure that the wife was paying. Most of the work is tracking down missing spouses for child support or to file divorce papers or something. The more exciting jobs, it looks like, are finding grounds for adultery. But this, somehow it just feels different. It shouldn't have been any big deal. I should have found him sooner. He shouldn't have jumped off the cruise ship in Mexico and he shouldn't have shown up in Aruba."

I laughed. "You should go back to grad school. You're wasted on this stupid job."

And he laughed and I laughed and the moment of vulnerability and revelations was gone.

And it was good and comfortable and safe between us, at least so long as I kept my big mouth shut.

chapter
TWENTY-FOUR

Desi met me in the bar at Public on very short notice. I called her when I got in to work on Tuesday and then I remembered I had a date with Nathan on Wednesday and I almost started to gibber senselessly on the phone.

We sat at one of the tables under the glass oil lamps that lined the wall. I sipped my drink, nothing frilly and no paper umbrellas here, but a good respectable glass of port.

"It's all a mess," I muttered as Desi tasted her Chardonnay. "There's Nathan and what do I tell him and why is he even bothering, and then there's the thing with Marten and I don't know if Azoked is just doing her job or using her job as a smokescreen for being a bitch."

"One at a time," she said. "First, we all know that Azoked is a bitch. She might be doing her job, but she enjoys making us miserable and we know that. The trick is going to be to use her information and not let her sadism affect us. And that's particularly hard because she's good at it, and for you because you're the one who has to deal with her. And she has it in for you because she doesn't want this job."

"It got her a weekend at the Royal Sonesta in

Oranjestad," I groused. "She should at least be grateful for that."

"Yes, she should," Desi agreed. "But she's a bitch, and you heard her make it sound as if she were doing us a favor by showing up. Anyway, we don't have to think about Azoked. She's useful. Not that we couldn't find the information ourselves, but it's easier for us to have her do the legwork. Besides which, a librarian in the Akashic can do a lot more a lot faster than we can, and it's her job. You don't have time, you've got a magazine to put together. So let's not think about her because we all know she's a raging bitch. Case closed. So what's this about Marten and Nathan?" She leaned forward, perfectly lacquered lips pursed, ready to listen.

I finished my second port and she signaled the barman for my third. At this rate of consumption, since I had been planning to drown my sorrows buying shoes at Hollywould after I finished all my alcohol, Holly would be very happy indeed.

"Nathan called as soon as I got in last night. He came over with a pizza. We talked, that's all. We have a date tomorrow night." I thought it best to get all the facts in order before starting the speculation. "He was very sweet. He told me a little about himself, you know, the getting-to-know-you kind of stuff. And then I had to tell him about seeing Branford, that pharmacist he's been looking for in Aruba and he was all stressed out but also excited. And he was unhappy with me because I didn't call him immediately when I spotted the guy. But I was with Marten at the time and I wasn't going to tell Nathan that, and I didn't think that he was really on the case anymore. I mean, he had tracked the guy out of the country and last I heard that was good enough. He didn't even know if he'd get paid to look anymore, so I didn't have any idea it was urgent or anything."

"Did you tell him that?" Desi asked.

Desi is so sensible sometimes. I didn't know if I'd told Nathan, but I'd thought it was obvious. "I don't remember. I know I asked why it mattered so much. And then he went into the bathroom to call his boss. But then we talked about it and he wasn't so upset anymore so I guess it was okay. It just seemed too weird to me and Eros would have told me not to call him from Aruba and I don't really know what to do."

"What do you want to do?" Desi asked.

I blinked. Want? What did my wanting have to do with anything? What did he want? What was going to happen? Would he satisfy me well enough that I would be allowed to let him live? And did I want to find out?

"I'm scared," I told her. "If he doesn't satisfy me first when we finally do get to bed, then he's toast. There's nothing I can do about it. And I don't want to kill him. Even if he's not a great lover I want him alive," I admitted.

"That's a problem," Desi agreed. "At some point, you either have to find out or leave. Those are your options. You can't tell him?"

I shook my head. The barman arrived with my third glass of port and as I sipped it I started to relax, just a little.

"So that's one problem with Nathan. Are there any others?"

I thought for a few minutes. "I don't know about

relationships. And I feel like I'm lying to him all the time. I mean, I can't very well tell him I'm a succubus, can I? He won't believe it. But if we actually end up dating at some point he'll have to know. It's part of my contract with Satan, that if someone falls in love with me, he's got to love me knowing that I'm a succubus. Which was bad enough in the bad old days, but now just convincing him that I'm not completely crazy would be almost impossible. And he has no idea that I'm Babylonian and he has a really weird accent in Akkadian, you know, and I can't tell him anything about how things were really pronounced. And he doesn't know what he wants to do and . . . I think I'm drunk. I think that I'm afraid that I'll tell him I'm a Babylonian succubus and he'll think I belong in a mental hospital."

"Wait a minute," Desi cut me off mid-meander. "So there are different problems here. The first one is whether he's a good enough lover that you have the option of keeping him alive. That, so far as I can figure, is the most important point. If he's not, or if you're not willing to find out, then you're off the hook about all the other stuff. Because you won't be dating him if you can't have sex with him. Is there anything you can do to tip the scales a bit? You know, some foreplay or something to get you more aroused? Tomorrow night's your third date? Because no one expects sex before the third date, but not much after it. Maybe you go as high as five dates, but that would be pushing it."

"Oh." I didn't know that because usually I only had the one. "So how do I count? Did the impromptu evenings when he arrived with take-out or pizza count as dates? Or did only arranged-in-advance events with stated forms of entertainment count?"

"His coming over with food counts," she said firmly. "You could have said no either or both times. You could have said that you were too tired or had an early flight the first time, which was true, or that you were just too zonked last night, which would also have been true. So yes, they count, which makes tomorrow date number four."

"That's worse," I said, and downed the rest of my drink far too quickly. Port should be sipped, not gulped, and I was already feeling the effects. Just not quite enough.

"Well," Desi said slowly in her considering voice, "desire has a lot to do with sexual satisfaction. That is something I know about. Mostly you pick up prey you don't want at all, so they haven't got a chance of pleasing you. Nathan, though, you like him. You're hot for him, you desire him, right?"

I nodded and blushed. When I thought about it, I did desire him. I got a kind of warm fuzzy sexy feeling just thinking about him touching me, holding me, kissing me. . . . I saw what Desi meant.

"Reading your current state, I think you don't have to worry about having to deliver him," she said matter-of-factly. "I know about desire, and if you have half as much as I'm reading off you right now, you're going to come way before you have anything to worry about."

"I'd be really happy not to worry about it," I said in a small voice.

"I think you'll be okay with Nathan," she reiterated. "You might want a drink or two first, just to lower your inhibitions. You're not used to having sex with men you actually want. So what does Marten have to do with anything? Wasn't he just a fling in Aruba?"

"That's what I thought," I told her. "But then I got this e-mail from Azoked, like I said. And in it she said that Marten is a ceremonial magician and he knew what I was and targeted me. In fact, she said that Branford in Aruba had been after all of us. But then he had found me, and Marten said that we'd had sex and he was still alive. Which is true. You know that. Anyway, Marten even told me, but he sounded as if he thought that was all superstition and he didn't believe any of it. And then Azoked said that he thinks he saved me from Craig Branford by telling him that he'd had sex with me and lived, and he might try to cash it in for a favor. And I *still* have the Nathan problem. What do I do if he isn't getting me off?" I asked as the barman brought Desi another glass of wine. "I don't want to have to deliver him."

Desi looked at me and rolled her eyes. "Kick him or something. Once you're all naked, if you're not having fun there isn't any reason he should be having fun. Squeeze his balls. Kick him out of bed. Come on, you're smart and creative, I'll bet there are fifty ways to get rid of a man before he comes that you could think of. You just have to try."

I was utterly and completely shocked. She was right. That would work. Only after three thousand years as a succubus, I couldn't imagine turning around and deliberately making sex no fun, and preventing myself from making a delivery at the same time.

"Anyway, really, why should any man get off if you're not, you know?" she went on, and I realized that she'd had enough to drink. "And if he's no good and you kick him out, you've still saved his life and you don't have to worry about telling him about your past, or what you do outside your job or anything."

"And what if I have a great time?" I asked, the three glasses of port taking effect and making me bolder, or more hopeful, than I had been.

Desi shook her head. "Then you have a great time. And you date him. And you be the person your ID says and you don't tell him anything. I'd never tell anyone I was dating that I'm a demon. The chances are very high he wouldn't believe it, and if he did it would only hurt the relationship. You don't have to tell all when you're involved with someone. Especially not early on. And for us, never."

What a mess.

chapter
TWENTY-FIVE

At this point I should know better. Somehow my e-mail always brings me bad news. My life would be much smoother if the Internet had never been invented. We always had much more time before Treos and cell phones and Bluetooth.

Getting a personal e-mail from Satan Herself is almost always bad, and this was just as bad as I had feared.

> *Dearest Lily,*
>
> *I have been quite lenient and understanding that you have not been in the correct astrological conjunctions to compel a delivery, and you have also been on vacation. I myself made a space for your holiday in Aruba so that you would have options. I hope you found him delightful—I do have my eye on that one.*
>
> *In any event, I would appreciate a delivery in the near future. I don't want to pressure you, my dear. This is not a command, it is merely an observation, but it has been a little while since you have sent a soul this way.*
>
> *I am looking forward to your next contribution*

to our population, and wish you the best with your beau.

Satan

Satan can be terrible. She can be a harsh taskmaster, she can be demanding. But she is also Martha, my mentor and friend and adviser, and to think I had disappointed her was far worse than any threat she could make.

She knows that, too. She is the Prince of Darkness, after all.

I was tired, but the port I'd drunk with Desi was wearing off. I couldn't put it off any longer. I had to hunt, and tonight. Nathan had taken my mind off my job, and off my delivery schedule. When the mojo is on, I have no choice. But Satan was accustomed to me sending Her little gifts from time to time when the astrological interval was particularly long.

So, a hunt. On a Tuesday.

I was tired and starting to get hungover. I wanted to deliver for Satan but I really didn't want to go all the way downtown and I especially wasn't in the mood for a bar. I took a quick look on Citysearch. And there it was, a Werner Herzog film and lecture at the Met that should be letting out just around the time I could get there, provided that I ran down right away. I hadn't delivered a pretentious intellectual in a while and they are just as annoying in their way as frat boys.

I was already dressed in black from work and had my subdued (intellectual) wool coat, so I ran out after only the most cursory check on my lipstick.

At least the cool air woke me up. At least I was

familiar enough with Herzog's work to wander into a random conversation. Once I'd tried this after a discussion of Pop Art that I hadn't attended and felt like a fool. Worse, being found out as a fake had scared off my prey, so I went home alone.

No chance of that tonight. I was going to deliver and prove myself the most loving of Martha's minions, one of those who showed real dedication to Her, not simply one of the demons who do the absolute minimum. I was one of the Chosen, and tonight I felt like I had to prove it.

As expected, when I arrived the street was full of people who had just left the lecture. Many of them were lined up at the bus stops in front of the museum, mostly for the crosstown bus to get over to the West Side. I hardly ever went over to the Upper West Side myself. It's all Columbia professors or intellectual wannabes, most of whom dress terribly and are more likely to debate the existence of the immortal soul than give it up. I generally find the type wearying and unattractive, and more time consuming than my usual quick pickup boys in the bars.

And wasn't Nathan an intellectual, writing a dissertation for a Ph.D. at Yale? That had to be at least as bad as the Columbia crowd.

I put Nathan firmly out of my mind and perused the crowd for a likely target. I noticed a knot of three young men, all of them talking with great animation and wearing the requisite leather jackets, jeans, and boots that comprised the standard university uniform the world over. There were no women with them. I sidled up to the three of them and caught snatches of their conversation.

"Herzog's fascination with the outsider can be seen as an extension of Nietzsche's notion of the superman," one of them was saying as he puffed on a cigarette. He was probably no more than twenty-five, though he assumed a professorial air. Grad student? No, Nietzsche is the intellectual armor of the semi-informed who want to impress. Wannabe? Likely. Columbia literature? NYU film program? Or someone who didn't make the cut but liked to talk. A likely victim in any event. He belonged in Hell—probably he made most of the people he hung around with feel like they were already there.

I joined the group on the edge and noticed that none of the others could quite get a word in. "Yes, it is always about the superman, a particularly Germanic construction, you would have to agree." Mr. Sententious hammered his point, and us, into the pavement. "Since you are most likely unaware of the supporting literature—"

"Let's get into this some other time, Lou. It's really fucking cold out here, in case you hadn't noticed," one of the other young men spoke up. "Later."

The other two muttered "later" as well and all three of them turned. Lou looked rather bereft as his audience melted into the night. Then he saw me.

"I'm not entirely convinced that Herzog is supporting the philosophical position of the superman," I spoke up. "Herzog's outsiders are often freaks; he is interested in what is repulsive to society, not the outsider so much as the outcast. There is a difference."

Lou was clearly taken aback. I smiled—I knew I had him. These types can't stand for anyone to contradict them, and for a woman to speak up and question their wisdom, that was tantamount to first evil. He would not be able to let it go, and all I had to do was play along. He would believe so easily that I was swayed to crave sex with him because of his towering intellect.

Many women are attracted to brilliant men. But Lou was not brilliant, he just wanted everyone to think he was. And since the worship-my-brains boys usually stuck to coffee, they couldn't even blame alcohol for their poor performance in bed. Not that they ever thought their performance was poor. How could it be? They were so overwhelmingly smart that they were doing women a huge favor to have sex with any of us. Because while we couldn't understand the reaches of their uberintellects, we could serve their little brains.

Or so they thought.

Lou, you're in for one interesting evening. And you're so smart you don't realize that I could be every bit as capable, and that you're my prey and not the other way around.

During the time I'd been thinking he'd been yammering on about the Enlightenment, German philosophy, and literature of the late nineteenth century, and his own remarkable achievements.

Good thing I hadn't been paying attention.

"It is cold out here," I said. "Why don't we continue this in that coffee shop across the street?"

They can never resist the lure of the coffee shop. Never.

"Not Starbucks," he specified. "I don't support corporate America and their stranglehold on the rest of the world."

So much for fair trade beans and a fast-food chain that offers health insurance to employees. He selected a Seattle's Best Coffee instead. Satan adores hypocrites. And Starbucks, one of Her favorite enterprises.

He got a double shot mochaccino and I got a small latte and we found a table where he could lecture me at length about everything the *Village Voice* had published an editorial about in the last two issues. I shrugged out of my coat and let him take a good look at my very delectable curves, subtly enhanced by Italian design. His eyes caressed my shoulders and breasts as he continued to mouth opinions that I'd read in last month's *New Yorker*.

I let him talk. That was what he wanted to do anyway. Talk at me and stare at me. Probably he had never been to coffee with a woman who looked as good as I did who wasn't ready to toss her latte in his face. I was certainly tempted and he really did deserve it. But since I had bigger plans for him, I resisted.

After half an hour I was getting tired. He walked me back to my building and was shocked when I said this was it. "You live here? In this neighborhood?" his scorn was so heavy it would have made a good winter coat for a Canadian.

I shrugged. "House-sitting gig," I improvised. "Some Fordham prof is on sabbatical, so I get paid to live here and take care of the houseplants. Want to come up and see it?"

"Oh, you're at Fordham?" he asked, his voice dripping condescension. I noticed that he hadn't said where he was, if he really was anywhere.

I didn't deign to answer, but let Vincent open the

door for both of us and ring for the elevator. I noticed Lou observing the lobby critically, taking in Vincent, the marble floor and walls, the thick brass fittings on the elevator, the Art Deco styling. Probably totaling up how much it would cost to live in this kind of building.

Nor did my apartment disappoint him. There were plenty of bookcases, there was a fabulous view, and there were Art Deco antiques in burled wood and blue glass. By Manhattan standards my place is huge, with a nonworking (but very ornamental) fireplace in the dining area with a black marble mantelpiece, a kitchen that two people could almost squeeze into, and the bathroom with my glorious claw-foot tub.

Sometimes I really resent bringing these men back to my place. I love my apartment. I love the art on the walls, the fresh lilies on the mantel, my clean Frette sheets with the blue embroidered edging, and my Aubusson carpet. I love the fact that my place smells fresh and clean, like flowers and Comet with a little hint of coffee. I don't like having men I despise like Lou up here, even though I know how it ends.

So I let him gawk as I hung both of our coats in the hall closet and made certain that my dress and boots were accenting just the right bits of my anatomy.

"Would you like to see the rest of it?" I purred.

Lou looked at me with wide eyes, as if it had never occurred to him that I might actually be willing. He probably had imagined this scenario a million times, the beautiful woman seduced by his superior intellect. But it had never happened and he had never really believed that it might. Lou knew that he was only third- or fourth-rate at best when it came to brains, and way below that on looks. Oh, he wasn't disgusting, hugely fat, or unkempt (though plenty of his ilk were), but his hair was thinning and he had the beginnings of a potbelly and a scholar's slouch. Which could be overlooked in someone who might pay attention to the person he was speaking to, but Lou's most unattractive feature was his opinion that his was the only voice worth speaking.

He talked. I led him to the bedroom by the hand, and in one motion (perfected by many years of this precise seduction) pulled the zipper down the back of my dress and let it fall in a puddle around me. There I was, dressed only in sea-green lingerie and knee-high stiletto boots.

That shut Lou up in a hurry.

I tugged lightly at his sweater, which smelled faintly of mothballs that I bet his mother sent him. The sweater lay on the carpet and he fumbled at the buttons of his oxford cloth shirt. Already I could tell he was ready, eager, not thinking about anything other than what was coming next.

I don't know why they all believe that I would throw myself at their feet. Thousands and thousands of losers, thousands of years of losers, and not one, ever, had paused to wonder "What does she see in me?" or "Isn't this going a little fast? Doesn't she want a date or something first?"

But they never think that. They think that they are so irresistible that a woman who looks like I do is just all hot and horny because they're so fill-in-the-blank. Smart. Rich. Handsome. Witty. Charming. Athletic. Masculine. Drunk. Whatever.

Only the ones who really are smart, rich, handsome,

witty, charming, or athletic don't usually take me or their luck for granted.

So, in a funny way, being willing to just have sex with me without wondering why I was there and what was going on was the final test of prey.

Lou flunked. In spades.

He practically tackled me on the bed, and didn't take his socks off. Yuck. At least he was easy. He didn't even try to satisfy me. After all, wasn't all the foreplay the brilliant display of his dazzling mind? Guess I was supposed to be all hot and gushy because he could say Nietzsche and Herzog, and at least three other German intellectuals all in the time it took to down one coffee.

He touched my breasts, but only to fill his hands and enjoy their size and weight. He didn't stimulate my nipples, didn't bend down to even lick them. No, he was doing me a big favor by having sex with me. So far as he was concerned, I was his reward for his achievements.

And I was. Only not in the way he thought.

He didn't even notice that I wasn't all that excited. He was ready, which meant that surely I must be, too. And—even bigger yuck—he didn't use a condom.

If I'd been a mortal woman, I'd have insisted, but I'm immortal and don't have to worry about STDs or pregnancy. He should have worried, though.

Fortunately, he had a lot more to worry about than the clap. He pumped a few times, grunted something like, "yeah, baby, take it all," when it really wasn't much, and turned to ash as soon as he came.

So much for that. I hoped Satan would be satisfied. I certainly wasn't.

Much as I wanted to just roll over and fall asleep, I felt skuzzy after the encounter and wanted to remove all traces of Lou from my bedroom. So I got up, changed the sheets, removed his wallet and valuables from his pockets and bundled up his clothes and stuck them in a Barney's shopping bag.

His wallet yielded only fifty dollars, a subway card, and a City College Staff ID. Staff, not faculty or even student. Creep.

I lay the wallet on top of the clothes. Vincent would take care of them in the morning. And that would be that. No trail to follow, last seen at the museum, just disappeared. Fine with me.

I took a quick shower to rinse the smell of him from my skin. Deliciously enveloped in the scent of honey, I felt clean and decent enough to go to sleep.

chapter
TWENTY-SIX

I slept through the alarm on Wednesday. By the time I actually woke up it was ten past nine, and I was already late for the office. At least, at a run, I would make the editorial meeting on time. So I threw on my reliable pink and olive tweed Prada suit and ran out, barely nodding to Vincent, who had a cab waiting for me. I didn't even break stride as I dashed from under the awning into the taxi.

I did my makeup on the way to the office and headed directly for the meeting, do not pass Go, do not collect two hundred. But I wasn't late and I wasn't even the last person to arrive. And Amanda Freemark, our editor in chief, looked so pleased with something that she hardly noticed when Danielle and I slipped into our seats.

When we had all assembled, Amanda beamed at us. "Before we begin our usual discussion of the issue, I have a wonderful announcement for us all. I'm certain that you are all aware of Lawrence Carroll, the top fashion editor at *Vogue*'s London office. Well, Mr. Carroll has accepted our offer and will be joining us here as the head of the Fashion division. So let us all welcome Lawrence Carroll."

Whereupon the door to the conference room opened

and Lawrence Carroll entered. He was at least six-four and weighed maybe one hundred and ninety pounds, including his floor-length cashmere coat. Something about the smug satisfaction in his face reminded me of Lou the night before.

"Thank you," he said, nodding at Amanda. "I am of course honored and pleased to be here and expect we shall have a wonderful working relationship. Etcetera, etcetera." Then he sat and sighed and stared out the window.

We managed a splatter of polite applause before Amanda took over again, leading the discussion on the two big spreads on American designers and one on the new styles of pants. Then the Features editor spoke about the major article already in the works on breakthroughs in breast cancer treatments. Throughout it all, our new colleague looked bored and leafed through Amanda's notes.

Before we left, he rapped the table. "I want our October issue to be dedicated to the white blouse," he announced. "We will have to arrange the incoming shoots and articles, but the white shirt will be the most important article of clothing this fall, and I want us to be on top of it."

We all looked at each other around the table, but he said nothing more for at least three minutes. *"The White Shirt!"* he shrieked. "Every one of you should think about it. Every one of you should think about nothing else. I want *The White Shirt*, and I want it to be daring, new, perfect, and exciting. And I expect exciting at our next meeting." Then he yawned and strode out.

After we left the conference room, Danielle cornered

me in the corridor. "What do you think of this Mr. Carroll? Why do we need him? I have heard stories . . . and I think they are planning to take over our departments and put us under Fashion."

I smiled. "Don't be paranoid," I said, mostly because I was fine with a lighter month. And I had the big shawl issue. "He only cares about the Fashion department and I'll bet he won't even notice us. Besides, he'll be too wrapped up in his white shirt project for a while so that you can plan something really killer—maybe even a cover article. You know, I just heard about something that I bet you could run with. Don't tell them. But anyway, I've heard a number of women buy high-end shoes, Manolos, Jimmy Choos, the best, wear them for a season or so, and then resell them on eBay. There's a whole secondary market out there, and it means that the women who can't really afford a full wardrobe of high-end shoes can still indulge, knowing that they'll recoup at least half or more of their investment. And we can coordinate that with something I've been toying with. Did you know there are purse-renting clubs?"

"No!" Danielle's eyes went as wide as a kid's on Christmas morning.

I nodded. "I don't know all the particulars, but it would be easy enough to find out for an article. The women join, pay a fee, and they get a high-end bag for a month. Chanel, Gucci, Hermès, Prada, Dior, things they could never afford. The very latest styles, and they pay only a tenth of the price. Or something like that."

"And they get the bag for a month?" she asked, not quite sure I wasn't teasing.

"That's what I've heard. But with reselling high-end

shoes and renting designer purses, we could take over an entire issue and show that the best is not only for the wealthiest. To show how fashion-conscious women who don't have a trust fund can still dress on a budget."

"You think Amanda will go for it?" Danielle asked, skeptical. "I don't think our advertisers and designers would be thrilled with our telling our readers how to get their products secondhand."

I shrugged. "We'll see. But you've got to admit, it's the kind of thing *Trend* is all about. How normal women can have high-fashion looks. It's on our masthead."

We had now passed the ladies' room and the reception desk and were at the end of the hall where our offices were located. "How long have you been thinking about this?" she asked me when we got to my office door.

I shrugged. "A while, just a little bit," I admitted. "I saw something about it online. You could probably take a quick look on eBay and see if there's any truth to the resale thing. I didn't actually do any research, I just thought it was an intriguing idea."

"I wouldn't want to wear shoes someone else had worn," Danielle said with a delicate shiver.

"I wouldn't rent a purse, either," I agreed. "But clearly, people do. That's worth some ink."

I ducked back into my office for the first time of the day, threw my coat onto the hook behind the door, and slumped into my chair. Danielle, no doubt, was perusing eBay entirely for the sake of an article. I didn't even turn on my computer. I'd just rest my eyes for a minute.

Hours passed as I blissfully dozed, no one the wiser. Until the phone rang and startled me back awake.

It was Sybil.

"Lily, have you talked to Vincent since you got home?" she asked without preamble.

"No, not really. I figured you would talk to him before me," I told her groggily. I wasn't really all that functional, and had used up at least a week's worth of creative ideas with Danielle.

"You didn't tell him anything about Aruba, about the guys I hung with?" Her voice held suspicion.

"I don't know what you're talking about," I said firmly. "I have said maybe five words to Vincent since I came back, and they were mostly things like 'I need a cab' and 'Where's my mail?' He's my doorman, and he's been a good doorman and that's the only conversation we've had. Why?"

"Because he's not talking to me," she sobbed. "He's not taking my calls. I've called his cell phone three times and all I get is voice mail and he used to always pick up for me before we went away. And he hasn't called back and he always used to call back immediately if I did leave voice mail. Which mostly I didn't have to. And we had a fight last night."

"Sybil, have you talked to Eros? Eros would tell you not to call," I said. Really, I was too tired for this. And since I wasn't all that good at following Eros's advice myself, I felt like a hypocrite suggesting it to someone else. Satan loves hypocrites.

But Eros was right. Right right right.

"Can I come over tonight to see you and maybe then I could run into him?" Her voice was so plaintive that I felt dreadful, but I had to say no.

"I've got a date tonight with Nathan," I told her. "I'm not even going to have time to get home after work. I'm going straight to meet him from here."

She just broke down sobbing on the phone. "It wasn't worth it. Those guys in Aruba, they were fun, but it wasn't worth losing Vincent."

"There's no reason to think you've lost Vincent," I interrupted. "And there's no reason to think that he knows anything about Aruba anyway. I certainly didn't tell him and I wouldn't. And Desi or Eros wouldn't either, and neither of them have been over since we got back. So they haven't talked to him here, that's for sure. You know, Sybil, it could be some other thing. He could be studying for an exam. You know how he's been taking extra courses and really working to advance. Or maybe he's got something else on his mind. You really don't know all that much about him."

"You think so?" An edge of hope sounded through the tears.

"I think it's reasonable," I told her. "We really don't know much about him, and there's no reason to think that he's found out anything about Aruba, or that he'd care if he did. He's a demon, not a human."

"Demons get jealous. There are demons who specialize in jealousy," Sybil sniffed into the phone.

"Yes, true, but we don't know what kind of demon Vincent will become yet. He hasn't even finished all the introductory classes, let alone begun to specialize. And at least he's good enough that he's doing that. He's ambitious. He isn't just some demon slug who's satisfied being my doorman for the next fifty years or so. It'll be okay, really, Syb, I think it'll be okay. Just give him a little time, you know. And remember what Eros always says. Let him have to work for you a little more. Let him have to make the effort. They don't value what they have too easily."

"I know that," Sybil said. "Thanks, Lily. I mean, I'm still feeling pretty freaky. Are you home tomorrow? Can I come by tomorrow if I need to talk about it more?"

"And have an excuse to run into Vincent? I don't think that's such a good idea." I said. "Let's go to dinner at Ono instead, and you can tell me everything and we can figure it out. I think you need to stay away from him for a little while and let him stew. But wait, I've got a question for you. You're an Oracle. What do you know about the Akashic?"

"I don't know much more than anybody knows," she said cautiously.

"Well, here's my question. When I came home I got an e-mail from Azoked and she says that Marten targeted me in particular, that he's a ceremonial magician and he thinks that I owe him a favor for telling Craig Branford the truth. That he'd slept with me and was still alive. Which means that he knows more about the rules than the Burning Men."

Sybil laughed, but it was a tight, frightened laugh. "Ceremonialists tend to be pretty intellectual and scholarly in their magic. They do a lot of research. I think they get caught up in the trivia a lot of times, but they do do their homework. Burning Men? They're fanatics and ignorant and proud of it. They've decided what the truth is before they've ever met a fact, and they're not going to let reality get in the way of their assumptions. The stupider the better.

And the Burning Men hate ceremonial magicians almost as much as they hate us. They assume that all magicians of any stripe, include the hippie pagans, are in league with us and do our bidding."

"Wouldn't that be great if it were true?" I mused. Wiccans do not help Hell. Nor do magicians, alchemists, psychics, or other dabblers in the arcane arts. Once in a great while we make a working convert, but that's so rare as to be historical. Last time might have been three centuries or more back.

But that meant that the Knight Defenders had not set Marten on me. Either he had come looking for his own reasons, or he hadn't known when he first met me but had figured out what I was. I didn't know how he could have done that, but I'm not all that conversant with ceremonial magic. Maybe they had ways of knowing.

"But the Akashic." I returned to my original line of inquiry. "Could Azoked have known in advance? Could she have told me when she showed up at Margit's?"

"I don't know," Sybil said carefully. "My own oracular gift is from Apollo and has nothing to do with the Records. I know that some ceremonial magicians and cabbalists do try to access the Akashic, but I don't know how successful they are. My impression is that it's a fairly difficult undertaking for a mortal. But what a librarian could get to, and how quickly, I have absolutely no idea. But you know, Lily, if you're asking whether Azoked is enough of a bitch to know something useful like that and hold out, she is."

"Thanks, Sybil," I said. "That's helpful. I might want you to talk about this some more when we have dinner."

"Then it's a date," she said. "I'll see you at Ono at eight."

"Sounds good," I told her, and hung up. And felt somewhat better. Just knowing that I would see Sybil and not spend the night alone after seeing Nathan, no matter how it went, was reassuring.

It was too late for lunch. I went downstairs and picked up two lattes with double espresso and two scones. How did we live before coffee? Imported Chinese tea had seemed so helpful in the court of James I, but thinking back the stuff did not even come close to a good French roast. Right at the moment coffee was my best friend. I was still so tired that I was afraid that Nathan would be sick of me or leave me off halfway through the evening. Two huge servings of tasty natural speed were going to take care of that. I hoped.

I managed to get through the afternoon somehow, answering my phone and my e-mails and even choosing accessories for our regular feature page for July and final photos for the page for May. Then I felt very productive for someone functioning with only half her brain intact, so I took two hours of sick time, lied and said that I had a doctor's appointment and went home at four. I fell asleep as soon as I saw my bed, and I'm only glad that I didn't sleep through the second alarm.

Two hours' sleep is a wonderful thing. I wasn't entirely refreshed, but I was feeling much better. No circles under my eyes, no yawning, and I could even think of snarky things to say about postmodern art if I needed them.

A long hot shower also helped, and by the time I

was in my lingerie and pulling wardrobe pieces out of my dresser and closet and discarding them on the bed I was feeling almost like myself. All black always works for an art opening, especially in Chelsea.

We were meeting at the gallery at seven thirty. So I studied myself one more time in the mirror, added heavier eyeliner because loads of black eyeliner always looks "artsy" (and goes with fatigue), kept the rest of the look very neutral and declared victory.

Chelsea is on the West Side, north of the Village. The West upper teens and twenties used to be industrial and warehouse areas and are full of chic, sophisticated lofts that once upon a time housed sweatshops and vast department stores. I remembered the days when I would go down to Seventeenth and Sixth and walk up the great avenue, stopping in the great ornate shops that lined the street.

Then the department stores moved up to Herald Square and Chelsea fell on hard times for a few decades. Now it has been reborn as the new SoHo, since the real SoHo has become way too expensive for not only the artists but for the galleries that represent them. Now SoHo has become the trendier satellite to the Upper East Side, and the actual art has moved to Chelsea.

The gallery was on a side street but the building was old and ornamented, the granite face carved with Egypto-Deco motifs, simplified lotuses and sphinxes and heads that were supposed to look vaguely pharaoh-like. As Babylon and Egypt were the leading rival great powers of their day, I felt vaguely threatened and very much at home. Inside, the gallery space was new and glistening with blond bamboo floors (so very eco-conscious), the white moveable walls required of any art space, and the requisite industrial ceiling with suspended utilities and lights. Just like every other gallery I'd seen in the past twenty years or so. Ho hum.

Nathan was standing near the drinks table in an animated conversation with three very well-dressed urbanites. I walked over and waited until he turned around. "Lily," he said, his whole face lighting up with a smile. "Come on over and meet my friends."

I covered the few steps and Nathan presented me with a glass of tolerable white wine before introducing me to his friends. "Everyone, this is Lily. She's a magazine editor. Lily, this is Shula Samuels, the artist. We went to college together, and would you believe back then she was a French major? Now she's starting to get attention from collectors and has started teaching at Cooper Union."

I muttered something complimentary about the work.

"And this is her boyfriend, Greg, who does something with finance, and the disreputable-looking guy with the red wine is Jonathan Fields, my college roommate."

I said hello to all of them and then stood quietly as they gossiped about people I'd never met and exchanged memories from days gone by. I hadn't expected a "meet the friends" date so soon. And I was sure that afterward he would care a lot about what they said about me. I tried to pay special attention to Shula, because I had no doubt that he would listen to her judgment of me.

"I would like to take a little time to look at the

paintings alone, if you don't mind." I excused myself gracefully from what was rapidly becoming an awkward situation. "I really like to have some personal space to interact with art privately the first time I look seriously."

Everyone took this as evidence of my artistic sensitivity and let me wander away on my own. Surprisingly, the paintings were interesting. Shula had combined painting, collage, and printing, and each was organized around a few samples of typography. I found myself entranced, especially by one that featured various samples of pastel blues and the letter *m*. Nathan was still busy, which was good because I didn't want him catching me. I went over to one of the assistants working behind the food table and said that I wanted to buy a piece.

The young man in the requisite all black and long but perfectly cut ponytail managed the transaction both efficiently and discreetly. As I munched on a canapé made of smoked salmon garnished with caviar, he wrote out all the details and affixed the red dot to the title.

Then Nathan came and found me, without his whole crowd. "So, what do you think?" he asked.

"I like her work a lot," I told him truthfully.

"Are you ready for some dinner?"

I looked around. His friends had split up, the artist talking to several people who obviously shopped at Barneys and the two men off in a corner. "Are we waiting for your friends?" I was a little off balance because I had no idea what to expect. Was this the date where he introduced me to his friends? It seemed a little early, but what did I know?

Nathan smiled. "I had kind of hoped we'd have dinner just the two of us. I did want to see Shula's work. She sent me an invitation to the opening and all, and I had to take a date."

"Had to?" I raised an eyebrow. This was more interesting.

"Shula and I went out for a while a very long time ago," he confided. "She's been with Greg for a couple of years now, but I did want to show up with a smart, beautiful woman so she would know that I was to be envied." Then he paused and looked at me, and his face fell. "Oh, no, I'm sorry. I didn't think it would offend you. I meant it in the most complimentary way possible."

I laughed. "Let's go eat," I said. "I'm not upset at all, so long as we're doing more than showing your old girlfriend that you've done better."

chapter
TWENTY-SEVEN

We went to Cafeteria. There was a line, there is always a line at nine forty-five, but we'd nibbled at the opening and standing on the corner of Seventh Avenue was no hardship. I had my usual blood orange martini and Nathan had a lychee mojito, and it was hard to hear him clearly even though we were sitting just across from each other. Cafeteria is a lovely place to impress someone with your knowledge of hip, but it's a bad venue for an apology.

"I'm really sorry, Lily, I wasn't thinking of what it might sound like," Nathan was saying. Since he spoke so that I could hear him, half the room had heard him as well. "When I asked you to come I hadn't thought that it would be anyone but Shula. I should have figured Greg, but I hadn't expected Jonathan as well. But let me tell you, all of them said that you were way too good for me. And they're probably right."

I thought the apology a little overdone, and not particularly necessary. But the drinks were really strong, so I figured that the mojito made him more morose than he had any reason to be.

"It's really okay, Nathan. What about that Branford guy you were following? Any developments?"

And I'll admit that this question was not entirely to get his mind off feeling badly. "You called your boss about him so quickly—did anything happen? Are you going to go to Aruba?"

He shook his head and looked even guiltier. "We informed the wife, who paid the bill and has disappeared herself now. I don't know what's going on, but it doesn't look like I'm going to get any mileage out of it. I don't know why I seem to keep screwing up with you. I wanted tonight to be really fun, really special between us."

I took his hand across the table. "It is fun and it is special and you haven't acted like a jerk at all. I've had a really good time, except for all your mea culpas."

"Because you're the most beautiful, most special woman I've ever dated," he continued. "The very first time I saw you I couldn't get you out of my head. And I told myself that it was just an image and that when I got to know you you wouldn't be interesting or smart and that I'm shallow and it was just that I'd never seen a woman so beautiful in the flesh before. And then I found out that you were creative and brilliant and cared about things that I cared about, and sometimes I think you might know almost as much about the ancient world as I do. And I could not stop thinking about you, Lily. I want to take you to New Haven and show you the Sumerian tablets that I'd been working on. I want to show you my apartment and I wonder if you'll like it, what you'll think. Yours is so elegant and sophisticated, just like you."

"Give him a kiss, honey, and tell him you'll go home with him. Otherwise the rest of us will never get a word in edgewise," a woman two tables over shouted in a heavy Long Island accent. She was a Nassau County tragedy, probably over seventy with her hair hennaed the color of a rust stain, plastered with drugstore makeup and draped with more Monet chains and bracelets than the end-of-season clearance stand at Marshall's. The younger woman with her, probably her granddaughter, turned bright red and stared down at her plate.

"Nathan, I like you a whole lot," I said. "Maybe a lot more than that. I'd like the chance to find out if it's more than that. You're one of the nicest, most interesting men I've met and I like your friends and I liked the art. I even bought a piece, but I didn't want you or Shula to know, because I bought it because I wanted it. Not because she's your friend. I've been around art long enough to know that you can't buy stuff just because you like the artist."

He looked up at me as if I'd started speaking Akkadian. Which I hadn't. He probably wouldn't understand my accent anyway.

"And if you're inviting me to have coffee at your place after dinner, then I accept. Though I've had a lot of coffee today and I'll have to take decaf. Do you have decaf?"

I was still holding his hand. He picked up his hand with mine in it and kissed my fingers. "Lily, Lily, you don't know what you've said," he said as softly as he could under the circumstances that I could possibly hear. "Yes, I have decaf."

We took the L train to his apartment in Williamsburg. Even though it boasted a fair number of trendy

clubs and shops, I'd never been there. His place, a
large industrial loft, was very close to the subway
stop and the main drag. The area seemed more edgy
than Chelsea, maybe more like the Meatpacking District had been a couple of years ago before everyone
started moving in. There were the clearly artsy types
and the old ladies and the teenagers hanging out in
the park. There was concertina wire over the entrance
gate to his building which made me wonder, but it
was probably just left over from a few decades ago
when the area was seriously sketchy.

His building was long and narrow, one of the original warehouses. Today a lot of places are built to look
like lofts. It's very chic in New York and probably
much cheaper for the developers, who don't have to
bother with a lot of walls and finishes. Nathan's loft
was the real thing, original, that had been retrofitted
with the current high-end designer kitchen (maple
cabinets, granite counters, stainless steel appliances—
I was impressed by a man who had a Sub-Zero fridge,
a Wolf stove and a Miele dishwasher. Though probably he didn't know how to use them). The entire
floor faced the river and through the twenty-foot-
high windows that made up the wall I could see the
Manhattan skyline in its full glory. That view was the
best advertisement for living in Brooklyn I had ever
seen.

He had to have had a designer, I thought. No guy,
not even the most sensitive and artistic metrosexual,
would manage that mix of the industrial furniture
and Art Deco woods and leathers. Scattered around,
on the coffee table and on a pedestal in front of the
view, were excellent reproductions of Babylonian

antiquities. Or at least I hoped they were reproductions. He (or possibly the developer) had installed a mezzanine above the kitchen and dining area, so they had what felt like twelve-foot ceilings while the living area fronting the windows appeared to be closer to twenty feet.

He settled me on the huge leather sofa, curved and sensuous and upholstered in warm chestnut leather, and went to get the coffee. In front of me on the coffee table was a tiny statue that I recognized out of my very distant past. Ishtar, adorned with fruits and nuts, was depicted as the Goddess of the Harvest. I picked up the piece and studied it carefully. I was certain I had seen it before. This particular statue had graced the small niche altar in the women's quarters of the Great King when I had been a young girl. I had been taught to make my first offerings before it, a piece of fruit or a particularly delectable honey cake.

I heard Nathan come in behind me. "Is this original?" I asked, my voice catching.

"No," he reassured me. "It's just a very good reproduction. Mom never did quite understand why I didn't want something that had been brought over in the nineteenth century before the exportation laws were in place."

"I'm really glad you convinced your mother not to try to find originals," I said slowly, moved by his care for the origins of the pieces.

I replaced Ishtar gently on the table, treating her with the same reverence as a statue originally made for worship. They were no different—the idols I used to venerate had been made recently, turned out in workshops by journeymen supervised by master artisans.

The artists carving the statuettes were on the job, following a pattern. They weren't praying all the time or thinking of the stone as the embodiment of Divinity. They were just guys with a shipment to deliver. But to me, she was my Goddess in all her glory.

"Why aren't you back there, working on your dissertation? Why are you here?" I asked. "You love it so much."

He looked down, slightly abashed. "My mother . . . Well, my family didn't approve of my choice of profession. That's putting it nicely. And there were some family politics and I promised to take some time to really look at their objections and try to deal with the world their way. So I got this gig, which they disapprove of as much as they dislike my Near Eastern studies. I can't win."

"Why do they have a problem with it?"

He looked away from me and shook his head. "I turned down a job offer at Goldman Sachs when I graduated from college. My mother will never forgive me for that. I refused to apply to law school. So far as she's concerned I'm an overgrown child who doesn't know anything about the real world and won't grow up and take responsibility. And I'm ashamed that maybe she's right in some ways. I take their money, or at least I use my trust fund. I don't live on what I earn as a PI, that's for sure. I didn't live on my TA stipend in school, either."

I could see this conflict was older than college. I wanted to comfort him because I didn't want to see him hurt. But I also understood why his mother was disappointed. Much as I was thrilled he was a Babylonian scholar, I was also certain that he wasn't merely pessimistic about his job prospects. And playing PI for the time being was only another way of getting back at his family, not really exploring to see if there was anything he could like in the life they had envisioned for him.

Still—I reached out and touched the back of his hand gently. "So many people just give in, go to Wall Street, don't stand up for who they are or what they want in life. I respect you more for having the guts to stand up to your family and pursue your own desires."

He smiled and reached over and caressed my hair. "You're really sweet. But I haven't stood up to them, and that's the problem. My mother tells me to drop the grad school thing, and here I am." He picked up the little statue and held it. "Ishtar was the Goddess of fertility, of the harvest. To her devotees, sex was sacred and fecundity was her gift."

As he replaced the small idol I drew him down on the sofa. And, blessed by the Goddess and with the glories of the New York skyline before us, he held me against his chest and began to kiss my forehead and cheeks. I raised my face and he looked at me for a long moment before he touched my lips.

We kissed for eternity. He was gentle but strong, not timid but slow and deliberate. When he leaned over to nibble at my ear, I sighed.

"What do you want?" he whispered urgently. "I knew you were the most beautiful woman I'd ever seen when you were all wrapped up in that bathrobe the night I met you. I've never been able to get you out of my mind. And the more I know you the more I know I've never met anyone like you."

"I want you, Nathan," I sighed. "I want to have sex with you and I want to have breakfast with you and I want us to date. And my friends all say that I shouldn't call you or send you e-mails and I did too much too fast but I couldn't help it. But you should know, I haven't really dated many guys."

He pulled a little away from me, so that we could see each other's faces more easily. "We can slow down if you want, Lily. That's okay. I want to date you and I think this may be for a long time. I can wait a little bit if that will make you happier. We can talk and cuddle and I'll put you in a cab back to Manhattan in an hour or two if you like."

"No. I want to stay. I want to be with you. I'm just . . . I'm scared of liking you so much so fast," I tried to explain.

"Me too," he said. "I'm scared of liking you so much so fast, too. And I'm sure that once I sleep with you I'm going to be in over my head."

"We can wait," I said. "If you want." Not my usual line. I found myself breathless, panting, thinking of how warm his hands felt on my cheek, how they were large and strong and enveloped my back. How protected I felt.

"I don't want to wait," he whispered. "I will if it will make you happier, but I want you in every possible way."

I almost moaned right then, with all my clothes on. I shook my head and ran my hands up under the fine-gauge cashmere of his turtleneck. The wool was unbearably soft but his skin was softer over a hard layer of muscle and his flesh was warm, oh so warm. And he tensed as I explored the bulges and valleys of his back, his ribs and the full definition of his shoulders under my fingers.

"Oh Lily," he whispered. "Oh my God, Lily."

He tore off the sweater and threw it on a chair. I looked at him in awe. Scholar, yes, but he had spent a good bit of time in the gym, too. Or hefting around those tablets; they were heavy. Marten had a lovely body, but Nathan had the smooth, defined look of an athlete. It may be a cliché, but there is something about six-pack abs and defined pecs and deltoids that are just delicious.

There is also something about a man's nipples, very small on a chest full of muscle, when they're clearly hard and tight. Aroused. Most men don't realize how sensitive their nipples are. I ran my finger very lightly over Nathan's and he moaned and half closed his eyes. I leaned over to lick them, but he pulled my head up. "Oh, no," he breathed heavily. "No fair."

I didn't understand what he meant, and then he peeled off my leather shrug and my tank top and tossed both of them on the chair with his sweater. He left my bra, though, and traced the outline with his lips.

"Mmmm, lingerie," he muttered the words into the skin of my breasts. "Pretty."

I wanted to get out of that bra as quickly as possible. I wanted to feel his hands, his lips, on my breasts. I wanted him to tease at my nipples as I had done his.

But he didn't unlatch my bra, didn't even pause, but continued kissing down my stomach and tracing my skin with his tongue. Then he played with my navel, darting his tongue in and out as his hands reached my thighs.

How I wished I'd worn a skirt, so I could rip off my panties and he could explore me the way I wanted him to. But I was wearing those very fashionable crop pants made out of fabric that was way too heavy to feel the way he touched me. He sat back for a moment and unzipped my high boots, and pulled them gently off my feet. Then he took my left foot and began to massage the bottom of my foot and my calf. I nearly melted, one little goblet of succubus left in the massive explosion of wonder.

I'd had men rub my feet before, fetishists who found this act humiliating and sexually stimulating at the same time. Marten had rubbed my feet as a form of seduction. Not Nathan. He was rubbing my feet because he wanted me to relax. He applied himself carefully, paying attention to the soft responsive places on the bottom of my foot that I'd never known I had.

And just when I felt so relaxed that I was no longer certain of skeletal support, he lay my left foot on a toss pillow and then applied himself to the right.

I could have gone to Heaven then and there.

Instead, I grabbed his shoulders and pulled him back down on top of me. This time he did remove my bra (with a minimum of fumbling—it always amazes me how grown men who supposedly have some experience with sex cannot manage to unhook a bra) and held my breasts in his hands. His hands were large but my breasts overfilled them, spilling out against my chest.

He touched my nipples gently this time, feeling the response, though they were already erect. Bending over me, he kissed each nipple lightly, and then took the right one in his mouth and began to suck softly, flicking his tongue. While I moaned and begged for more, he took his time, as if he knew he was uncovering some new Babylonian treasure.

"We could be more comfortable," he whispered in my ear.

I nodded enthusiastically and started to get up, but he pushed me back into the sofa. "Wait." And then he got up and lifted me off the couch into his arms.

Yes, he certainly *had* been in the gym. He carried me out of the living room and up the stairs onto the mezzanine bedroom. Right at that moment all I noticed was how long it took and how badly I wanted all of our clothes off.

He lay me gently on the bed, kicked off his own shoes and tumbled next to me before he turned and buried his face back in my breasts. I was breathless, excited, ready. Almost too ready. I started to fumble with his belt and he immediately bent and relieved himself of his trousers, underwear and socks with a single practiced movement.

And he was utterly beautiful and obviously quite enthusiastic about me. Obviously.

I reached out to caress him but he shook his head. "Shhh, you first," he said. And he pulled the elastic from his hair and let his long black hair tumble free over his shoulders. Thick and straight and well past his shoulder blades, it made an ink-dark shadow against his pale skin. I breathed in sharply, wanting nothing more than to run my fingers through that hair. He leaned over me and let his loose hair tickle my ribs, my breasts, and my belly. His hands went to my waistband and oh so very slowly he unbuttoned and unzipped, and slipped the capris off, leaving my panties.

No, no, no. I wanted them gone, I wanted everything right then. I wanted him inside me desperately. But he bent down again and ran his hands up my thighs and traced the outline of my panties as he had done with my bra. I was quivering, a mass of sensation without thought. When he ran his hand lightly over my still-clothed mound I thought I would expire from the need that had built inside me. And he matched that need, I could see quite plainly that he wanted as much as I did. But still he waited, teasing, drawing the seconds out cruelly and deliciously.

He slipped one finger under the thin lace of my panties and I shuddered and practically came right then as the tip of his finger grazed the outer edge of my labia, already slickly lubricated with my own desire.

"Mmmm," he said, smiling. I wriggled and tried to ditch the panties, but he wasn't having it. He wagged his finger at me and with a decidedly devilish expression went back to toying with me, panties in place.

Even with all my squirming he managed to keep me just on the edge and avoided the one final release I desperately desired. The pressure and warmth built inside me, built and built until I was beyond thought. Frustration drove my hips as the orgasm I so deeply needed was held just barely out of reach. "Please please please," I begged him.

He still did not remove the offending La Perlas, but merely moved them aside and flicked his tongue expertly over my mons. And I exploded with the most overwhelming tidal orgasm I could remember in three thousand years as a succubus. Wave after wave rode me and my legs spasmed with the aftershocks.

"Satisfied?" A whisper in my ear.

I shook my head. "Want the rest," I managed to sputter, though I'm not sure my words were entirely intelligible. So I reached up and stroked his cock and he shuddered. "Want."

My mental processes were orbiting Mars.

He leaned over to the bedside table and put on a condom while I removed the dripping remnants of my eighty-dollar five inches of lace.

And then he entered me, so slowly that it was almost painful. I wanted him, wanted his strength and energy, but he was showing far more strength in holding back. Then, finally, there was satisfaction, that utterly delicious replete feeling with all the stimulation in all the right places.

Nathan was not the largest man I'd ever had, but he was plenty large enough. And I was already so sensitive and stimulated that it was all I could do to wait before falling over again into a second orgasm and then a third.

And then I really wanted him to come. I needed his response, needed to know that I could bring him as much pleasure as he had given me. My skill, my desirability, my beauty were on the line as I increased the pace. "I want you to come, I need you to come," I chanted over and over.

Suddenly he changed his own rhythm, speeding up so that he was practically pounding me the way I wanted. I needed him raw and powerful, for my own power was on me and I was channeling it, increasing his desire and need in a way that would magnify his experience.

He shuddered and bucked, out of control. Then he threw his head back and his mouth opened with a soundless cry as I finally brought him over the pinnacle into release.

I had the power in me and with me and I held him and coiled it around him. It was a power that could mean death but I held it firmly disciplined. And that power, which I could release to deliver a soul to my Master or withhold wrapped around us both and surged with another level of sexuality.

Death and sex are one. No one knows that better than a succubus. And so, for the first time in three thousand years, I did not simply withhold the death but transmuted it. So he came and then he relaxed and was hit again and came again even more powerfully than before.

And the second time he screamed aloud, and he screamed my name.

We lay in bed too limp to move, both of us covered with a sheen of sweat though it was February and the streets were covered in slush and the thermostat was turned down to 68. A shower would be nice. Sometime later. I could not move, could not speak, could not bother to roll away from the dampness beneath me.

I heard Nathan breathing beside me, but I could hardly turn my face enough to look at him, and I'm not sure how long the two of us lay as if we were dead.

After some time I was able to move again, just a

little. Nathan rolled over and sat up. I turned enough so that I could see him remove the condom. Then he rolled over and managed to burrow into the covers, and threw an arm over me.

I removed the arm. "I'd like to rinse off first," I said.

He grunted and I moved out of the bed. I just was too sticky and gross to sleep. A few minutes of water and soap would make me feel much better.

The bathroom, like the rest of the apartment, was perfectly beautiful. Definitely there had been a designer involved. The bathroom was floored in flagstone with a deep two-person Jacuzzi set into a deck that was influenced by Japanese aesthetic. The shower was separate, floored and tiled in flagstone, with lemongrass soap, shaving gear, and two plants on a knee-high ledge. When I got out of the shower I found a cabinet with clean fluffy white towels. I wrapped one around my body and, clean and fresh, I felt suddenly very wide awake.

The entire mezzanine level was bedroom and personal space. Nathan appeared deeply asleep. I looked out the massive windows overlooking the city and saw the faintest lightening in the sky.

Restless, I started to explore. A large modern desk, glass on steel, dominated the far wall. Amazing how good it looked with the Deco antiques. I wandered over and saw the bookcase beside it and a credenza in the shadow. Idly, both bored and curious, I nosed around the items on the desk. I thumbed through his calendar and saw little of note—work meetings and one that read *Mom*, 8 pm. Cute.

A fine notebook lay neatly in the corner. One of

those elegant journals with handmade paper sold in elite stationery shops, it was bound in hand-stitched blue leather.

I opened it with no thought of what I might find. Men do not keep diaries, not that I'd ever noticed. So I thought it might be a picture album or book notes or something. But what I saw startled me beyond belief.

It was a handwritten series of triangles, some with short tails and some with long. Sometimes the smallest were enclosed in a fence of long-tailed triangles.

It was Akkadian. Handwritten. In a hand that was neat and legible and carefully schooled but looked nothing like any Babylonian scribe had produced. I sat in the desk chair and started to read.

I started near the back, not that I wasn't curious about everything he had to say but I wanted most of all to see if there was any reference to me. And there, on the third to last page, I read an entry that, roughly translated, began, "I met a beautiful girl. A girl who thinks. A girl who is like all the stars. I hope I see her again."

I heard a voice behind me. "What do you think?"

He had moved so quietly that I hadn't heard him get up, hadn't smelled him or felt his warmth as he moved behind me.

"You write in Akkadian," I said weakly, not knowing what to say. I'd been caught reading his private diary, when men don't write diaries. I looked up at his face, fearing the fury that I was certain would be there.

There was only humor and satisfaction in his expression. "Yes, I do write in Akkadian," he said, quite pleased with himself. "I started keeping a diary as an exercise to write the language regularly. It was something we started doing in second year and I've always liked it."

"But," I protested very shakily. "Aren't you worried about anyone reading it? About how I was just looking at it?"

And then Nathan laughed out loud. "That's exactly the beauty of it, Lily. You were looking at it. And I don't care. Because there are only thirty people in the world, maybe, who can read this. And I know most of them in this country. It's the best security device I know, kind of like the code talkers in World War Two. Look all you want. I've got all my detective notes in here, too."

I put the book down and he grinned at me, took my hand and pulled me up. "You are welcome to look at my notes and my journal anytime you like. You're welcome to look at it all night, but I'm tired now and I was asleep and I knew you weren't there. Aren't you tired, Lily? You can look at the book tomorrow, but why don't you come to bed now?"

So I went to bed, so relieved that I wanted to laugh and jump and shout for joy. I went to bed curled up against Nathan and I thought I would be too happy to sleep, so I was surprised to find that when I looked at the clock I had already missed the first meeting of the morning.

chapter
TWENTY-EIGHT

Sybil and I met for dinner at Ono in the Meatpacking District. Just a year or so ago this area was still rough, full of actual meat warehouses and leather bars. Now the good shops have started to move in and the clubs are trendy and full of people strutting their best designer duds.

Ono is one of the most beautiful restaurants in the city, modern and spare with a curtain of crystals hung over the bar. Their Asian fusion cuisine is innovative and exciting. When I first lived in New York I missed the fine sauces and interplay of flavors that I'd grown used to in Italy and France. Then Americans ate steak and salad and potatoes. I used to go to the premier French restaurant in midtown at least once a week to give my palate a perk. The only other foods that were interesting and reminded me of better times were the traditional Italian trattorias in the West Village and Little Italy, and the Chinese on Mott Street.

Ono was a welcome addition to what had become one of the most eclectic and exciting array of restaurants of any place and time where I had lived.

I was there early and Sybil arrived in a fluster of taxi and flowers. I was already seated when she collapsed at the table, laid a bouquet of pink tulips and roses on the extra chair, and burst into tears.

"What's wrong, Syb?" I inquired gently, and pushed my drink over to her. It tasted something like a cream-sicle and packed a lot more alcoholic punch than I had expected. She gulped it down as if it were water and I was certain it was the sweet she wanted and that she had no idea of just how much booze was in there. But the way she was crying she needed the alcohol. In fact, I thought we should order two more of these.

"Vincent," she sobbed, and drained the rest of the drink. "He found out about the guys in Aruba and he's angry at me and I don't know if he wants to break up and I knew I shouldn't have done that but I didn't know how Vincent felt and . . . I think I might have broken up with him."

"You think you broke up with him?" I was completely confused. "You aren't sure?"

She shook her head. "He accused me and I got angry that he would do that because why should he get all huffy at me and act like he owned me and believing anything he heard—"

"Wait a minute," I interrupted her. "First of all, how did he find out? Who told him? Did you?"

She shook her head and looked at me in wide-eyed disbelief. "Lily, there are some things you never ever tell a man. Honesty is one thing, but there are things you just shouldn't ever really tell. I know that. I didn't tell him. I don't know who did." Then she sniffled heavily and looked at me. "At first I thought it was you, because you live there and you have the opportunity and you don't know how delicate these things can be."

"Wasn't me," I said, aghast. "I may sometimes be the elephant in the china shop, but I've got more sense than that. Besides which, I've hardly been home and all I've seen of Vincent is that he opened a cab door for me. I was so late that he didn't even come up for the ashes and clothes from my delivery."

"Oh," she sniffled. "He came up to your apartment and took care of that when you were at work."

"Oh." I'd never had a demon doorman with that much initiative. He really was going to move up the ranks and out of his doorman position really soon if he kept this up, and that made me sad. The next one would have to be trained and wouldn't do all the little services that Vincent performed.

"So tell me, you had a date on Wednesday night, right?"

She nodded.

"What happened?"

"Well, you were out most of the evening, I think. Or something. Anyway, we met early, before his shift. We went out for dinner and he said that he thought that I'd been running around in Aruba and had dates there."

"What did you tell him?" I prompted her.

"What could I say? Of course I told him it wasn't true. I told him that I didn't date people who don't believe me and trust me. And then I reminded him that we hadn't ever discussed exclusivity and he was new to being a demon and how did I know that he felt that way about me anyway."

At that moment our fresh drinks arrived, topped with a froth of sabayon sauce. How did anyone think of putting that on top of a drink? But it was wonderful, rich and comforting and sweet and very potent. I almost giggled when I thought of that word and thought of the night before, but Sybil was in too much distress for my levity.

"I'm not real experienced at the whole dating thing, we know that," I began carefully. "But I think you did the right thing. I don't think you actually broke up with him, but you're right. Why should he get some crazy jealous idea in his head? Even if it is true. And that doesn't even begin to mention the fact that you and Vincent did not have any agreement and had never talked about having an exclusive relationship or anything like that. So I think you're completely in the right."

"But I was so angry with him and then I walked out," Sybil protested.

I nodded, backed up with the authority of too much alcohol. "And you did the right thing. If he wants you, he'll come back and he'll apologize and treat you better in the future. And if he wanted an exclusive relationship he should have talked about it. Would you have blown up at him if he'd gone to Aruba for a weekend?"

"Yes," Sybil wailed. Then she thought for a moment. "No. I may have been sad at his going off without me, but I wouldn't have accused him without any evidence."

"So he's being a jealous idiot when he has no reason at all to think anything of the kind, except in his fantasies," I insisted.

"But he's right," Sybil said, and sniffled.

I shook my head. "Doesn't matter, and it's none of his business. You don't need some hair-trigger jealous maniac watching your every move. And you're going to wait and do nothing until he comes crawling and grovels appropriately because that's the least you deserve." I sounded so much like Eros I shocked myself. Had I really learned the lessons, or was I only good for telling someone else to do things I couldn't do myself?

"And," I added for further measure, "you're going to have to be sure something like this never happens again. That he knows he has to trust you and treat you with respect and let you spend time with your girlfriends. In Aruba, if that's what we're doing. He isn't allowed to interfere."

"Do you really mean that?" she asked, dazed.

"I have an idea," I said slowly, thinking as I went along. "Why don't we have brunch on Saturday this week instead of Sunday? Then we can all talk about things, because you need to hear everyone's point of view. Which will agree with mine, but I think it will help if you hear from all of us. And I could use all your input, too, before I see him again."

Sybil blinked. "Nathan, you mean. You have a date on Saturday night?"

I nodded. "And I need advice, really I do. I got caught reading his diary."

Sybil looked startled. "Guys don't keep diaries," she protested. "What did it say? What did he say?"

"He said it was language practice, and he keeps the diary in Akkadian. And he doesn't know that I can read it, so he said I could look at it all I wanted. And I felt so caught, Syb, because when he found me reading it I was sure he knew that I knew everything. And he didn't. He doesn't have any clue that I can read it.

Which makes sense, since there really are only a few dozen scholars who can make any sense of cuneiform these days. And to tell the truth, his grammar is a little shaky in some places and he could probably use my help. His accent is horrible."

"Lily, promise me that you won't tell him. I can't begin to tell you all the reasons not to. You'll have to explain everything about being a succubus and being Babylonian and it's too much this early in the relationship. And that says nothing to his feeling like he can't impress you anymore when your Akkadian is better than his."

"But it's my first language," I protested. Sometimes the fragility of the male ego is incomprehensible.

"Yes, but even still he's going to feel like he hasn't got anything to offer you. They're like that, Lily, you know it. And I know it. Do not tell him anything. And read it. Not just for yourself, but to make sure he isn't one of *them*."

"What?" I was horrified. "There is no way Nathan is one of them."

Sybil's eyes grew wide and she sipped on her third drink. Or was it her fourth? "But he could be. Anyone could be. Look at Desi. That was horrible for her. No, I'm just saying we all should be sure. And you told him where we were going in Aruba."

"And what about you and Vincent?" I asked, more to change the subject. "He knew where we were, too."

Sybil shook her head. "I'm sorry. I didn't mean that. I don't think either of our guys are leaking information. And I won't send Vincent an e-mail tonight. But maybe I'll come back with you and run into him in your lobby. I think he's working tonight." And then our seared ahi came and we drowned our sorrows in delicious food and topped it all with seconds of dessert. Because we needed it. Because life sometimes is just like that and the only thing that makes it survivable is brioche bread pudding and cheesecake and molten chocolate cake on top of that.

But I still felt guilty. I wanted to tell Nathan everything. I wanted him to know about me and still love me. I wanted his support and his commitment even though I knew I was asking too much.

Or was I? I could help him so much with his understanding of the ancient world that clearly was his passion. I could help him with his pronunciation and grammar in Akkadian, I could give him some of the more subtle nuances of court etiquette, I could teach him so much about the practice of religion. He would have scholarly publications for years.

Or was Sybil right and he would hate me for it?

Or was I too drunk to be thinking well? That was for sure.

Sybil decided not to come in. She was too drunk to confront Vincent, so I got out of the taxi alone.

And there, across the street from my building, I saw Craig Branford staring at my front door. He was standing on the curb and just—staring. I'd looked at his picture long enough that I was certain it was him. Yep, same stringy blond hair, same watery eyes, same sullen expression.

If I hadn't been drunk I probably would have just ducked inside and tried to hide. Maybe I would have called Nathan and whispered. Maybe that's what I should have done, used the cell phone and let him know that Branford was not only back in New York, but standing outside my building.

But I was drunk, outrageously drunk, so I ran between the parked cars and confronted him dead-on. "Just what do you think you're doing?" I demanded. "Standing here in front of my building. Are you stalking me? What was that whole deal in Aruba? I saw you and my date told me about what you'd said to him so I know you're up to something. And if you don't disappear, just leave us alone, I'm going to call the police and get a restraining order and maybe press charges."

"Are you a succubus?" he asked, point-blank.

That startled me into a moment of silence. I couldn't believe that he'd actually come out and asked me. "Oh, so the fact that I was dating someone in Aruba didn't convince you?" I attacked. Maybe it was a good thing that I was drunk. "Why are you following me anyway?"

He shook his head. "I had very good information. I thought I had excellent information, at least until Aruba. You—surprised me. And you have made my life very difficult."

I had made his life difficult? "And why do I care?" I asked loudly enough that a couple of people on the street turned in our direction. "You have no business here. You have no business anywhere and I suggest that you get lost. Permanently."

He shook his head slowly. "We have some questions about you and your friends," he said slowly. "Even if you are not the enemy you are in league with forces of sin. But I think something is wrong. Some of my brothers are convinced that you are innocent, true

women, but I know that Satan is the master of lies.
And I intend to discover what is wrong."

"Nothing is wrong except you," I almost shouted
in his face. "I'm going to call the police if you don't
get out of here right now, and if you ever come back
you're going to get into more trouble than you can
handle."

"Please understand, Lily, your ruses do not work
on me and you do not frighten me at all. Take this as
a friendly warning. We will find out what you are and
we will destroy you, and your Master as well." Then
he turned and walked toward the avenue, where he
turned the corner. I wanted to run after him, but my
motor control had gone somewhere around my
fourth drink and my four-inch Christian Louboutins
looked fantastic but weren't made for running, even
cold sober.

Stupid, righteous, self-proclaimed savior of humanity, I thought, fuming. If I hadn't been drunk I might
have taken in what precisely he had threatened me
with, but as it was he had just made me more furious.

Vincent was on duty when I staggered back across
the street. He opened the door when I arrived and I
told him to come upstairs with me. Which was fortunate, because he caught me around the waist and held
me on the elevator. He also inserted the key into the
lock when I couldn't make it after the third attempt.
He dropped me on my sofa and took a seat across the
coffee table, perhaps so that there would be no mis-
taking our propriety.

"Was there a problem with that guy across the
street?" he asked gently. "I've seen him before, just

staring at the building. I thought he was a real estate agent. Or maybe someone who wanted to move in."

"That was the Burning Man who was in Aruba," I hissed at him. "Are you the one who told them we were there? Is that how you got your jealous nutcase ideas about Sybil, because those liars will say anything about us and you believed them? Have you been passing information when that man, whose name is Branford, by the way, came by so you could tell him what you know about us?"

Vincent sat in startled silence. He opened his mouth and shut it again. "He was in Aruba?"

"Yes," I said. "He knew. He was there and they were tracking us. He set someone on me even, and I wouldn't be surprised if any of the people paying attention to any of the four of us were their agents. But how did he know? Who would have told him? You?"

"Me?" His shock and injured innocence were textbook, so good that it looked more like he was lying than responding honestly.

"Well, it has to be someone in the Hierarchy," I said reasonably. "Because there weren't any mortals who knew we were going. And there weren't that many demons, either. And you're ambitious. Maybe you set us up just so that you could save us later and win our gratitude and even Satan's approbation."

The blaze of anger in his look was impressive indeed. "You know, that's so low and devious that only Hellspawn would have thought of it. So now you're accusing me out of the blue and I don't deserve it and I won't forget this either." The flash of anger flared down, but his eyes still smoldered.

"I'm accusing you out of the blue the way you accused Sybil. You go and apologize to her," I told him. "For being an asshole. If you really care for her, if you want to see her again, you apologize. I hope you're not such a big jerk that you actually told anyone anything. Or are you just jealous of any life she has that isn't all about you? I don't care. My friend is crying and it's all your fault whether you said anything, or you believed bullshit, or what—"

"You're drunk, Lily. You're very, very drunk. But even drunk off your ass, you've made your point. Taken. Thank you. Now I'll see you tomorrow. I happen to be at work, in case you had forgotten." He got up and let himself out, and I managed to peel off my clothes before I collapsed back onto the couch.

Friday was another overcast slushy February day. My weather clock said the high today was expected to be in the twenties. I hadn't realized how badly I was ready for winter to end. Part of working in fashion is that you're always out of sync with the season.

We're putting together our summer issues at the end of the winter and looking at spring clothes in October. When I look at the photo spreads for the issue we're working on, I get all excited about clothes that won't be available or make sense for six months.

I'd been away in Aruba and then I'd been too tired and distracted to concentrate on my job since I'd returned. Even though I wanted to spend the day mooning over Nathan and figuring out the problems with Sybil and the Burning Men and dealing with my hangover, I did have to pay attention to work. And that was a nice thing, because I got all wrapped up in the shawl feature and helping a fashion editor choose luggage for a four-page spread on what to bring for a weekend in the Hamptons. I forgot about Nathan and Sybil and Vincent. I even forgot Satan and Aruba and Azoked. For just a few hours I forgot everything but suitcases.

There is a special satisfaction about doing one's job well. I've had enough of them, jobs that is, in my life. And while I often hate the time and necessity, especially since I don't particularly need the money, I enjoy being challenged and able to solve a problem for someone else. I enjoy being competent at something besides sex.

That was true even when I was a girl, why I really wanted to enter the Temple rather than be married off. My mother wasn't high enough for me to be useful in a diplomatic marriage, but there were more than enough families that would have been thrilled by an alliance with the royal household. I had had some choice in the matter, and it was my own desire to become a Priestess. I wanted the opportunity to do things myself, and that pleasure has never changed. In three thousand years I'd learned a lot about sex and about life, but I still loved being competent in a completely different world.

So work on Friday left me happy and fulfilled, feeling smart and capable and ready to take on the challenges of the world. Even if said challenges were only luggage.

I was so entranced with my own creative energy that I decided to pick up some take-out Chinese and play around with some project ideas a little more when I got home. I didn't have any plans for the evening, and while we'd changed our brunch to Saturday, I didn't want to think about the problems with Vincent and Nathan and all.

No, I wanted to put together a great feature idea and send it off to Amanda and eat egg rolls and Crispy Orange Beef in my pajamas. I picked up my takeout a block from the office and caught a cab home, happily anticipating a quiet evening indulging in my own company and being a slob. I would wear my Ozzy tee shirt and fuzzy slippers. I would eat out of the cartons! I would pig out on Ben and Jerry's! I would watch my *Pirates of the Caribbean* DVD and drool over Johnny Depp and Orlando Bloom. Sounded like Heaven to me.

chapter
TWENTY-NINE

I entered the building smiling, anticipating the heavenly-smelling takeout. Vincent was on duty and he was sticking to his job. No acknowledgment of my drunken tirade of the night before, even though it would have been entirely justified.

Nor did he tell me that there was a surprise waiting in my living room.

Azoked sat shedding on my sofa, licking the last of the Cherry Garcia. That was two strikes against the evening's success. The program had not included going out for more supplies. Strike three, my dinner would get cold while she said what she was here for, though no doubt the real reason she had showed up was to torment me. Sadistic librarian.

She looked at me and took a deep sniff, her whiskers quivering.

"Oooh, good, Crispy Orange Beef is my favorite," she said by way of greeting.

I have been trained to have good manners. In nearly a hundred different societies in thousands of years I have known how to be a good hostess, a good guest, make people feel at home, and be polite in any situation. I lost all of them at that moment.

"This is my dinner. I don't recall inviting you," I

said sourly. "And you just finished off all my ice cream and I wanted that. So why don't you just tell me what you came to tell me and then get out? If you want Crispy Orange Beef, you can get your own."

"I would have thought you were a better hostess than that," she sniffed. "I would have thought you would have welcomed me and my information."

"You're not my guest when I didn't invite you," I groused. "And the people I do invite don't help themselves to the contents of my freezer without even asking."

"What was I supposed to do?" she asked, completely unrepentant. "I knew that if you'd been home you would have offered. And you still don't have any Florentines, and I specifically asked for them."

In three thousand years I have not hated many beings. Human and demon, there have been many I disliked and a large number I wouldn't want to socialize with, but by and large I didn't go all the way to hate.

I made an exception for Azoked.

"How did you get in, anyway? Did Vincent let you in?" I was ready to kill Vincent for letting this demon into my sanctuary.

"Oh, no," she giggled.

Disgusting. She actually giggled. And I felt thwarted since I couldn't really blame Vincent for her presence.

"I manifested here. I have the coordinates and the visualization now. The Akashic is everywhere. Librarians manipulate that record. We can be wherever the record is."

"So that's why you stayed at the Royal Sonesta in

Aruba?" I wasn't curious, I was snarky. She deserved it. In fact, she deserved more, but I could smell my dinner and I was hungry and I was not in the mood to share.

"Why don't you serve me some of that orange beef while I arrange my notes?"

I growled. "I will serve you orange beef over your head," I threatened, and I meant it.

"I will report you to Satan," she countered. "Satan won't like you treating a librarian so badly."

She sounded just like the kind of smug dancing girl who'd pleased the King for a night and thought she was about to be elevated to a wife. I'd seen it in the women's quarters enough times, the young girl of no family who started giving orders and herself airs, to later discover that one good night, or even two or three, didn't make her a favorite. That was one lesson my mother managed to avoid. She knew that a farmer's daughter wasn't about to be elevated to wife, no matter how pretty or charming, no matter that she had given the King a daughter. And she had made very certain to teach me precedent and social awareness very young.

"I am one of Satan's Chosen," I said carefully. "I am not some lackey sent out to fetch your favorite dinner. You do not have the right to just show up in my apartment uninvited when I've been at work all day. You do not have the right to go through my place, eat my food, look at my private papers."

"Oh, but I do," she hissed. "I look at everyone's most private thoughts and dreams. What do you think the Akashic is? Something like a telephone book? No, I see what it is that people think and dream and desire. I know their future and their past, their fate. And I know what is hidden in their souls."

"I am not a person," I told her. "I am a demon. I know you can't access our information. We don't register in the Akashic at all; even I know that. So maybe if you stopped treating me like a not-so-bright servant, if you tried to respect my home and my privacy, we would get along a lot better. And then we could both do our jobs and try to endure what minimal contact with each other we could not avoid. Why do you insist on being so nasty? I mean, you could perfectly well get your own Chinese food."

She blinked twice. "Nasty? I'm not being nasty. I didn't know I wanted Chinese food until I smelled yours. Why shouldn't I want it?"

And suddenly I understood. She was a Bastform. She was a cat who claimed what she wanted and didn't think about manners. I let the computer and the talking and the glasses fool me, but her personality was all kitty. And not a nice kitty, either.

Understanding did not make me hate her any less.

But it did mean that I was able to redirect my rage. I hated her and I would have been happy to see her in the worst torments of Hell, but I needed her and I could use her, and that gave me an advantage.

Besides, the orange beef only came in the large dinner-size portion, which usually lasted me for three meals.

"If I give you some orange beef, you will give me the information you came to deliver," I said. There was no question in my tone. "And you will let me know in advance in the future when to expect you. We will make appointments like civilized beings. What if I had been out hunting?" Bargaining is an important skill in Hell.

"Why should I make an appointment?" she asked, genuinely confused.

"If you make an appointment I will be ready for you and will have plenty of ice cream and cookies. And we will conduct our business efficiently."

She appeared to think about this as if the idea were new to her.

"But you will give me orange beef now?"

"Yes," I said, doing my best not to think of slamming her face through the window. And then maybe dropping her out of it as well. Even if she was immortal. "But you will make appointments in the future. Mutually convenient and agreed-upon appointments. No surprise visits anywhere. Ever."

"And this will be more efficient for me?" she inquired seriously, as if she were not in danger of imminent dismemberment.

"Far more efficient. We will work together better. And you won't have to wait for me, and will get all the snacks you like."

I'm good at bargaining. My mother taught me, and she could drive a hard bargain. The only being I've seen who's better is Satan Herself.

She nodded. I brought my food into the kitchen and dished out white rice and a few pieces of Crispy Orange Beef and a large chunk of broccoli, stuck a pair of chopsticks in the bowl, and brought it back to the living room. She leaned forward eagerly. "Tell me first," I said, holding the food close to me. I could smell it, and I wanted to scarf even the small serving I had doled out for Azoked.

"Several items. First, there is dissension among the Knight Defenders, since it has been proved that you did not kill the man in Aruba, but Branford is not entirely ready to give up on you or your sisters. They are in a leadership crisis now, but Branford is by no means out of it. They appear to have enough financial backing to dismiss Branford's expenses while pursuing you, but the fact that his information appears to have been faulty has made the others doubt him. We've seen groups like this before. They will regroup and possibly be even more dangerous than before, but whether Branford will last is an open question at the moment."

I nodded. Fanatics cannot be dissuaded and we had thousands of years of experience of that. They can be distracted by their own internal power struggles, at least until a leader emerges. Branford could be eliminated or he could emerge much stronger, and I didn't know which would be better for us. We could watch for them now, though it was reassuring to think that we were a bit safer, at least for a few months.

"Go on," I said, holding the bowl out and letting the scent of dinner waft in her direction. "You didn't come here just to tell me that. I hope this entire visit wasn't just about Branford and the Knight Defenders, which we had mostly figured out anyway."

"Marten in Aruba is a ceremonial magician and believes that you owe him a favor," she said. "He knows what you are and he targeted you specifically."

I shook my head. "Old news. I've got that already. And honestly, I probably wouldn't mind doing a favor for Marten. But that's not it. So spill."

She ruffled her fur and pinned her ears back. "You know there is a high-level demon involved," she replied carefully. "Who is giving information to Branford. I cannot access the thoughts and actions of demons. We are not truly alive, and therefore are not inscribed in the Book of Life. But Vincent did not come by his jealousy unaided. If you find out who whispered that he might have reason to be jealous you might find out more."

The only reason she did not go out my window then and there is that she actually sounded like she was not trying to bait me. "Tell me more," I said.

She shook her head. "Truly. I swear on Satan's name. I have a pattern with Branford and Balducci and connections to other groups. There are spaces, blank places, puzzle pieces missing. It would make the most sense if there were more than one source. A higher demon who is using Branford, and someone who is privy to your information. Who told Vincent? Are you certain that it is not Vincent giving out details to someone he wishes to impress in the Hierarchy?"

She arched her eye in a way that looked particularly humanoid. Then she settled the empty bowl gently on the table. "I will leave now. I do not like you, Lilith, nor you me, I think. But we both serve our Master."

I nodded. "Thank you," I said sincerely. "And if you could make an appointment next time that would make both of our lives easier."

She nodded and vanished. And I called Vincent upstairs on the intercom.

He arrived and I told him to sit on the sofa. I was acutely aware of my dinner getting colder by the minute on the counter, but some things were more important. My friends, for one. And my duty to Satan above all. "Vincent, why did you think something happened with Sybil in Aruba? Did someone say something to make you suspicious?"

He thought for a moment. "I told a friend in my class, a demon who came in about when I did, that my girlfriend had gone to Aruba with her friends. And she said that I didn't know the half of what went on there."

"Who is this demon?" I asked quietly. "And why did you believe her? Does she have any reason to know?"

He shook his head. "No, she's a friend. Really. I think she was just speculating, but it got me crazy."

I winced. "You told her where we were? You know that we were going because we had been attacked, because Sybil had a premonition that there would be another attack this weekend. And you told someone where we were? Do you realize you could have been the one who set Branford on us? You don't know who this friend could be working for, do you?"

"No." Vincent was adamant. "I didn't tell her where you were at all. She just said—"

And then we exchanged a look that said we both understood. "Oh my goodness," he said softly. "I'll rip her apart."

"No, you won't." I shook my head. "You will not say a word. We have to know who she is working for, how she got that information if you didn't tell her. You are sure you didn't let it slip, maybe casually?"

"I'll think it over more carefully, but I really honestly don't think I said anything at all," Vincent said, studying his fingernails. "But Lily, can I ask you something about Sybil?"

I nodded assent.

"Do you really think she cares?" he asked softly. "She's one of Satan's Chosen, and I'm a brand-new demon still studying to pass my third level. I don't even have a specialty yet. I don't have anything to offer her."

"You're ambitious," I said. "You have plenty to offer her. And you do have a future in the Hierarchy, that's clear. So you may be a new demon, but you're on the way up. And Sybil should have a boyfriend who cares for her and is willing to take care of her. She's been through some hard times and I want her to be happy."

"I want her to be happy, too," he agreed. Then he hesitated and seemed to pull himself together. "Thank you, Lily. I couldn't deal with the idea that Sybil didn't love me."

"Were you jealous?" I asked carefully.

He thought about it for a moment, which was reasonable. Jealousy is a reasonable sin and could be an excellent specialty for him, but I didn't think that would be so good for Sybil. "I should have been. But mostly I was just crushed because I thought her going with someone else in Aruba meant that she didn't care for me. That I was just some newbie demon boy toy for her, that I didn't matter."

Looks like jealousy wasn't about to be his forte after all. "You matter. Trust me, you do matter to her," I said.

"Thank you, Lily." He crushed me in a hug, and for a moment I glimpsed the very young, scared mortal he had been. Then he left.

Alone at last, so wonderfully alone. I made up a large bowl of rice and orange beef for myself and put it into the microwave. The egg rolls were cold, but I didn't want them to lose their crisp skins so I ate them at room temperature and dripping with duck sauce.

Brunch. Saturday, not Sunday, so it wasn't quite the same and the menu was a little different. I didn't care. Having my quiet recuperative evening at home wrecked by a nasty cat-demon did not put me in a great mood. Reheating my Crispy Orange Beef in the microwave eliminated a lot of the crispy. I resented that. I resented a lot of things just then.

For once I was not the last one to arrive. Desi, Eros, and I stood on the pavement, looking at the funeral monuments across the street in the stonecutter's lot. Sybil was late. Sybil was almost never late. I was almost always the last one to arrive, and if it wasn't me it was Desi. Eros's collection of antique Rolex watches was not simply an affectation; for all the fifteen hundred years I'd known her she had not been late once. Not ever that I could remember. Even in the days before watches she was always there before we arrived.

Sometimes I felt really sorry for her and thought we must all try her patience. Eros was born a demigoddess and was preternaturally prompt. If I were she I would take a little more time and not be so anal about it, but I'm me and I'm almost always the last to arrive anywhere.

"I hope nothing bad is keeping Sybil," Desi said. She wore a long wool coat that was just the right weight for jumping in and out of taxis, but not quite warm enough for a prolonged sojourn on the street. She had her arms wrapped around herself and had jumped up and down a few times on her toes, though her high-heeled boots didn't give her a whole lot of play. Finally the cab pulled up and Sybil climbed out. She was glowing, almost giggling, as she ran for the door.

We followed like a clutch of baby ducks up to the hostess stand, and we were seated immediately. And, well, sometimes we get benefits for being immortals. The hostesses and waitstaff don't know we're not human, but they sense something different about us. And they defer.

We hadn't even looked at the menu when Sybil started chattering. "Vincent called this morning and apologized," she announced. "And then he came over—with flowers and hot mocha lattes—and apologized again."

"I don't know if that's enough," Eros said as she folded her menu. "He should be on his knees. In the street. In the snow."

Desi shook her head. "You're the goddess, Eros. The rest of us get flowers and mocha lattes. I think Vincent made a decent effort. Besides, there isn't any snow in the street now."

The waiter showed up with our Bellinis and we ordered quickly.

Sybil just glowed, though that might be partly due to caffeine. "Vincent and I are back together again and it's great. It's great." She looked at each of us, her face full of hopeful innocence. "None of you have been married," she said carefully, trying to make her point without hurting us. "You're sex demons and everyone desires you and you've all had a million lovers. But sex demons don't have long-term relationships in general. And that's about all I've had, really.

At heart, I'm still a good girl who doesn't have sex on the first date, or even the third, really."

"Have you had sex with Vincent?" Eros asked, with only curiosity in her tone.

Sybil blushed and shook her head.

"But what about those guys in Aruba?" Eros continued.

Sybil went from pink to red and looked at the table.

"It's different on vacation in a place like Aruba," Desi told her. "I was raised to be a good girl, too, and I know how Sybil felt. Far away from home for just a few days you can try on a new persona, play at being someone else. I think Sybil was playing at being us. But it didn't mean anything, which is why she was able to do it. That once. Isn't that it, Syb?"

Mutely Sybil nodded without removing her eyes from her silverware.

"Then you're saying that in some dating situations, it's okay to lie," I said, thinking of my own situation.

Desi shrugged. "The truth is, sometimes it's necessary. Because they don't understand."

Sybil nodded in agreement. "It doesn't matter that Vincent is a demon, he still thinks like a mortal. And in every marriage I've had I've known there were things it was just better not to say. If I had, it would have destroyed the relationship, and really, no one would have benefited. I believe in honesty in general, but sometimes people can take it too far. Honesty is fine for most situations, but my experience is that sometimes telling is far worse than not."

"What about my situation?" I asked. "What about me and Nathan? Because I've been thinking about it over and over and part of me really wants to tell him everything. I want to tell him that I'm a succubus and that I'm Babylonian, and correct his weird grammar and accent on occasion. Part of me thinks he ought to be thrilled by this and part of me thinks it's a very bad idea."

"It's a very bad idea," my friends pronounced in chorus.

"This is exactly the kind of thing I mean," Sybil said. "There are two separate sets of facts that you want to tell Nathan. One is about being a succubus. That's not a good idea because he probably doesn't believe in us in the first place. So he could easily think you're a nutcase. How would you prove it to him? How would you get him to believe that there is an Underworld, let alone that we walk the Earth? He's a secular well-educated American man. He isn't going to believe that some woman he's dating is really an immortal servant of Hell. That's just for starters.

"Then there's the particular kind of service. He might be confident, but he's going to feel insecure when he thinks of all the men you've had sex with. And he really won't like you continuing," Sybil went on, and it sounded like she was just warming up.

"The Babylonian part is entirely separate. It would have to come if he accepts that you're a succubus, and that's already massively problematic. But just for argument, say he can deal." She paused for a breath but the rest of us were rapt. We were the sex demons, but she knew so much more about mortal men than I had ever dreamed.

"So he can deal with the fact that he's dating an immortal demon who has sex with men and then kills them. Which, if you look at it pretty blatantly, is going to be hard for him to take. But say he does. Now you're going to tell him that you know more about his special area of study than he does? He's spent all these years learning Akkadian and you're going to correct his grammar and pronunciation? There is nothing on Earth he would hate more. And he'll know that you could read his notes and that his security system isn't all that safe. Which will make him upset about what he's revealed that he never meant to reveal because he never thought you could read it. Even if you give in to a weak impulse and tell him you're a succubus, no matter what, you should never tell him that you know more about Babylon than he does."

She stopped for a sip of her Bellini and we all took the opportunity to take a little alcohol.

"Nathan is really better than most," Desi said. "At least he asks Lily about what she knows and is interested in. He does want conversation, not just an audience."

I was horrified. What they were describing was the kind of men I delivered, the ones who could only talk about themselves and their work and never asked me anything about myself. Ever. Nathan wasn't like that at all. Which was what Desi said, but I was feeling very protective.

"Obviously he's far better than most," Eros observed dryly. "If he weren't, Lily, you would have delivered him and this conversation would be pointless."

The waiter arrived with our food, and we ate. I thought about what they had said as I chewed and paid attention to my lunch. "So, you think I shouldn't tell him anything?" I asked after I swallowed the last bite I could manage without a rest. "I should just let him think that I'm the mortal woman that shows up on my ID?"

"That's exactly what I think," Sybil said. "I've been married fourteen times as a demon, and not one of my husbands ever knew. It wasn't useful for them and would have only upset them."

I said little but thought about the concept. It had never occurred to me to simply pretend to Nathan to be the person I was set up to appear to the world. All of *Trend*'s articles on relationships stressed honesty and communication, and I pointed that out to the girls.

"That's in an ideal world." Desi jumped into the conversation. "In real life, all that honesty and communication kills relationships. Guys hate relationship talks. Communication means that you discuss what to do for the evening, where to eat, and stuff like that. But don't talk about your feelings or you'll scare him off."

"I just hope I scared off that Branford character," I mused. "I was so drunk I don't remember most of what I said, but he threatened us. He said he didn't understand and he wasn't sure of his information, but he said that he wasn't done with us yet."

"But didn't Azoked say that the group was in disarray?" Desi interrupted my train of thought.

"Not for long, I'm sure," I corrected her. "There is a leadership dispute because it appears that Branford was wrong about me. They doubt his information and he might even be wondering about how reliable his contact is. But they're not done by a long shot and I expect they'll come back worse than ever.

"I hope he goes after a certain catty librarian," I muttered. "I wouldn't mind seeing her pursued by the Knight Defenders. Maybe they'd give her something to complain about besides not having a six-month supply of her favorite cookies."

Eros pushed her empty plate away from her place. She had managed to devour a huge bacon and onion tart and a pile of home fries that had been almost as tall as the Chrysler Building.

"I asked Beliel if he'd help us, and while Security is really for internal affairs, he said he might be willing to. If we're still having problems," she said.

I looked each of the others in the eyes, shoulders squared as if I were playing Patton in a fashion shoot. "We're Satan's Chosen. It's our job, whether or not we're in danger. And truthfully, I expect the demon will still try to eliminate us. Because we are loyal and capable and now it's personal, since he hasn't managed to eliminate us so far."

"And the Enforcers are goons," Desi added, just in case we'd forgotten. "Insanely powerful goons. They can demolish a good-sized town with some motivation, but they're not all that bright."

"That's true," I agreed, my mind, for once, not entirely focused on Nathan. "But maybe now we have some time to do a little searching on our own." I thought briefly about Marten. He had saved us, but I wondered if he could help even more in finding out who in Hell was feeding information. Perhaps I could make his favor just a touch more expensive than it had been.

"We should still enjoy the fact that no one should be able to find us here, especially not on a Saturday," Desi suggested. "I plan to celebrate with some dessert. Anyone with me?"

chapter
THIRTY

I had a date with Nathan that night. It was good that I'd talked to the girls, though it was hard advice to accept. Don't tell Nathan the most important things about me. Keep silent. Keep mum. Isn't that what women had always done? Weren't we supposed to be breaking the mold, behaving as if we believed that we should actually interact with men instead of manipulate them?

I obsessed about whether to tell or not as I went about my usual Saturday afternoon errands. I bought flowers and a few groceries at the corner market, picked up the dry cleaning, paid a few bills, and got my nails done. After running around in the cold I treated myself to a long hot bath with an eye mask. By the time I got out and dried, and massaged four different kinds of moisturizer into various parts of my anatomy, it was past five and I needed to think about what to wear for the evening.

Tonight—I had no idea what Nathan had in mind tonight. Dinner, I expected, though he hadn't told me where. We'd done the art opening and the museum, so it could be an intimate evening or we could be out on the town. Clubbing maybe? Or a movie?

Finally, I gave up and decided on my newest pair of

Citizen jeans, a romantic blouse with thick lace cuffs, and a pair of actually sensible low-platform boots.

I was still putting things into the bag I'd chosen for the evening when Nathan rang the bell. At least I'd thrown in the clean underwear and toothbrush before he arrived. It was okay if he saw me transfer my wallet, keys, and cell phone. Which he did.

He was smiling and his face glowed with more than the cold. In his right hand he brandished tickets. "Anonymous Four at the Cloisters," he said. "Are you starving? The show starts at seven thirty and I thought we could get dinner afterward."

Okay, I was now officially impressed. Museum, art opening, and now concert of the most famous early-music a capella group in New York. At the Cloisters, no less. What had this guy done, taken dating lessons?

"Sounds wonderful," I said. "Who did you kill to get the tickets?" I knew those tickets couldn't have been easy to come by, not unless he'd ordered them ages ago with only hopes of a date or plans to scalp one of them.

He shook his head. "My mother had them, decided that she was doing something else this evening and called me yesterday," he said. Then he shrugged. "Well, I had planned something different, but I thought you were probably into this music."

We took a cab across the park and way uptown. The Cloisters would be one of my very favorite places in the city if only it were closer to anything and if there were shops and restaurants convenient. Unfortunately, it's on the West Side near the George Washington Bridge in Fort Tryon Park where martial arts groups work out and people let their dogs run during the day.

Nathan held my hand in the cab as we sped toward the most romantic date spot in New York City. The Cloisters was an amalgamation of five real French cloisters that had been brought over and reconstructed in New York. I remember when it first opened, back before John D. Rockefeller gave the money for the Met to buy it and relocate the entire thing to its present location.

Most of the structure houses a collection of medieval art and artifacts, but the chapel is used for events like charity balls and weddings. And concerts. According to the program we were given, it is considered acoustically exceptional and performers do not need microphones.

I had never been to the Cloisters in the evening, especially a cold winter evening when the strangely transplanted medieval building was glowing with warm yellow light. Most of the galleries were closed at this hour, but we did have to traverse the cloister itself to get to the chapel, and I stopped to admire the subtle colors of the marbles in the golden light. I noted four colors of marble, the columns all of pink or yellow, black or green.

Nathan held my hand as we moved through the sheltered walkway. Utterly enchanted, I found myself remembering times when this would be the very latest design.

We entered the chapel and were handed programs. When we took our seats I almost gasped aloud. I remembered hearing of Hildegard von Bingen when she had been alive. I had been living in Paris then, when Abbot Suger was building St. Denis, the first Gothic cathedral in the world. And I'd heard whispers even there about Hildegard, a woman with talents that dwarfed the men of her generation. She had been a composer, painter, poet, and the abbess of not only her own establishment but also the local authority for a thriving and populous region in Germany.

Yes, I remembered more clearly now. When she had been very old she had submitted her papers and her work to the University in Paris to be considered as a Doctor of the Church, and she had been turned down. Because she was a woman. All my sisters and I had been horrified, though I had to admit we hadn't been surprised.

But it was the end of the Second Crusade and the men were returning, and the women who for years had tilled the land and run the businesses and practiced the trades and professions, all these women were told that they should return home to be wives and mothers and leave the work of the world to the men. And so Hildegard, a genius to rival Leonardo, was shunted aside and forgotten.

I had been angry then, as I had been angry when the same thing had happened at the end of World War Two. In eight hundred years, not all that much had changed.

Now, in New York, in the most medieval setting in the New World, four women performed music that I had never heard before. Four women doing all the parts that in the Abbey of Bingen must have been sung by a hundred or more, and yet in the acoustic glory that had been transplanted from France, we could hear every note unamplified. Hildegard von Bingen died eight hundred years ago, but her music was as alive and thrilling now as it must have been at the end of the Third Crusade, when Philip Augustus of France and Richard Coeur de Lion had retreated in shame.

I was transported. Back in time but also into my own soul, the soul I had sold to my Beloved Master Satan to do Her will forever. In the world in which this music had been written, we had been understood. People knew that Satan walked among them. They were wary of demons and angels alike. They lacked technology and education and even basic hygiene, but they knew there was more to reality than molecules and telescopes, TV and the Internet. They knew the unseen world, knew not only that we did, in truth, exist, but also that we were ranked and organized, that we had jobs and damnation, that we were both their tempters and their deliverers.

They knew the Hierarchy. They talked to us daily, mostly to Upstairs, but many had called on us as well. We were powerful then and we were paid in worship and respect and awe.

So I remembered as I listened to the music, and the music alone without the associations was beautiful enough to strip me down and leave me vulnerable.

I wanted to think that what happened that night would never have happened had we had some other date. If Nathan's mother had used her own tickets, if he had dragged me out to some boring art film or pretentious jazz club, everything would have been fine. I would have done exactly what I knew was right, what my girlfriends had counseled me. I would have been strong, would have been firmly anchored in right now.

But we did go to the Cloisters and we heard the most amazing music that I'd heard since the Beatles first landed in North America.

By the end of the concert I was sobbing, softly, just tears running down my face and my chest heaving a little. Nathan turned to me after the third upwelling of applause and wiped away a tear with his thumb. "Are you all right?" he asked, concerned.

I nodded, not able to speak.

"Come," Nathan said quietly, using my hands to raise me from my seat. "We'll get some food into you and you'll feel better. I'm sorry, I'm really sorry, I didn't know it would affect you this way."

At that point he was leading me out and this time I didn't notice the magnificent museum that surrounded us. "Don't be sorry," I said. "It was beautiful. It was so beautiful and it just—there are so many things, Nathan. So many things that I need to tell you and I'm so afraid and the music brought them all back to me. And I'm so afraid."

"Shhhh, don't be afraid. Nothing to be afraid of," he said soothingly, as if I were a child. "Come on, we'll get a cab, there's a whole line of them here. And we'll go get some food and you'll feel better."

I only nodded. I could do no more, so he steered me into a taxi and gave the driver instructions and we ended up at a place that was quiet and dark with intimate tables that were well separated. It wasn't a place I knew, not a place well known or written up in CitySearch, but clearly an elegant bastion of Old Money.

My menu swam before me and Nathan ordered for

both of us, scallops and salad and then simple steaks. I could hardly eat. I cut and chewed and pushed food around on my plate, but somehow my throat and stomach had closed, and although the food was delicious I could barely swallow.

"I am so sorry, Lily," Nathan finally said after we'd let the waiter clear our nearly untouched plates. "I only wanted to do something special for you, something you'd really enjoy. I didn't mean for it to hurt you."

I shook my head. "It was wonderful, Nathan. It was the most beautiful music . . . I had no idea. But . . . it brought up things, things about me, about my past. My friends said that I shouldn't say anything to you, that I should wait or that it wouldn't matter, but the memories started to crowd me out and now—"

"You don't have to tell me anything you don't want to tell me," he said quickly. "We're both adults in the modern world and we've both lived and things have happened. I expect that. Okay, maybe you've done some things you would rather not have. So have I. But we learn from those things and we go on and they're what make us who we are. And I'm falling in love with you. With who you are. Not the airbrushed, perfect Lily, but the one with the red nose in the bathrobe that I met that first night at your door."

I was falling in love with him, too, had been since I met him. But if this was the real thing then I had to tell him. I had to be honest. If he thought he loved me, then he had to know me, had to know who I was. And that meant . . .

"Nathan, I'm crazy about you and that's why I'm so afraid. Before we go any further there is something really important you need to know about me. Because maybe you won't be able to love me if you know and I don't want that to happen and I'm so afraid."

He reached for my hand across the table. "Don't be afraid, Lily. Truly, really, don't be afraid. I can't think of anything you could tell me that could change the way I feel and what I want with you."

I was insane.

I looked up, looked into his warm, bright eyes, shining with sincerity and love. I felt his fingers around my hand, engulfing and protecting. And I looked at him dead-on and I said, "Nathan, I'm a succubus."

chapter
THIRTY-ONE

"What?" he asked, as if he hadn't heard the word. "You said you're a what?"

"I'm a succubus," I repeated. "I'm a demon who lures men to their death, but don't worry, I only deliver the bad guys to Satan. I would never ever deliver anyone decent. I never would have hurt you. But that's—that's what I am."

Suddenly I had said all the words and he was glazed and frozen, his mouth gaping open and his hand slack.

"And Satan promised me, too, that if someone knows what I am and loves me anyway, I can leave. I can stop being a succubus. I could even become a mortal and there's nothing I want more, Nathan. I want to be a mortal woman with you, and marry you and live like totally normal people."

He withdrew his hand from the table. "Lily, there is no such thing as a succubus. There is no such being as Satan. You're having delusions. Are you in therapy? Have you tried medications? There are some very good drugs these days—"

"No, no, Nathan," I protested. "Really. What if I could prove it to you? Would you listen to me? Would you at least try?"

"How could you prove it?" he asked gently, sadly, as if speaking to a crazy person.

"Give me a minute," I said.

Satan, I thought in a manner that was half magic and half prayer. *Satan, this is Your servant, your Chosen, Lily, and I am in great need. And there is none but You can help me. Please, show this mortal that we exist. That the Hierarchy exists and that I am a demon as I have said. Please convince him that I am not crazy. I ask this as the boon You granted me.*

All my heart and love I put into that plea, all the need and desire and hope that I had ever had.

And in She walked, Martha/Satan, in pastel Dior.

"Please, tell him what I am," I said, my voice all scared and little girl.

I wondered how he would know She was Satan. She looked like any Upper East Side president of the Junior League who had a thirty-room cottage in the Hamptons and threw brilliant parties. She did not look like most people's image of the Prince of Darkness.

She reached Her right hand as if to shake his, and, being well trained, Nathan rose and shook Her hand. But She didn't let go. Instead She grasped my hand in Her left and said, "Let's go then, shall we?"

And there was a sickening lurch of color and light and a whoosh like a jet taking off, only louder and surrounding us and then suddenly we were not in some Old-Money steak house anymore. We were on the terrace of a mountain palace, and before us lay Hell.

The terrace was strangely familiar, nearly Babylonian

if I thought about it. The floor was tiled in cobalt blue and a small table had been set with fine linen and crystal and a large pitcher of iced tea. Sugar and lemon lay in silver bowls and three long iced-tea spoons were laid out beside them. A vase of purple flowers, tulips, roses, and calla lilies graced the center of the table, and for some reason I found the elegance and yet ordinariness of the iced-tea service more frightening than anything else.

Around us the air was hot and dry, like the desert. The sky appeared mostly yellow with streaks of red, as if it were near sunset. I did not venture too close to the wall at the edge of the terrace, trying to keep my focus on the iced tea.

"That's for later," Satan said. "It's rather warm, don't you think? We'll be needing it soon, I expect." Then She turned to Nathan. "Would you care to take a brief look at the larger picture here, before we go on a bit of a tour? Lily, of course, is quite familiar with the setup, being one of My Chosen. She has great status here, you understand. She is not simply a succubus—I have hundreds—but one of My inner circle. An ordinary succubus, working under several layers of supervisors, would never have met Me, let alone come into the position where I consider her a personal friend."

Satan had changed as well. She no longer looked like the president of the Junior League. Here where She ruled Her beauty blazed, harsh and exotic. Her hair was still that deep, rich chestnut but now it was a great mass that shone in the unnatural light, loose down Her back and thick around Her face. Real humans only dream of hair like that but no living being actually has it. Nor was She dressed in designer pastels. Now Satan wore a tight gown in a style vaguely based on a cheongsam that appeared to be made of light and flames and shadow, constantly changing over Her skin so that at one moment it appeared to expose Her arms and at the next had long complicated sleeves. Her nails matched the oriental ambience, ridiculously long and brilliant scarlet to match Her luscious mouth.

Nathan stared at Her openmouthed, as if he could not look at Her enough and as if he couldn't quite believe what he saw. Which was fairly reasonable because unless you were prepared for Satan She was overwhelming.

"I, this is, it's a shock," Nathan stammered when he finally recovered his voice. "And is this real? Did you slip something into my drink and I'm hallucinating or maybe hypnotized . . ."

"It is all quite real," Satan responded. "Clearly you have little experience with hallucinogenic drugs or hypnosis if you believe this could be either. In those situations there remain both the basic structure of the world you know and an awareness that your perceptions are altered. Here you should be quite clear that you are sober, in full possession of your faculties, and that there is not even a passing resemblance to the restaurant, or even anyplace in New York City. Certainly not in February."

We were outside on the terrace and it was as hot and dry as a sauna, leeching the moisture from my skin. When we arrived the blazing red and yellow sky looked like imminent sunset, but the colors had not changed. The burning sky of Hell remained the same.

Neither daylight nor darkness covered the landscape, only ever this fire overhead, flickering and unsteady, sometimes brilliant and sometimes smoky and dim. Long layers of what looked like cloud from a distance could be seen to be carbon gray smoke as they passed overhead. Just a trace of the scents of sulfur and brimstone wafted through the still air. The flowers on the table, which had appeared fresh when we arrived, had begun to droop, the tulips curled over and turned downward, the roses shedding petals on the tablecloth.

"Well, come along then," She said, gesturing with one of those bloody talons. Then She turned and walked briskly through the open doors into the welcome shade of the palace—Her palace.

Nathan and I followed mutely into the Throne Room. Here against a vast wall, up at least twenty feet of stairs, was the Throne of Hell, formed of steel and bone and the bodies of the tortured damned, who screamed in agony as they contorted their bodies to hold a structure that could only very loosely be thought of as a seat. Satan did not mount the stairs; those were for the damned and the supplicants. She merely blinked and She was seated, now three times as large as She had been, and at Her feet her gown became a river of fire tumbling over the black stone step.

I had seen Her in this aspect many times but it never ceased to inspire my awe.

Only this time She had positioned me standing to Her left as her Maid of Honor. My dress had changed, too, and now I was dressed in emerald and gold in a style that was half Periclean Athens and half Bollywood.

Nathan, on the far side facing both of us, gaped.

"Perhaps this is the easiest place to begin," Satan said conversationally. "The seat of power, as it were. Supplicants come here or manifest, and if I'm in the mood to hear petitions I might see as many as ten in a day. Of course, you will notice that you are at the front of the line right now, and if you look behind you, you'll notice that there are thousands waiting."

Nathan turned and saw a sight that could not be anything but Hell. We were inside but also on a mountain. A single narrow path led deep into a valley, and every inch of the path was packed with souls. Some were damned, others (most others) were in Purgatory. Some were the righteous dead who came with petitions on behalf of their loved ones in either place. Here and there along the line, mostly near the front, were a few ceremonial magicians resplendent in their robes, lamens and headdresses, bearing wands, swords, and sigils.

"But this is still the traditional interpretation of Hell," Satan said only to Nathan. "If you want more information you could do far worse than read Dante. What he wrote was not entirely fiction, you understand. There was a Beatrice and he did indeed glimpse My realm before he wrote it. I made certain of that. So let us go on and see some of the more modern innovations."

In a flash we were in a huge, comfortable room furnished in Philippe Starck. With crisp tan walls, blond bamboo flooring, and Lucite furniture neatly placed between the stone fountains, it brought to mind one of the public rooms of a very elegant, very modern boutique hotel. Everything was sleek and streamlined, but not sterile. Which had been the curse of eighties minimalism when nothing had any softened lines. Here a few plump cushions upholstered in rich gold and coffee brocades exuded luxury and ease, and brought in the traditional note required for the postmodern punch.

A delicate antique escritoire held a laptop running Windows. Satan ran a red fingertip over the keyboard and caressed the function keys. "Just in case you were wondering, yes, we do run Windows in Hell. It's one of our premier acquisitions. But, enough of that, come on."

She touched one of the softly backlit panels and it slid open to reveal a set of offices that were all well appointed and quiet and populated by a team of demons who looked the part. Which means, they looked demonic in business dress. Many had horns or were colors not seen among humanity. There were even a few Bastforms and one who appeared to be more nightmare than humanoid.

We knocked on the thick wooden door of the first office on the left, and were admitted by a receptionist wearing something from last year's collection in H&M who just happened to have skin that resembled a tangerine peel that had been marked with blue sigils on the forehead and both cheeks. One wall of the reception area was covered with a beautifully decorated mural of a map of all the world with clusters of colored fairy lights thickly layered over the inhabited areas. There was no time to gawk, as we were brought directly through to the inner office where a big window overlooked the burning sky and a brass nameplate. Meph was there looking out the window, tiny horns poking out of his news anchor hair just lightly frosted with silver at the temples and a tail hanging out of his pinstripe Brioni suit, but otherwise the very picture of a CEO of a Fortune 500 company. He must have morphed those on just to make the point.

He looked up as we were ushered in. First he made reverence to Satan, a crisp nod of the head that indicated something much deeper but was kept restrained because a stranger was present. Then he turned to me.

"Lily," he exclaimed, "I haven't seen you in ages, not since we had dinner. And I saw that you've gone to Ono. What did you think?"

"We're just stopping in for a very brief visit," Satan interrupted. "I'll command that she blog it and you can read all about it. And maybe the two of you can even have a dinner together in the future, but right now we're giving Nathan the tour."

Meph crossed his office in rapid strides and held his hand out to Nathan. "Lily's young man? So very pleased to meet you. You saw us outside of Butter, didn't you? You take good care of our Lily, she's very special to us."

Nathan did shake his head as if in agreement, however reluctant he appeared to me.

"Well, enjoy the tour, but remember, this is only Headquarters. We operate in every corner of the world, on all seven continents, and yes, that does include the installation on Antarctica. Though we don't interfere with the penguins. Those belong to Upstairs. We just take care of the scientists."

"This is Mephistopheles." I made the introduction in case Nathan hadn't noticed the nameplate. "He's

Satan's lieutenant, which makes him the most senior executive after Satan Herself."

Meph smiled. "Well, nice of you to say, Lily. But be careful because you know that Beliel and Beelzebub and Moloch and Marduk would claim that all of us are equals. And Moloch with his airports." Meph turned to Nathan. "I'm head of all the functions and departments under Satan, but I hope you have the opportunity to meet the others soon if they're not available right now. Beez is in charge of Operations, Beliel is the Chief of Security and Marduk runs the Budget."

"Marduk?" Nathan asked, confused. "But he was one of the Babylonian pantheon. Head of it at various times."

Meph pulled a face. "Exactly, and he never lets us forget it. He was a god and the rest of us were never more than mere angels." Meph shrugged. "Office politics doesn't change just because we're not among the living. But . . . he does a good job. Runs the department efficiently and is a real hardnose with Accounting."

Satan ushered us out. The receptionist demon bowed low to Her before closing the door after us.

"What is his relationship to you?" Nathan asked after we were out of earshot.

"Avuncular," I replied crisply. "Meph loves good food and likes good company, and he's looked out for me since I first arrived. But in case you're thinking of being jealous or something, don't bother. Meph isn't interested in female demons that way."

"If we were doing a full tour I would take you to meet Moloch and Beliel and Beelzebub and Marduk, but my schedule is rather constrained, as you might appreciate," Satan said. "I'm needed elsewhere at the moment. Lily, you can continue to show Nathan around. If you need assistance, call on Sariel. I believe she's available. And now, I must be off. So lovely to see you, Lily. You know I couldn't resist."

I hugged her and kissed her on both cheeks. "Thank you, Satan," I whispered in her ear. "Thank you a million times, thank you."

She smiled. "Well, we all know how things work. One favor deserves another, after all."

"Yes, Satan." That was the formal acknowledgment and seal. Satan had granted me a great boon and I would have to pay. But I knew that and I didn't care. There wasn't anything I wouldn't do for Her anyway, so it was a great privilege that She had answered my prayer.

She disappeared in a puff of sulfur-scented smoke and we were back on the terrace. Only two iced tea glasses remained, and the flowers were now completely wilted.

I added sugar and lemon to the iced tea and handed it to Nathan before I fixed one for myself. He didn't sip, but put the glass down directly. "Lily, can you get us home? I've had enough of this."

"Then you believe me?" I asked, hopeful.

"I believe you," he answered.

"But there are other things you need to know," I added. "Yes, I can get us home. Not a problem. But I need you to know, Nathan, while I'm a succubus I have only really ever loved one man before. And I think I'm falling for you. And you know that Satan will let me go if someone truly loves me."

He nodded mutely. "Lily, please, I need to go back now. I believe, but I want to be out of here."

I understood. Hell can be oppressive. It's supposed to be oppressive. It's Hell.

I returned us to the lobby of my building. Vincent would have been the only one who noticed that we hadn't entered through any door.

"Would you like to come up?" I asked.

Nathan shook his head. "I need to think," he said, holding my hands. "This is all very . . . unexpected. I need to clear my mind. Lily, it's just been a few weeks and we've only seen each other a few times, and in that bit of time I've come to care for you as much as I think I've ever cared for anyone. I wanted—but I have to think. I have to assimilate all this. I need a little time."

I dropped his hands and my head. My heart felt like lead in my chest. I knew.

He turned away without even a hug and went into the night. Vincent came over wordlessly and hugged me close, held me while I sobbed. I had cried so much tonight and it wasn't going to stop anytime soon.

Vincent took me upstairs, took off my boots, and made me a cup of tea. A demon who can brew a cup of tea, who would have thought? Though maybe Sybil had taught him.

My brain was not working right. I felt like I was thinking in a haze. Vincent got me settled on the sofa with tea and the remains of my last pint of Chunky Monkey, which was woefully low. "I'll run out and get you some more on my break," he said.

Vincent came back at three a.m. to find me bawling

and a puddle of ice cream dripping onto my antique carpet.

He cleaned up the mess and put the new pint in the freezer. Then he fed me a little yellow pill with the now tepid tea that I hadn't touched. I don't know where he got the Valium and I didn't care. I rarely take drugs so this one worked fast and I was grateful for it. The worst of the misery dulled and I fell asleep under Vincent's care.

chapter
THIRTY-TWO

I woke fully dressed—but in my bed—on Sunday morning.

Sunday. At least I would be seeing my friends at brunch and they would take care of me . . . or not. We'd changed our brunch date this week. No nice comforting banana-stuffed French toast, no endless alcohol, no best friends clustered around to hold my hand.

Maybe it wasn't so awful. Maybe he was in shock but it would wear off and he'd see the advantages. Maybe he'd heard the part about me becoming mortal.

Maybe I'd been a total idiot.

I lay in bed and pulled the covers up, but I was uncomfortable in my clothes and they smelled from being slept in. Sighing, I got out of bed, stripped my carefully chosen outfit straight into the cleaning bag, and went for the shower.

If I lived in a house with my own water heater, I would be showering in ice water by now. Thank all there is for the heavy-duty plumbing in a luxury apartment building.

But my skin had wrinkled up and I'd stopped crying for the moment. I got out, toweled my hair, got dressed. No careful choices today.

I thought about coffee but I couldn't work up the energy. A bagel would be nice, a fresh one slathered with butter (which Desi would consider heresy, but I didn't care, I like butter more than cream cheese). A big fat poppy seed bagel and then a pumpkin muffin or an orange walnut scone. And hot chocolate, that would be the perfect beverage, a nice big hot chocolate.

Maybe the girls would come and we could have brunch anyway. Maybe they'd be willing to meet me for a carb-out at the Carnegie Deli, and I'd have the matzoh ball soup.

I was thinking about the telephone when it rang. My heart leaped. Nathan? Had he reconsidered? I grabbed the receiver.

It was Sybil. "Vincent told me," she said without preamble. "Can I come up?"

"Sure," I said, not thinking. Five minutes later she was at my door with a bag of fresh bagels, still hot from the oven, and lattes and cream cheese and capers. I couldn't move while she set out plates and knives and put the bagels into a bowl. Dear Sybil had even bought extra poppy seed, which were my favorites.

She cut a bagel open for me, slathered it with butter, and set it in front of me. "Eat," she commanded, sounding far more like a Jewish mother than a Delphic Oracle. "You look like Hell."

"I feel worse."

She shook her head and sighed, then cut a sesame bagel for herself. "We told you not to tell him, Lily. We told you, you knew. Why did you do it?"

I couldn't explain. The place, the music, my own

memories, all of them had overwhelmed me. I tried to tell Sybil but the words all sounded trite and silly.

"You wasted your boon on *that*?" She was clearly horrified when I explained how I'd asked Satan to prove my sanity. "He's right, you're crazy."

Then she sat down next to me and rubbed my back. "The others are coming soon," she said. "I called them before I left, but I wanted to come up alone for a bit. Because you helped me with Vincent and he was really worried about you last night. And because I have this feeling. It's not a true oracle, you understand, but I've been around these things long enough that I sometimes have a sense of the future. Maybe it's like the Akashic in a strange way."

I blinked at her and shook my head. "What do you mean?" I asked, not daring to hope.

"I don't know if I should tell you this," she said softly. "Hope is a dangerous thing. It can be cruel, it can be worse than despair. But . . . I have this feeling that you will see Nathan Coleman again. And your magician from Aruba, I think he will return as well. I can't promise but I'd still bet money on it."

This was Sybil speaking. If she would bet money then I would listen. I generally do, and my finances have always benefited. And Nathan was definitely a high-risk investment.

"Nathan is shocked and he can't handle it and you knew that would happen," she continued. "But I have a strong premonition that he also can't stay away. He loves you, I think, Lily. That may not be a good thing, you know. But I sense that he will be back. And I'm sure Marten will."

I blinked and swallowed hard, and took another

bite of my bagel. It tasted good. The latte was hot and calming. And Sybil, my friend who sees the future, not only from Apollo but the stock market as well, said that there was still some hope. Nathan would be back.

Maybe.

I can hope. I can be patient. I have lived for three thousand years. Nathan Coleman can't outlast me. And I have Sybil's sense that he would return. I'd take those odds any day.

Epilogue

My girlfriends are wonderful. No matter how hard or harsh our lives, no matter how scared and broken I am, my best friends are always there for me.

All three of them showed up bearing food. I was reminded of the Three Kings, only this was the Three Demons who came bearing bagels and chocolate and ice cream. They fed me and Eros gave me a handful of tiny yellow pills ("Just a few, use them only when you can't deal at all because they can be addictive," she warned me).

Sybil stayed and called my office the next morning. Desi called her travel agent and got me a first-class ticket on the next Lufthansa flight, connecting in Frankfurt to Venice. They packed my bags and Vincent drove me to the airport and the girls were all there and saw me to the security gate.

Even in first class, with the wonderful wide seats that fold back into flat beds, with the eye masks and the airline pajamas, I couldn't sleep. So I drank myself across the Atlantic, away from Nathan, away from New York and my life.

Only for two weeks—that was the longest I could get away. But my features were all on track and I'd planned the photo shoots through the end of August, and Danielle said she'd cover if some fashion editor really could not manage appropriate jewelry or hand-bags.

Even Satan gave me the two weeks. No deliveries needed, though if I really wanted to take out my hurt and rage She would be happy to give me the excuse. And She gave me a ruby and diamond ring just so that I could wear it and remember that She was always there for me.

Men may hurt and tear us apart, but girlfriends are forever.